Volume 1

Story by Anthony Andora
Art by Lincy Chan

HAMBURG // LONDON // LOS ANGELES // TOKYO

Rhysmyth Volume 1
Story By Anthony Andora
Art By Lincy Chan

Lettering - Star Print Brokers
Production Artist - Jennifer Carbajal
Graphic Designer - Jose Macasocol, Jr.

Editor - Alexis Kirsch
Digital Imaging Manager - Chris Buford
Pre-Production Supervisor - Erika Terriquez
Art Director - Anne Marie Horne
Production Manager - Elisabeth Brizzi
VP of Production - Ron Klamert
Editor-in-Chief - Rob Tokar
Publisher - Mike Kiley
President and C.O.O. - John Parker
C.E.O. and Chief Creative Officer - Stuart Levy

A  Manga

TOKYOPOP and 🐱 are trademarks or registered trademarks of TOKYOPOP Inc.

TOKYOPOP Inc.
5900 Wilshire Blvd. Suite 2000
Los Angeles, CA 90036

E-mail: info@TOKYOPOP.com
Come visit us online at www.TOKYOPOP.com

ISBN: 978-1-4278-0088-6

First TOKYOPOP printing: May 2007
10 9 8 7 6 5 4 3 2 1
Printed in the USA

CONTENTS

RhysMyth

LOADING>>>>>

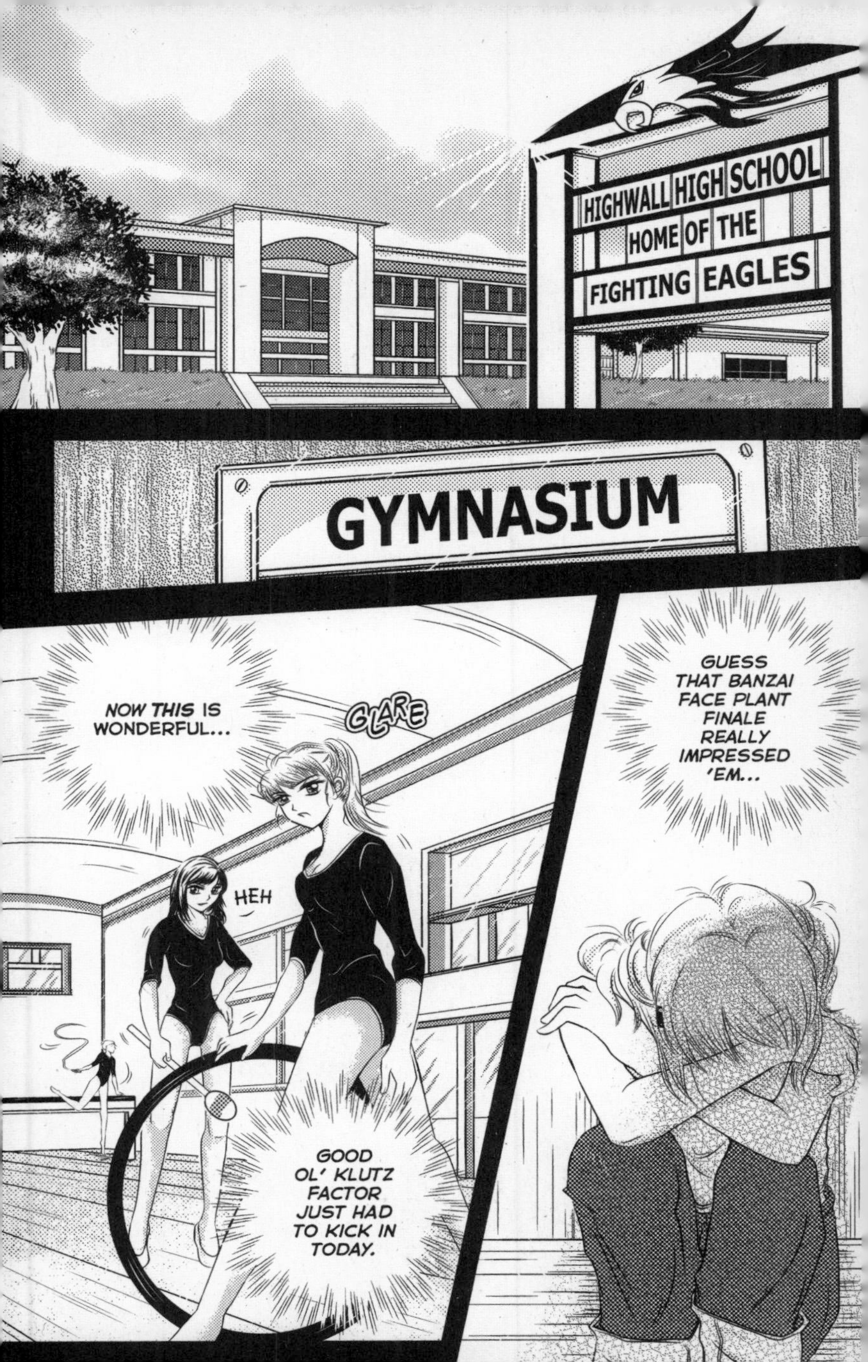
HIGHWALL HIGH SCHOOL
HOME OF THE
FIGHTING EAGLES
GYMNASIUM
NOW THIS IS WONDERFUL...
GLARE
HEH
GOOD OL' KLUTZ FACTOR JUST HAD TO KICK IN TODAY.
GUESS THAT BANZAI FACE PLANT FINALE REALLY IMPRESSED 'EM...

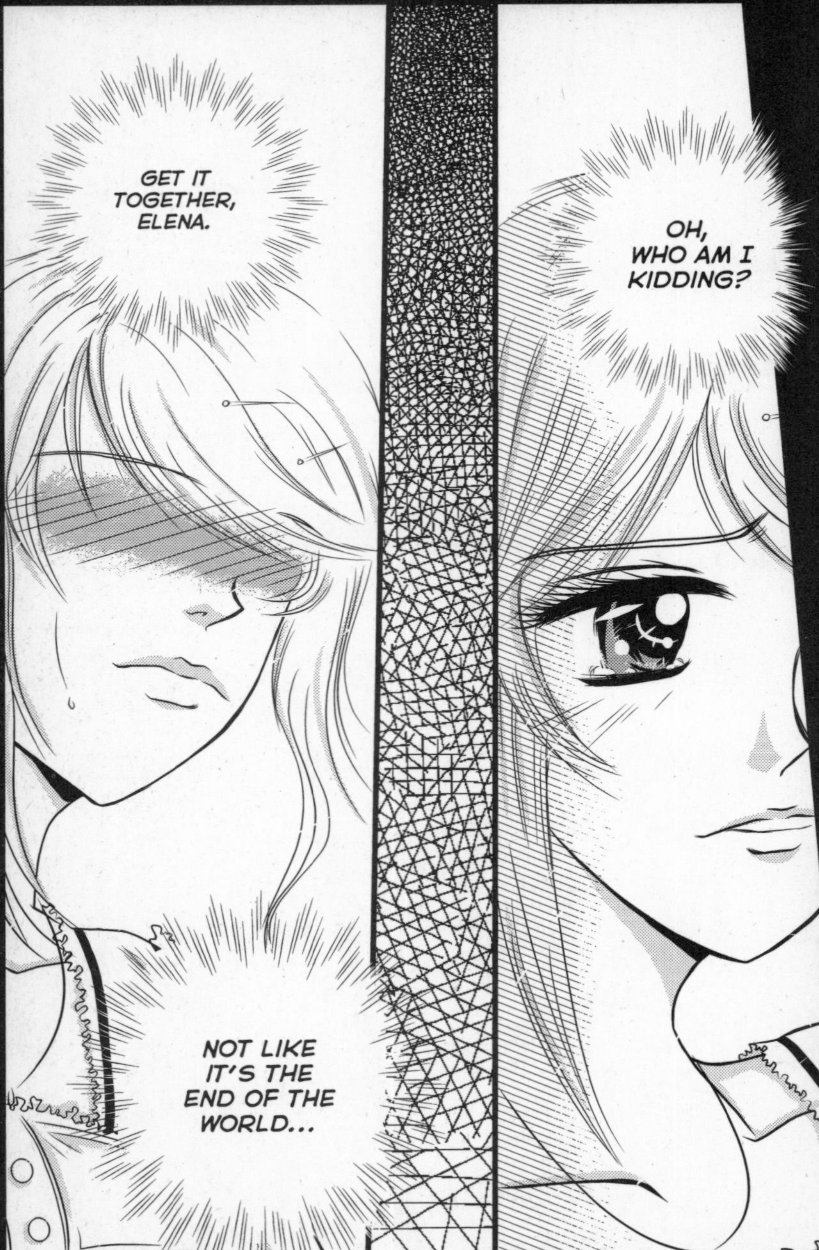
GET IT TOGETHER, ELENA.
NOT LIKE IT'S THE END OF THE WORLD...
OH, WHO AM I KIDDING?

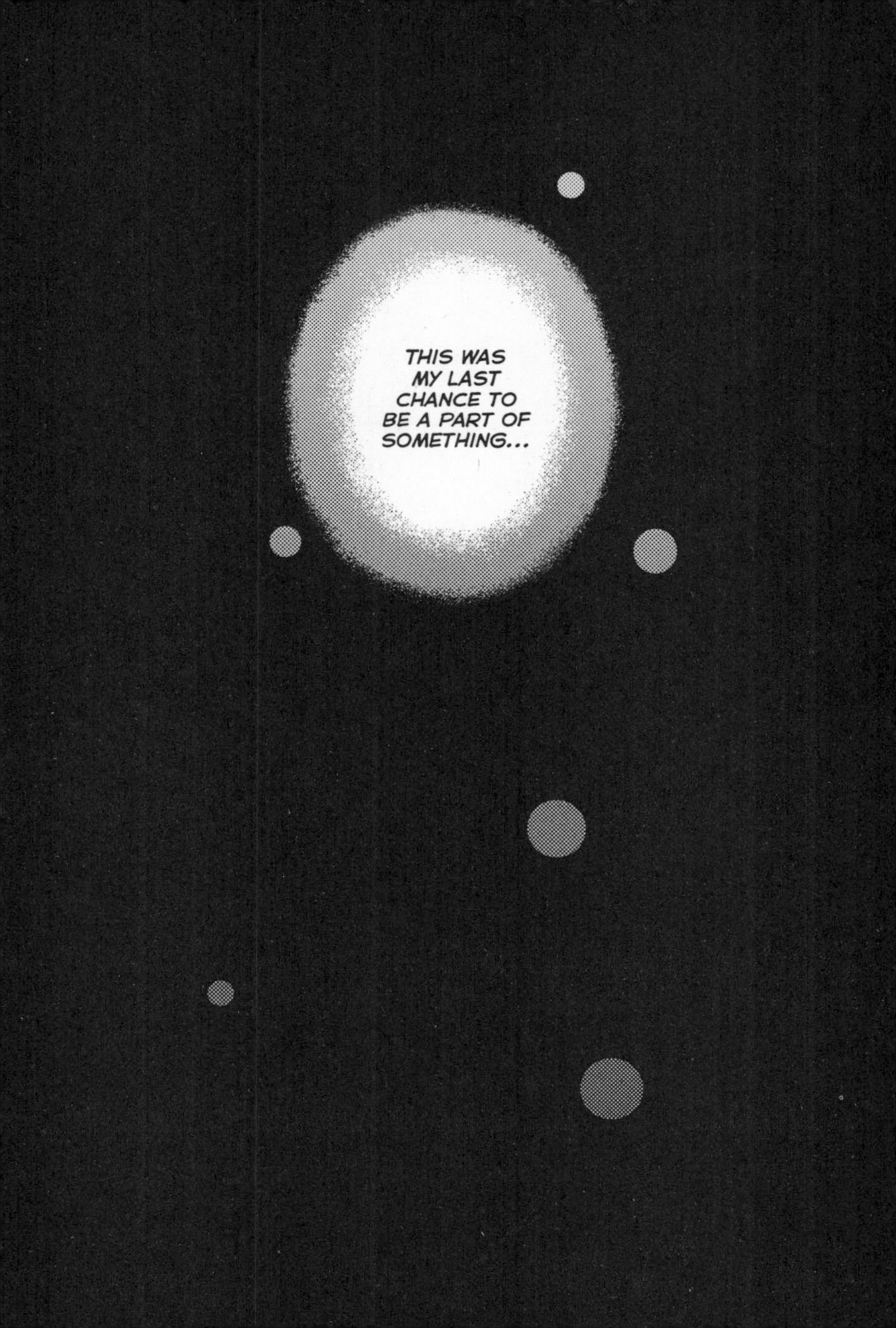
THIS WAS MY LAST CHANCE TO BE A PART OF SOMETHING...

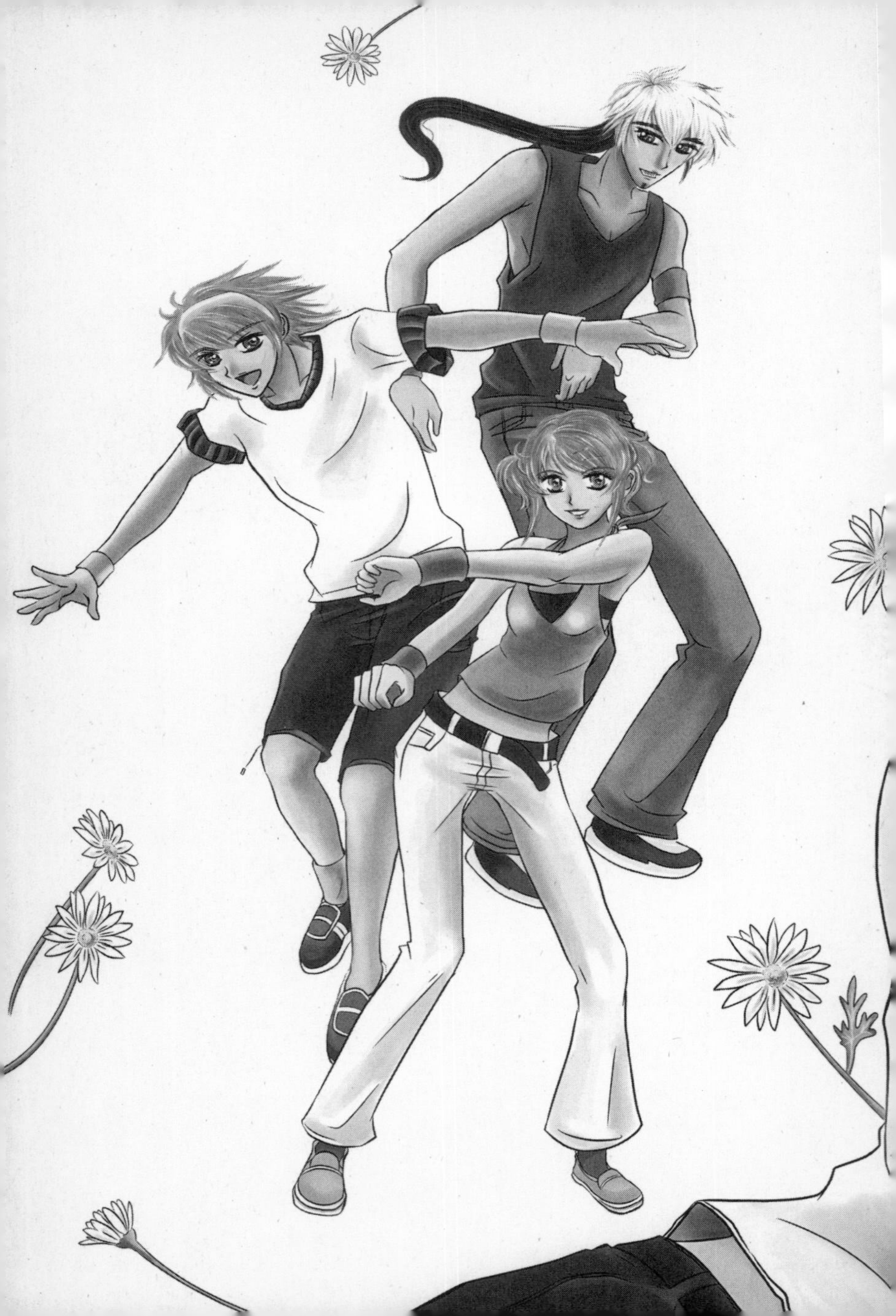

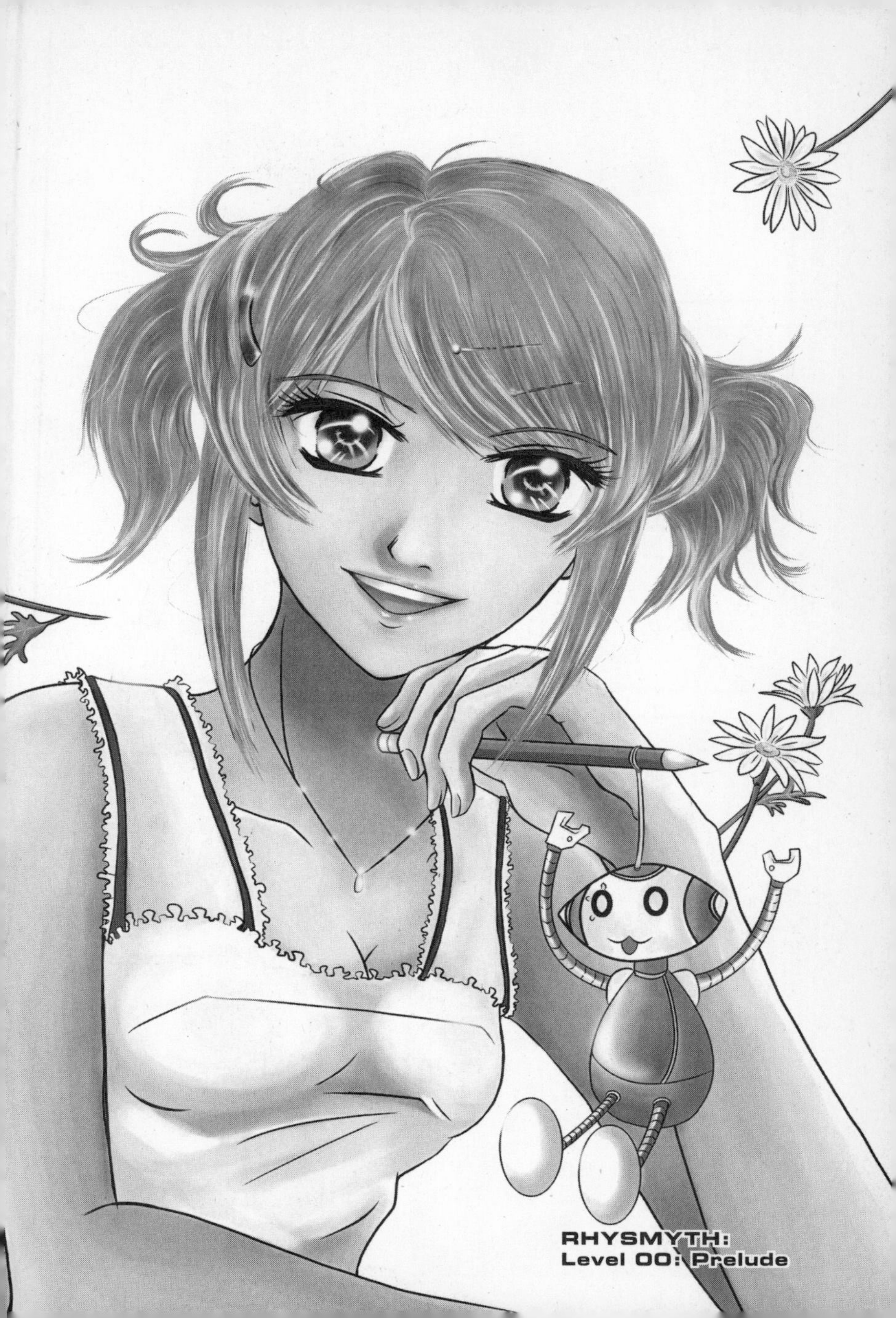
RHYSMYTH:
Level 00: Prelude

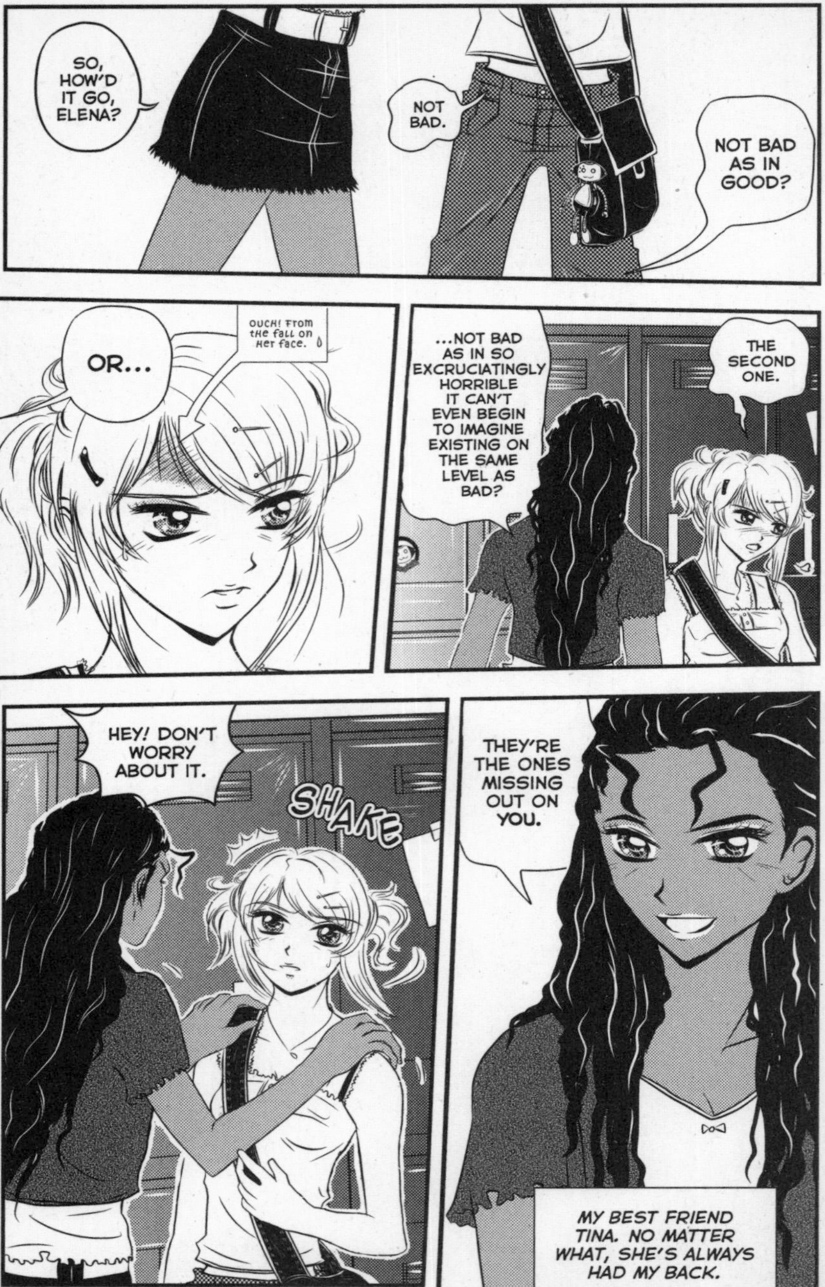
SO, HOW'D IT GO, ELENA?
NOT BAD.
NOT BAD AS IN GOOD?
OR...
OUCH! FROM THE FALL ON HER FACE.
...NOT BAD AS IN SO EXCRUCIATINGLY HORRIBLE IT CAN'T EVEN BEGIN TO IMAGINE EXISTING ON THE SAME LEVEL AS BAD?
THE SECOND ONE.
HEY! DON'T WORRY ABOUT IT.
SHAKE
THEY'RE THE ONES MISSING OUT ON YOU.
MY BEST FRIEND TINA. NO MATTER WHAT, SHE'S ALWAYS HAD MY BACK.

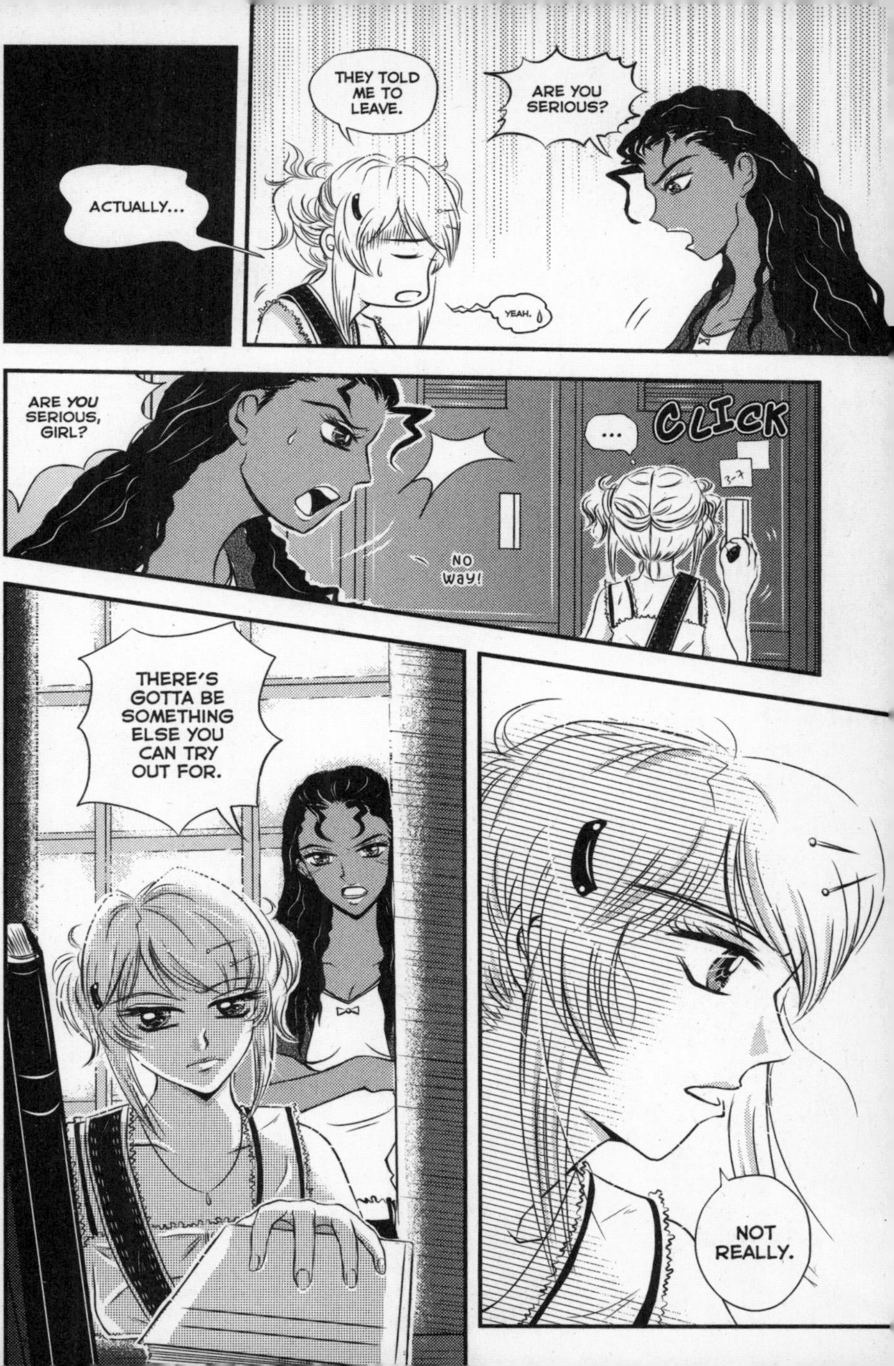
ACTUALLY...
THEY TOLD ME TO LEAVE.
ARE YOU SERIOUS?
YEAH.
ARE *YOU* SERIOUS, GIRL?
NO WAY!
...
CLICK
THERE'S GOTTA BE SOMETHING ELSE YOU CAN TRY OUT FOR.
NOT REALLY.

REMEMBER MIDDLE SCHOOL?

SOFTBALL

SOCCER

BASKETBALL

I'M NOT EXACTLY A NATURAL IN HAND-EYE COORDINATION.

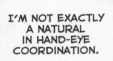

WHICH MEANS I GET HIT IN THE HEAD EVERY TIME.

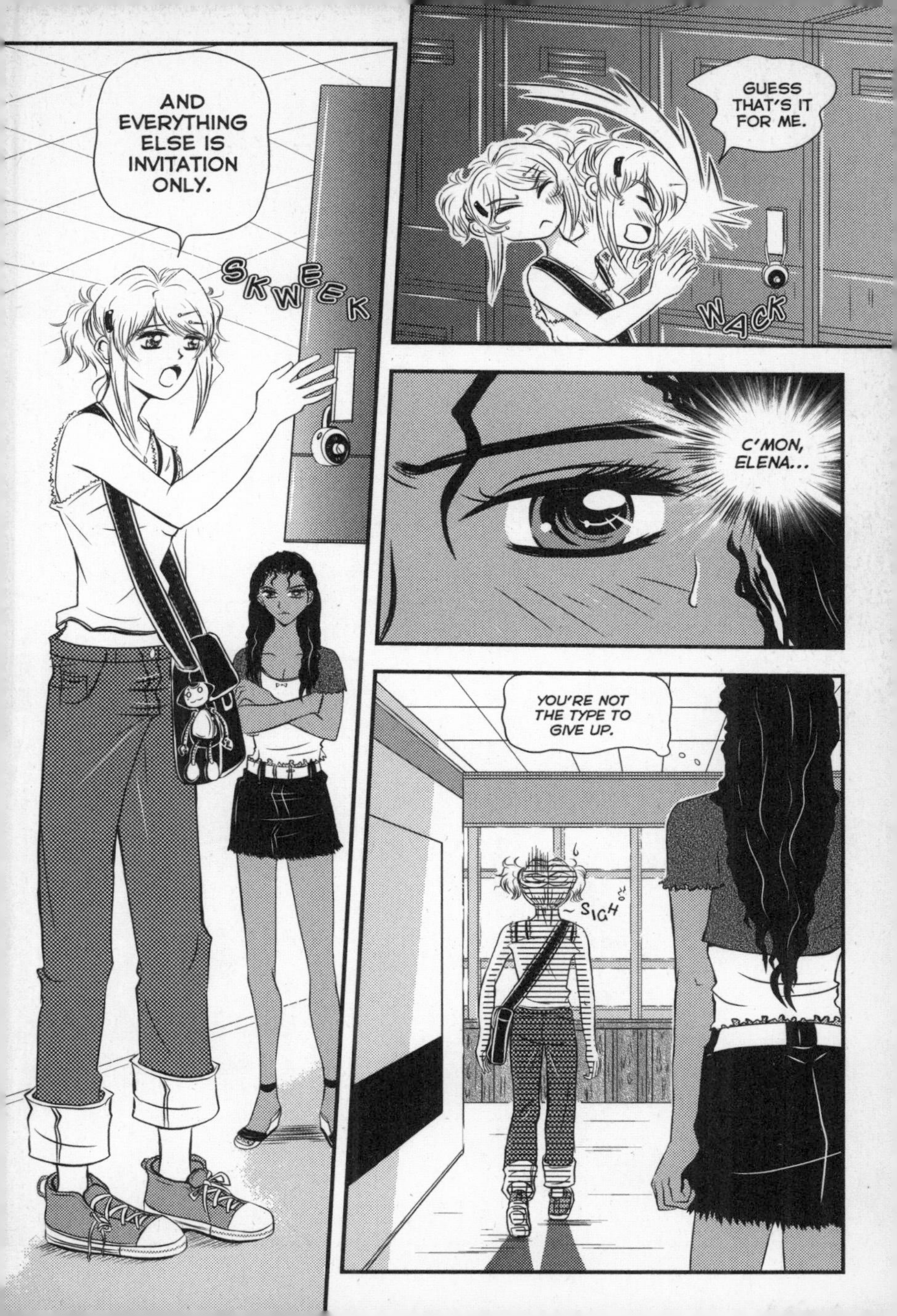
AND EVERYTHING ELSE IS INVITATION ONLY.
SKWEEK
GUESS THAT'S IT FOR ME.
WACK
C'MON, ELENA...
YOU'RE NOT THE TYPE TO GIVE UP.
~SIGH

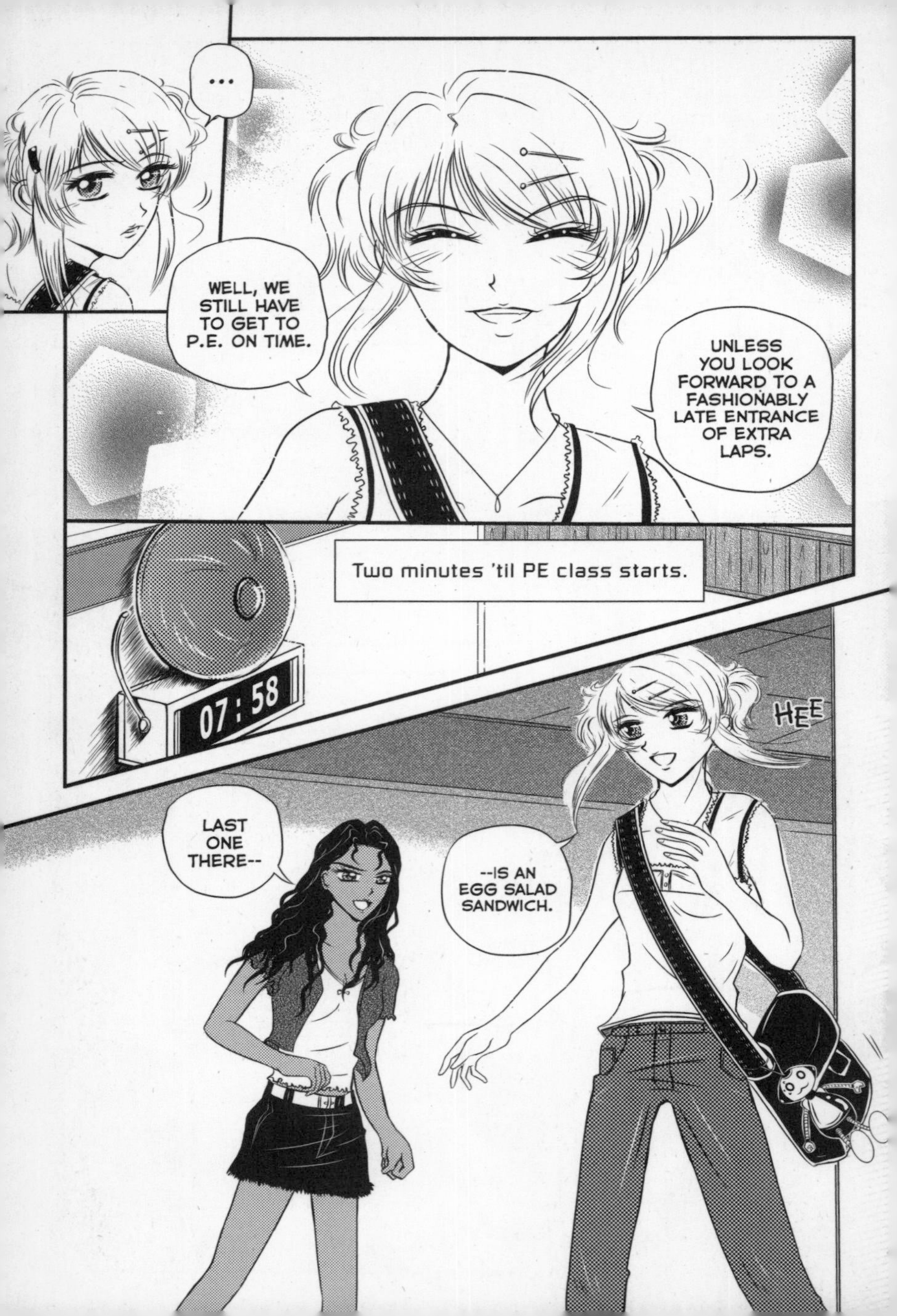
...
WELL, WE STILL HAVE TO GET TO P.E. ON TIME.
UNLESS YOU LOOK FORWARD TO A FASHIONABLY LATE ENTRANCE OF EXTRA LAPS.
Two minutes 'til PE class starts.
07:58
HEE
LAST ONE THERE--
--IS AN EGG SALAD SANDWICH.

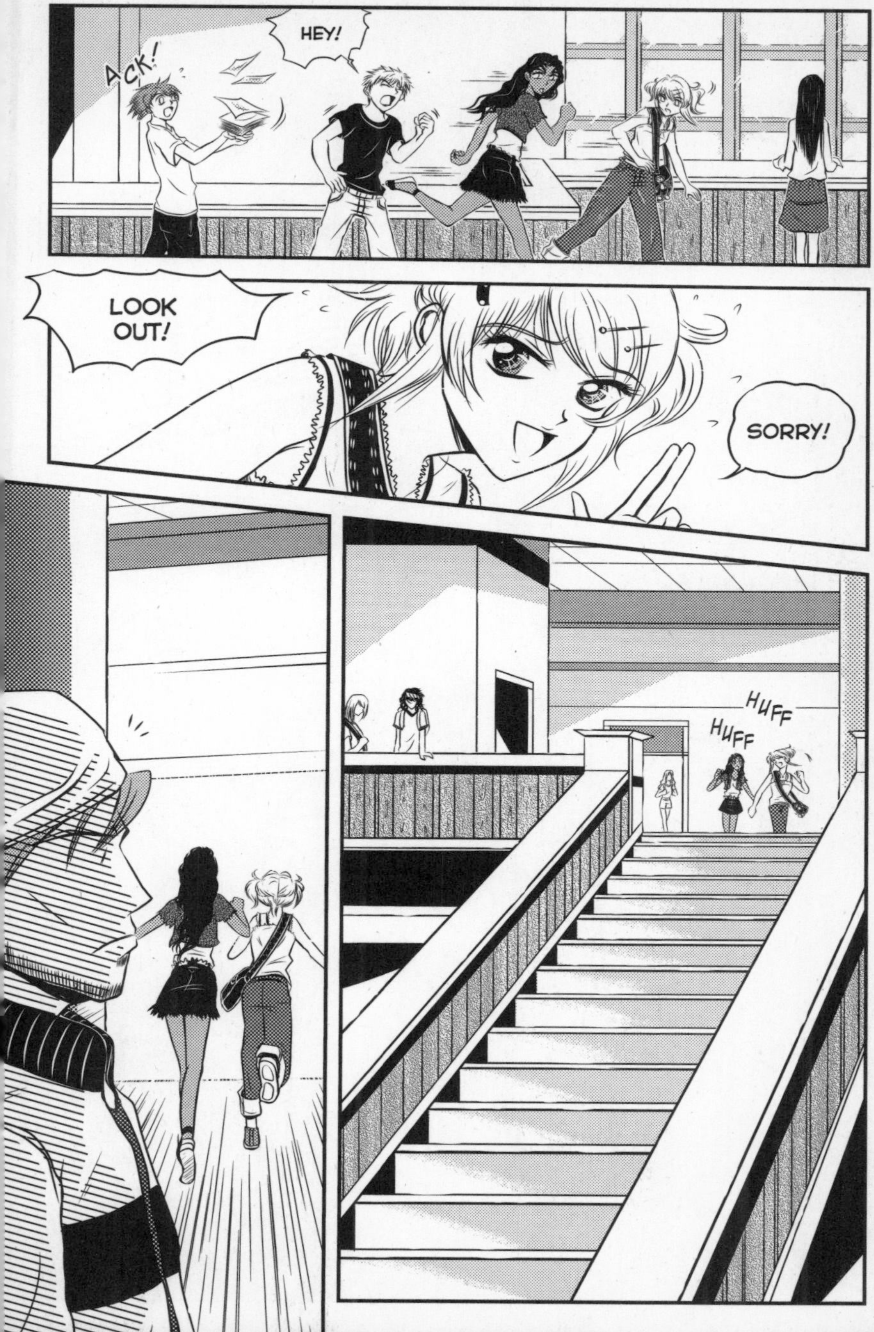
ACK!
HEY!
LOOK OUT!
SORRY!
HUFF
HUFF

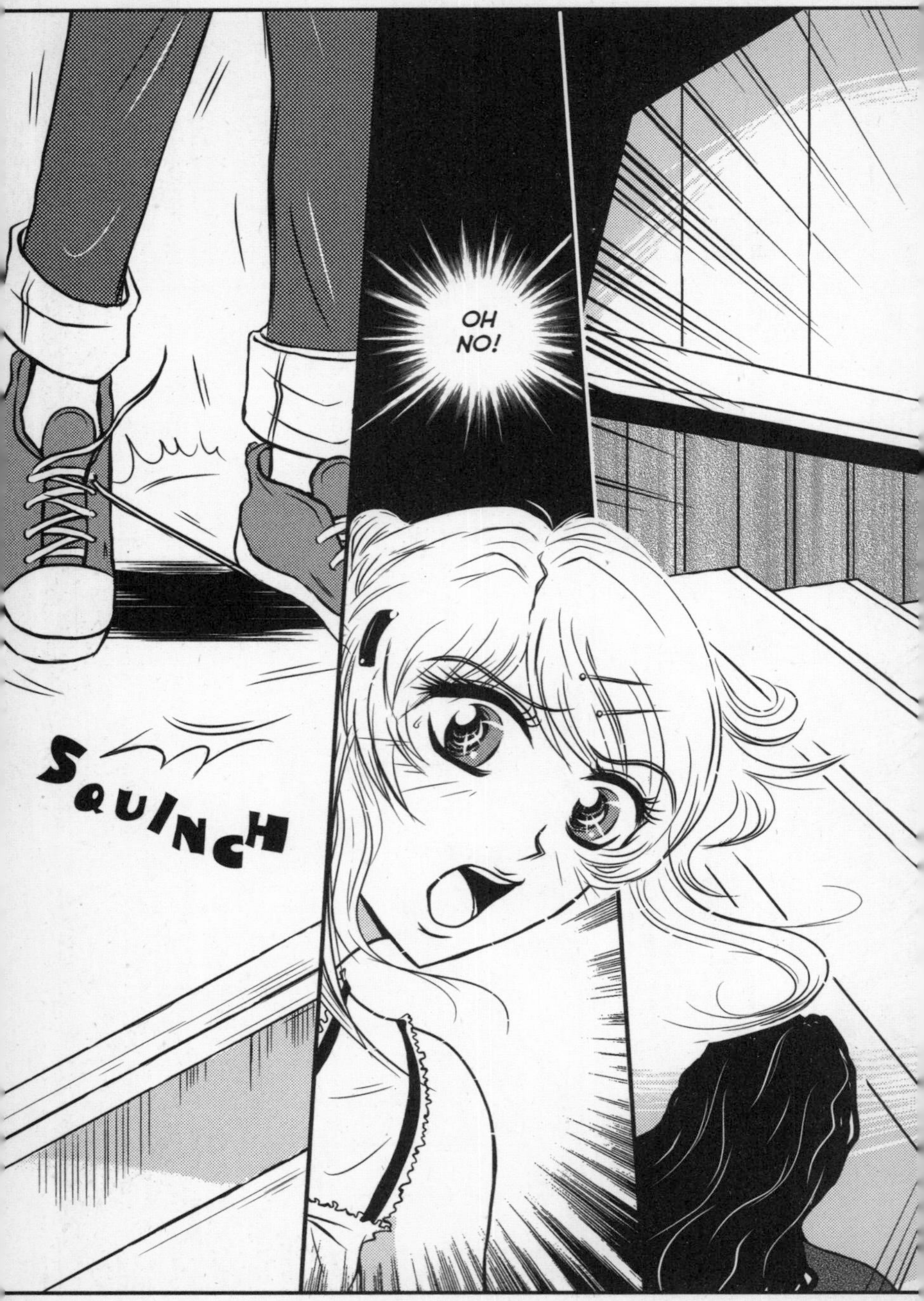
OH NO!
SQUINCH

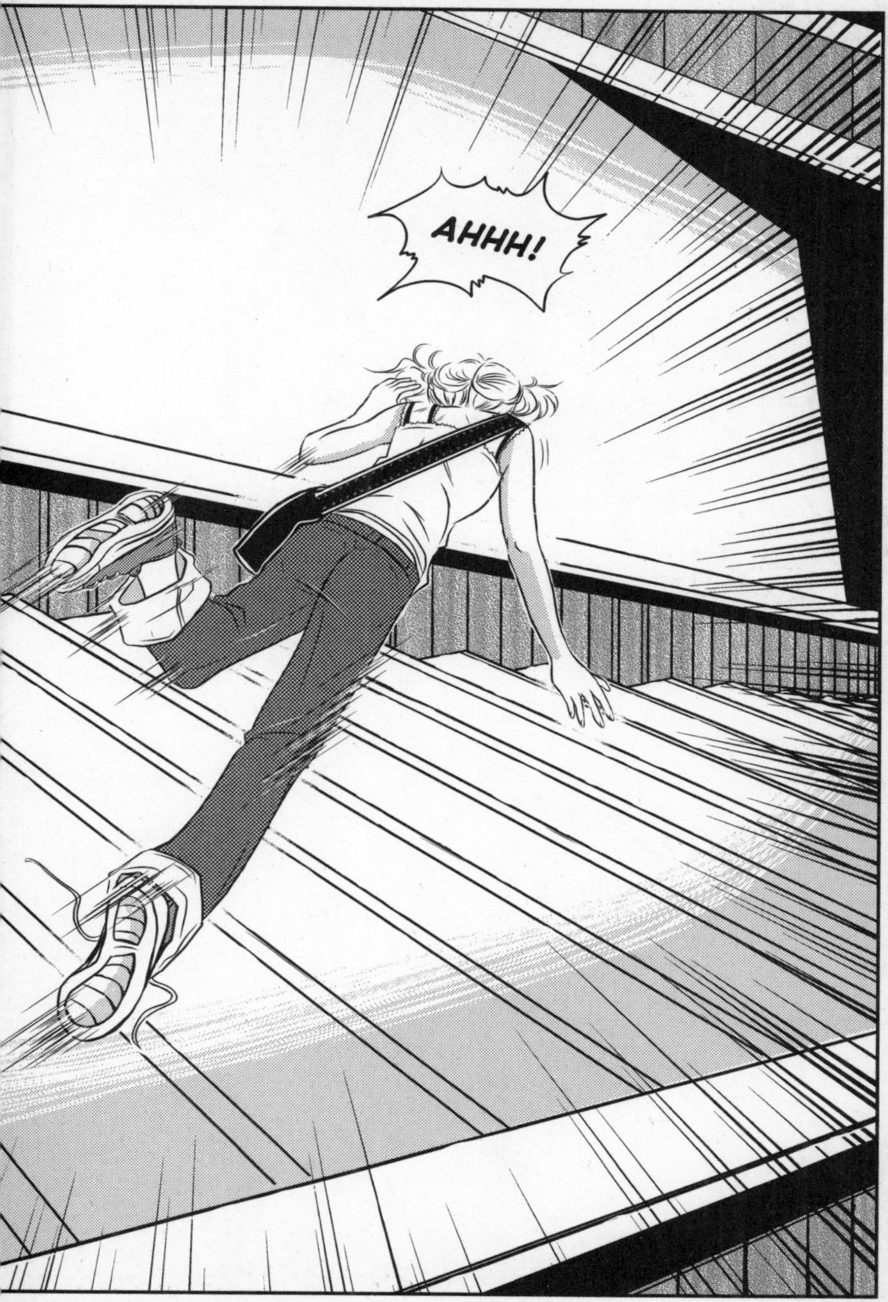
AHHH!

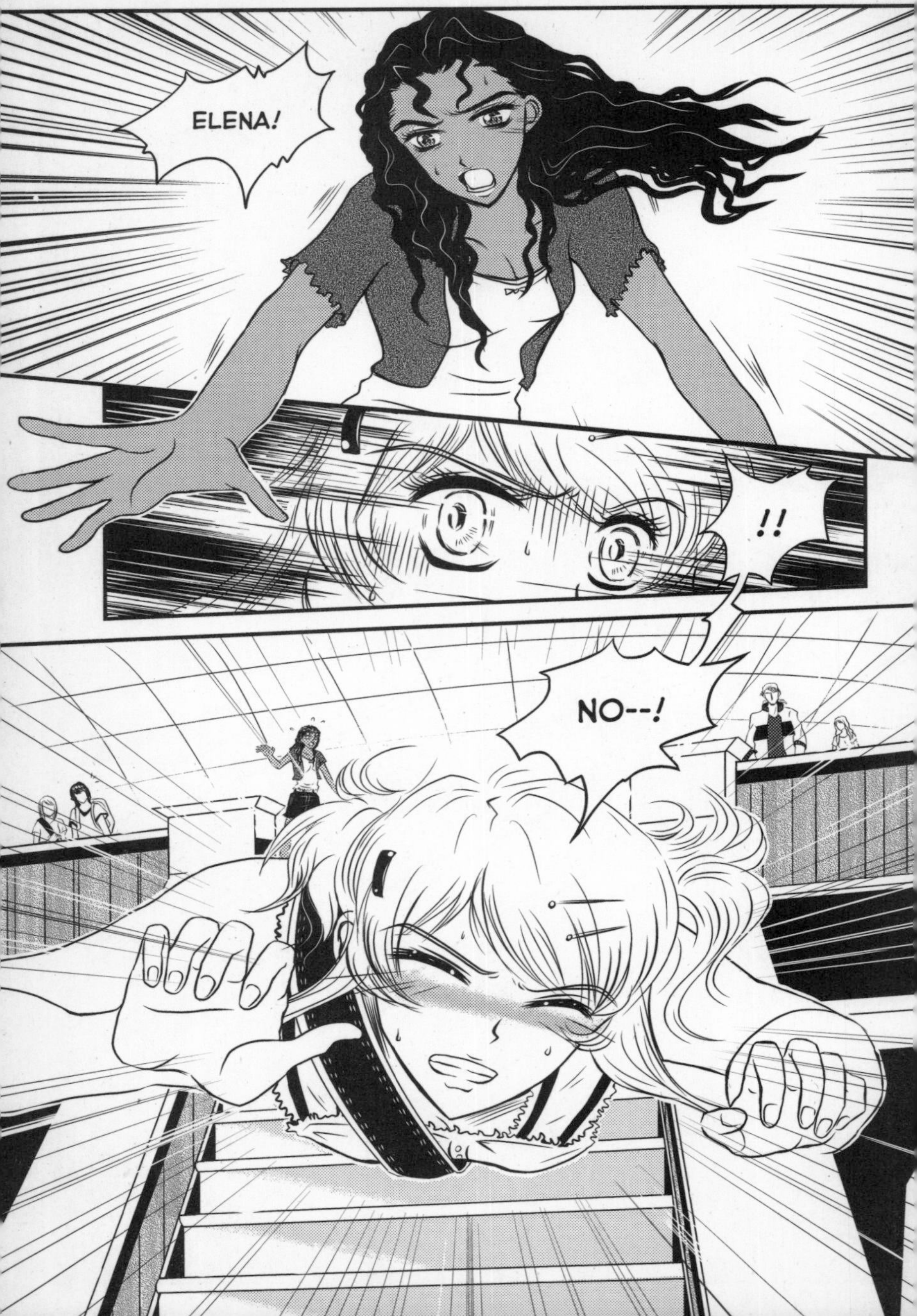
ELENA!
!!
NO--!

RHYSMYTH:
Level 01: Falling

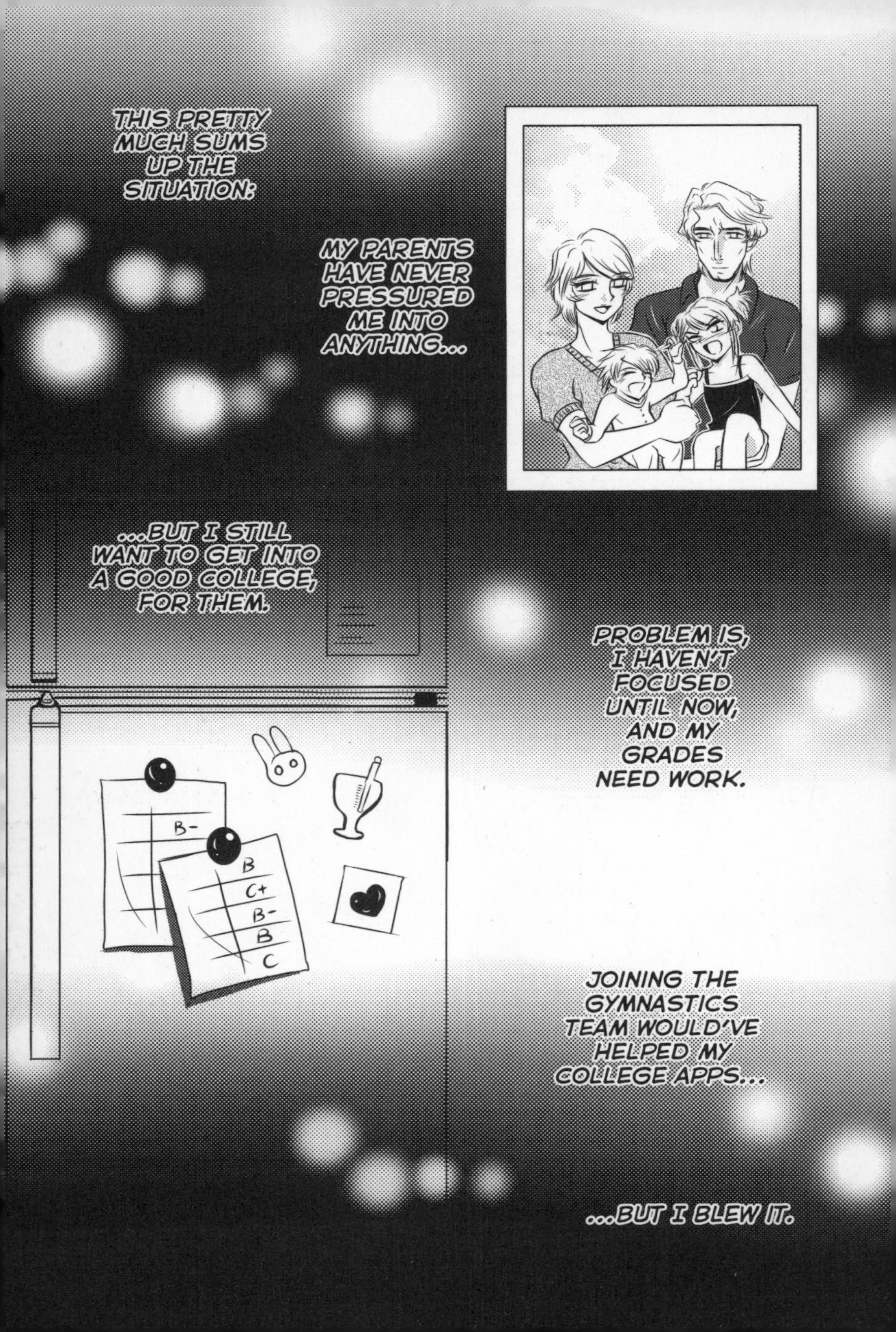
THIS PRETTY MUCH SUMS UP THE SITUATION:
MY PARENTS HAVE NEVER PRESSURED ME INTO ANYTHING...
...BUT I STILL WANT TO GET INTO A GOOD COLLEGE, FOR THEM.
B-
B
C+
B-
B
C
PROBLEM IS, I HAVEN'T FOCUSED UNTIL NOW, AND MY GRADES NEED WORK.
JOINING THE GYMNASTICS TEAM WOULD'VE HELPED MY COLLEGE APPS...
...BUT I BLEW IT.

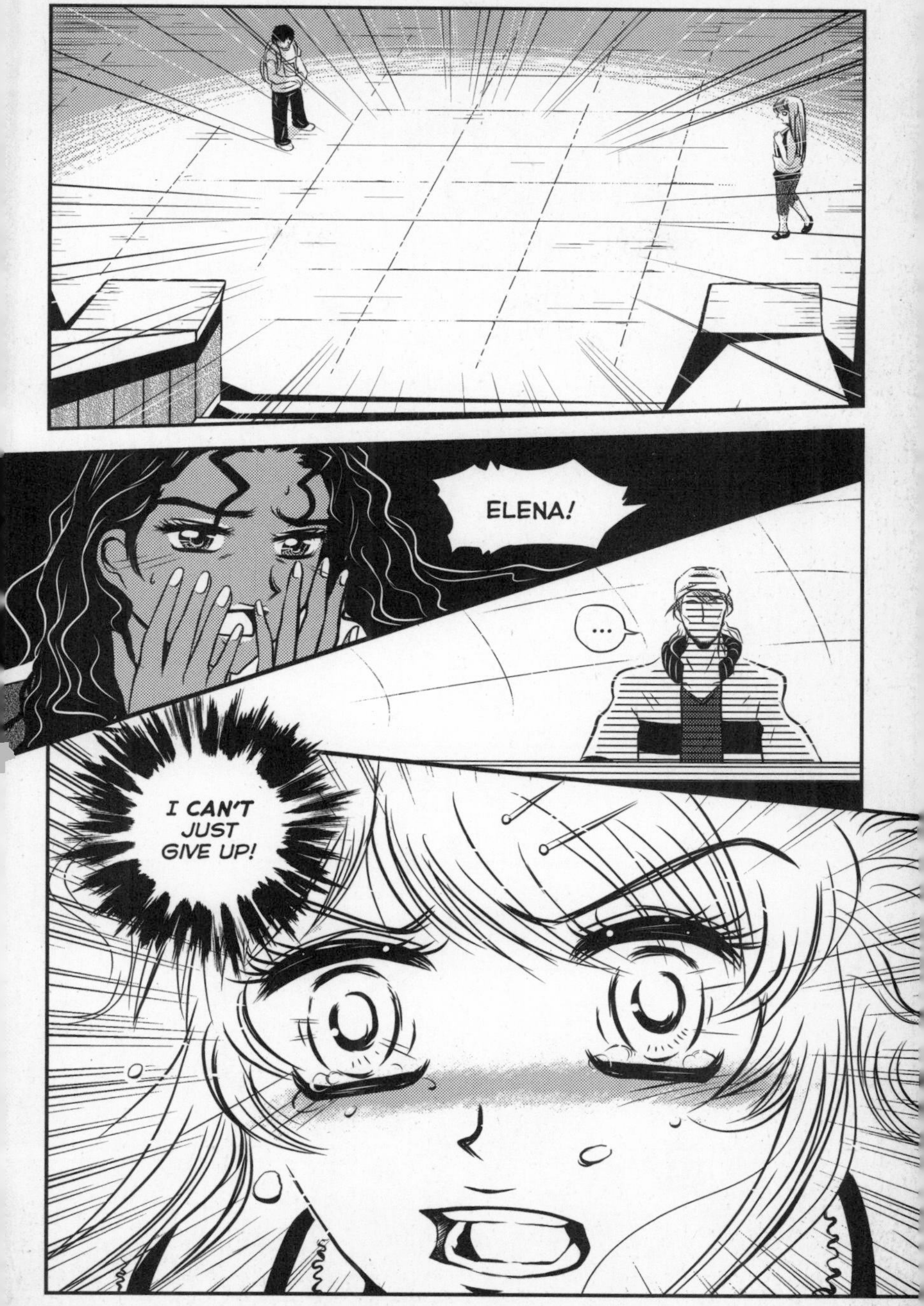
ELENA!
...
I CAN'T JUST GIVE UP!

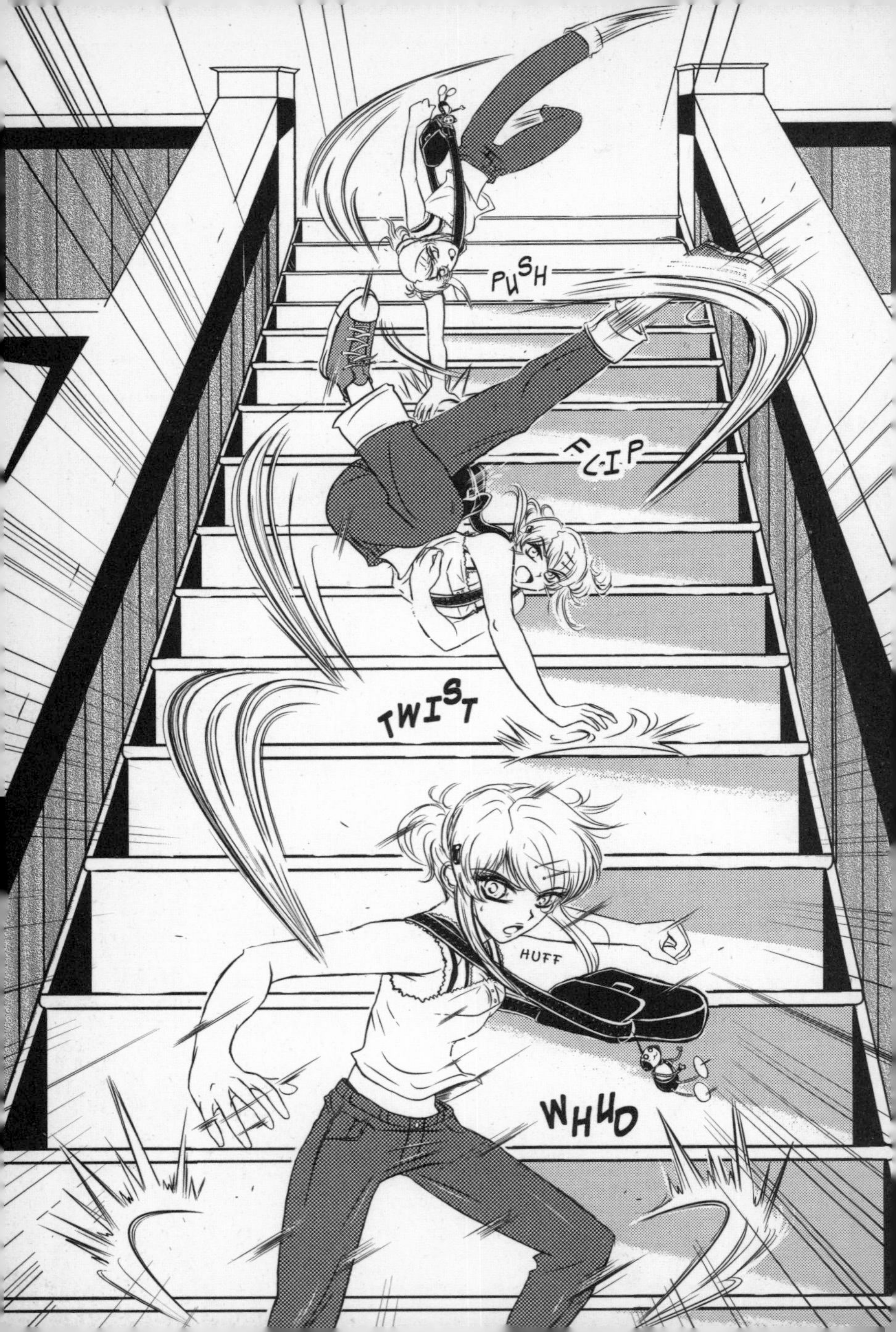
PUSH
FLIP
TWIST
HUFF
WHUD

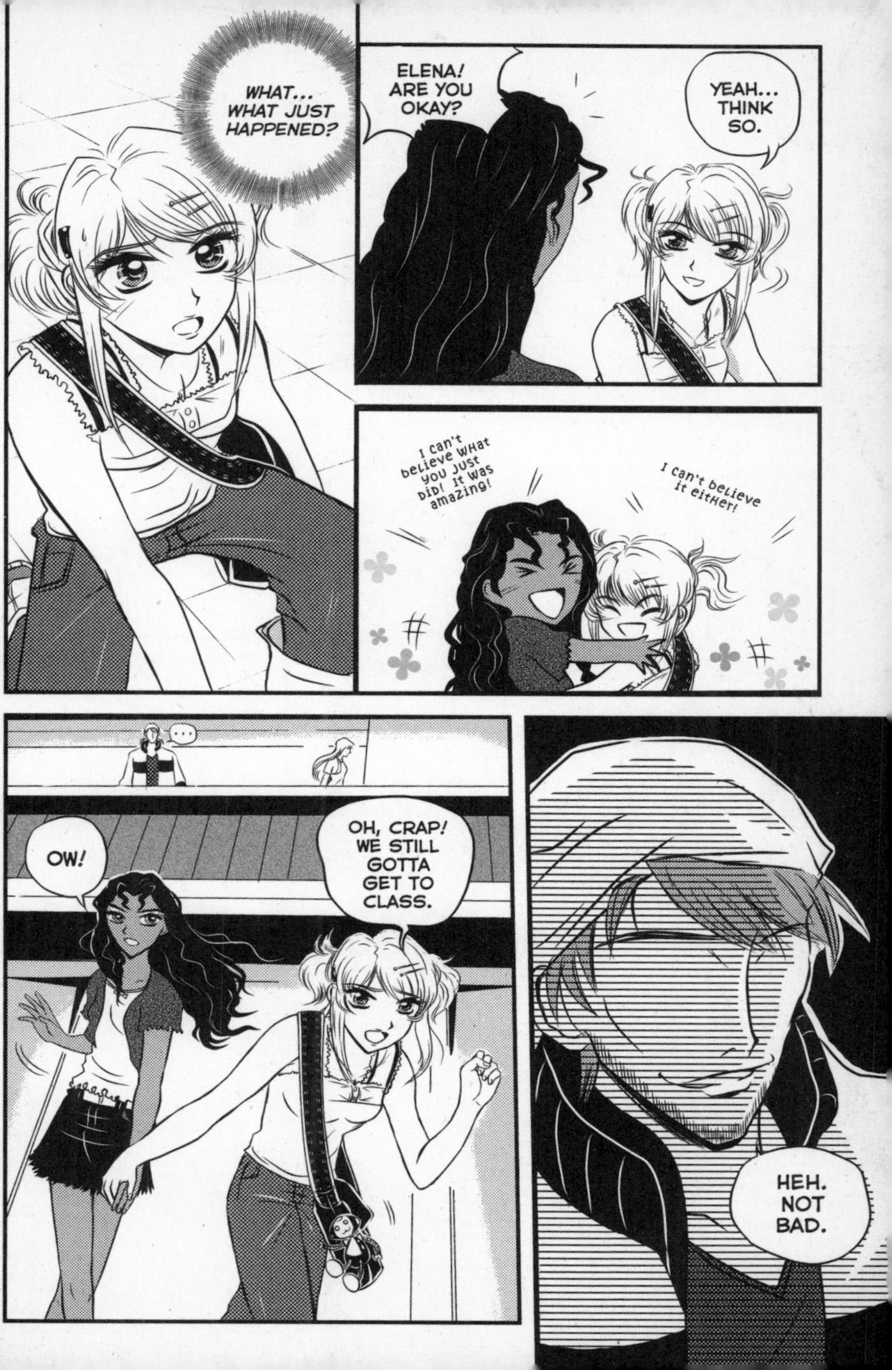
WHAT... WHAT JUST HAPPENED?
ELENA! ARE YOU OKAY?
YEAH... THINK SO.
I can't believe what you just did! It was amazing!
I can't believe it either!
...
OW!
OH, CRAP! WE STILL GOTTA GET TO CLASS.
HEH. NOT BAD.

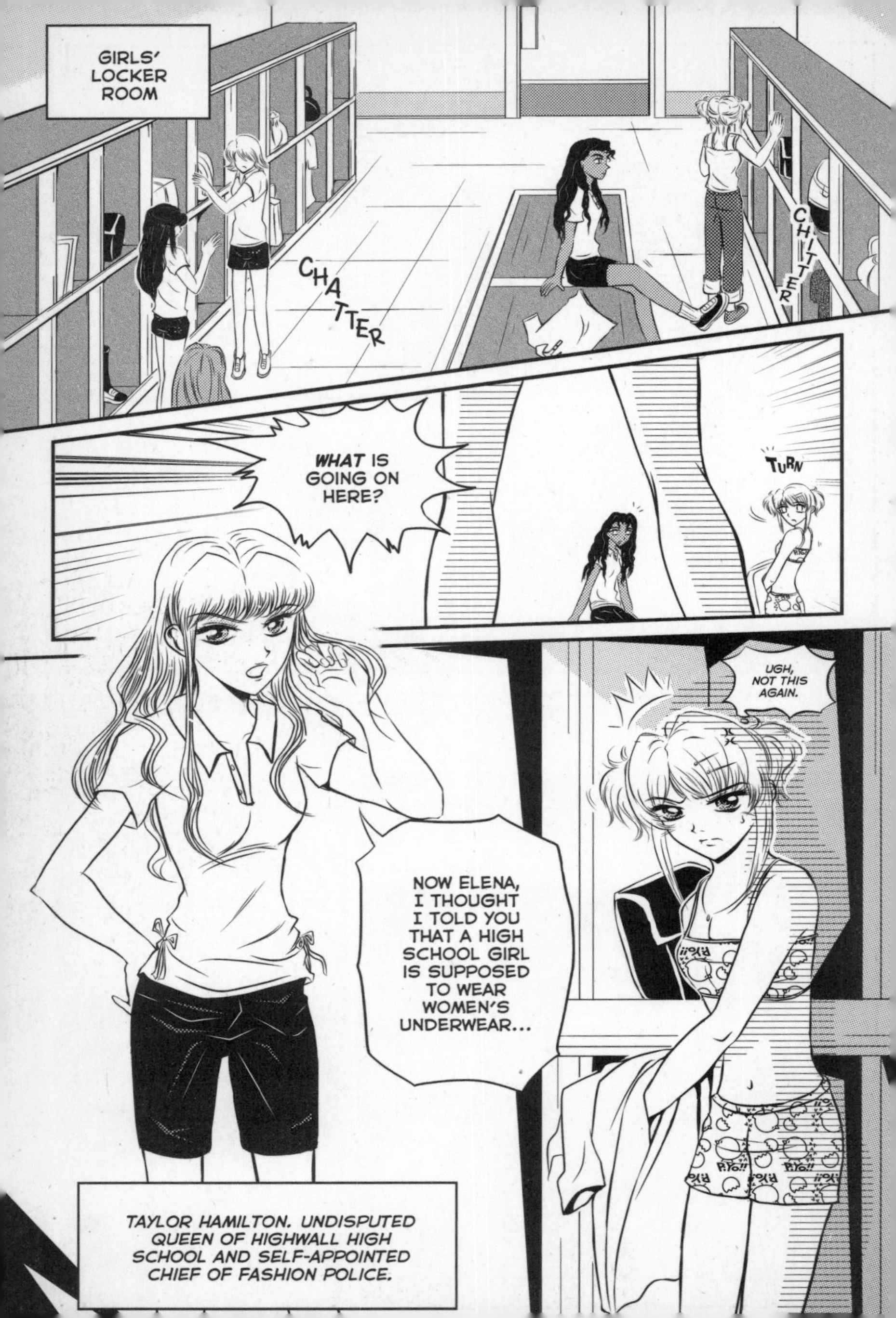
GIRLS' LOCKER ROOM
CHATTER
CHITTER
WHAT IS GOING ON HERE?
TURN
UGH, NOT THIS AGAIN.
NOW ELENA, I THOUGHT I TOLD YOU THAT A HIGH SCHOOL GIRL IS SUPPOSED TO WEAR WOMEN'S UNDERWEAR...
TAYLOR HAMILTON. UNDISPUTED QUEEN OF HIGHWALL HIGH SCHOOL AND SELF-APPOINTED CHIEF OF FASHION POLICE.
PIYO!!

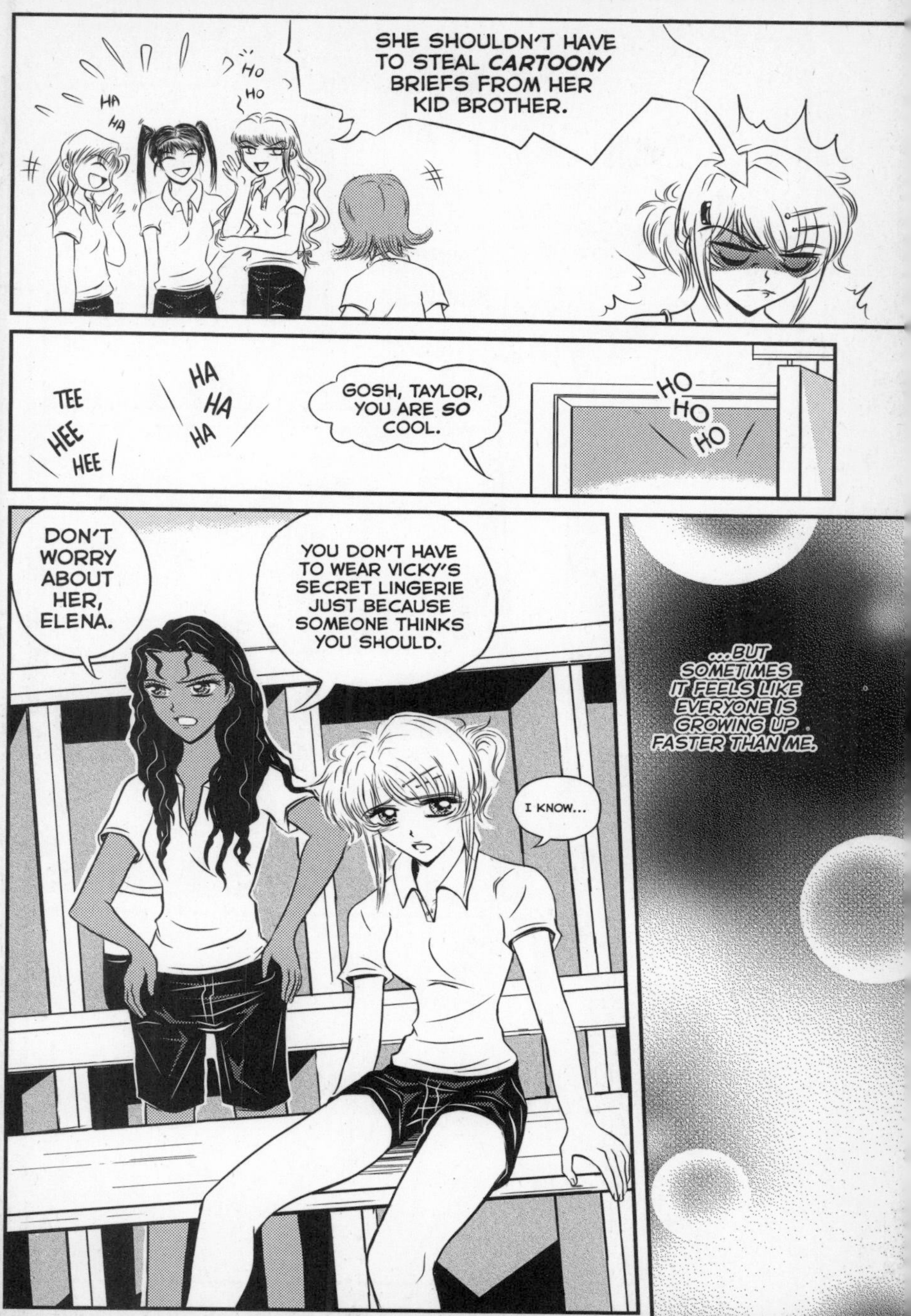
SHE SHOULDN'T HAVE TO STEAL CARTOONY BRIEFS FROM HER KID BROTHER.
HA HA
HO HO
TEE HEE HEE
HA HA HA
GOSH, TAYLOR, YOU ARE SO COOL.
HO HO HO
DON'T WORRY ABOUT HER, ELENA.
YOU DON'T HAVE TO WEAR VICKY'S SECRET LINGERIE JUST BECAUSE SOMEONE THINKS YOU SHOULD.
I KNOW...
...BUT SOMETIMES IT FEELS LIKE EVERYONE IS GROWING UP FASTER THAN ME.

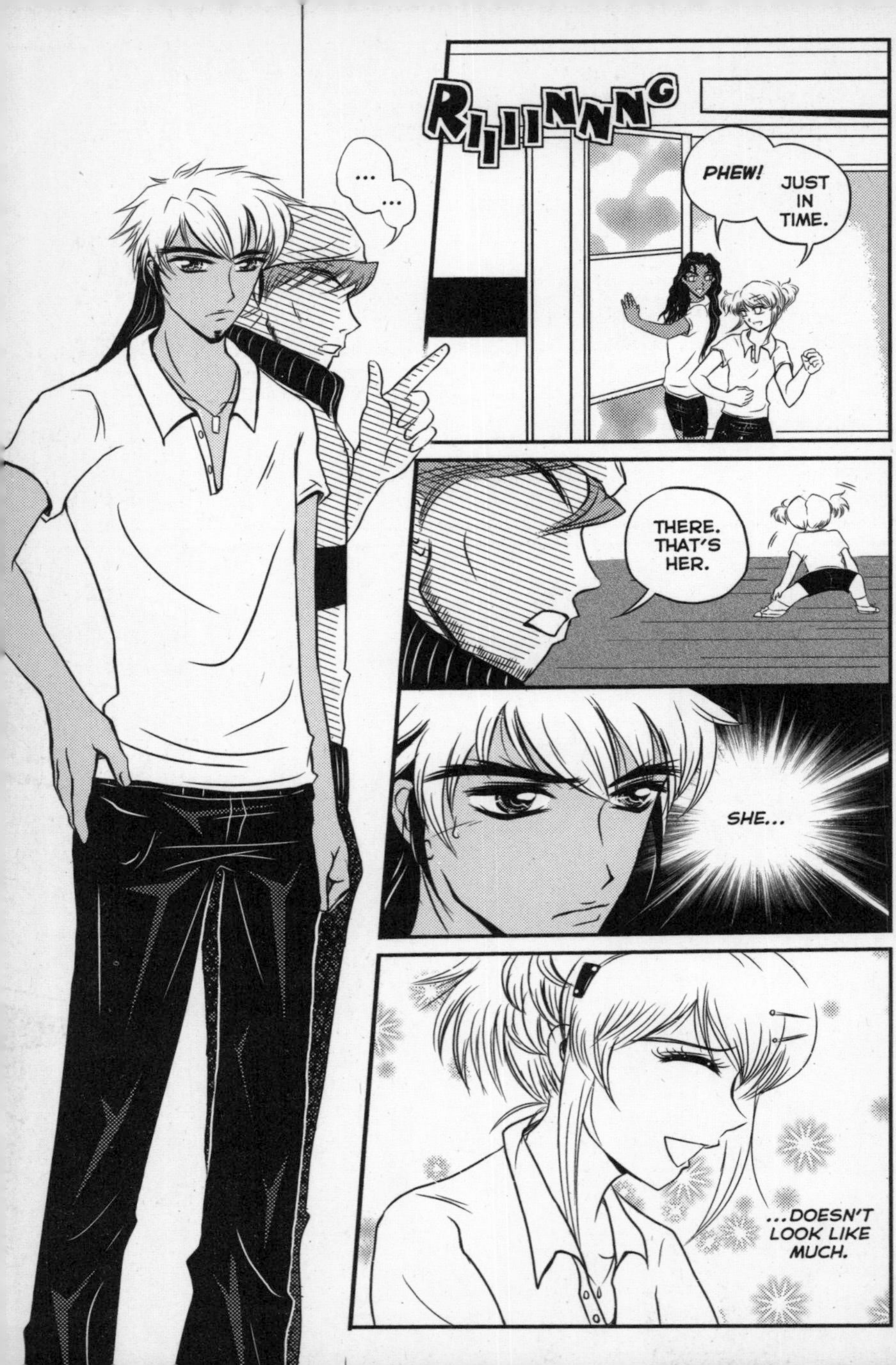
... ...
RIIIINNNG
PHEW!
JUST IN TIME.
THERE. THAT'S HER.
SHE...
...DOESN'T LOOK LIKE MUCH.

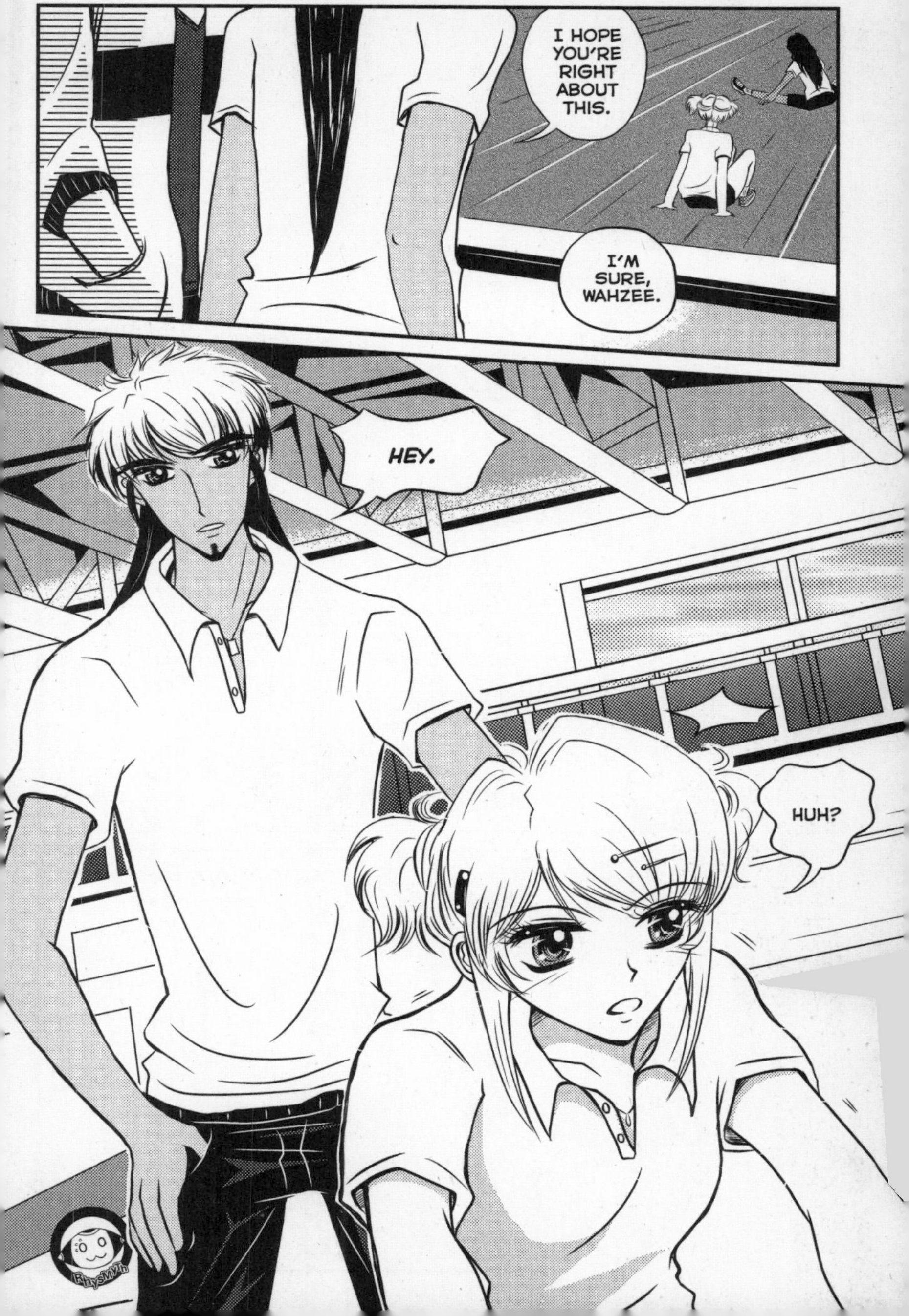
I HOPE YOU'RE RIGHT ABOUT THIS.
I'M SURE, WAHZEE.
HEY.
HUH?

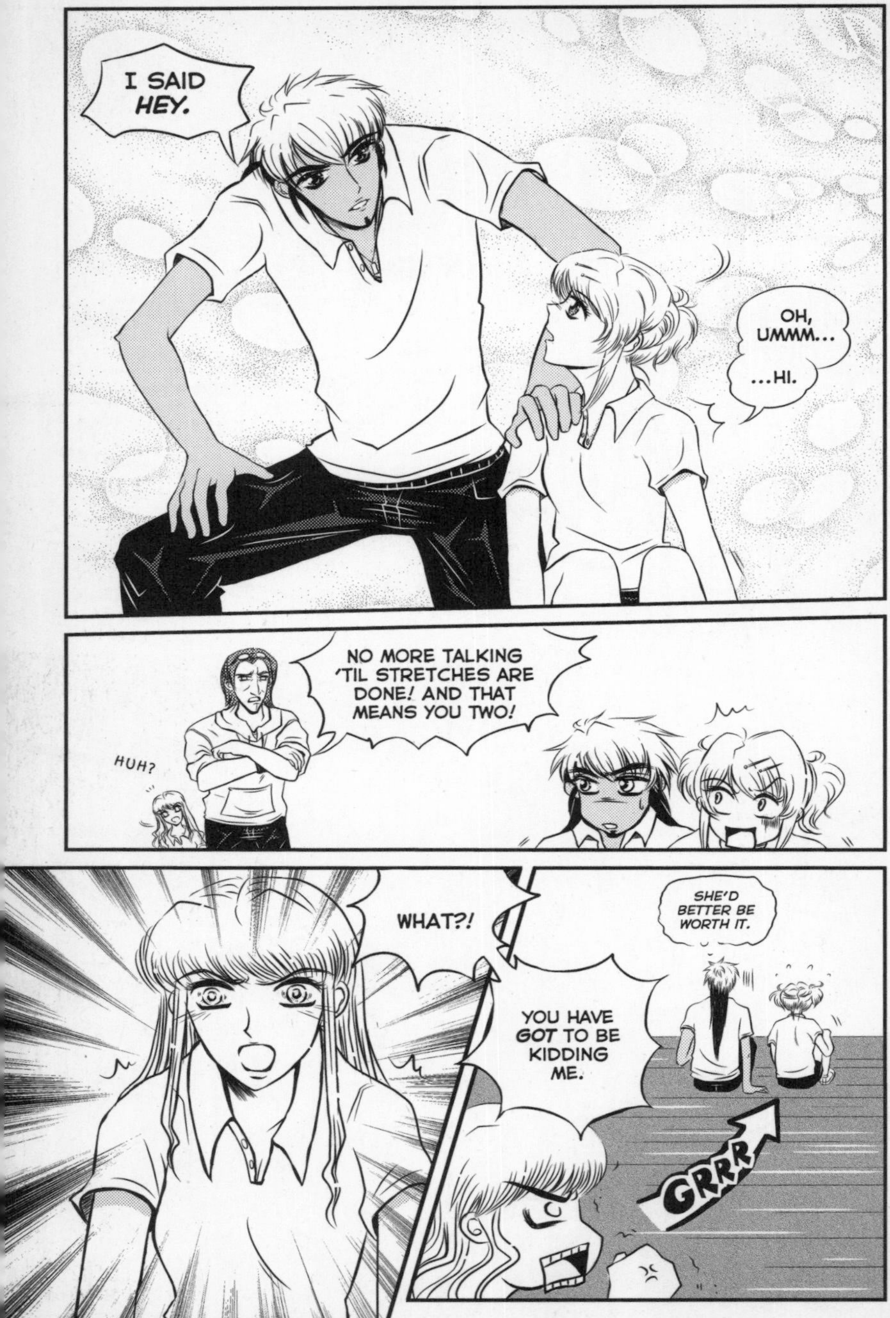
I SAID *HEY.*
OH, UMMM...
...HI.
NO MORE TALKING 'TIL STRETCHES ARE DONE! AND THAT MEANS YOU TWO!
HUH?
WHAT?!
YOU HAVE *GOT* TO BE KIDDING ME.
SHE'D BETTER BE WORTH IT.
GRRR

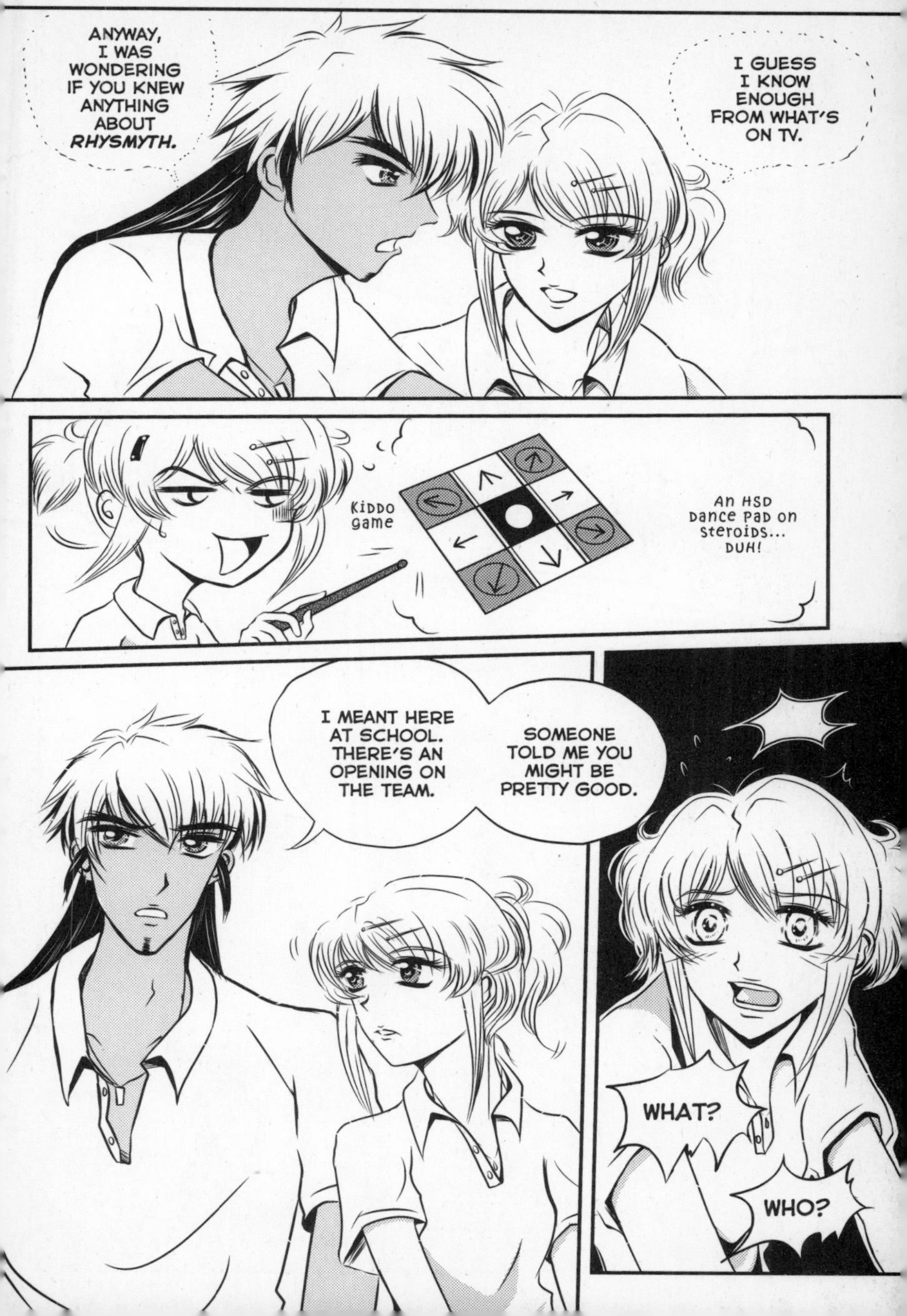
ANYWAY, I WAS WONDERING IF YOU KNEW ANYTHING ABOUT *RHYSMYTH.*
I GUESS I KNOW ENOUGH FROM WHAT'S ON TV.
Kiddo game
An HSD Dance pad on steroids... DUH!
I MEANT HERE AT SCHOOL. THERE'S AN OPENING ON THE TEAM.
SOMEONE TOLD ME YOU MIGHT BE PRETTY GOOD.
WHAT?
WHO?

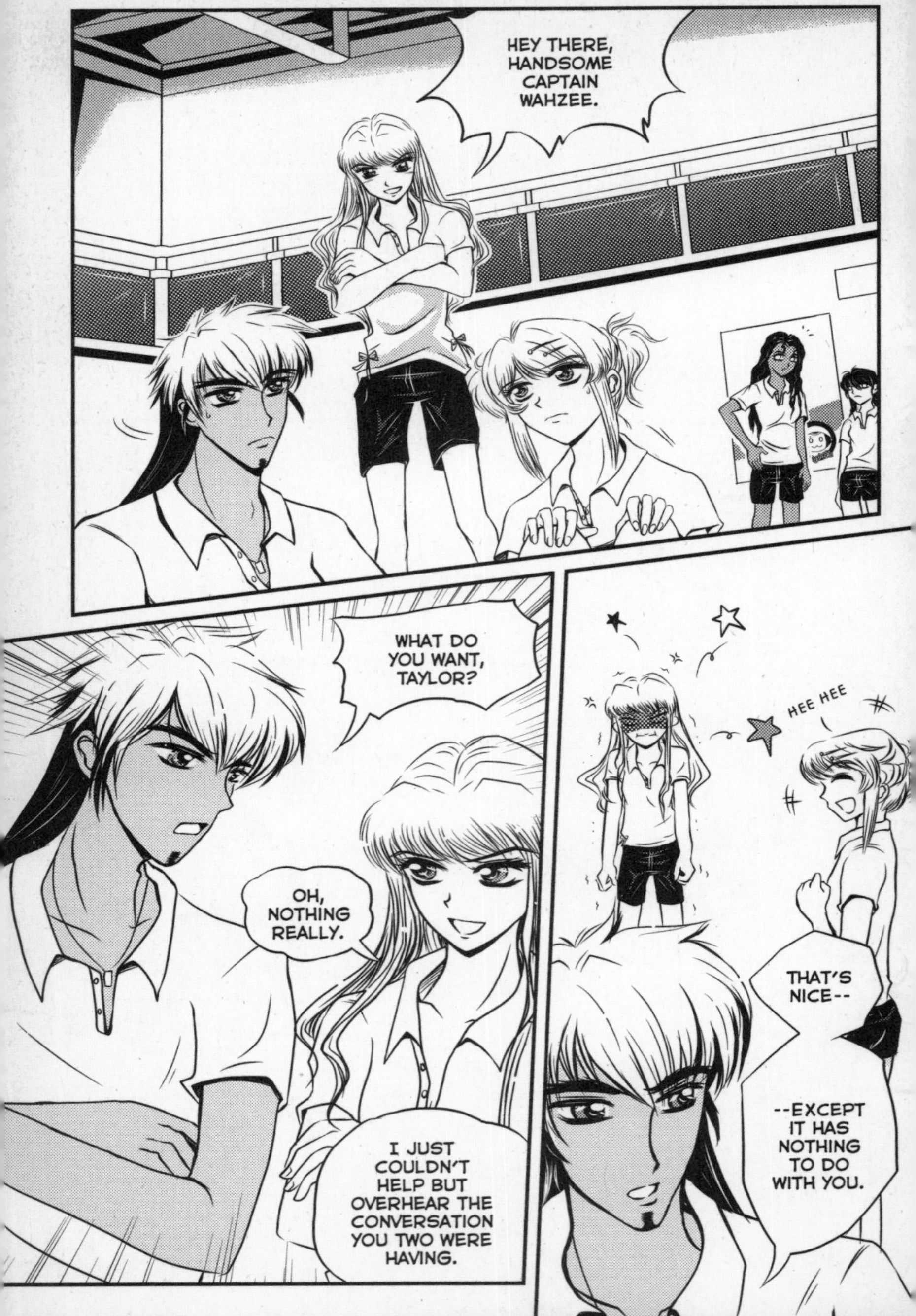
HEY THERE, HANDSOME CAPTAIN WAHZEE.
WHAT DO YOU WANT, TAYLOR?
OH, NOTHING REALLY.
I JUST COULDN'T HELP BUT OVERHEAR THE CONVERSATION YOU TWO WERE HAVING.
HEE HEE
THAT'S NICE--
--EXCEPT IT HAS NOTHING TO DO WITH YOU.

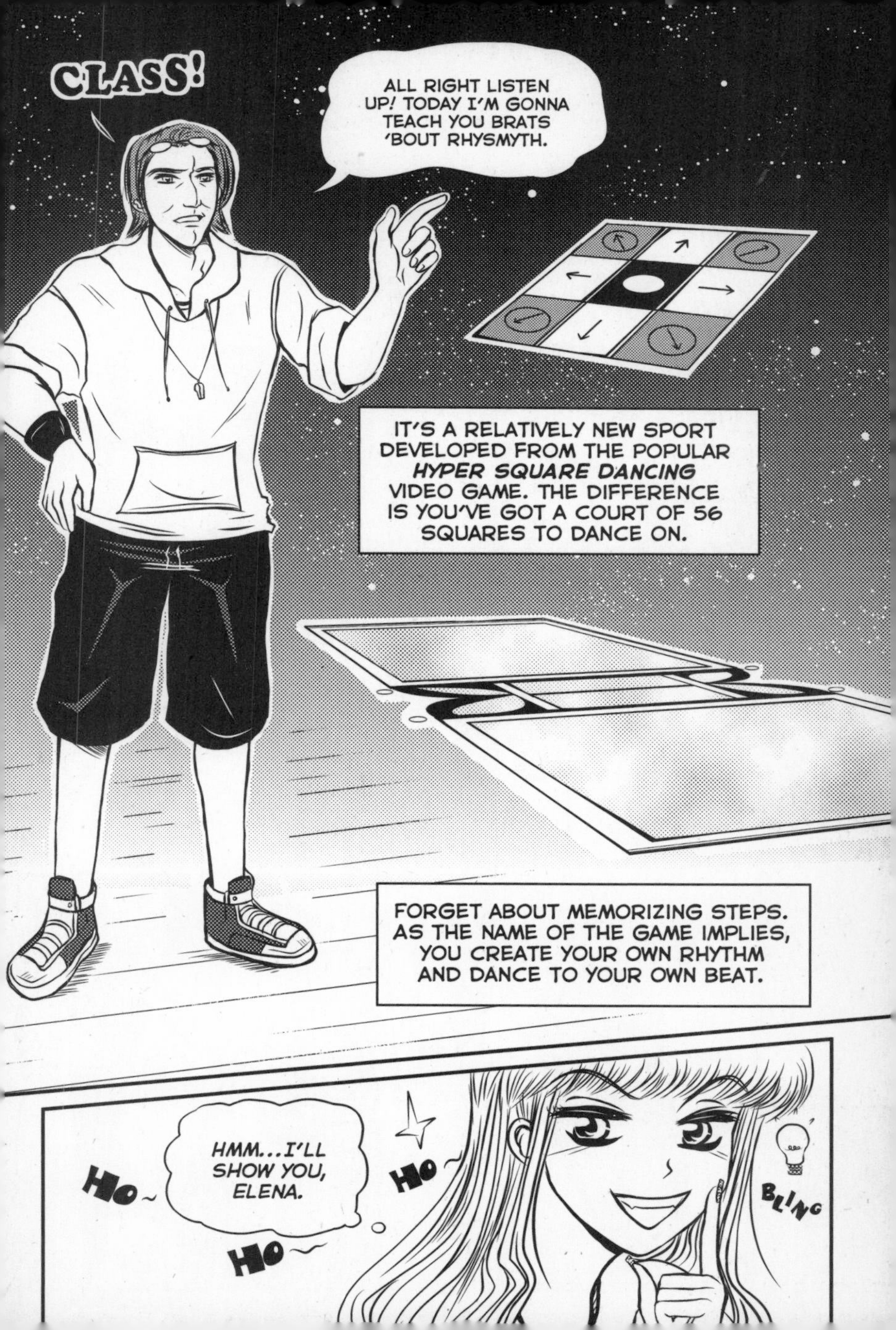
CLASS!
ALL RIGHT LISTEN UP! TODAY I'M GONNA TEACH YOU BRATS 'BOUT RHYSMYTH.
IT'S A RELATIVELY NEW SPORT DEVELOPED FROM THE POPULAR *HYPER SQUARE DANCING* VIDEO GAME. THE DIFFERENCE IS YOU'VE GOT A COURT OF 56 SQUARES TO DANCE ON.
FORGET ABOUT MEMORIZING STEPS. AS THE NAME OF THE GAME IMPLIES, YOU CREATE YOUR OWN RHYTHM AND DANCE TO YOUR OWN BEAT.
HO~
HMM...I'LL SHOW YOU, ELENA.
HO~
HO~
BLING

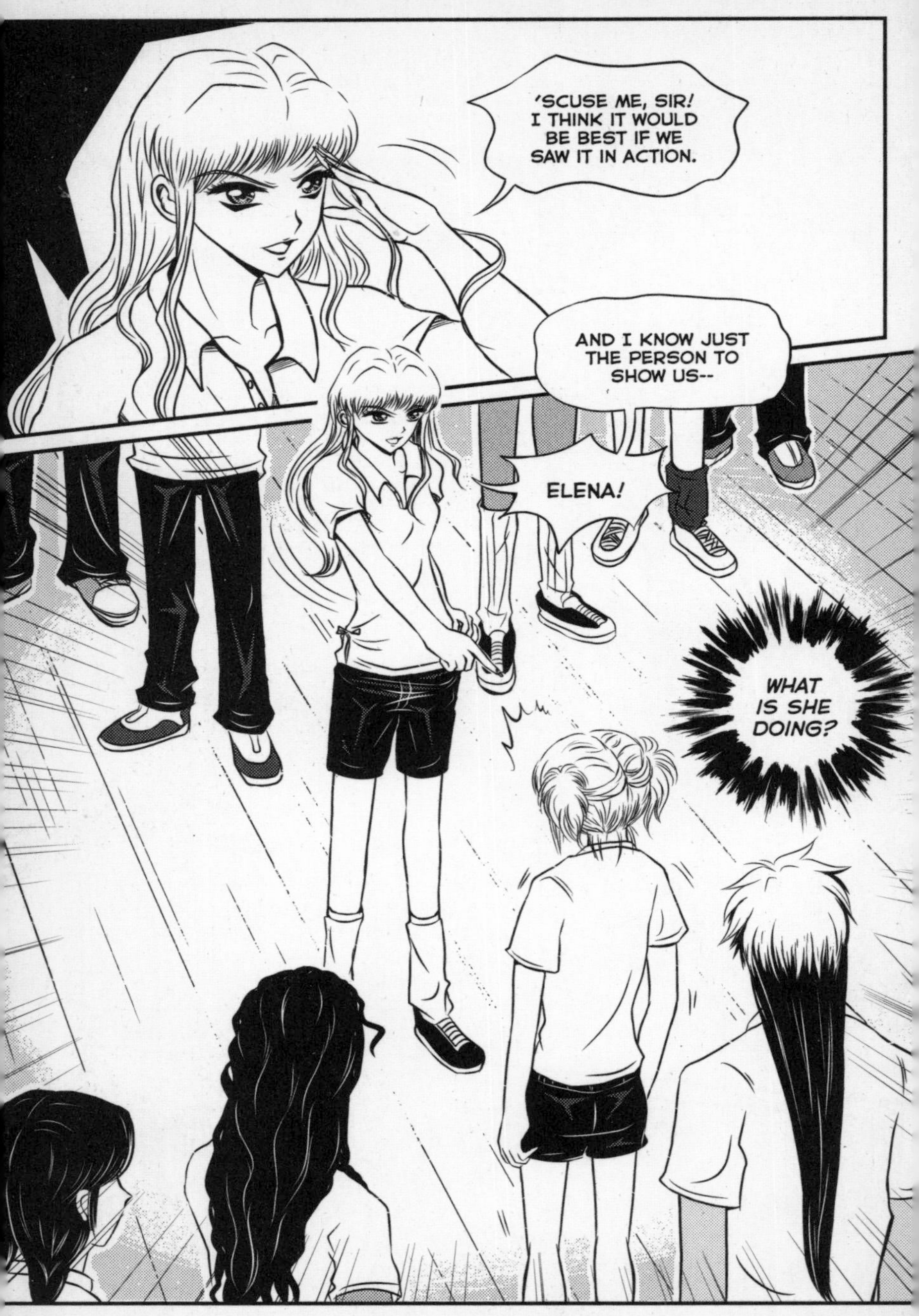
'SCUSE ME, SIR! I THINK IT WOULD BE BEST IF WE SAW IT IN ACTION.
AND I KNOW JUST THE PERSON TO SHOW US--
ELENA!
WHAT IS SHE DOING?

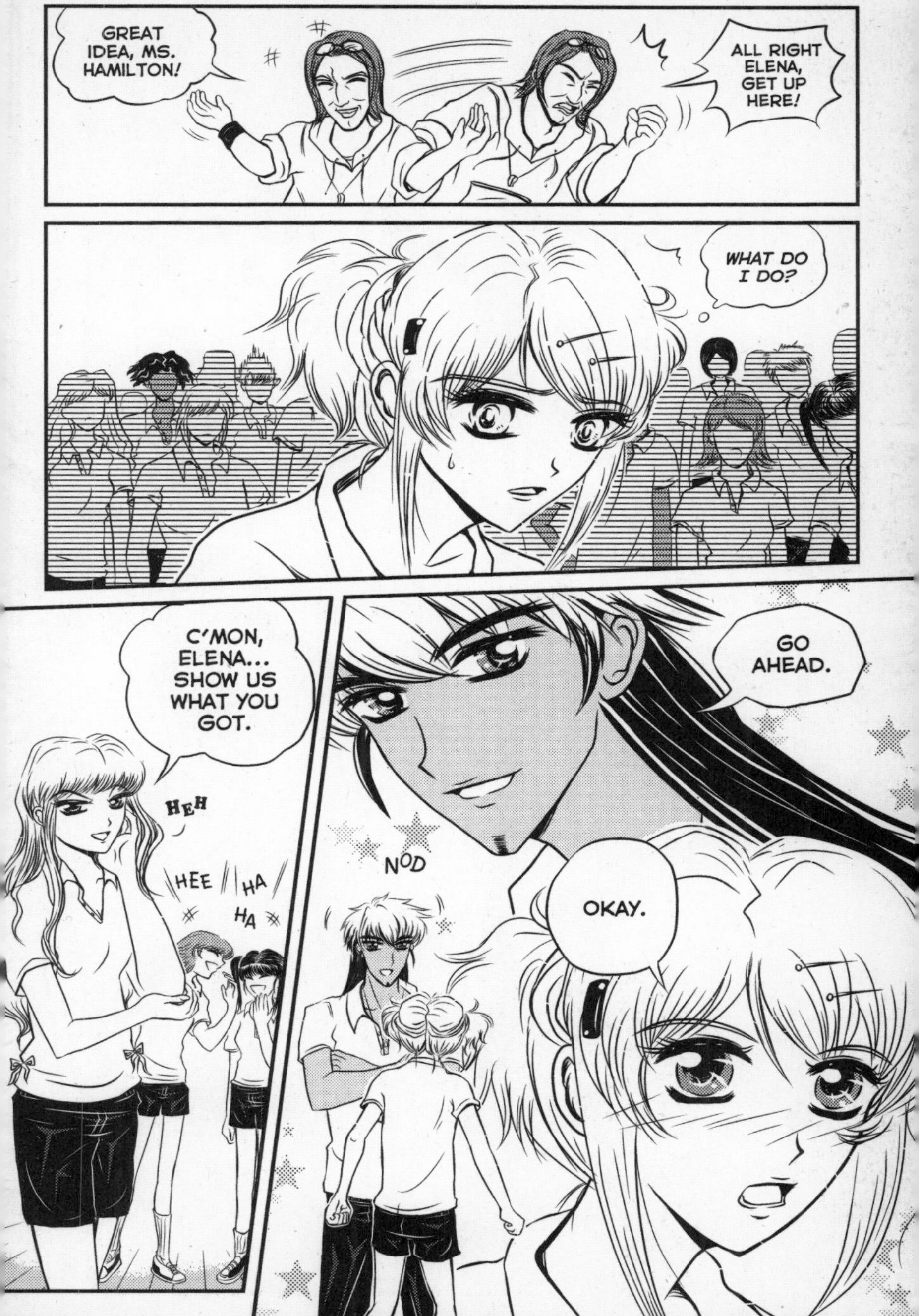
GREAT IDEA, MS. HAMILTON!
ALL RIGHT ELENA, GET UP HERE!
WHAT DO I DO?
C'MON, ELENA... SHOW US WHAT YOU GOT.
HEH
HEE
HA
HA
GO AHEAD.
NOD
OKAY.

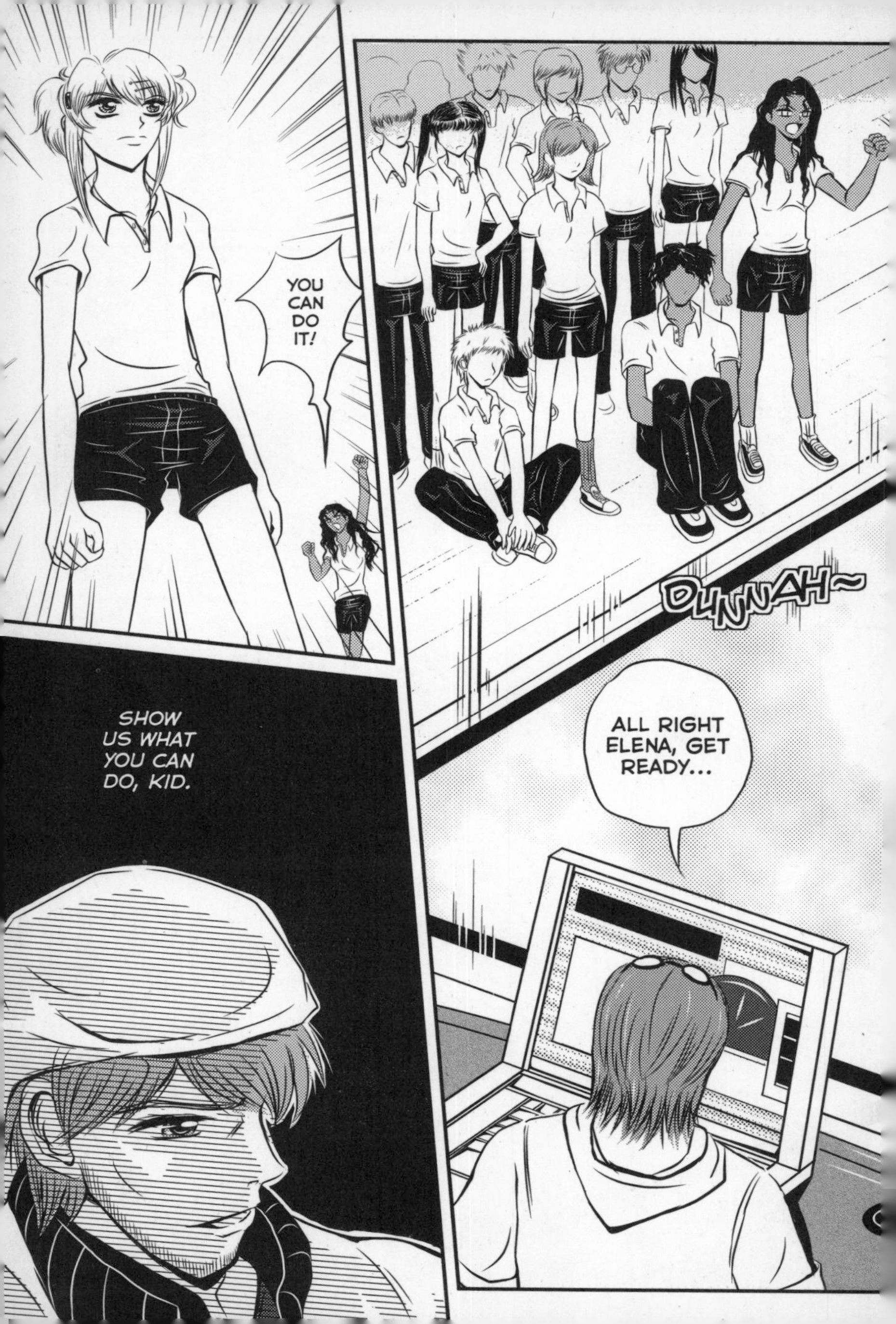
YOU CAN DO IT!
DUNNAH~
SHOW US WHAT YOU CAN DO, KID.
ALL RIGHT ELENA, GET READY...

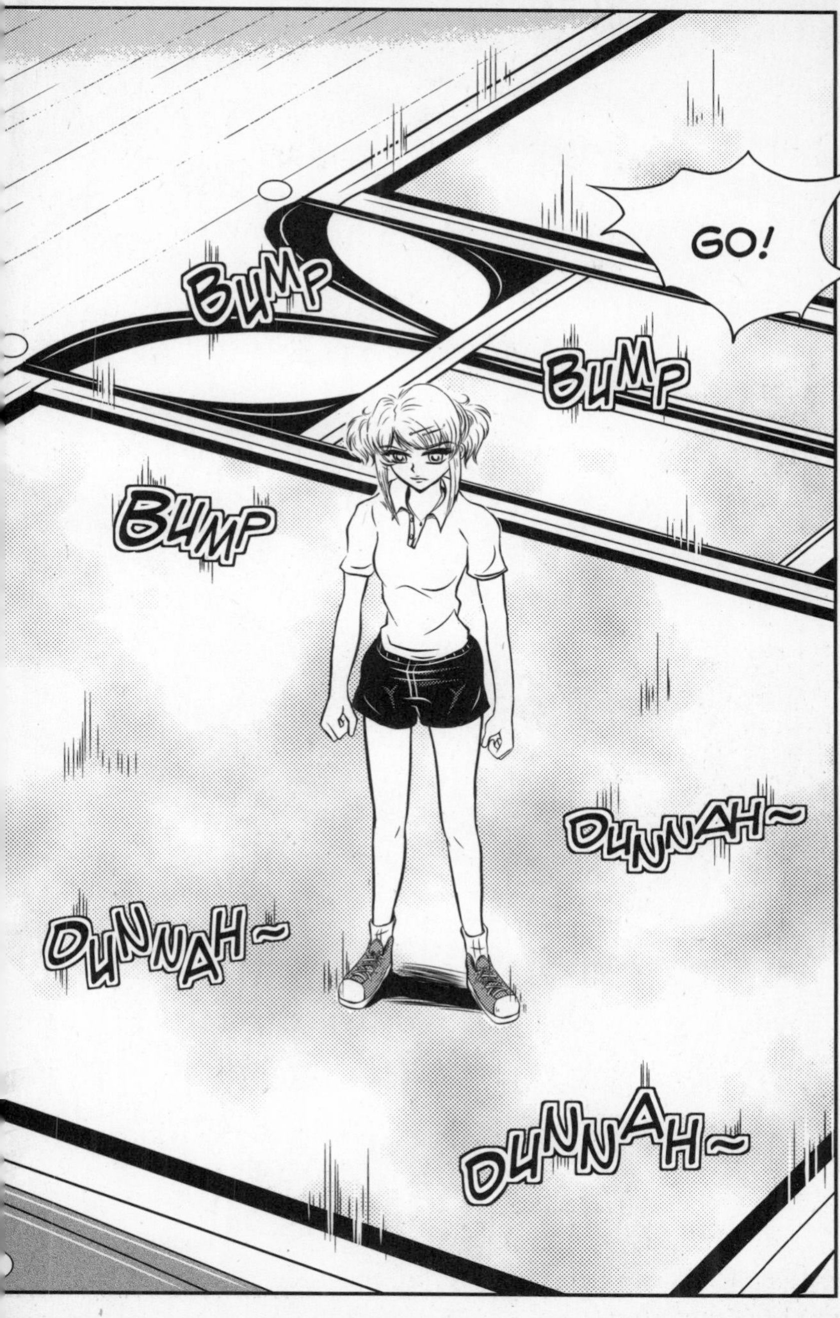
GO!
BUMP
BUMP
BUMP
DUNNAH~
DUNNAH~
DUNNAH~

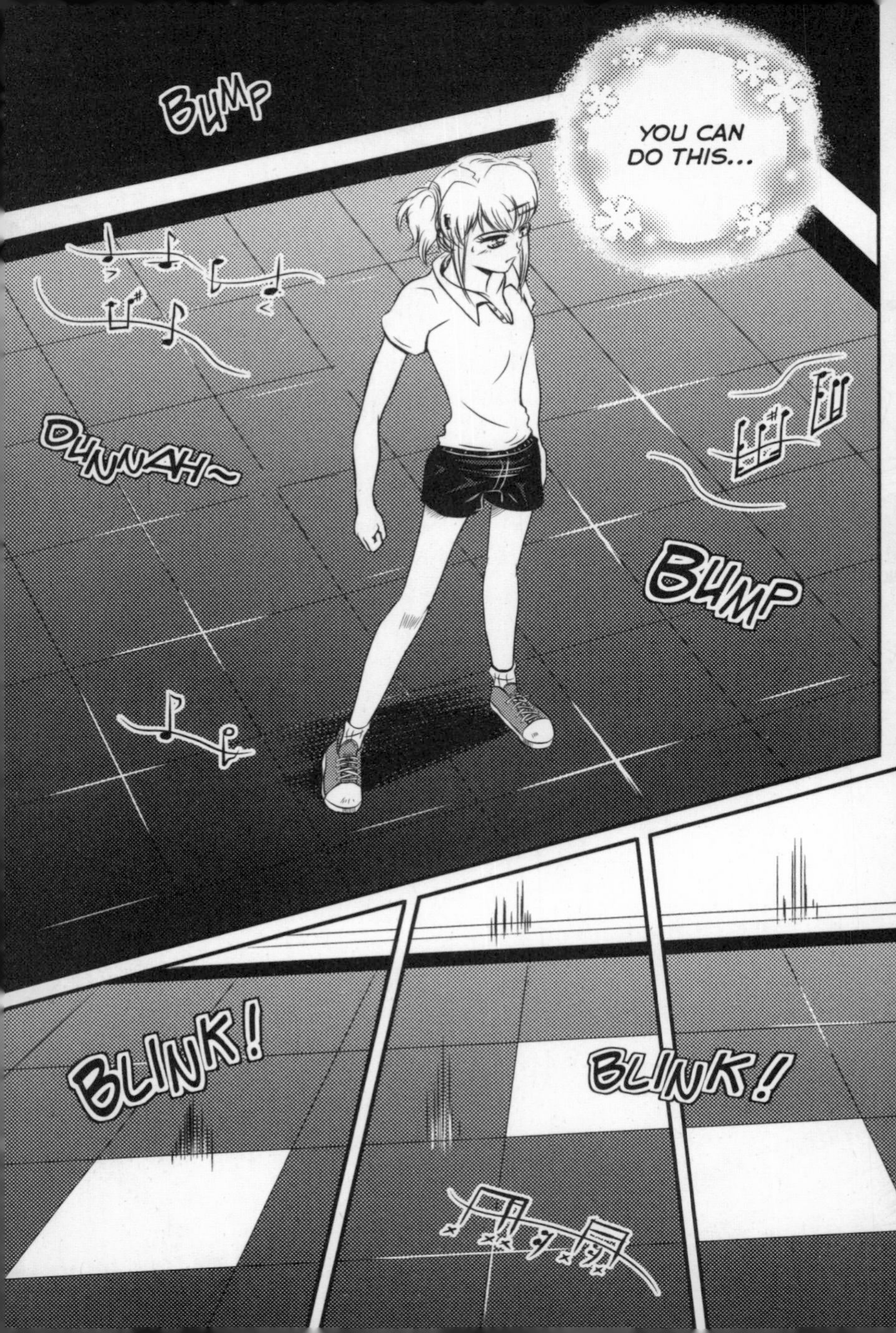
BUMP
YOU CAN DO THIS...
DUNNAH~
BUMP
BLINK!
BLINK!

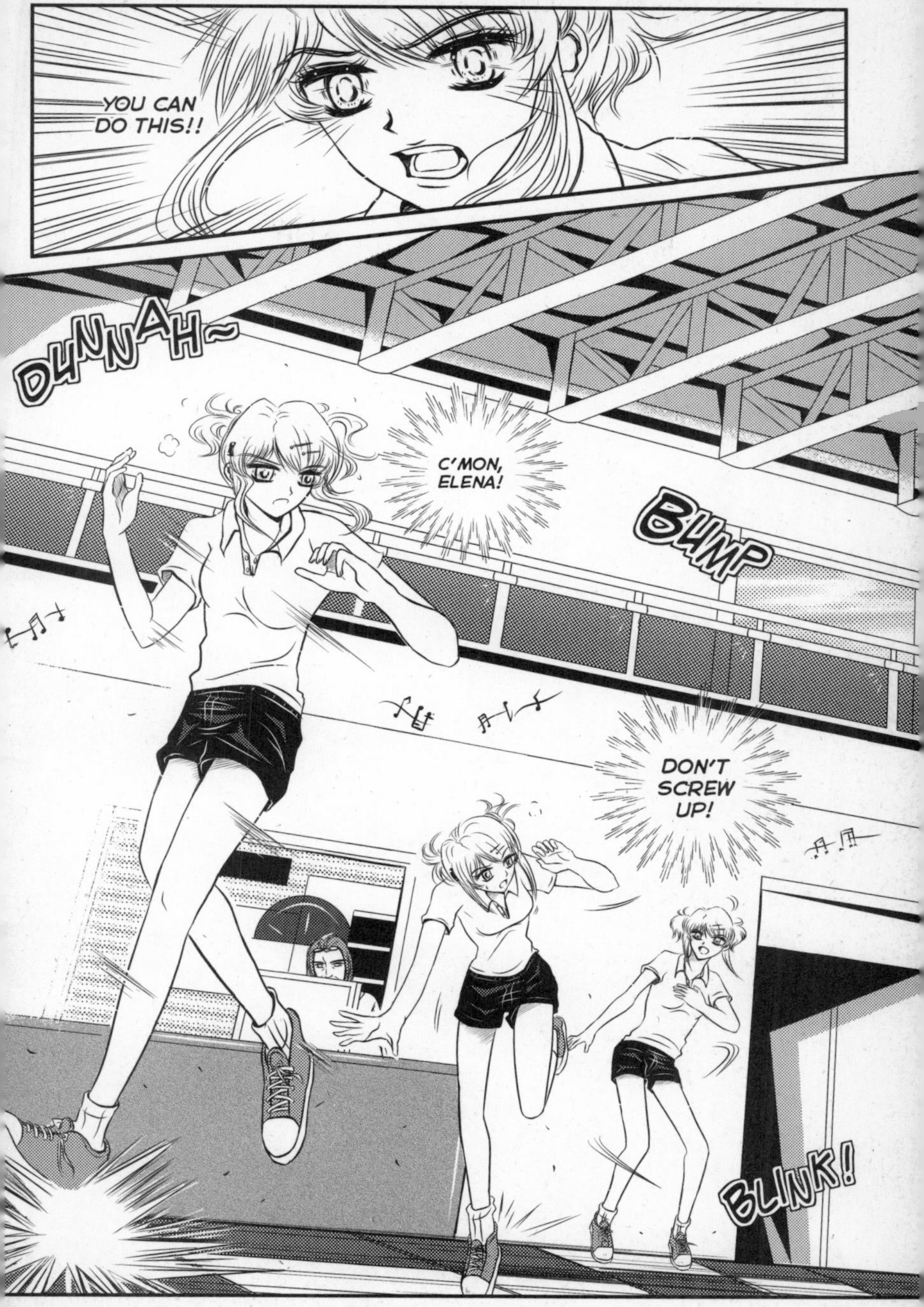

YOU CAN DO THIS!!
DUNNAH~
C'MON, ELENA!
BUMP
DON'T SCREW UP!
BLINK!

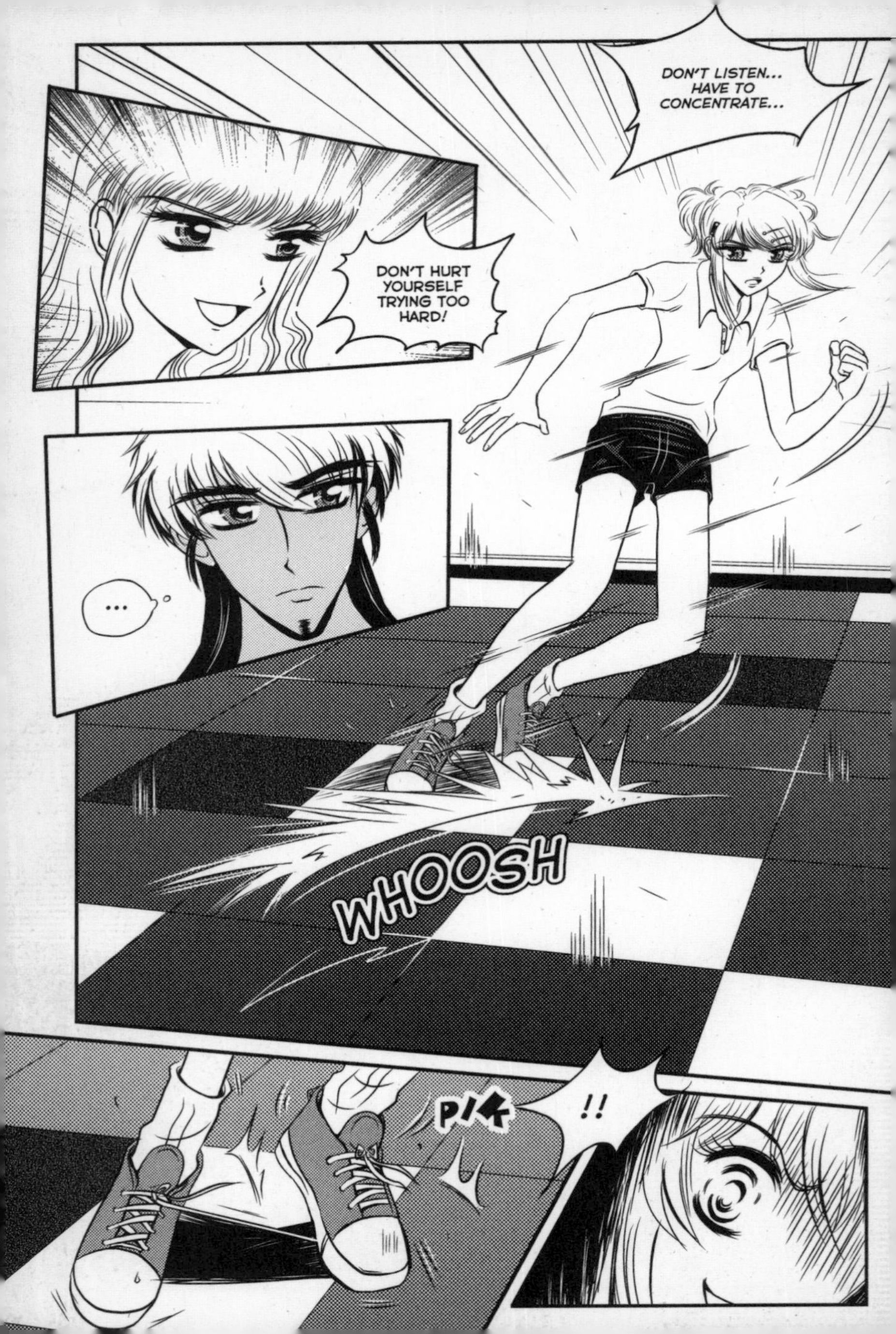
DON'T HURT YOURSELF TRYING TOO HARD!
DON'T LISTEN... HAVE TO CONCENTRATE...
...
WHOOSH
PIK
!!

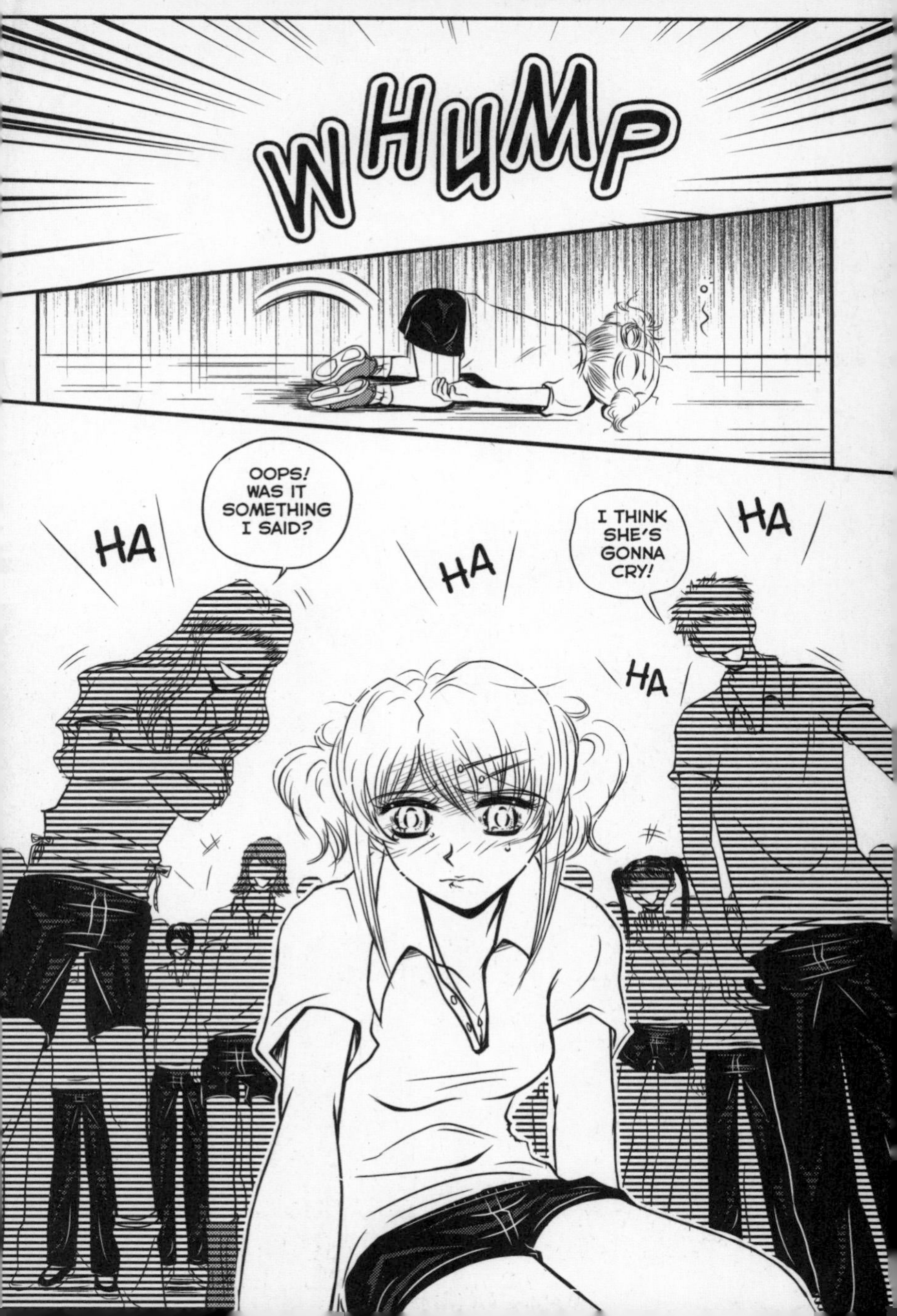
WHUMP
HA
OOPS! WAS IT SOMETHING I SAID?
HA
I THINK SHE'S GONNA CRY!
HA
HA

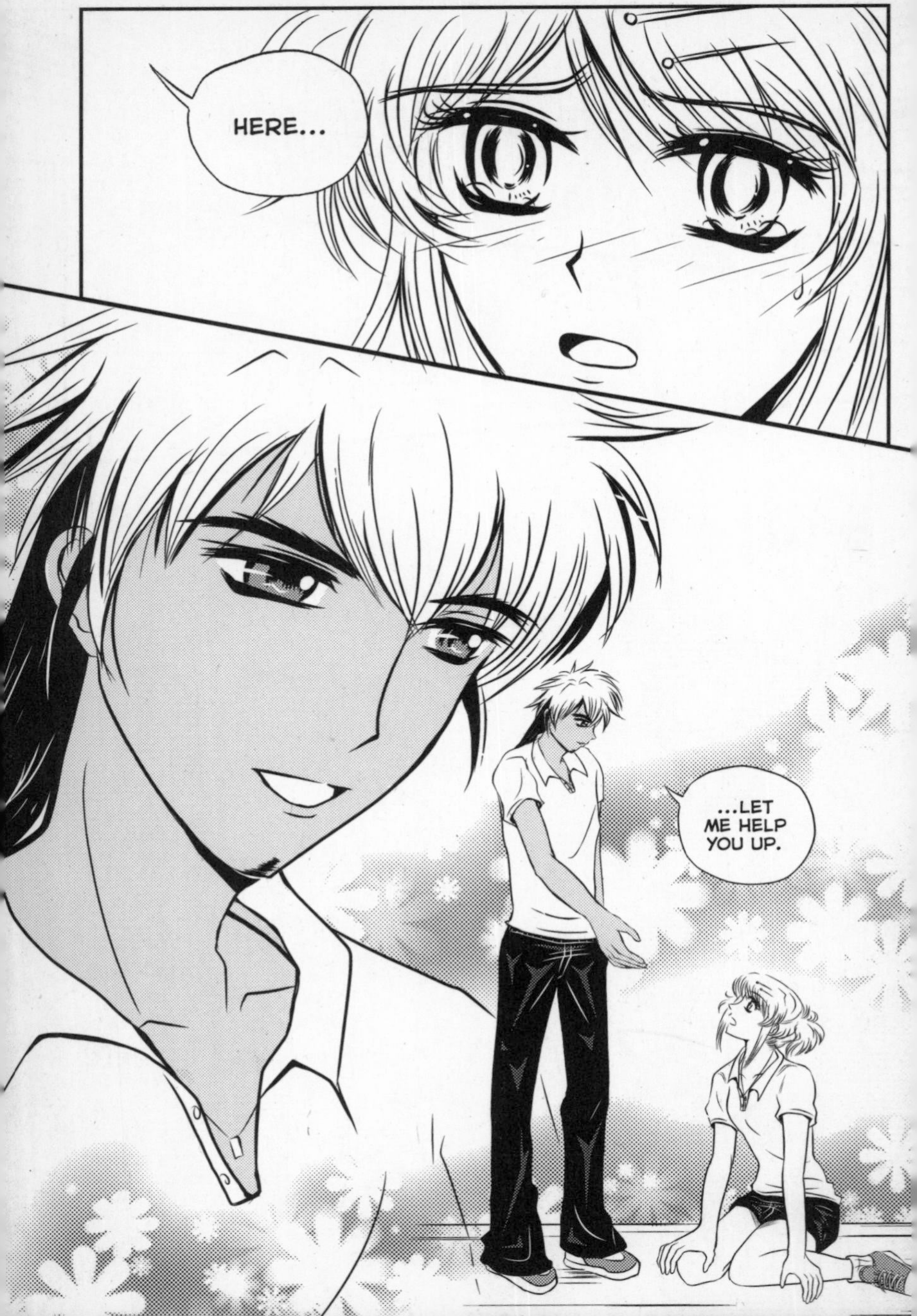
HERE...
...LET ME HELP YOU UP.

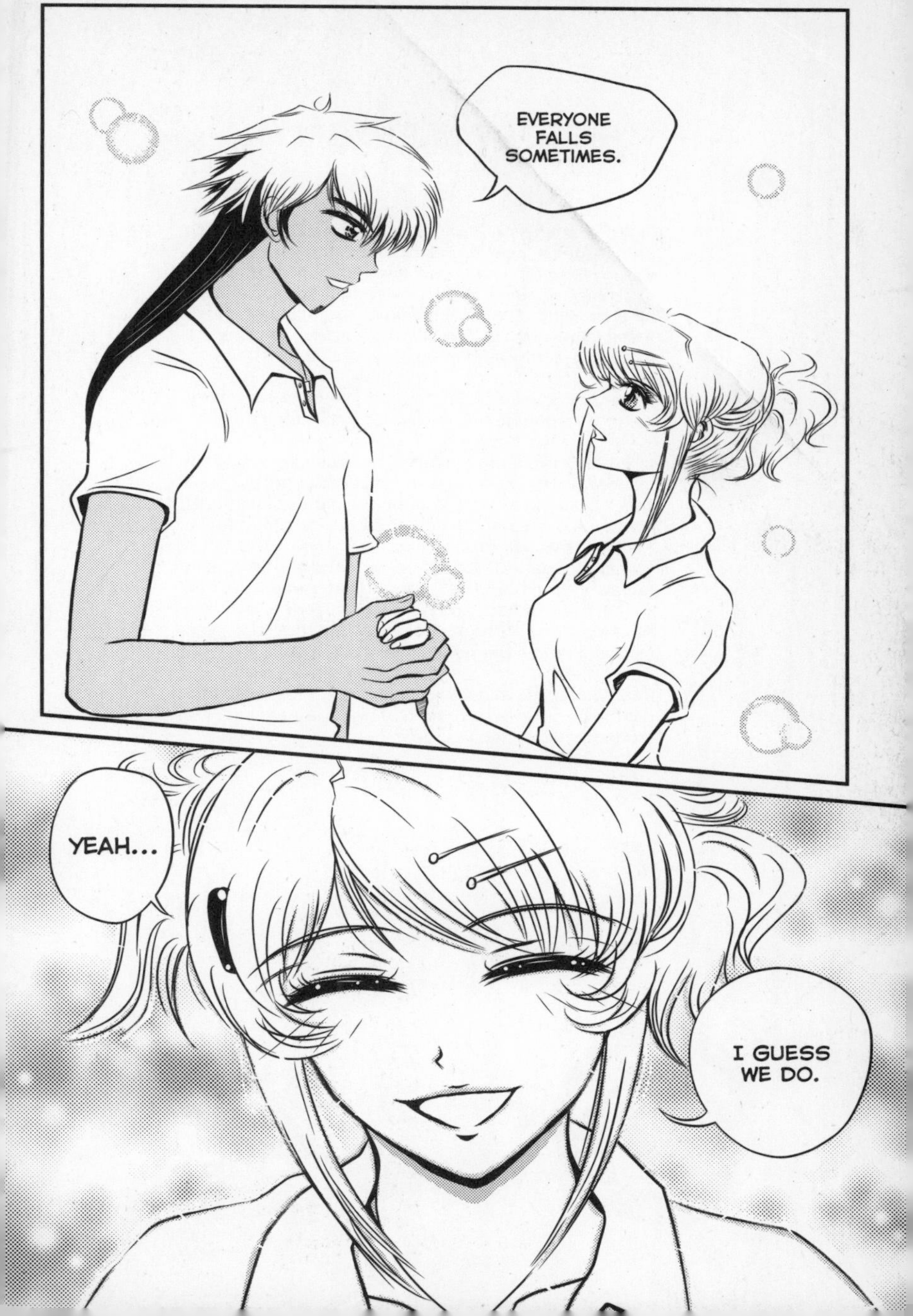
EVERYONE FALLS SOMETIMES.
YEAH...
I GUESS WE DO.

HISTORY of RHYSMYTH

In 1997, the very first Hyper Square Dance (HSD) arcade game was released and took the world by storm. People of all ages lined up, pockets full of quarters, awaiting their turn to join in the newest gaming sensation. After a successful home video game conversion in 1998, HSD went on to become the #1 selling video game of the year and 3rd all-time.

Through the years, HSD has sustained its popularity despite competition from various knockoff games.

In 2002, a rabid fan following composed of freestyle players openly criticized the rigid structure of HSD and the game's inability to punish players who only memorized step sequences and refused to actually "dance" during songs. Together they developed Rhysmyth, an HSD-based game that simultaneously rewards style and strategy. With an expanded dance floor and the potential for limitless creativity, Rhysmyth has surpassed its predecessor and continues to garner new players every day.

Anything but a fad, Rhysmyth recently joined the pantheon of American sports with the opening of a professional league last year.

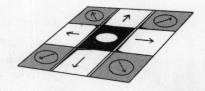

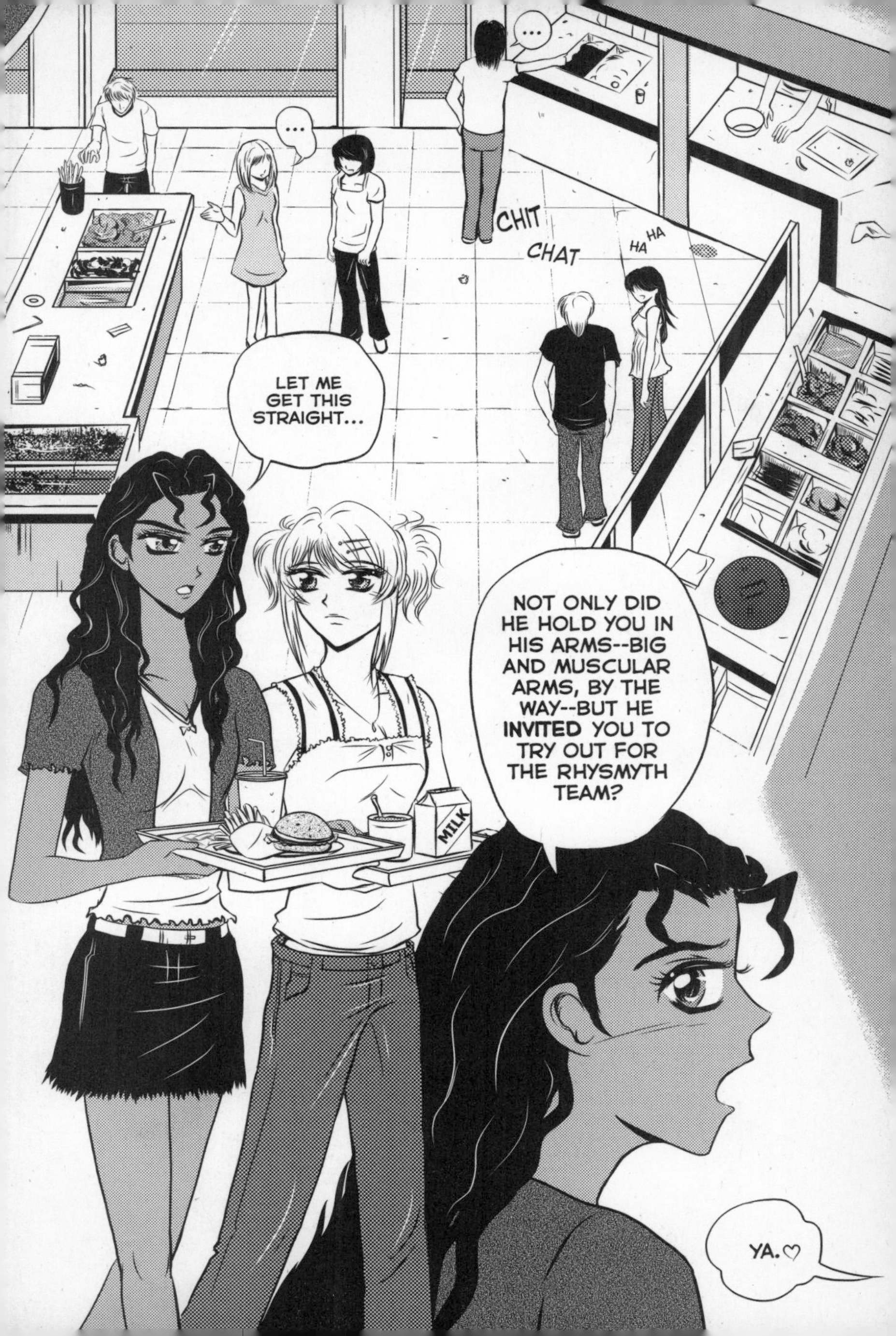
...
...
CHIT CHAT
HA HA
LET ME GET THIS STRAIGHT...
NOT ONLY DID HE HOLD YOU IN HIS ARMS--BIG AND MUSCULAR ARMS, BY THE WAY--BUT HE INVITED YOU TO TRY OUT FOR THE RHYSMYTH TEAM?
MILK
YA.♡

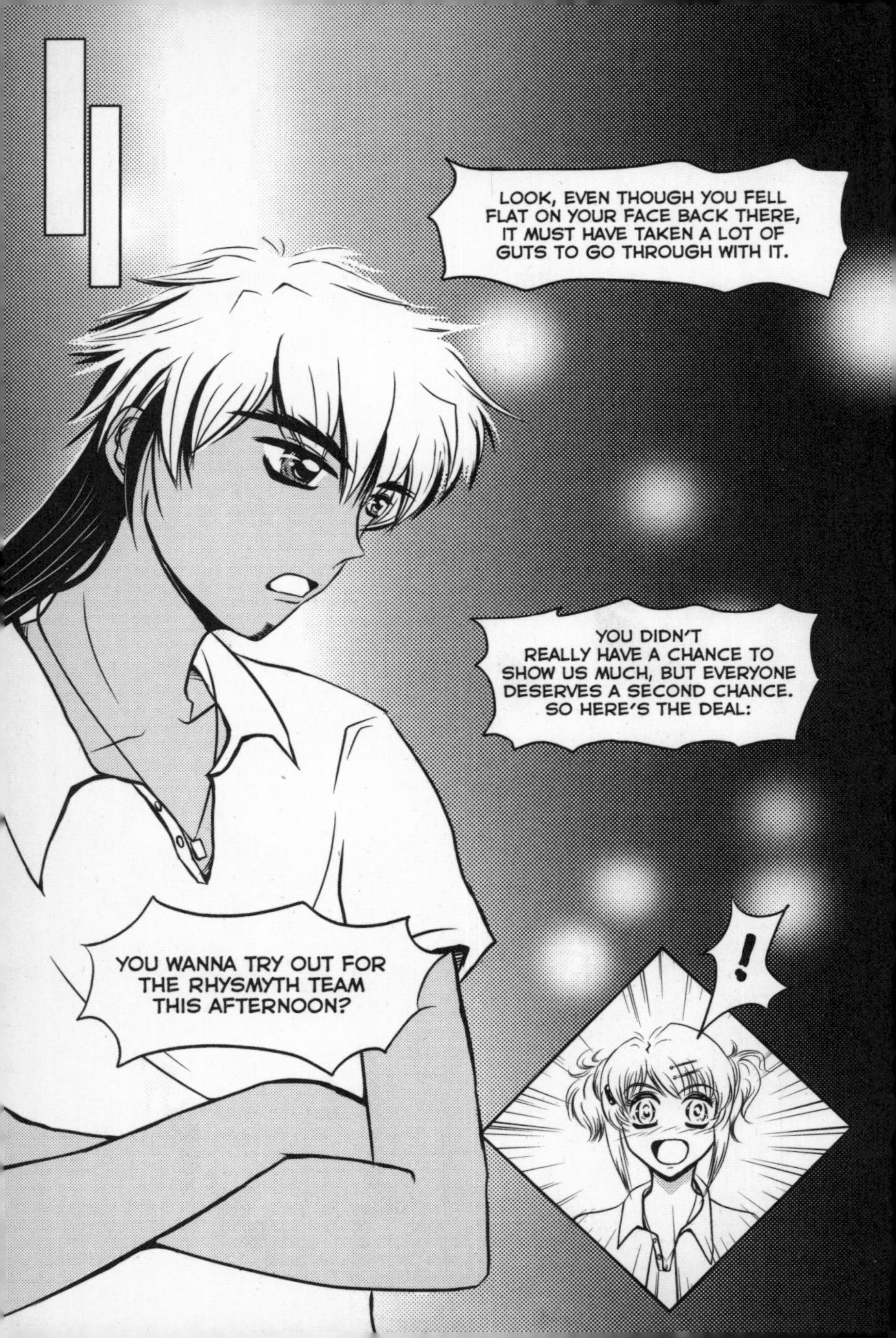
LOOK, EVEN THOUGH YOU FELL FLAT ON YOUR FACE BACK THERE, IT MUST HAVE TAKEN A LOT OF GUTS TO GO THROUGH WITH IT.
YOU DIDN'T REALLY HAVE A CHANCE TO SHOW US MUCH, BUT EVERYONE DESERVES A SECOND CHANCE. SO HERE'S THE DEAL:
YOU WANNA TRY OUT FOR THE RHYSMYTH TEAM THIS AFTERNOON?
!

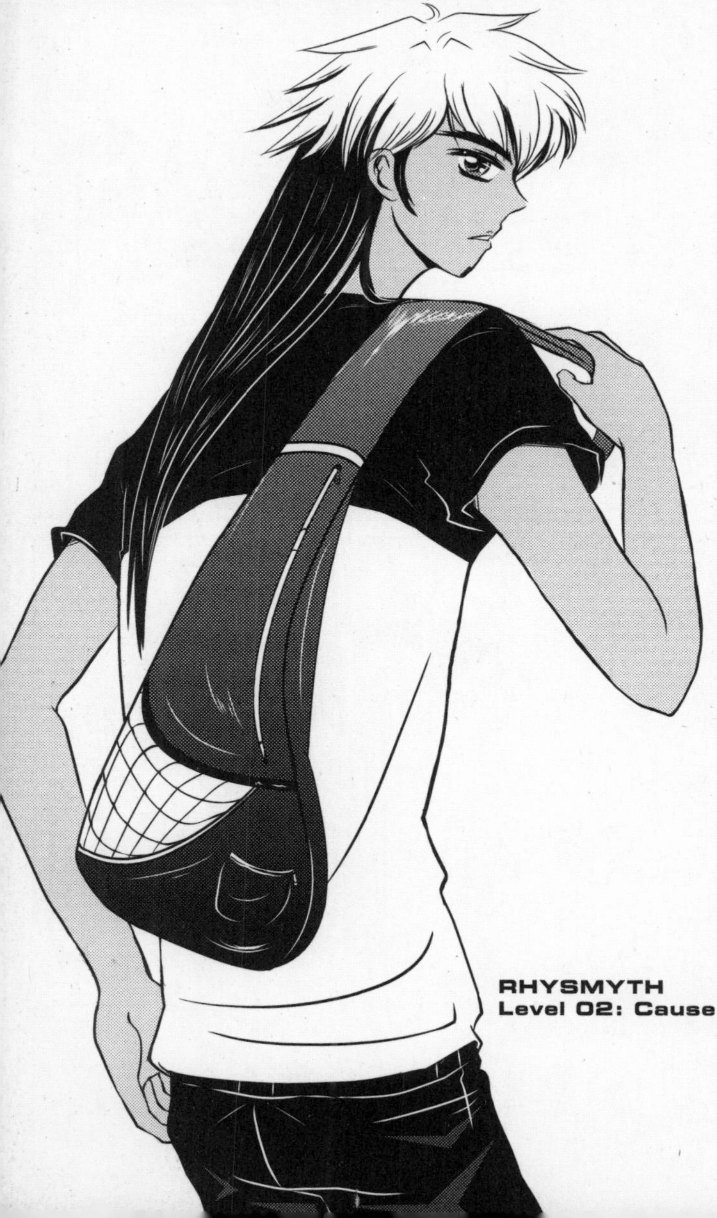

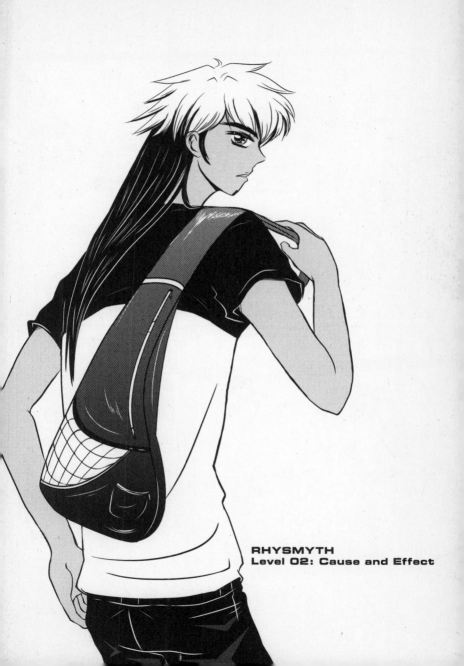

RHYSMYTH
Level 02: Cause and Effect

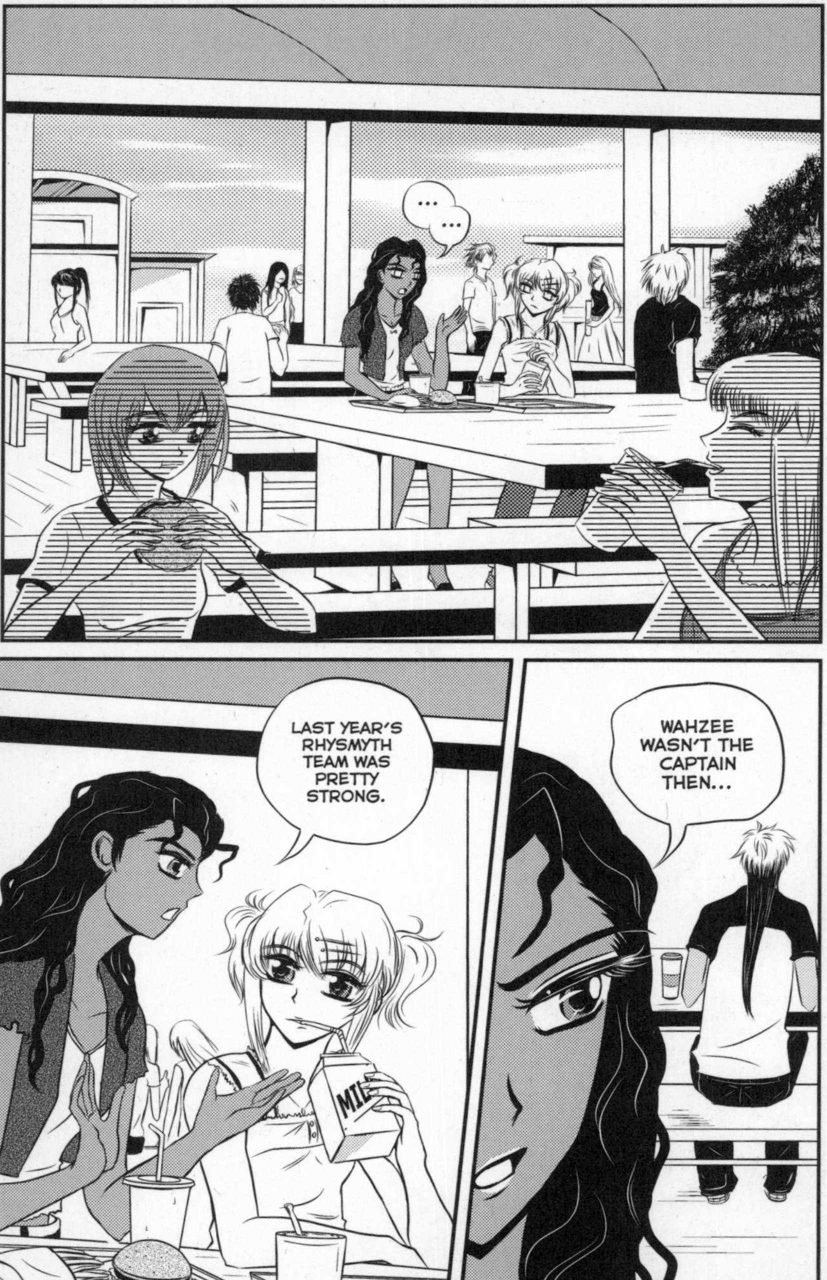
...
...
LAST YEAR'S RHYSMYTH TEAM WAS PRETTY STRONG.
WAHZEE WASN'T THE CAPTAIN THEN...

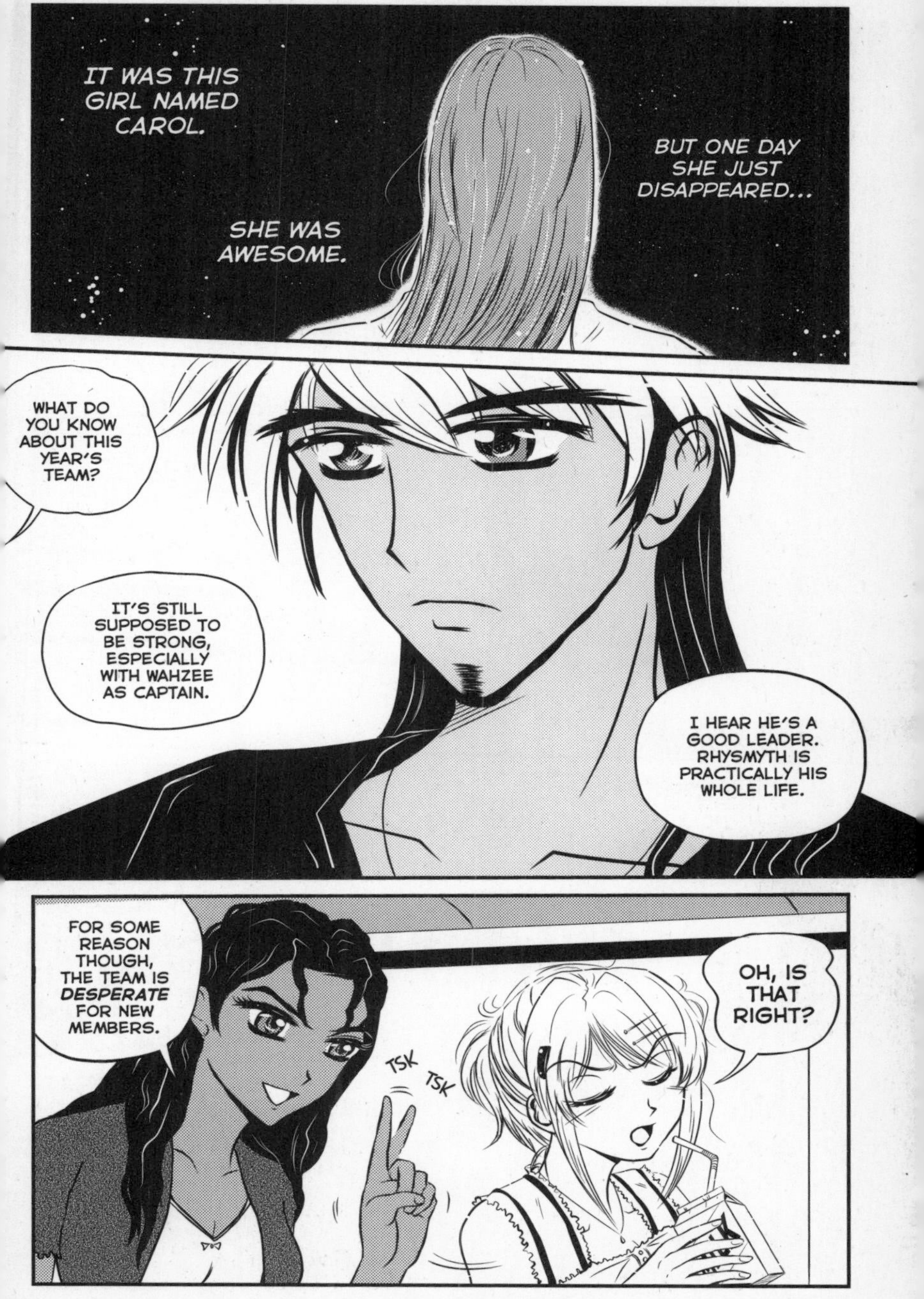
IT WAS THIS GIRL NAMED CAROL.
SHE WAS AWESOME.
BUT ONE DAY SHE JUST DISAPPEARED...
WHAT DO YOU KNOW ABOUT THIS YEAR'S TEAM?
IT'S STILL SUPPOSED TO BE STRONG, ESPECIALLY WITH WAHZEE AS CAPTAIN.
I HEAR HE'S A GOOD LEADER. RHYSMYTH IS PRACTICALLY HIS WHOLE LIFE.
FOR SOME REASON THOUGH, THE TEAM IS ***DESPERATE*** FOR NEW MEMBERS.
TSK TSK
OH, IS THAT RIGHT?

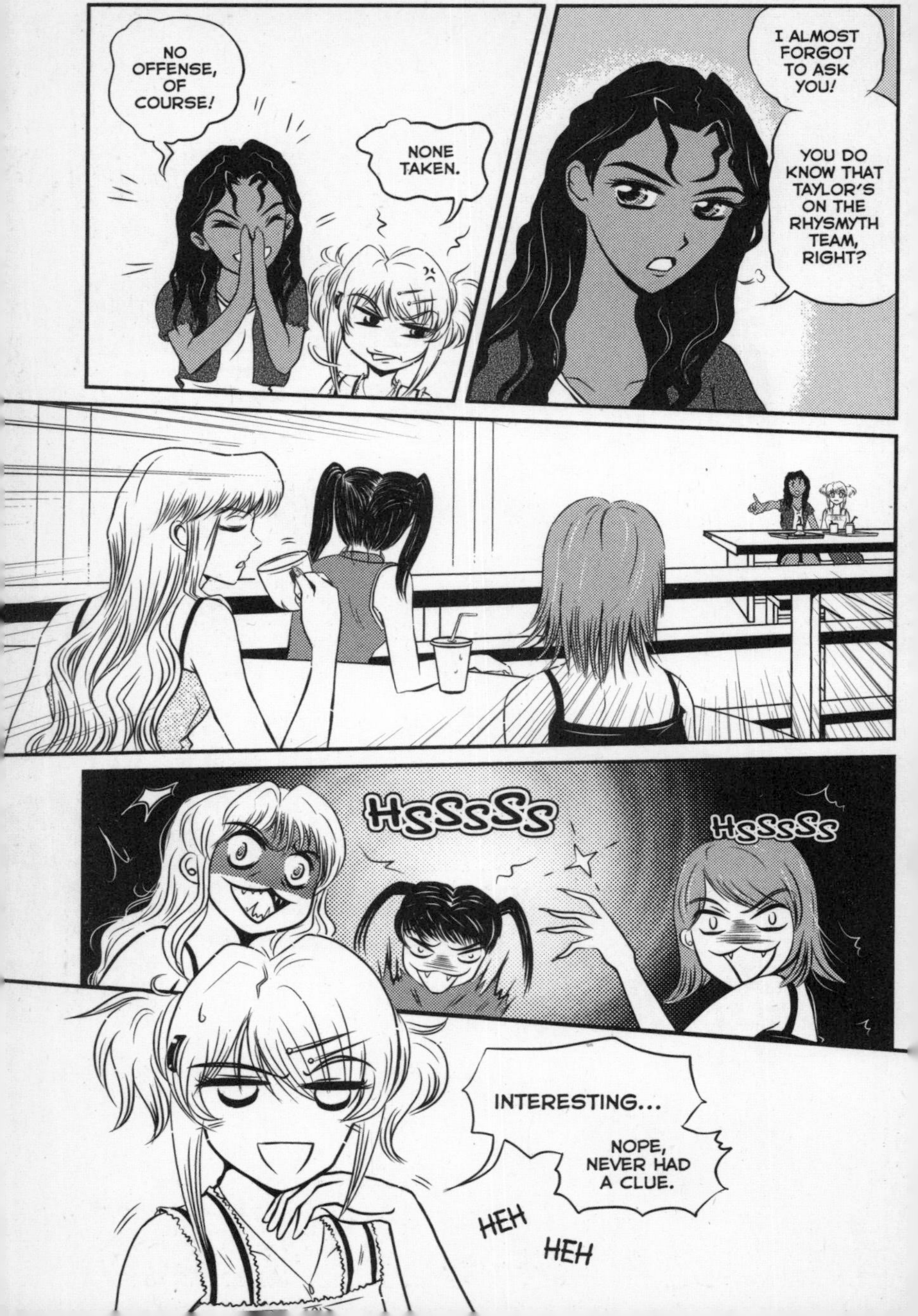
NO OFFENSE, OF COURSE!
NONE TAKEN.
I ALMOST FORGOT TO ASK YOU!
YOU DO KNOW THAT TAYLOR'S ON THE RHYSMYTH TEAM, RIGHT?
HSSSSS
HSSSSS
INTERESTING...
NOPE, NEVER HAD A CLUE.
HEH
HEH

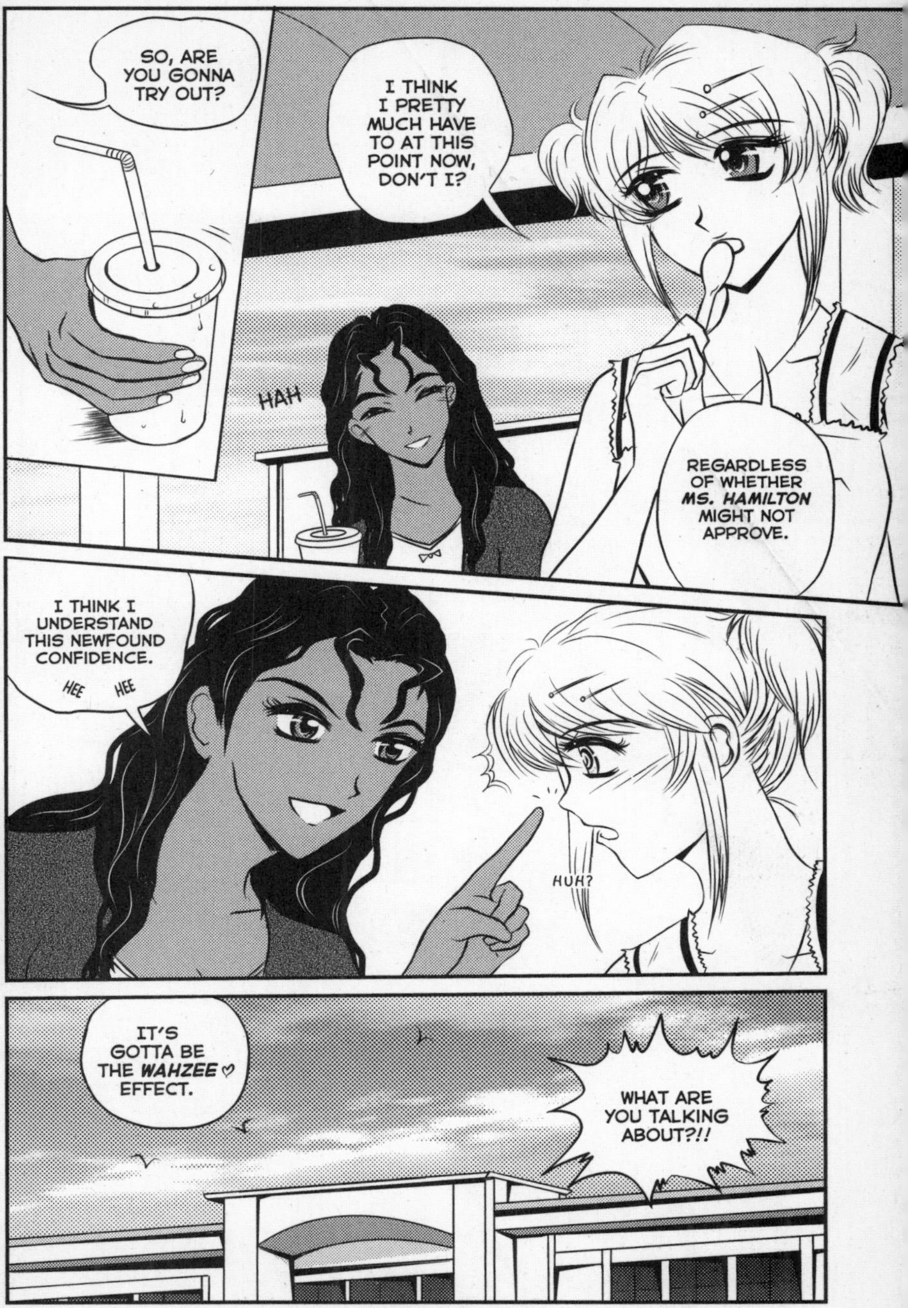
SO, ARE YOU GONNA TRY OUT?
I THINK I PRETTY MUCH HAVE TO AT THIS POINT NOW, DON'T I?
HAH
REGARDLESS OF WHETHER ***MS. HAMILTON*** MIGHT NOT APPROVE.
I THINK I UNDERSTAND THIS NEWFOUND CONFIDENCE.
HEE HEE
HUH?
IT'S GOTTA BE THE ***WAHZEE*** ♡ EFFECT.
WHAT ARE YOU TALKING ABOUT?!!

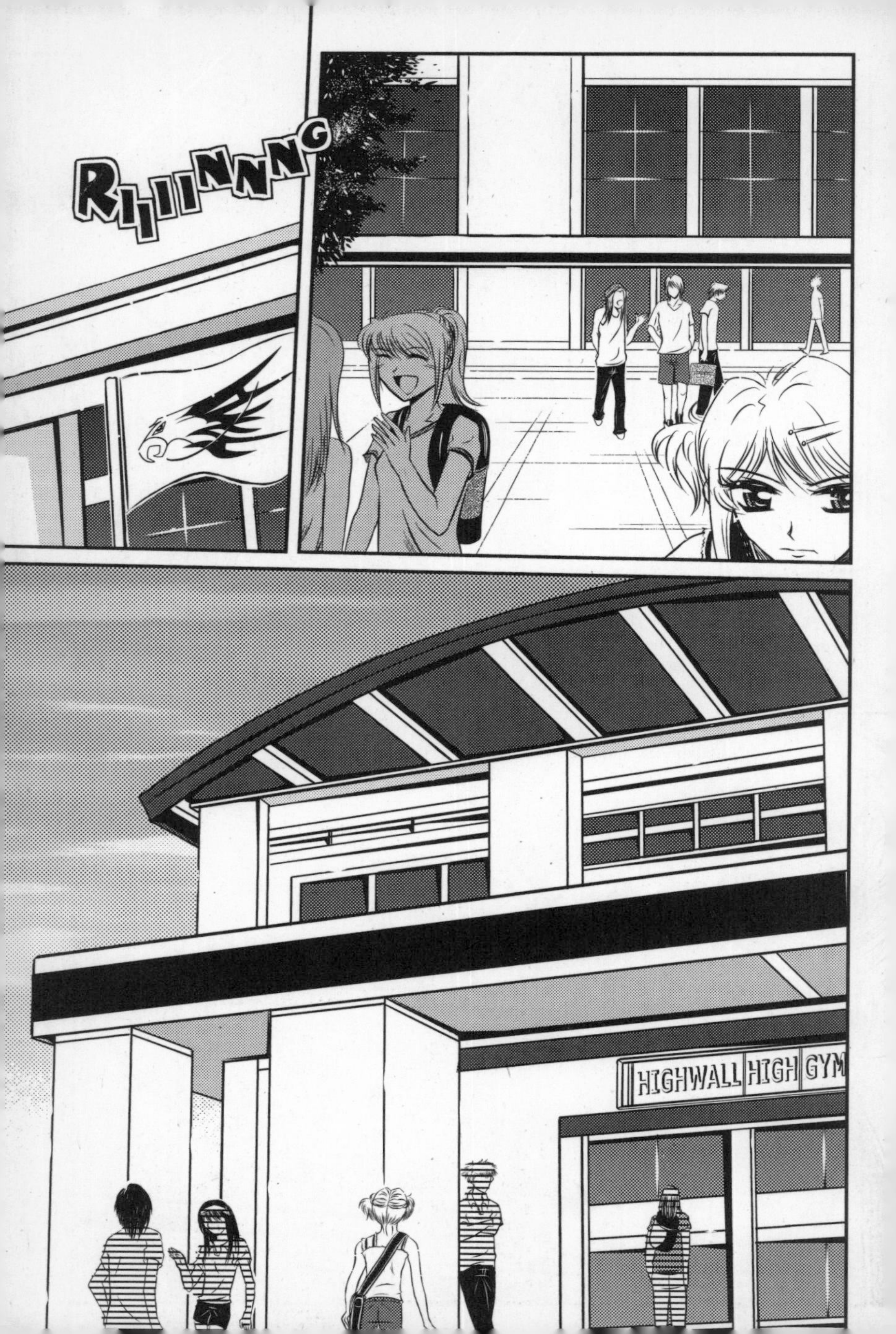
RIIIINNNNG
HIGHWALL HIGH GYM

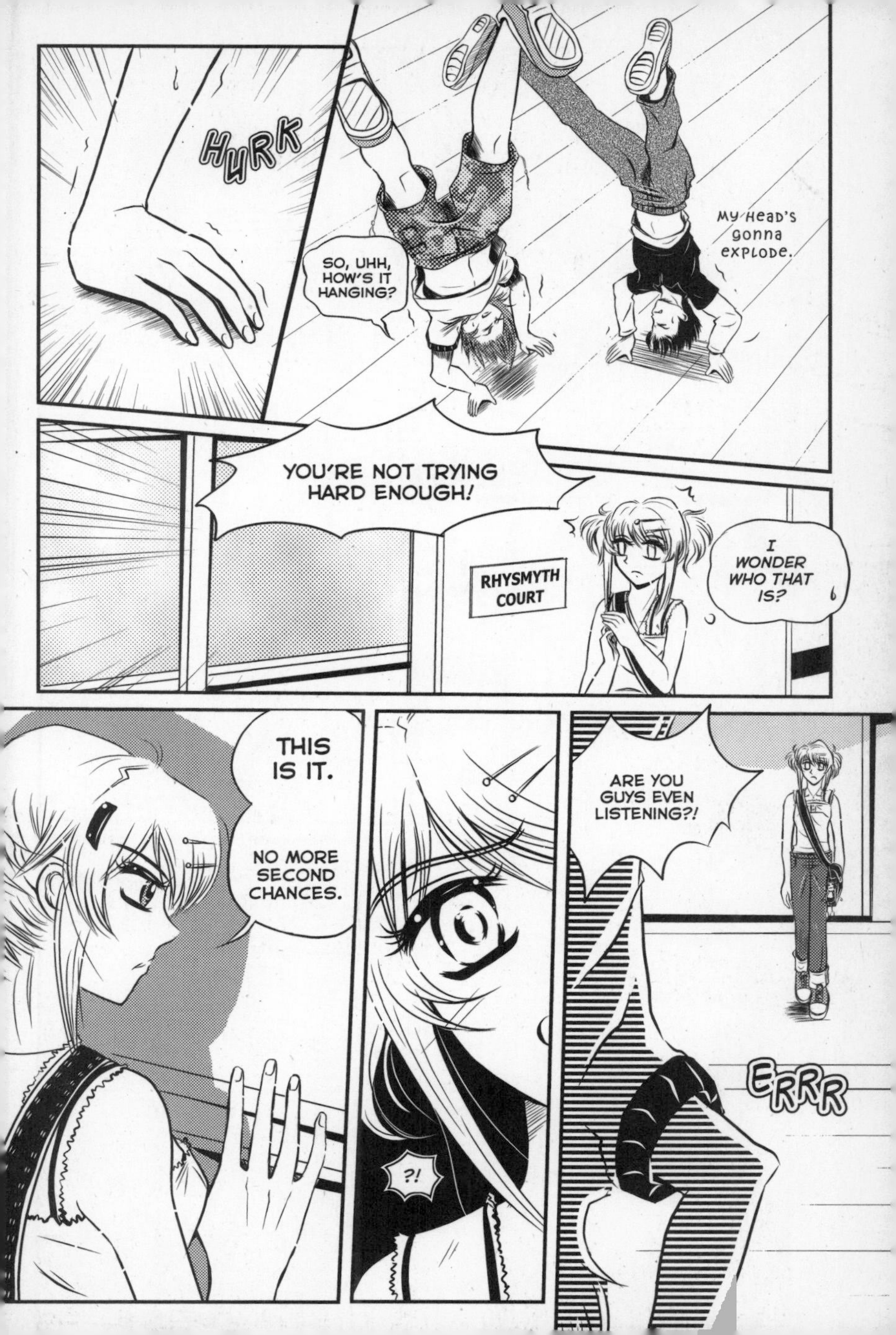
HURK
SO, UHH, HOW'S IT HANGING?
MY HEAD'S gonna explode.
YOU'RE NOT TRYING HARD ENOUGH!
RHYSMYTH COURT
I WONDER WHO THAT IS?
THIS IS IT.
NO MORE SECOND CHANCES.
?!
ARE YOU GUYS EVEN LISTENING?!
ERRR

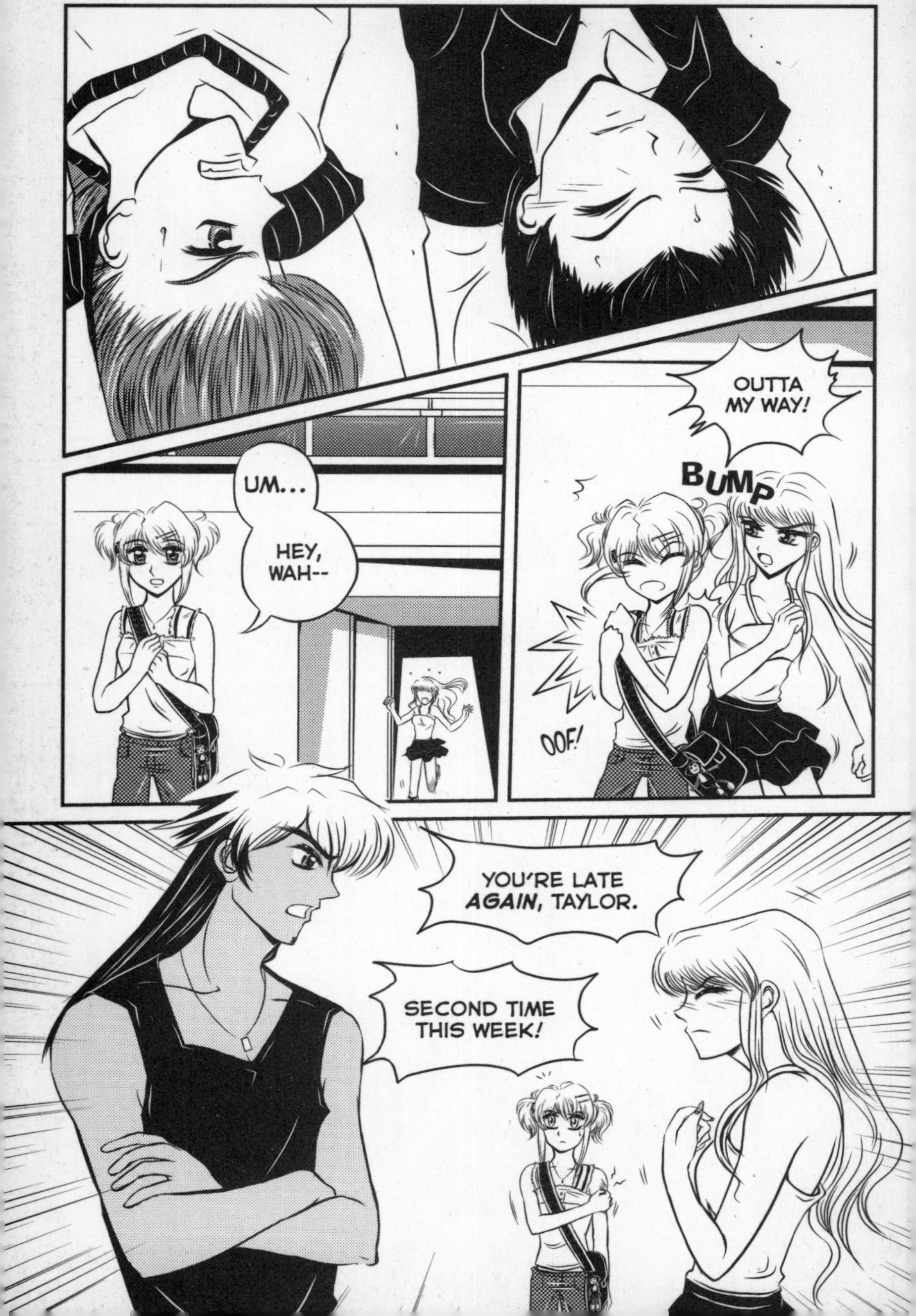
UM...
HEY, WAH--
OUTTA MY WAY!
BUMP
OOF!
YOU'RE LATE *AGAIN*, TAYLOR.
SECOND TIME THIS WEEK!

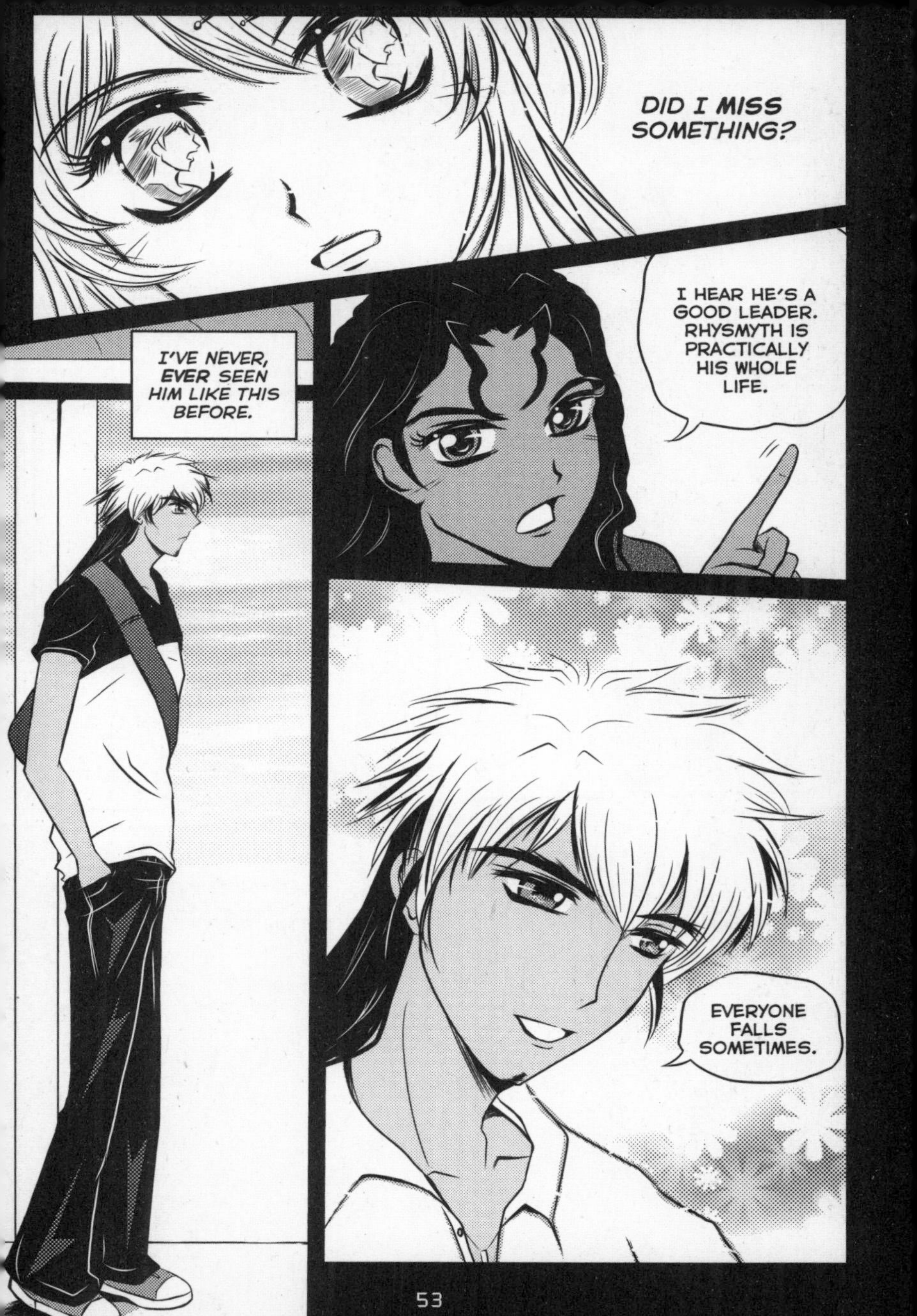
DID I MISS SOMETHING?
I'VE NEVER, EVER SEEN HIM LIKE THIS BEFORE.
I HEAR HE'S A GOOD LEADER. RHYSMYTH IS PRACTICALLY HIS WHOLE LIFE.
EVERYONE FALLS SOMETIMES.

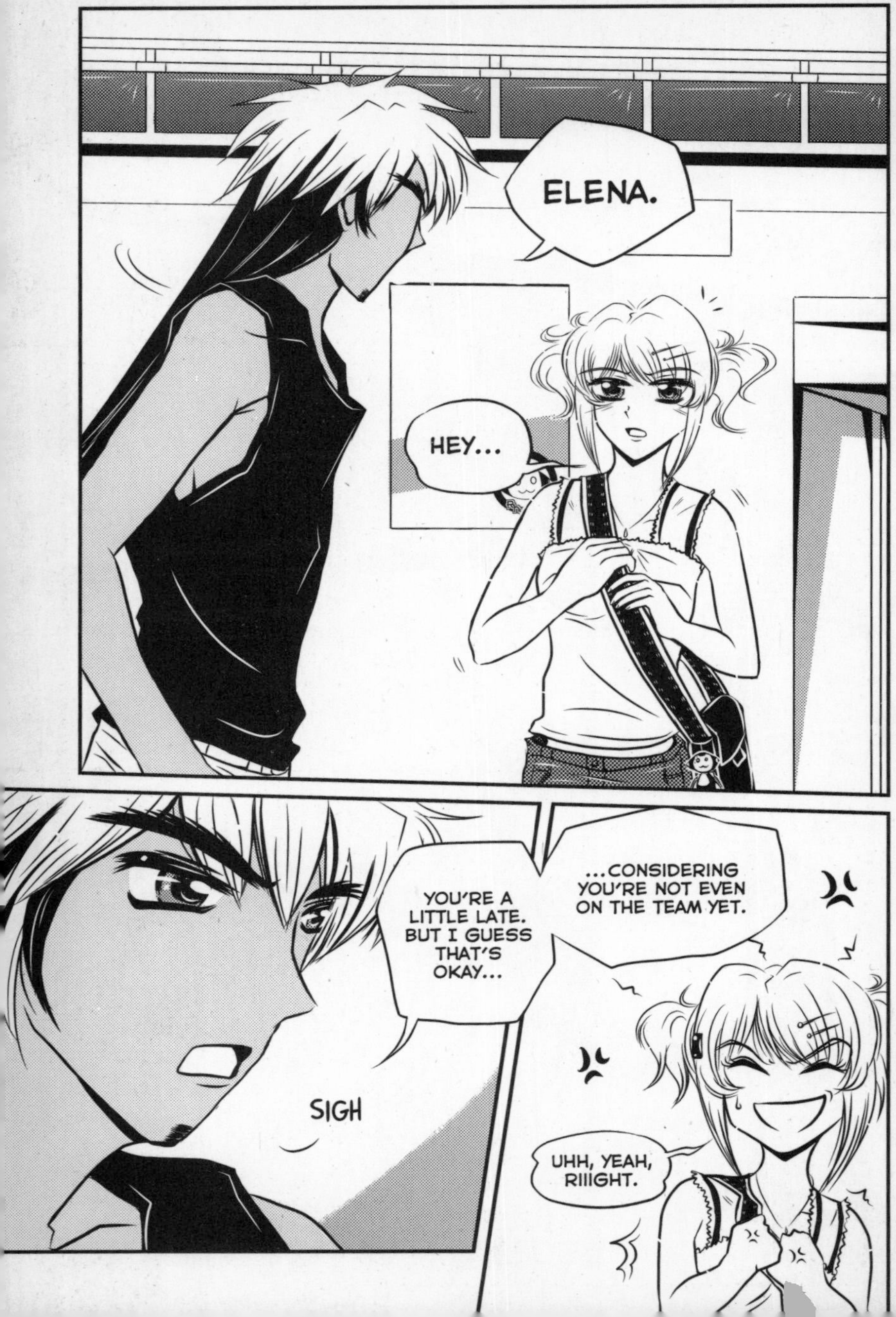
ELENA.
HEY...
YOU'RE A LITTLE LATE. BUT I GUESS THAT'S OKAY...
...CONSIDERING YOU'RE NOT EVEN ON THE TEAM YET.
SIGH
UHH, YEAH, RIIIGHT.

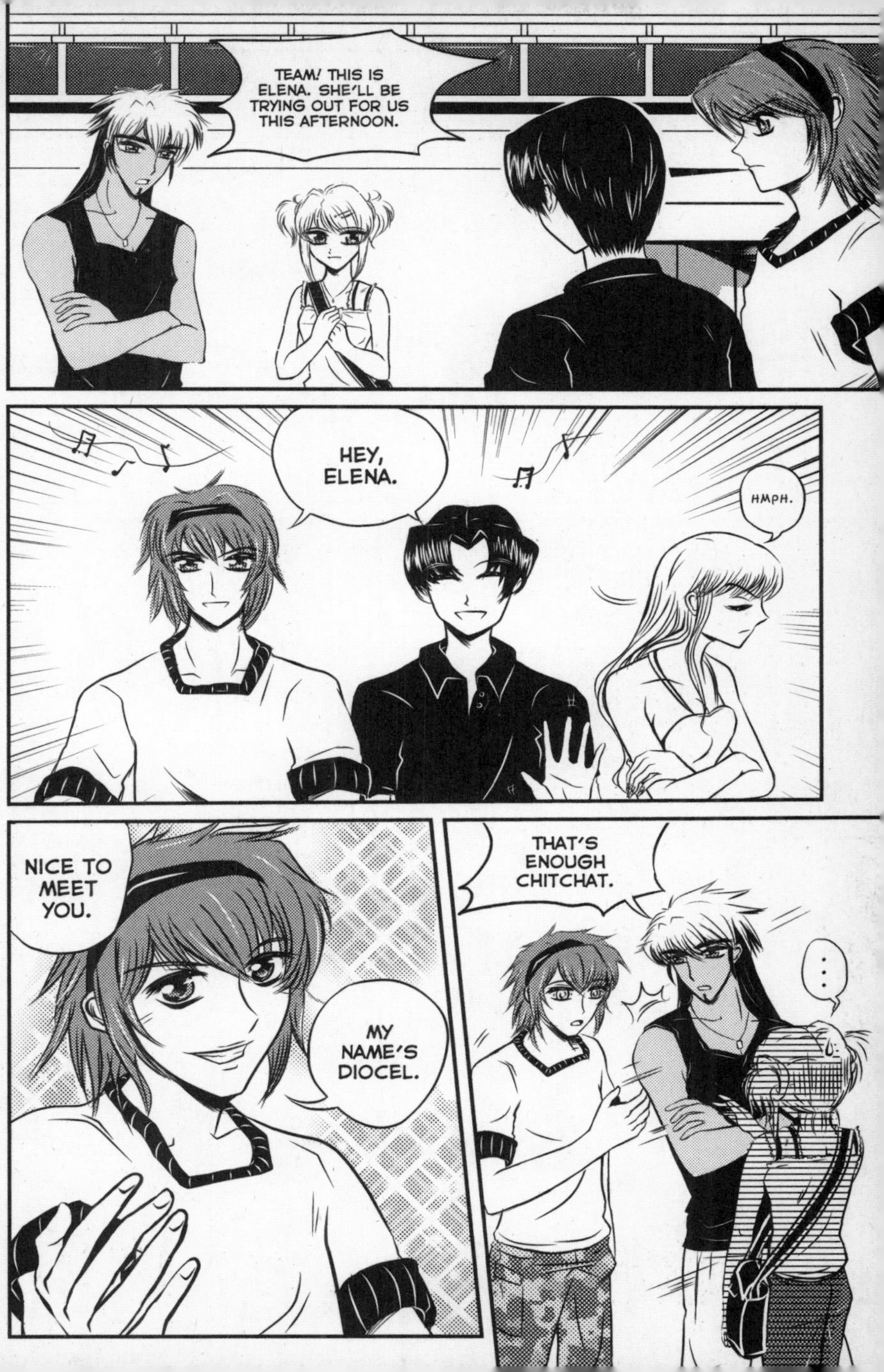
TEAM! THIS IS ELENA. SHE'LL BE TRYING OUT FOR US THIS AFTERNOON.
HEY, ELENA.
HMPH.
NICE TO MEET YOU.
MY NAME'S DIOCEL.
THAT'S ENOUGH CHITCHAT.
...

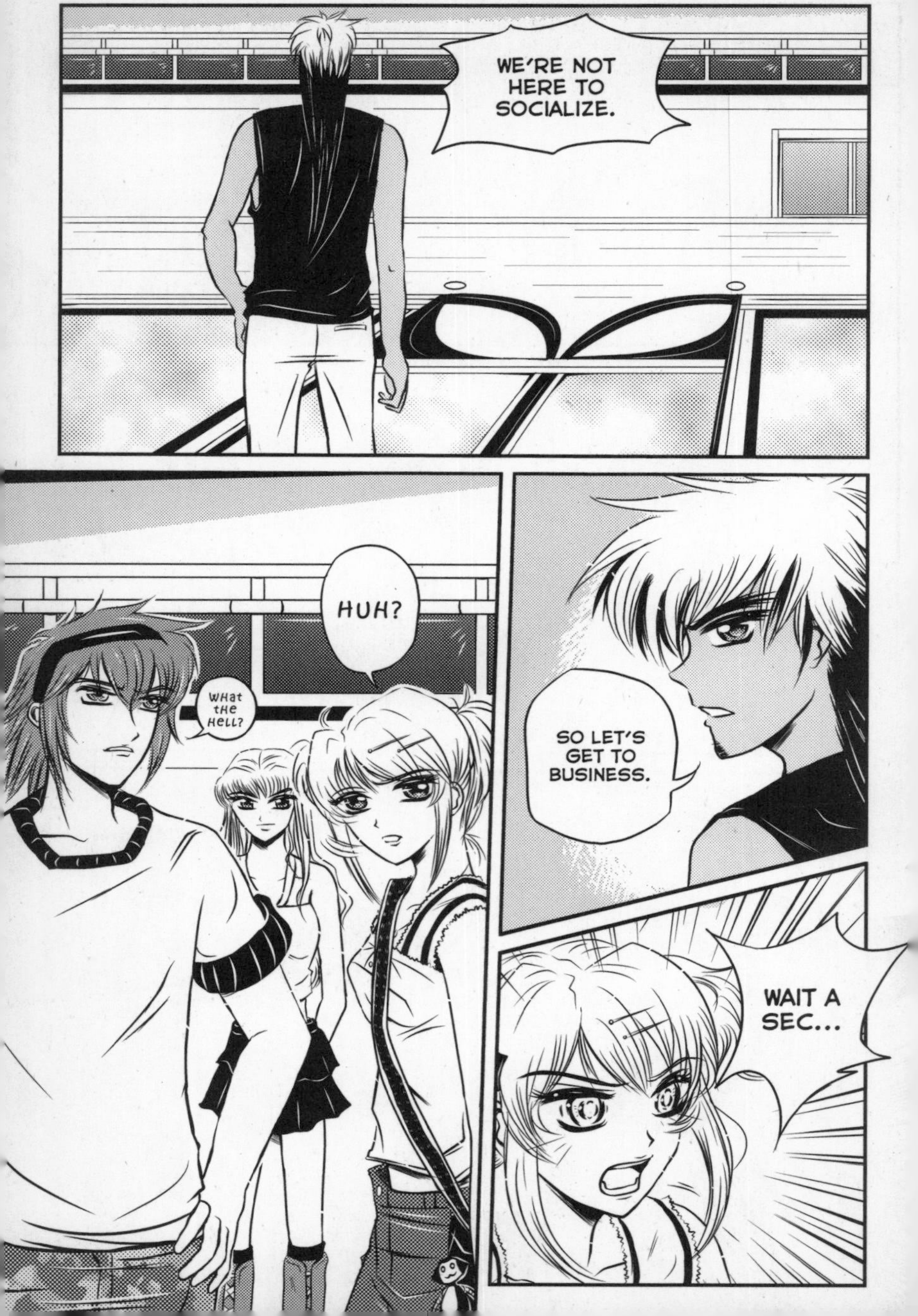
WE'RE NOT HERE TO SOCIALIZE.
HUH?
What the Hell?
SO LET'S GET TO BUSINESS.
WAIT A SEC...

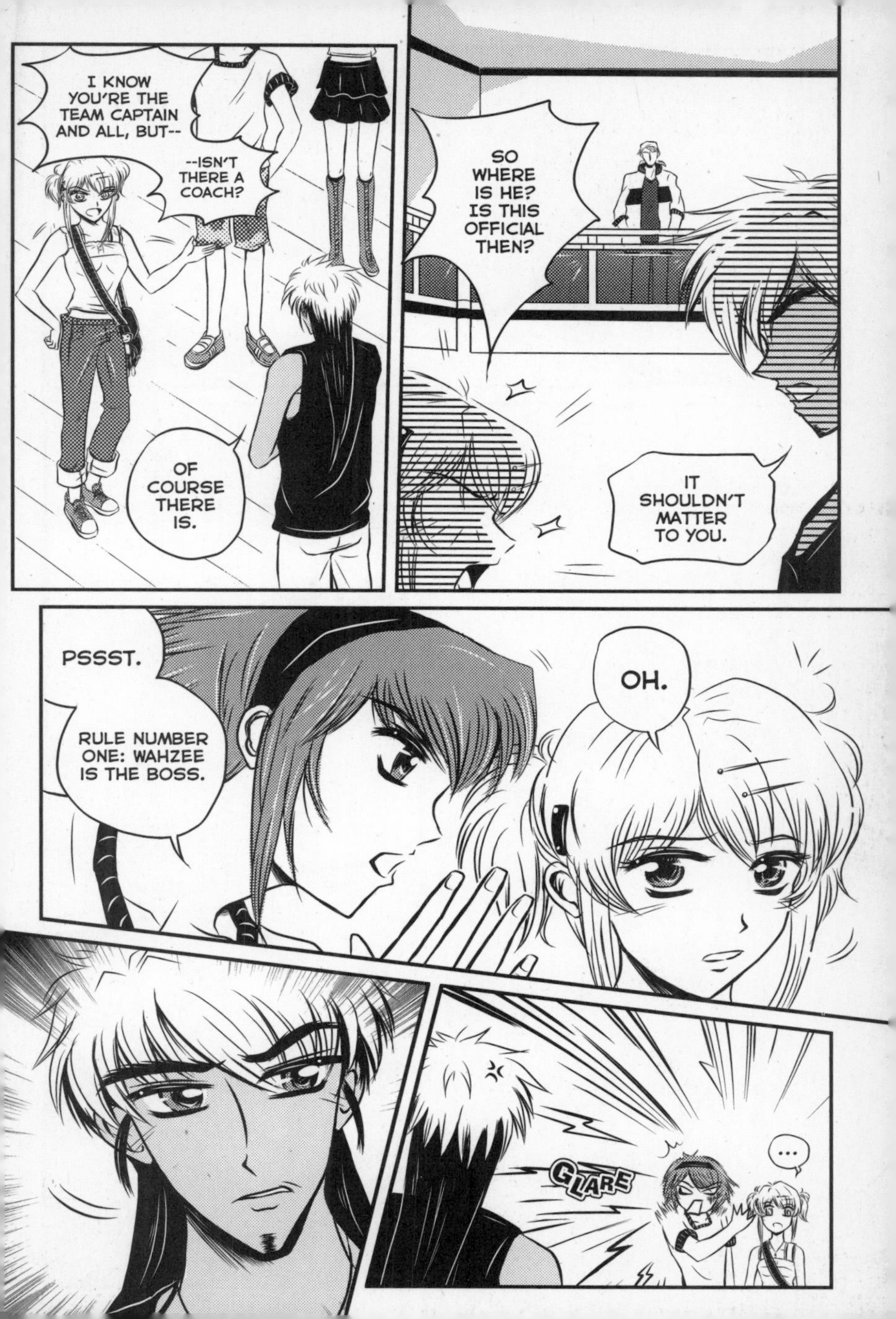
I KNOW YOU'RE THE TEAM CAPTAIN AND ALL, BUT--
--ISN'T THERE A COACH?
OF COURSE THERE IS.
SO WHERE IS HE? IS THIS OFFICIAL THEN?
IT SHOULDN'T MATTER TO YOU.
PSSST.
RULE NUMBER ONE: WAHZEE IS THE BOSS.
OH.
GLARE
...

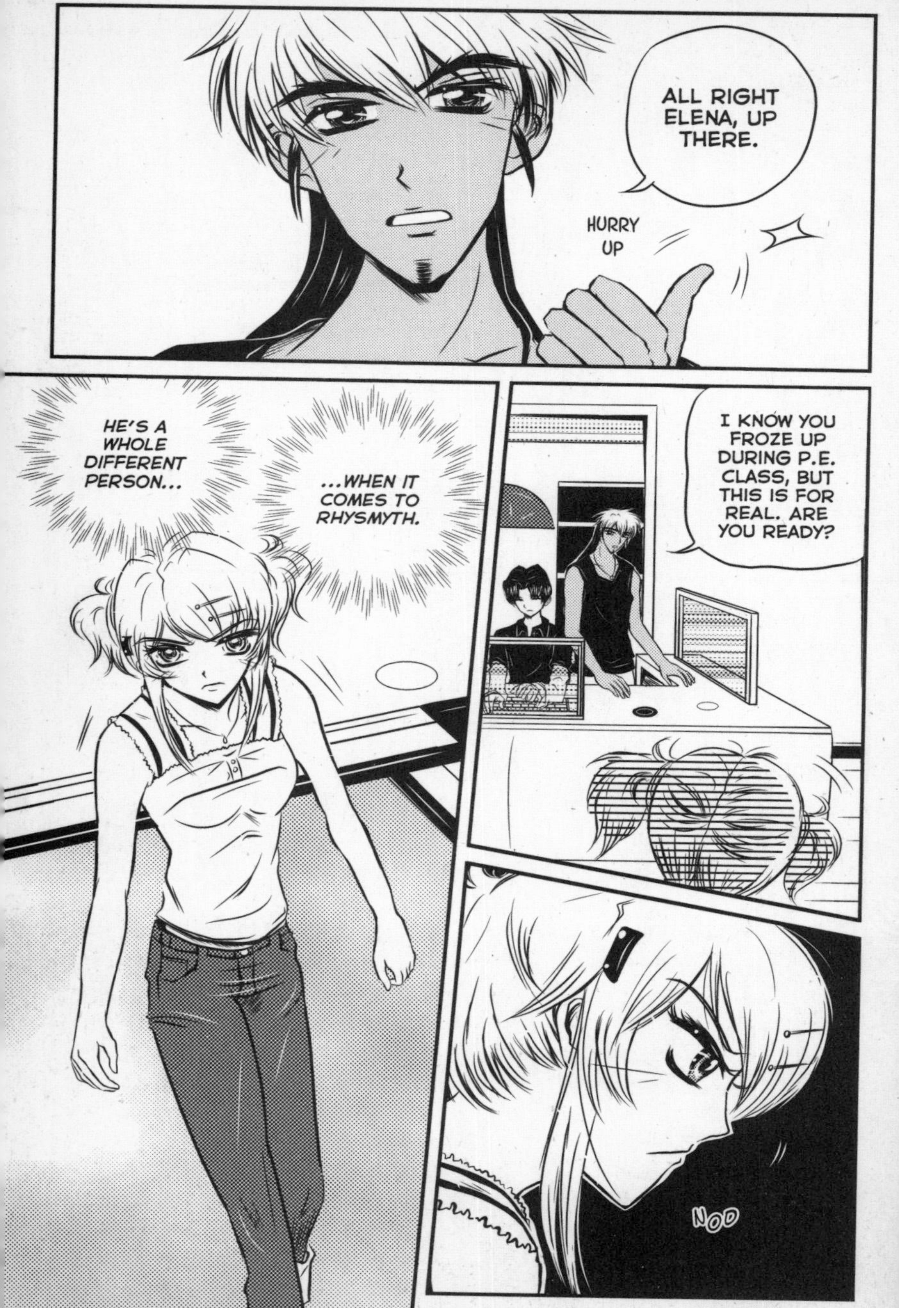
ALL RIGHT ELENA, UP THERE.
HURRY UP
HE'S A WHOLE DIFFERENT PERSON...
...WHEN IT COMES TO RHYSMYTH.
I KNOW YOU FROZE UP DURING P.E. CLASS, BUT THIS IS FOR REAL. ARE YOU READY?
NOD

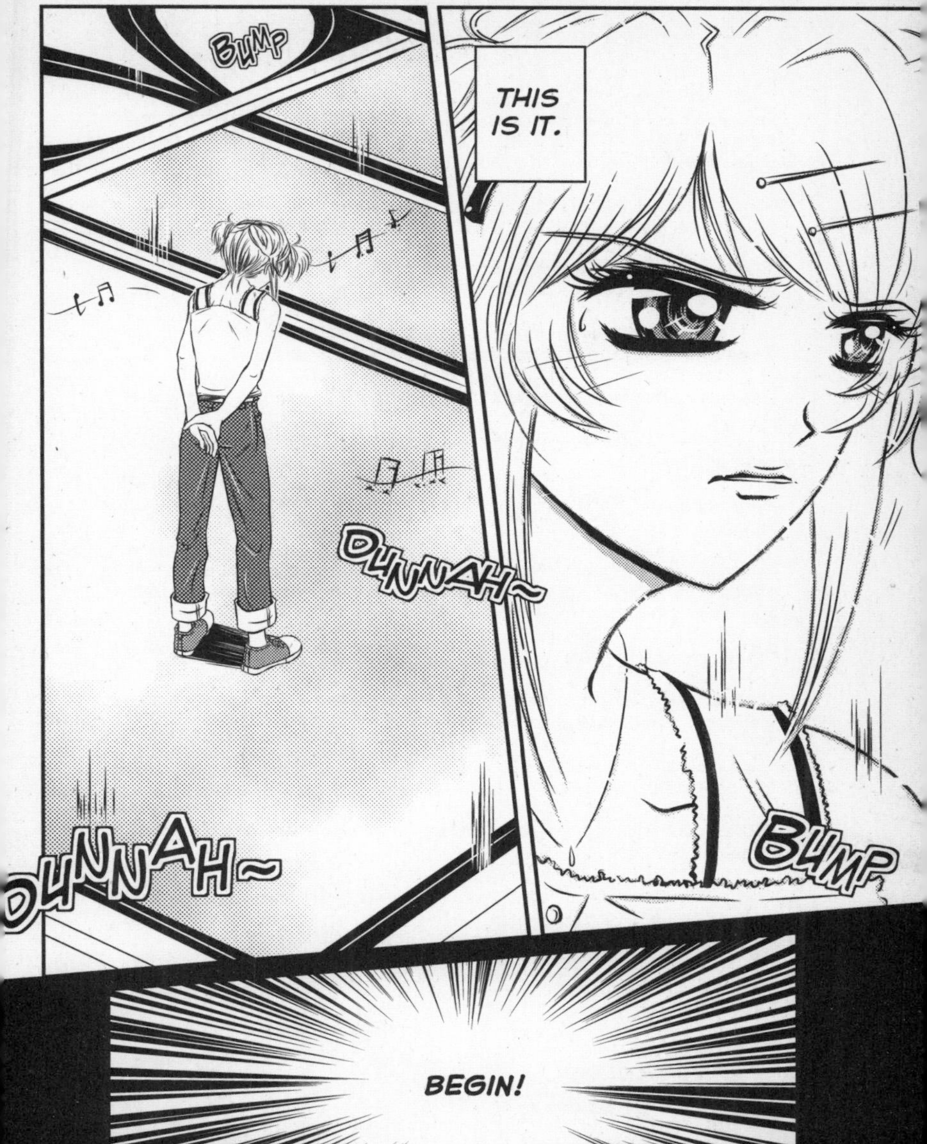
BUMP
DUNNAH~
DUNNAH~
THIS IS IT.
BUMP
BEGIN!

RHYPER: the BIRTH of a MASCOT

June 23rd, 2002. San Francisco, CA. A group of four friends have a heated dinner discussion. Their baby, the newly-developed Rhysmyth game, is missing something to set it apart from other HSD imitations.

"We needed something to really bring people to the game," recalls head programmer Lindsay Chond. "Sure, you dance. So what?"

"Besides being more difficult, what else could Rhysmyth offer to the casual HSD fan?" co-designer Kenji Toriyama muses.

With pizza crusts and empty beer bottles spread across the floor, the Rhysmyth team looked at one another with blank faces.

"Stumped. Absolutely stumped," says Antonio Maples, music composer.

That's when co-designer Damien Sanchez walked over to his pet monkey's cage and let him out.

"He's my muse." Sanchez laughs out loud. "When I can't think, he always helps me out."

Hyper, a small capuchin monkey, lived up to his namesake and charged straight out onto the prototype HSD dance pad for a sequence of backflips and, more often than not, spectacular crashes.

"It was magic. Absolutely magical," says Maples.

The team glanced at one another, slow acknowledgement crawling across their faces: they were missing a mascot.

"See, mascots are all about forging an identity, something for the masses to identify with your product," says Toriyama.

And so robo-monkey Rhyper was born that night over another round of pizza and drinks.

"Besides, monkeys are cute," Lindsay says with a smile. "Slap a monkey on it, I'll buy it."

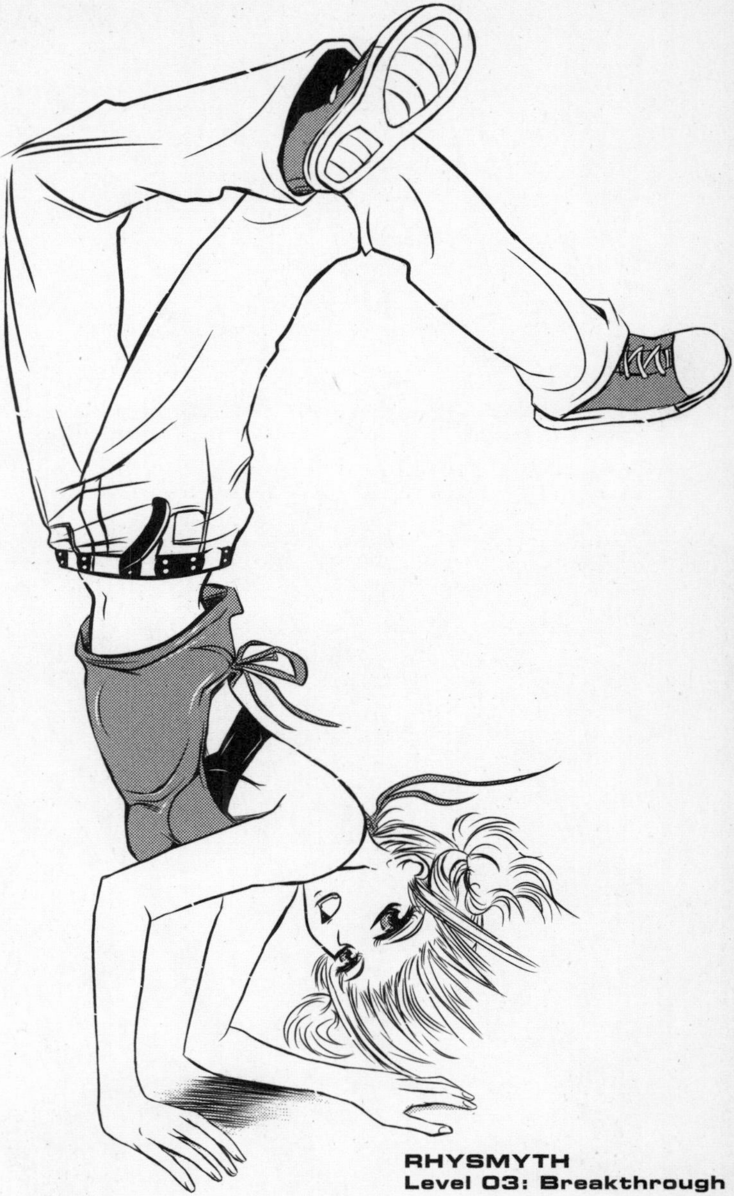

RHYSMYTH
Level 03: Breakthrough

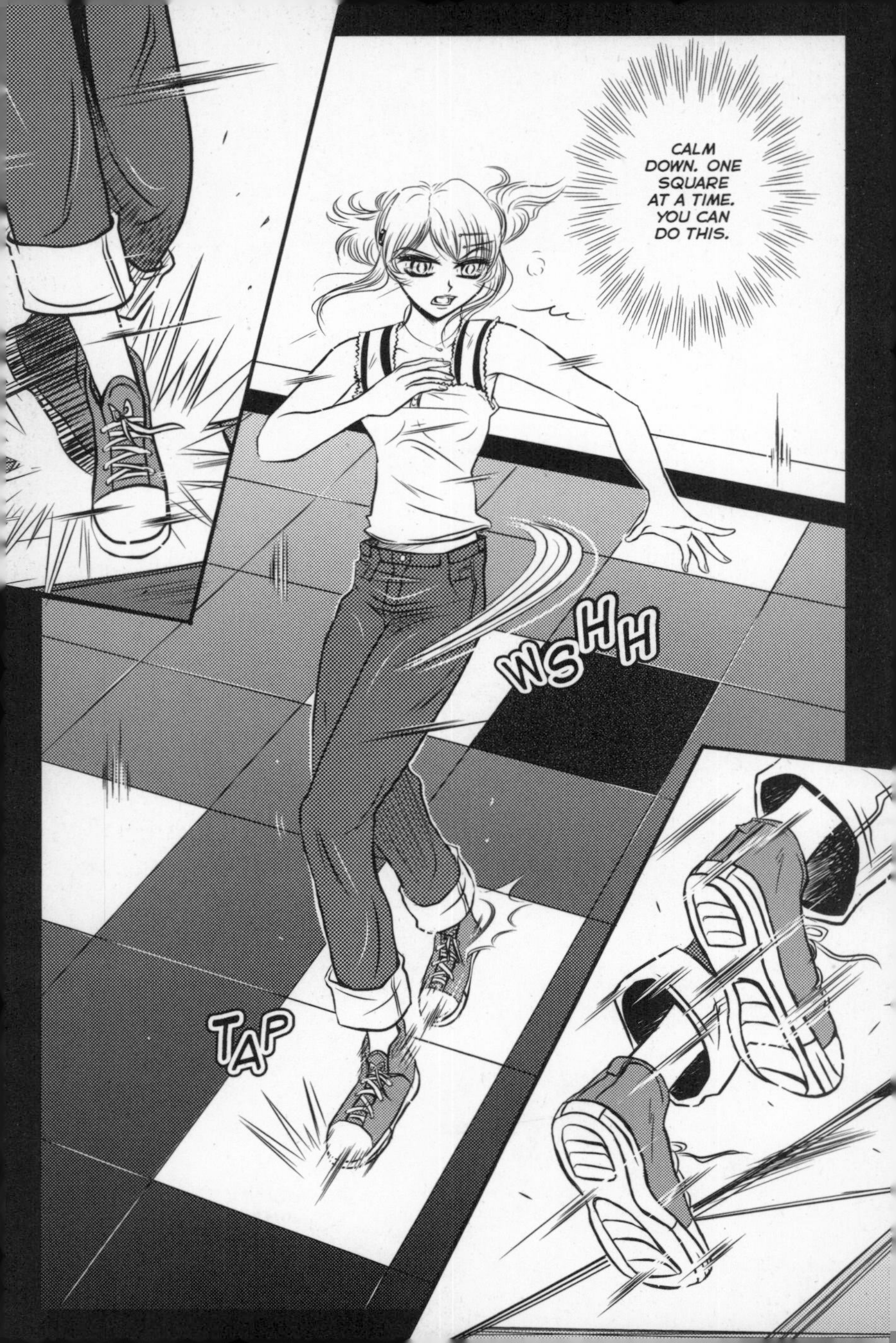
CALM DOWN. ONE SQUARE AT A TIME. YOU CAN DO THIS.
WSHH
TAP

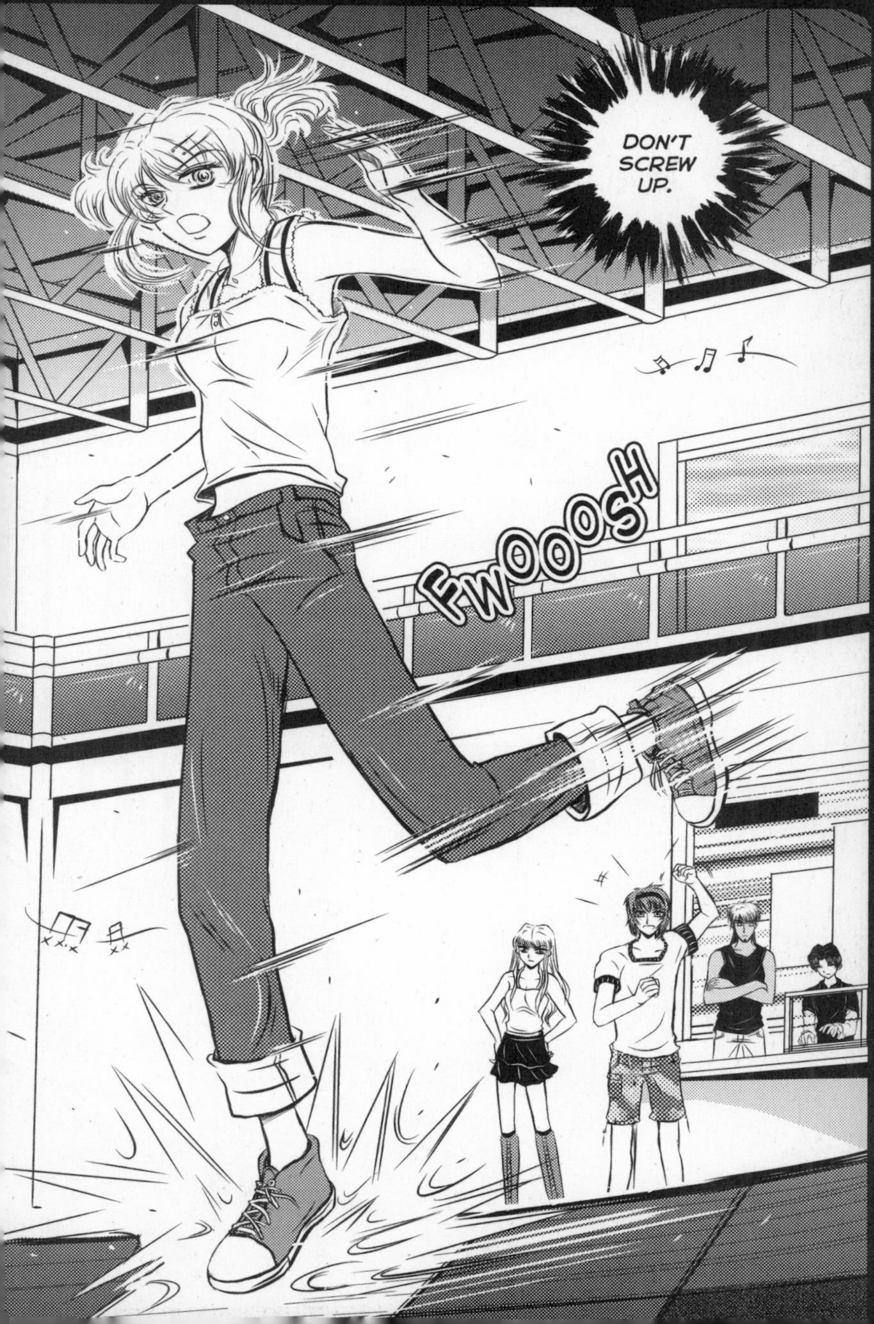
DON'T SCREW UP.
FWOOOSH

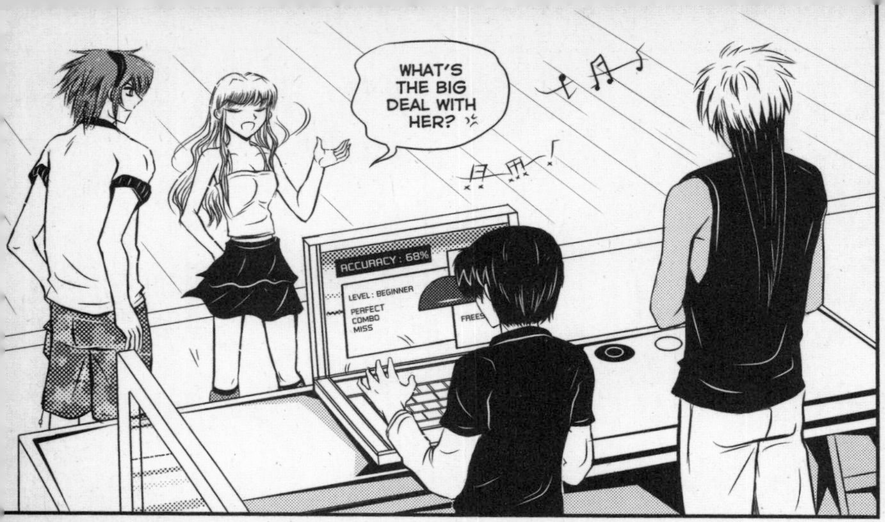
WHAT'S THE BIG DEAL WITH HER?
ACCURACY : 68%
LEVEL : BEGINNER
PERFECT
COMBO
MISS

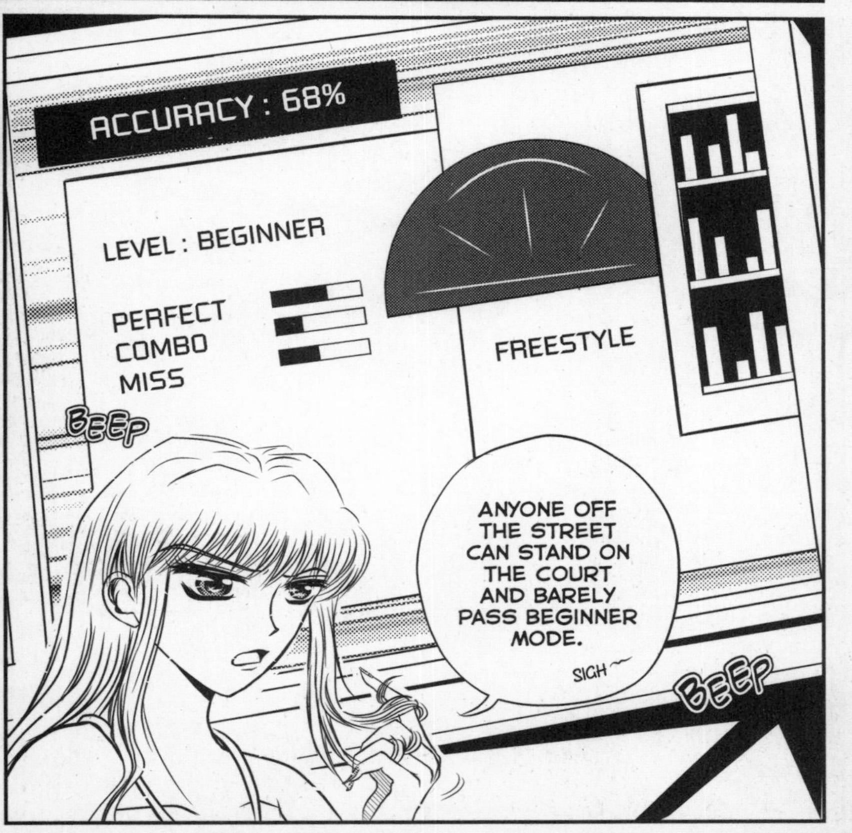
ACCURACY : 68%
LEVEL : BEGINNER
PERFECT
COMBO
MISS
FREESTYLE
BEEP
ANYONE OFF THE STREET CAN STAND ON THE COURT AND BARELY PASS BEGINNER MODE.
SIGH~
BEEP

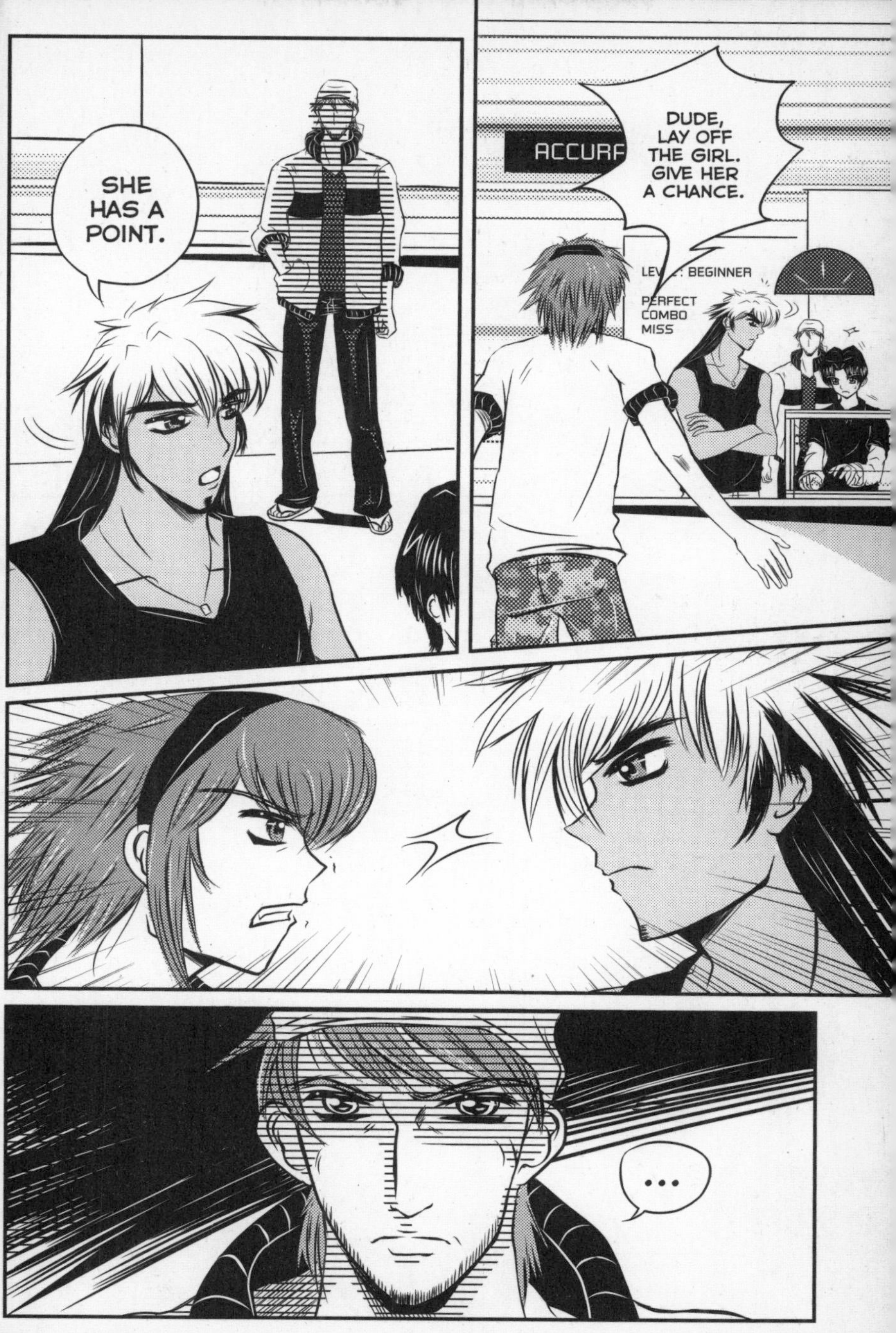
SHE HAS A POINT.
ACCURA
DUDE, LAY OFF THE GIRL. GIVE HER A CHANCE.
BEGINNER
PERFECT
COMBO
MISS
...

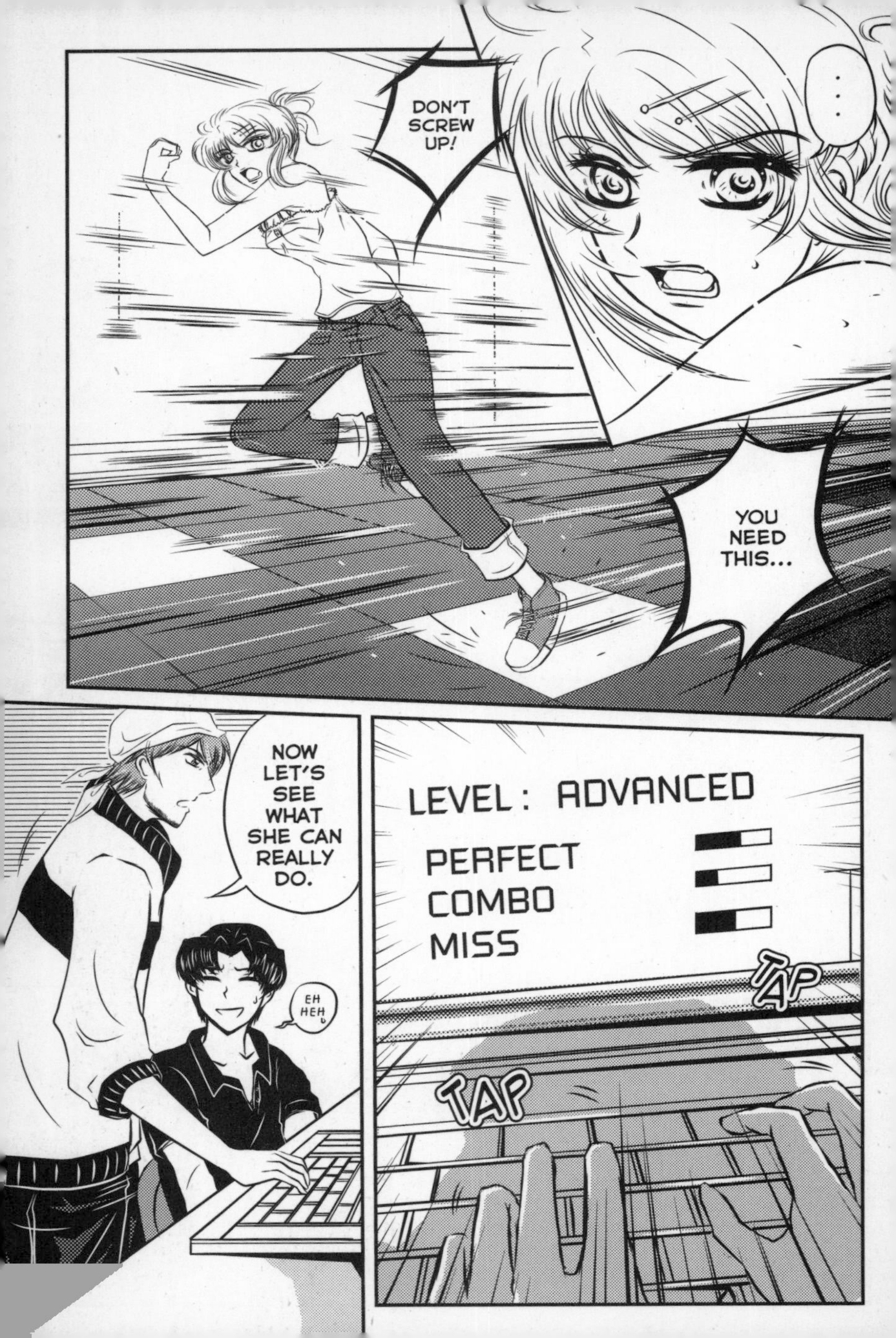
DON'T SCREW UP!
...
YOU NEED THIS...
NOW LET'S SEE WHAT SHE CAN REALLY DO.
EH HEH
LEVEL: ADVANCED
PERFECT
COMBO
MISS
TAP
TAP

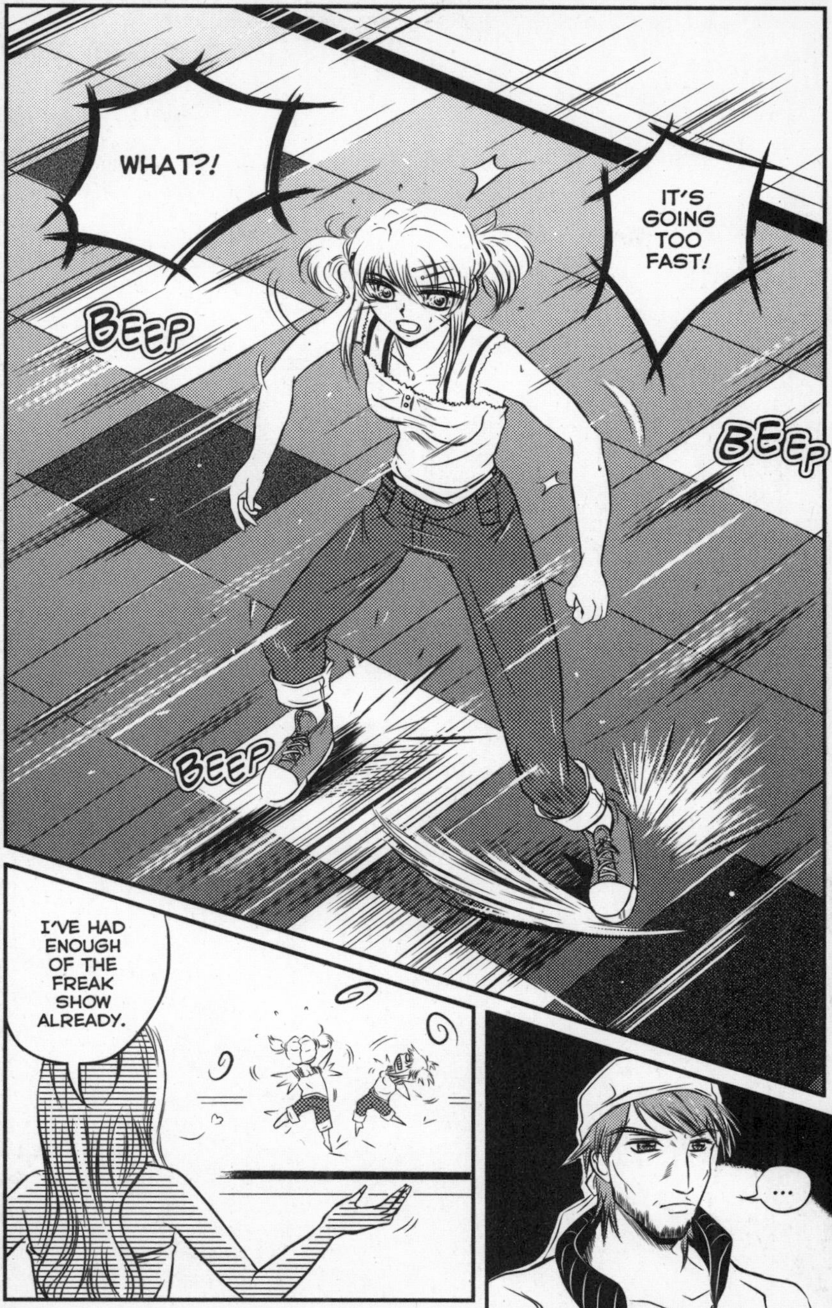
WHAT?!
IT'S GOING TOO FAST!
BEEP
BEEP
BEEP
I'VE HAD ENOUGH OF THE FREAK SHOW ALREADY.
...

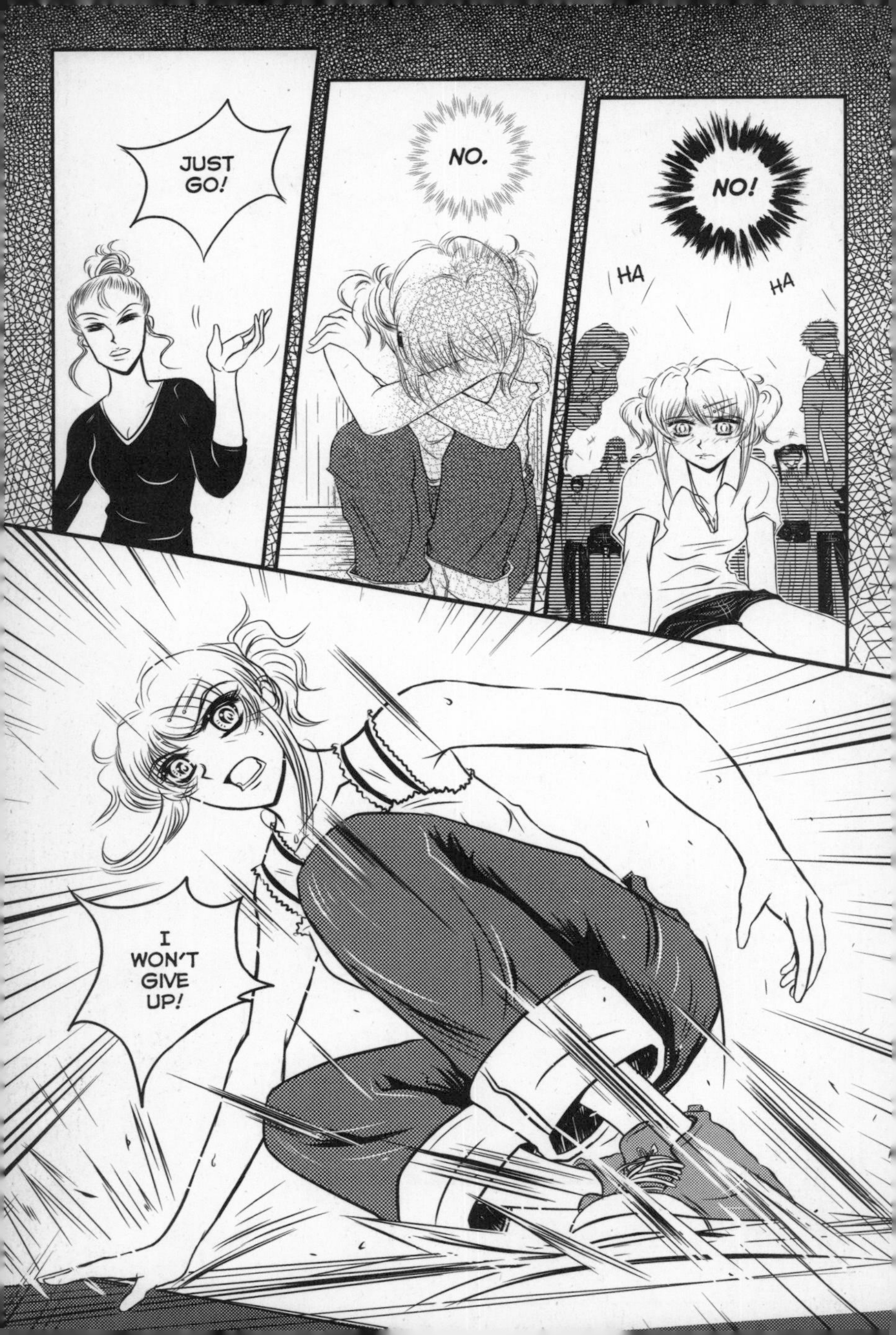
JUST GO!
NO.
NO!
HA
HA
I WON'T GIVE UP!

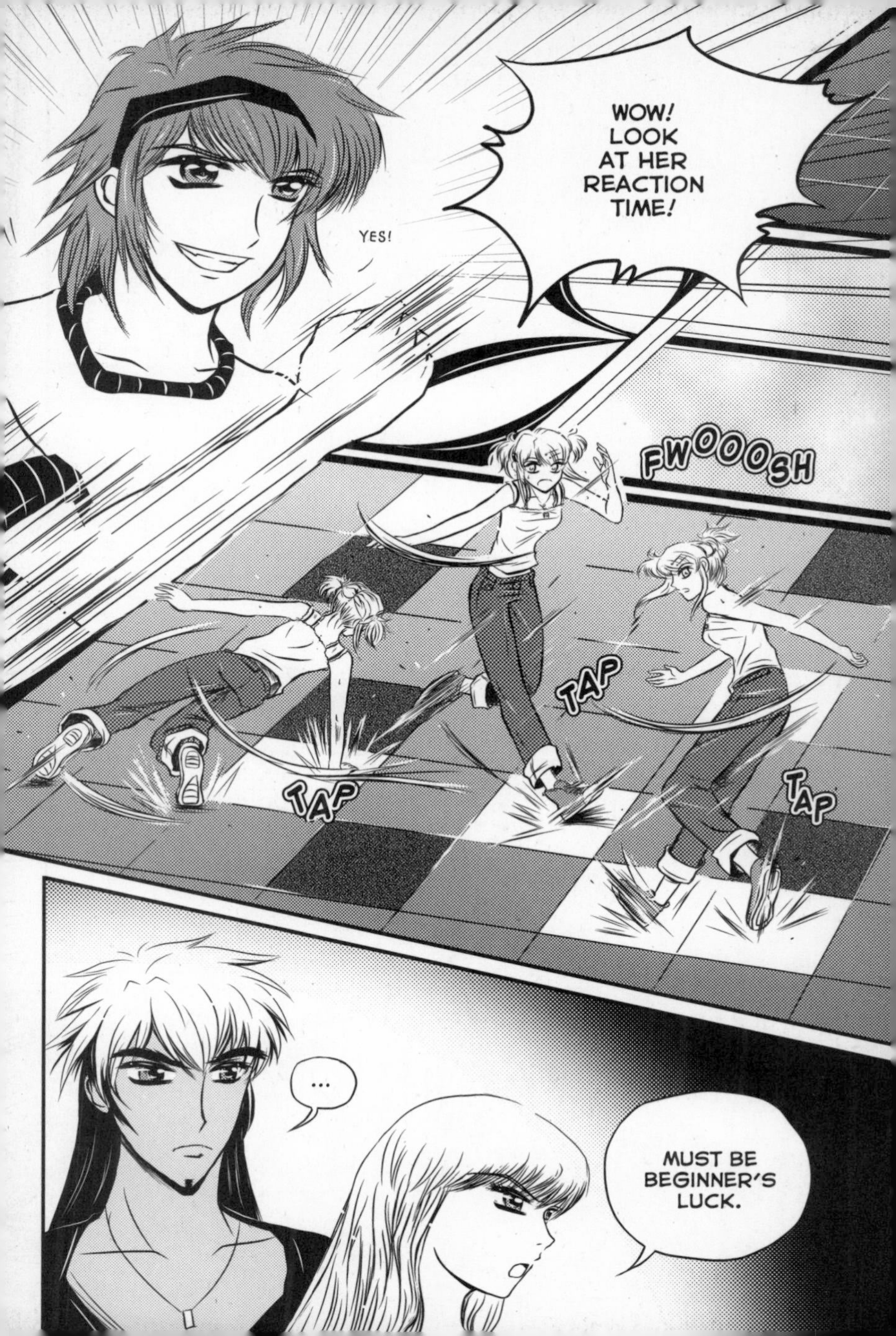
YES!
WOW! LOOK AT HER REACTION TIME!
FWOOOOSH
TAP
TAP
TAP
...
MUST BE BEGINNER'S LUCK.

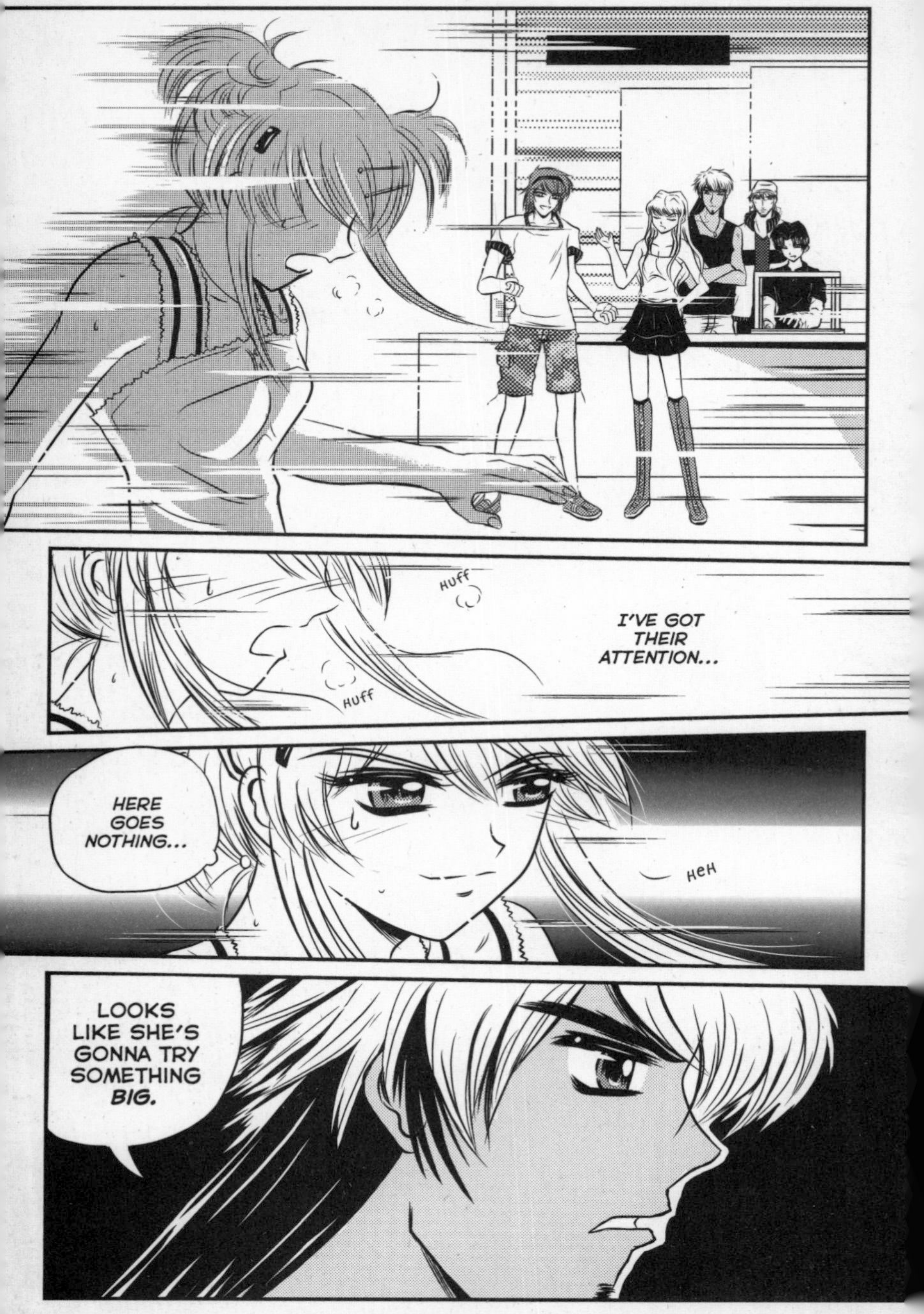
HUFF
I'VE GOT THEIR ATTENTION...
HUFF
HERE GOES NOTHING...
HEH
LOOKS LIKE SHE'S GONNA TRY SOMETHING BIG.

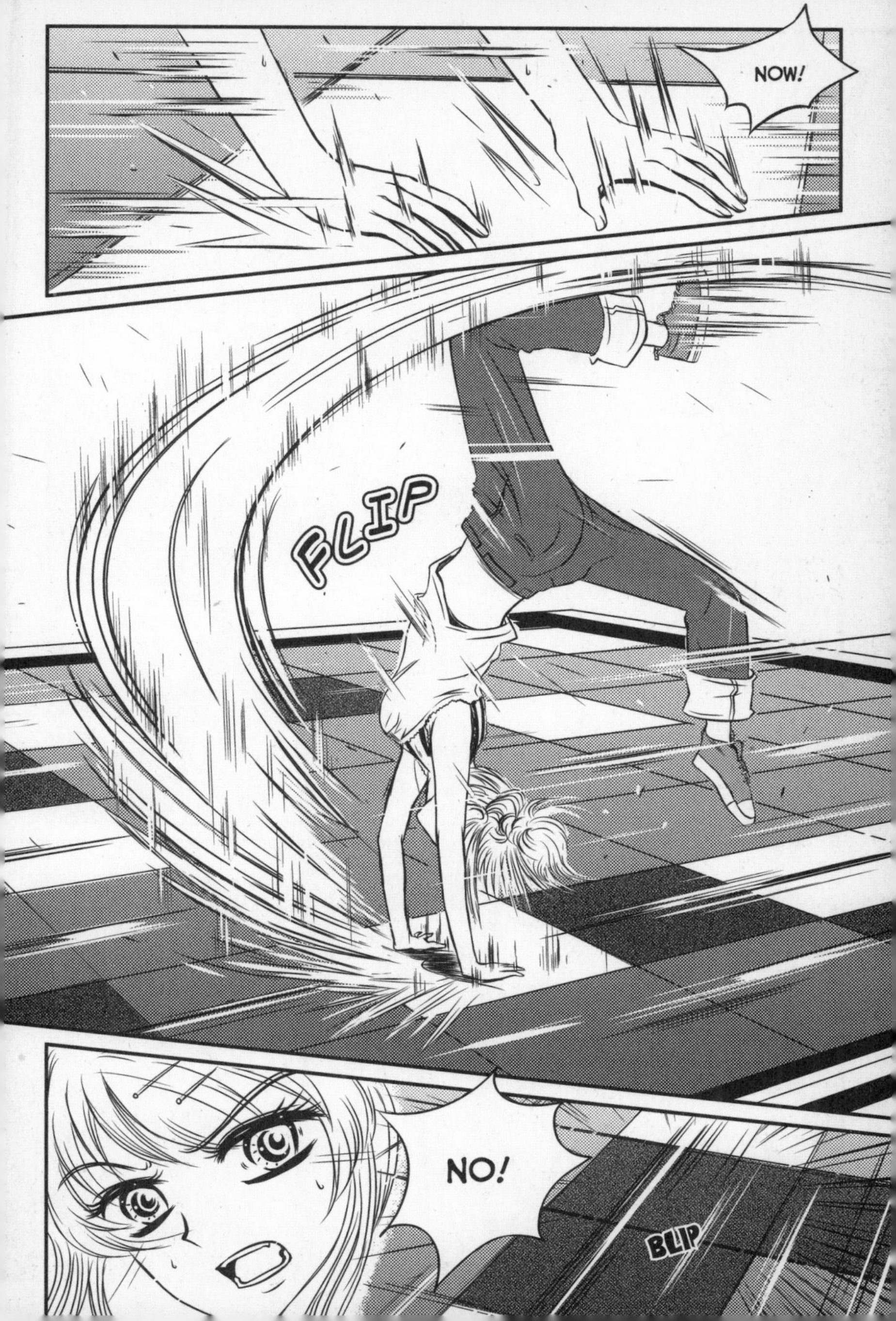
NOW!
FLIP
NO!
BLIP

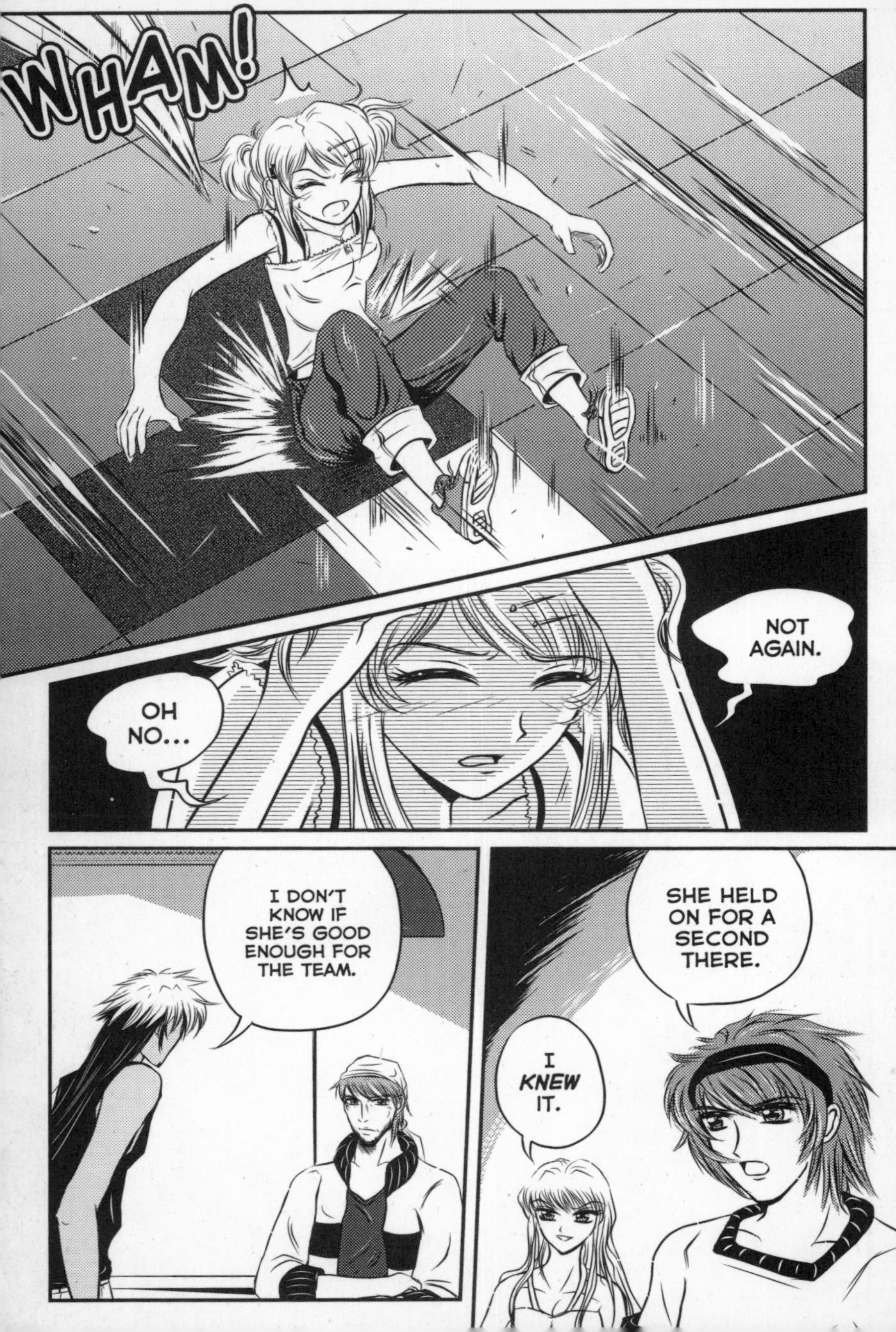
WHAM!
OH NO...
NOT AGAIN.
I DON'T KNOW IF SHE'S GOOD ENOUGH FOR THE TEAM.
SHE HELD ON FOR A SECOND THERE.
I *KNEW* IT.

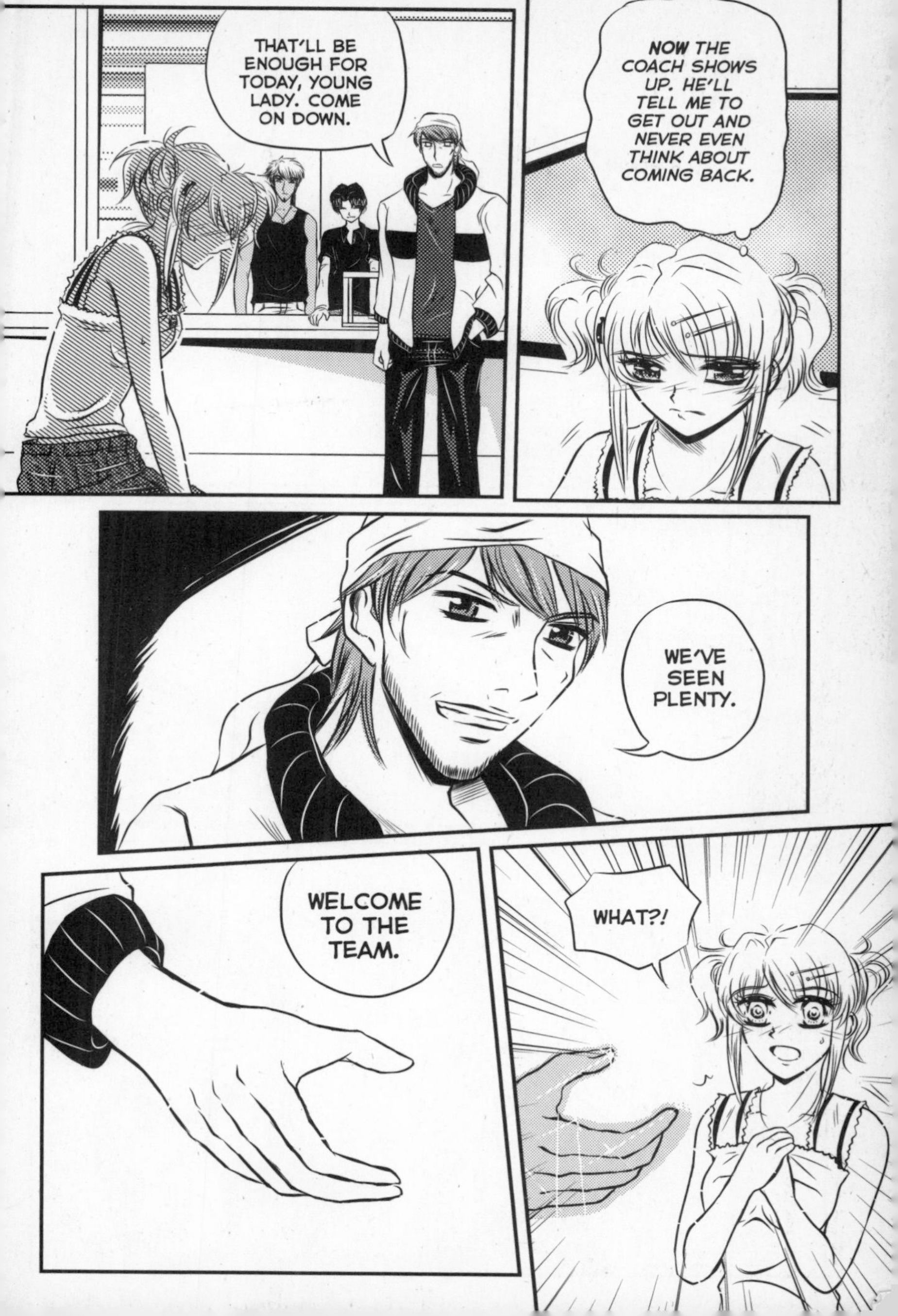
THAT'LL BE ENOUGH FOR TODAY, YOUNG LADY. COME ON DOWN.
NOW THE COACH SHOWS UP. HE'LL TELL ME TO GET OUT AND NEVER EVEN THINK ABOUT COMING BACK.
WE'VE SEEN PLENTY.
WELCOME TO THE TEAM.
WHAT?!

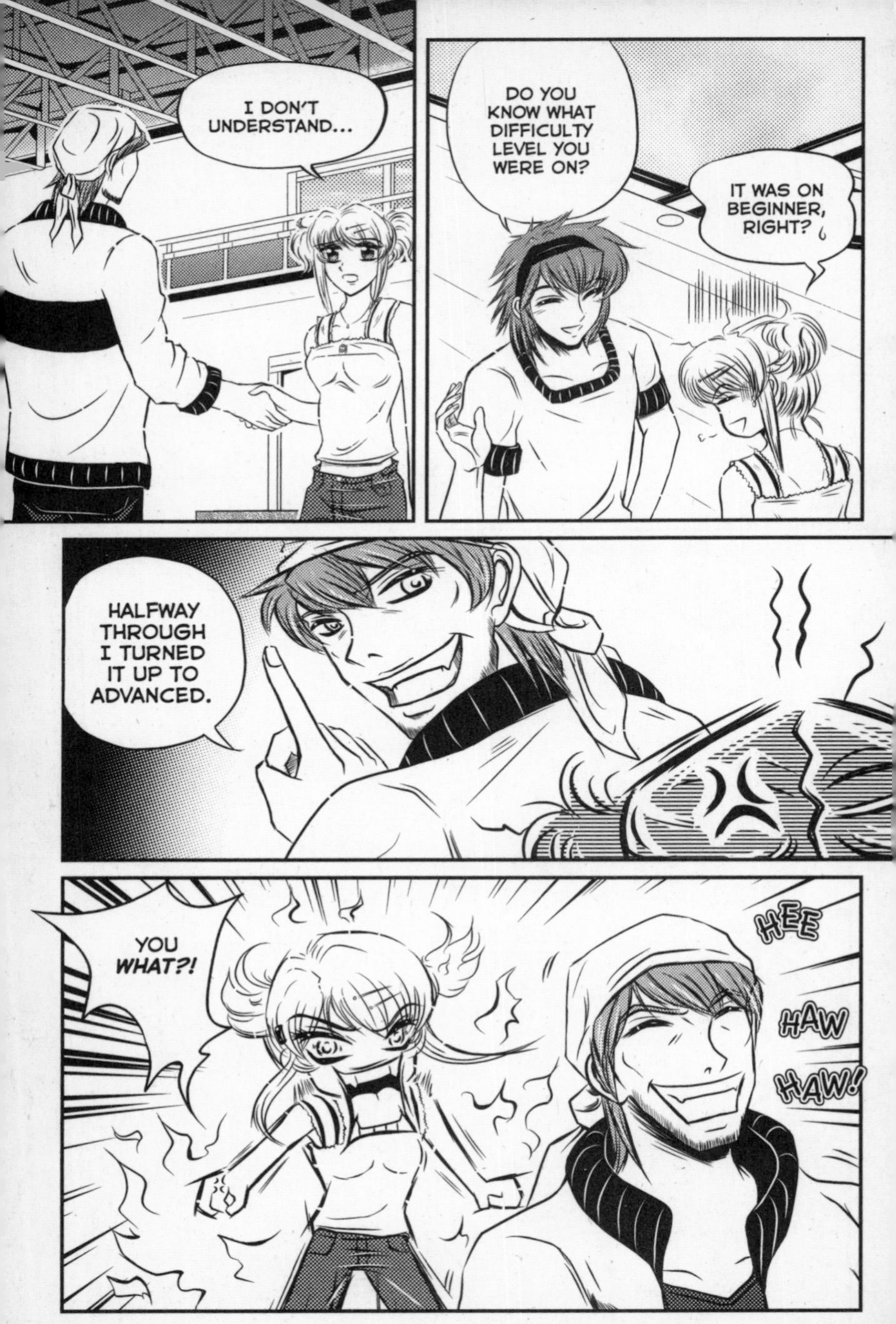
I DON'T UNDERSTAND...
DO YOU KNOW WHAT DIFFICULTY LEVEL YOU WERE ON?
IT WAS ON BEGINNER, RIGHT?
HALFWAY THROUGH I TURNED IT UP TO ADVANCED.
YOU WHAT?!
HEE
HAW
HAW!

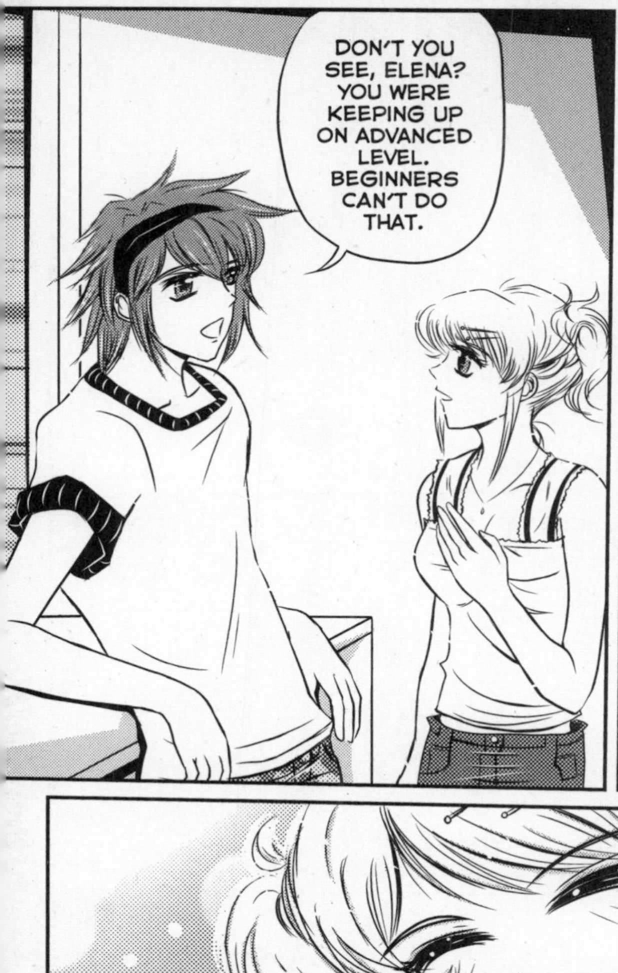
DON'T YOU SEE, ELENA? YOU WERE KEEPING UP ON ADVANCED LEVEL. BEGINNERS CAN'T DO THAT.
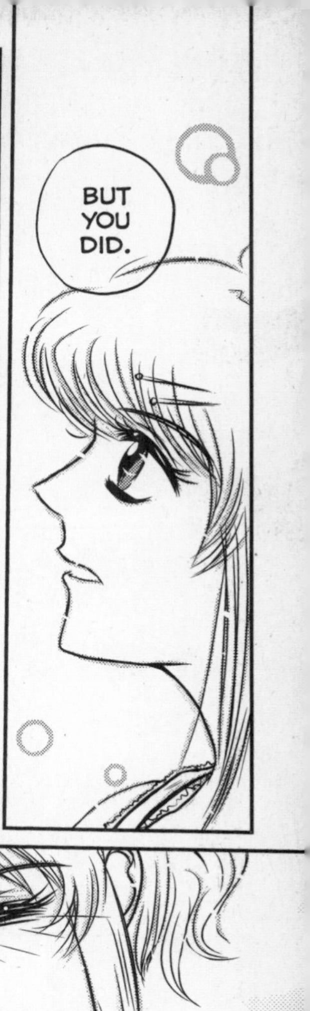
BUT YOU DID.
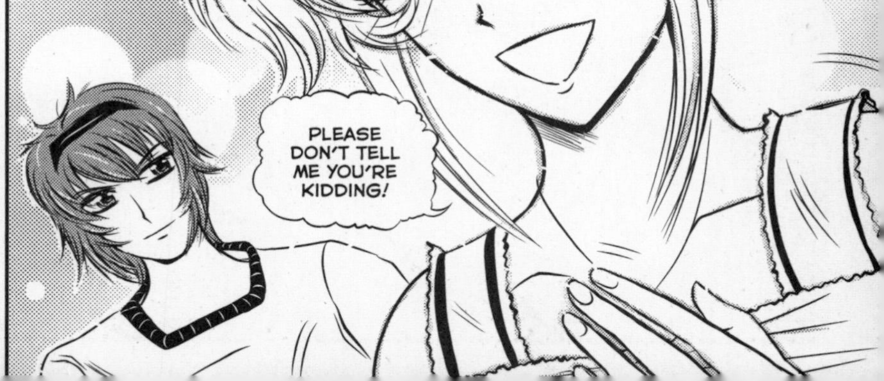
PLEASE DON'T TELL ME YOU'RE KIDDING!

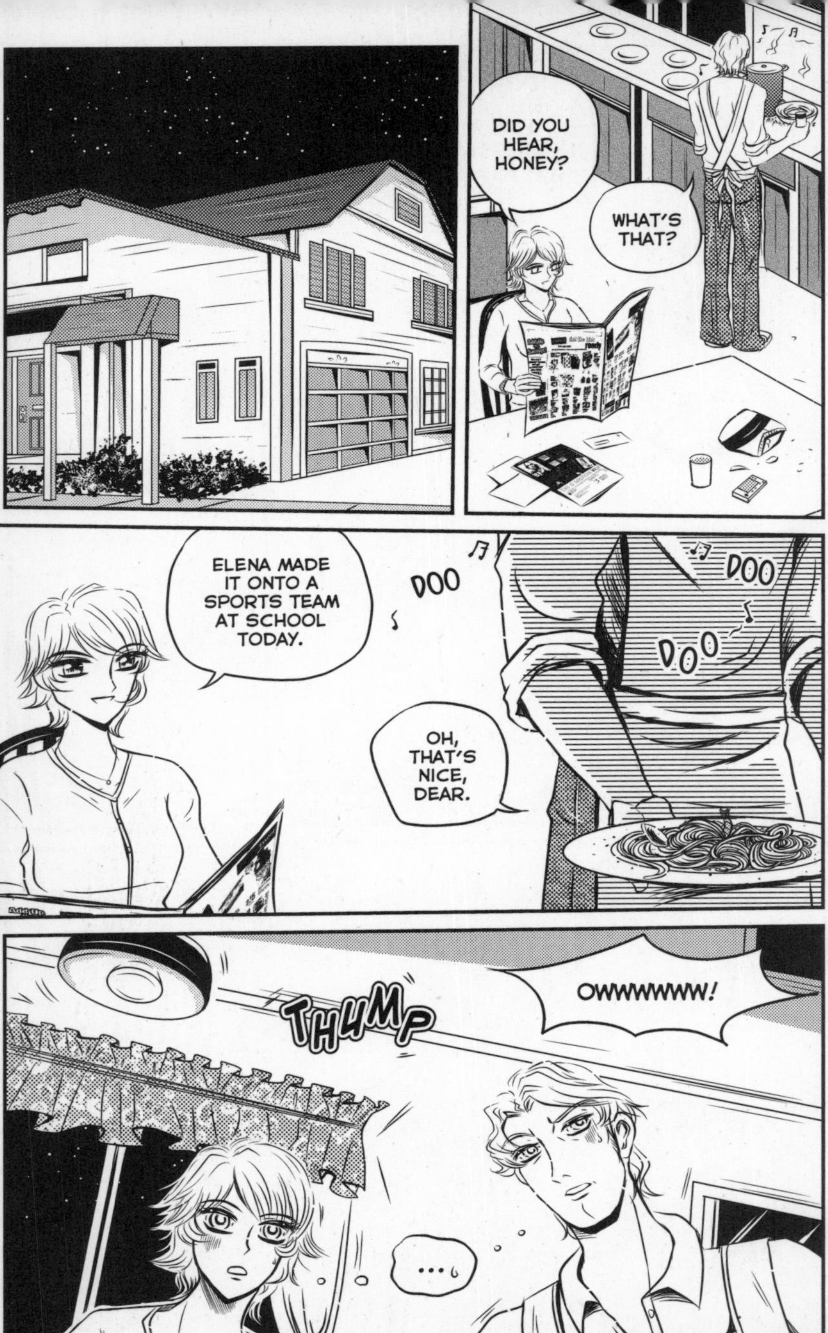
DID YOU HEAR, HONEY?
WHAT'S THAT?
ELENA MADE IT ONTO A SPORTS TEAM AT SCHOOL TODAY.
DOO
DOO
DOO
OH, THAT'S NICE, DEAR.
THUMP
OWWWWWW!
...

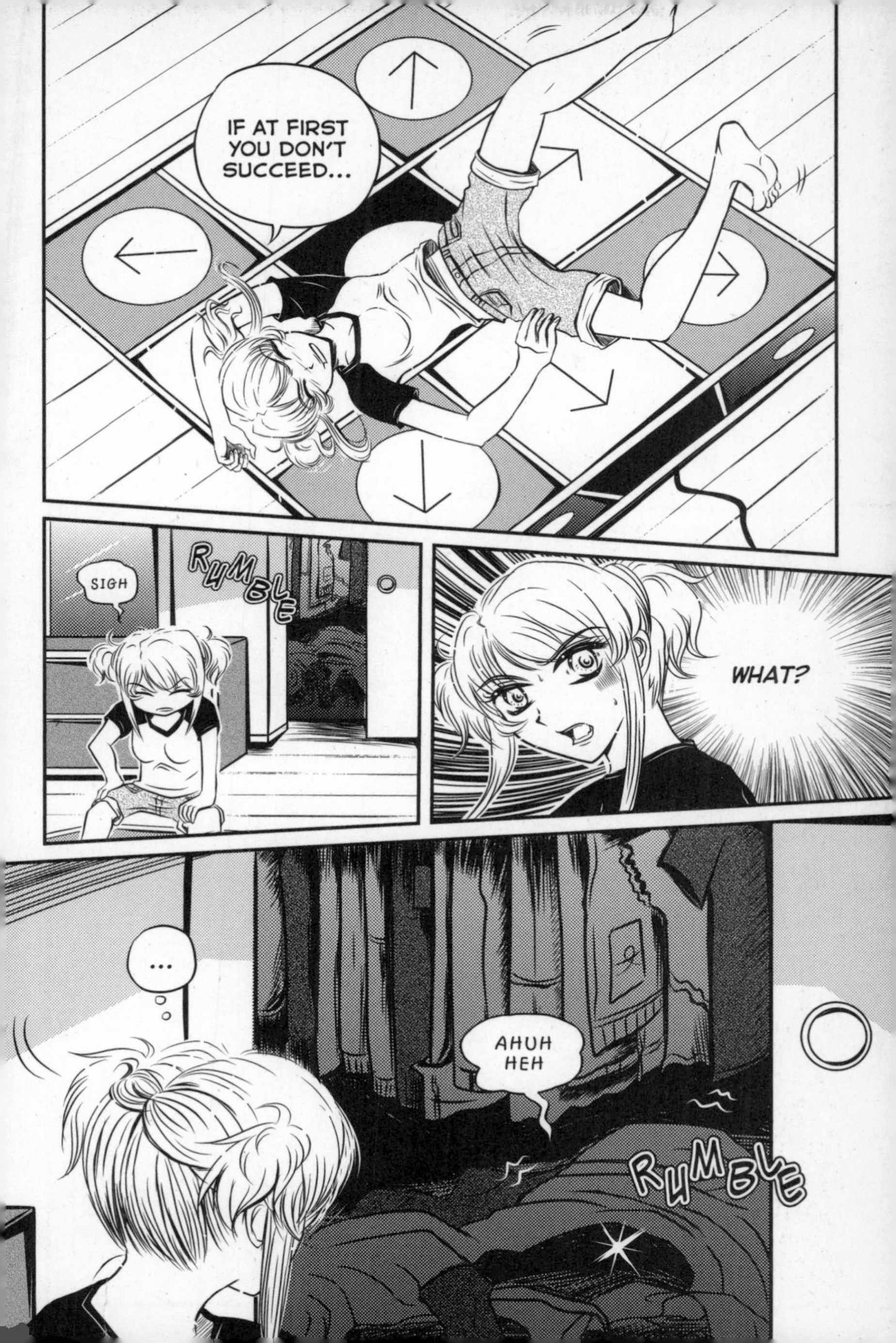
IF AT FIRST YOU DON'T SUCCEED...
SIGH
RUMBLE
WHAT?
...
AHUH HEH
RUMBLE

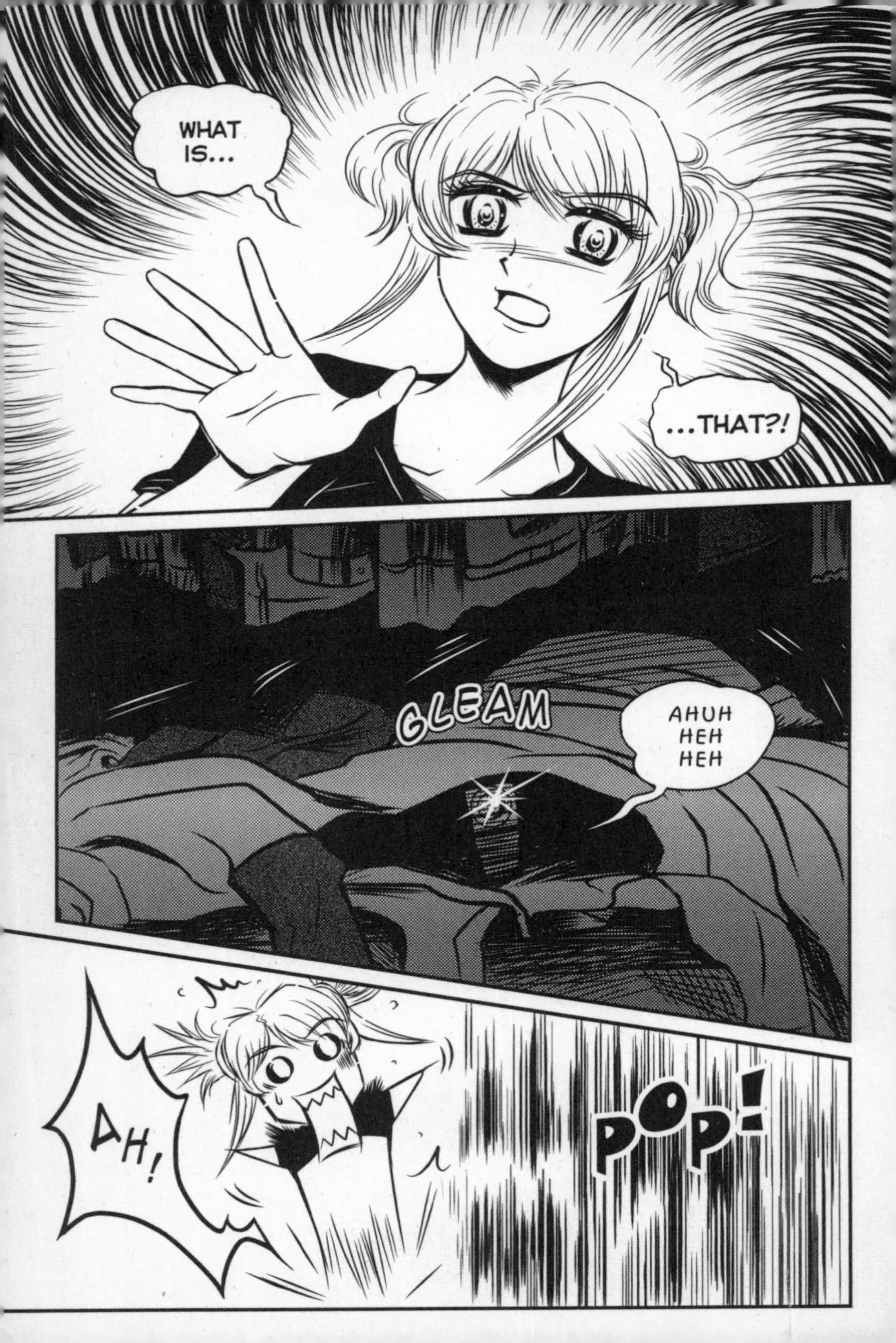
WHAT IS...
...THAT?!
GLEAM
AHUH HEH HEH
AH!
POP!

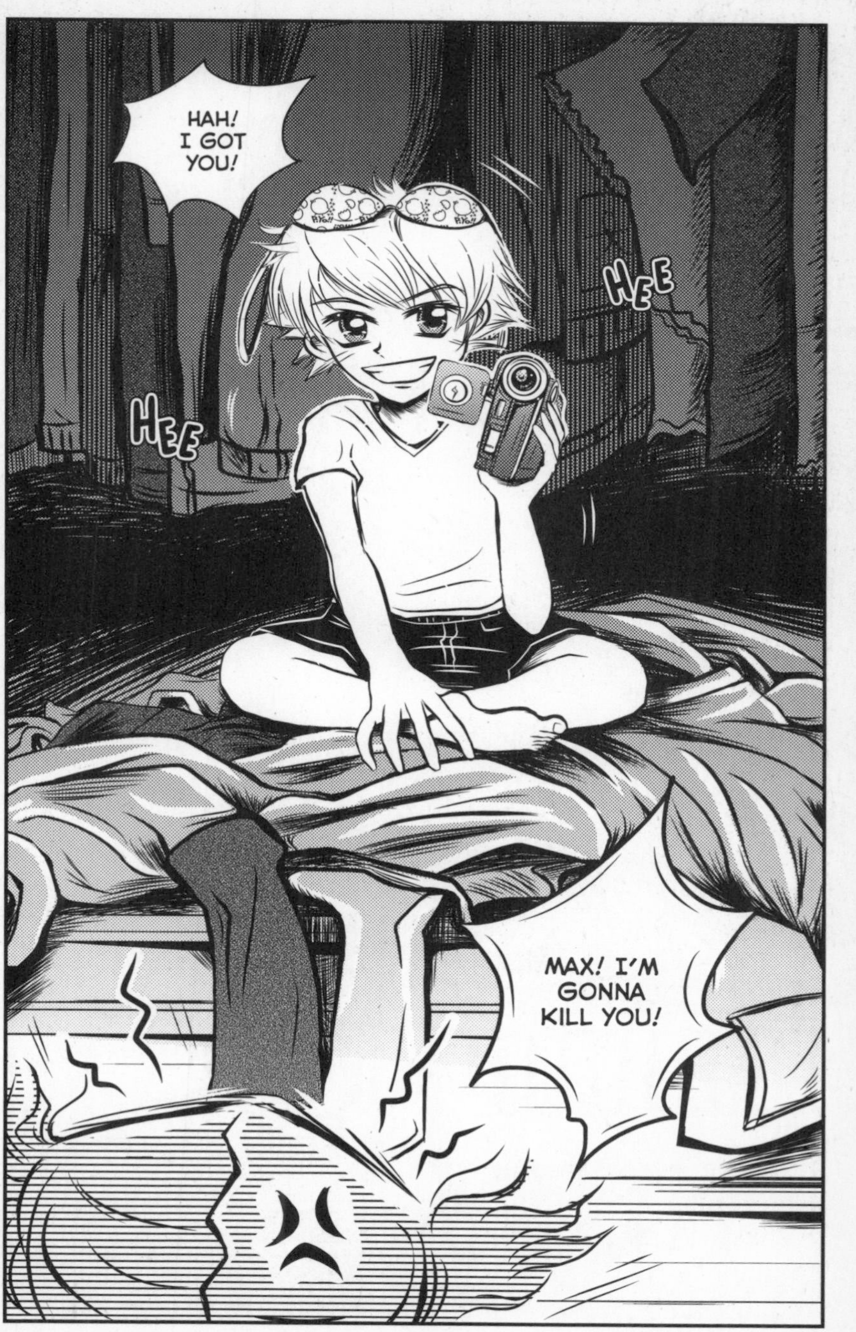
HAH!
I GOT
YOU!
HEE
HEE
MAX! I'M
GONNA
KILL YOU!

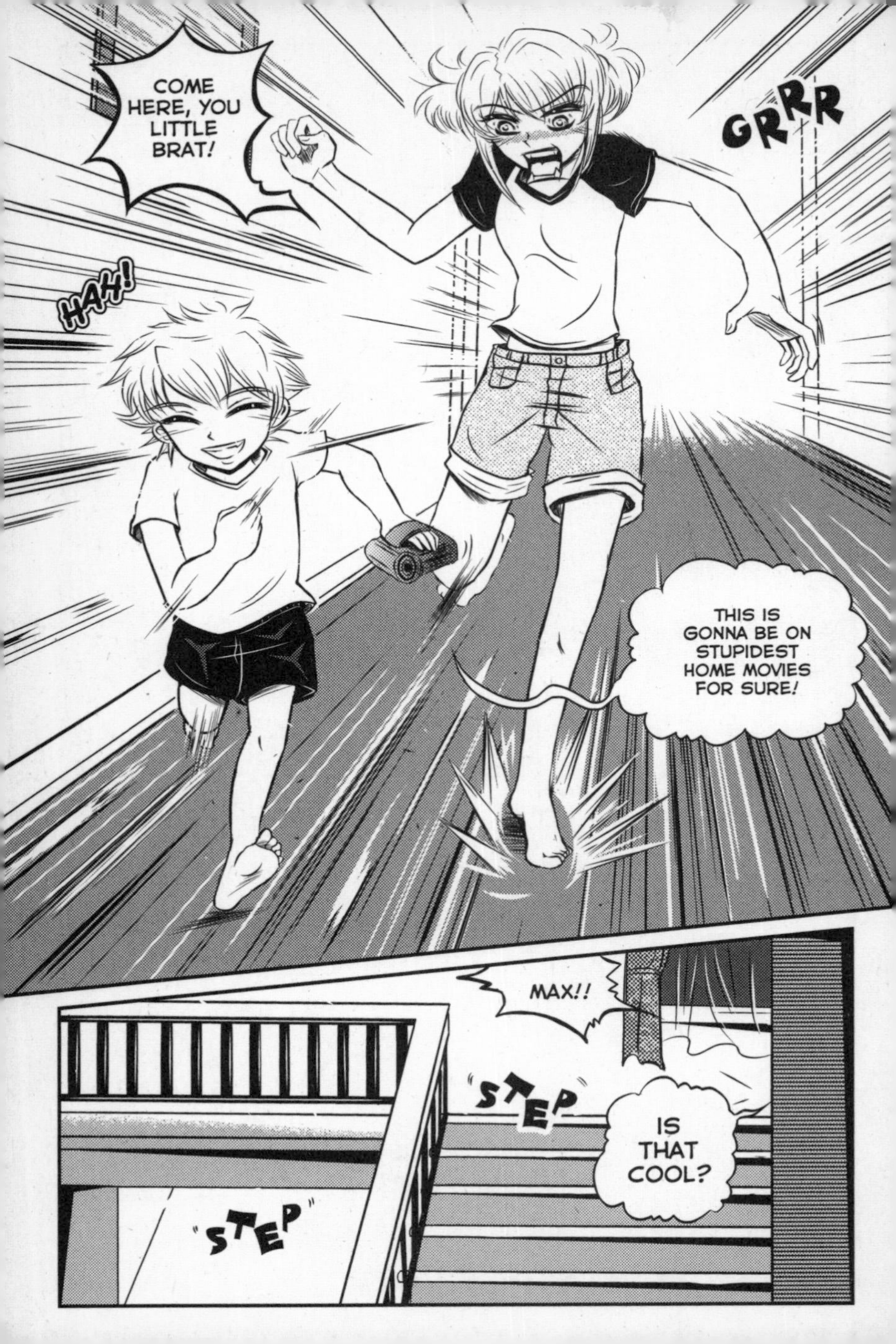
COME HERE, YOU LITTLE BRAT!
GRRR
HAH!
THIS IS GONNA BE ON STUPIDEST HOME MOVIES FOR SURE!
MAX!!
STEP
IS THAT COOL?
STEP

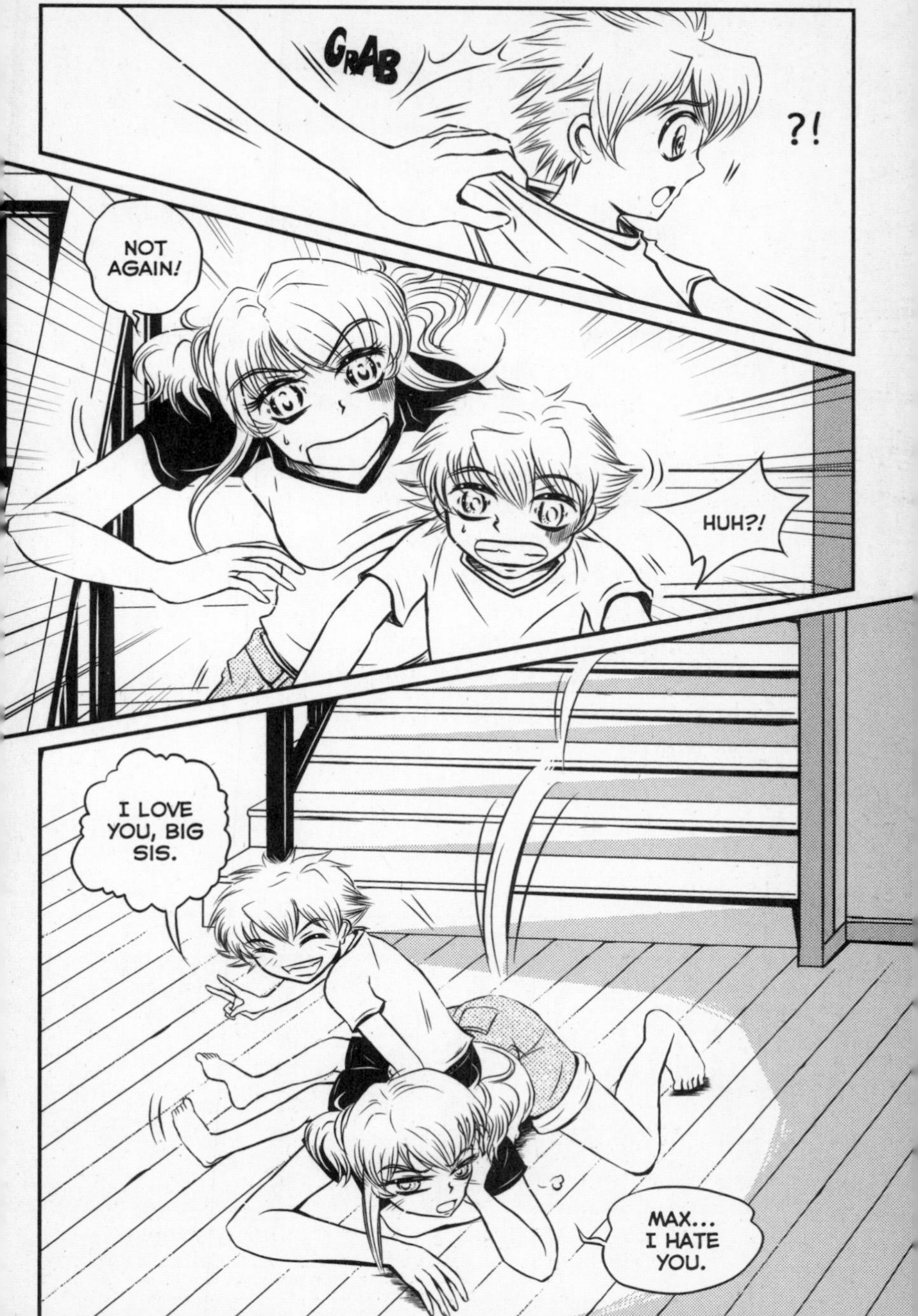
GRAB
?!
NOT AGAIN!
HUH?!
I LOVE YOU, BIG SIS.
MAX... I HATE YOU.

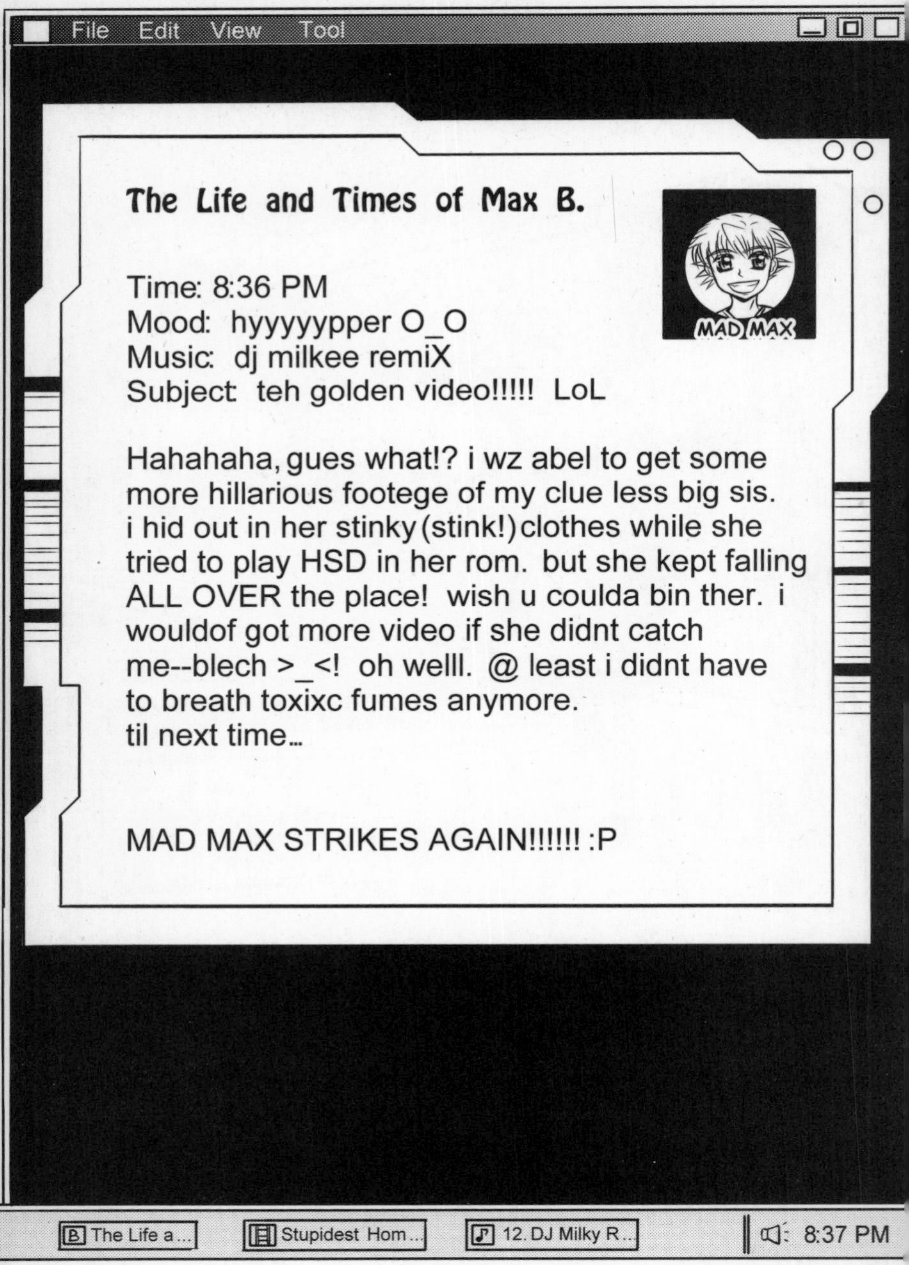
File Edit View Tool
The Life and Times of Max B.
MAD MAX
Time: 8:36 PM
Mood: hyyyyypper O_O
Music: dj milkee remiX
Subject: teh golden video!!!!! LoL
Hahahaha, gues what!? i wz abel to get some more hillarious footege of my clue less big sis. i hid out in her stinky (stink!) clothes while she tried to play HSD in her rom. but she kept falling ALL OVER the place! wish u coulda bin ther. i wouldof got more video if she didnt catch me--blech >_<! oh welll. @ least i didnt have to breath toxixc fumes anymore.
til next time...
MAD MAX STRIKES AGAIN!!!!!! :P
The Life a...
Stupidest Hom...
12. DJ Milky R...
8:37 PM

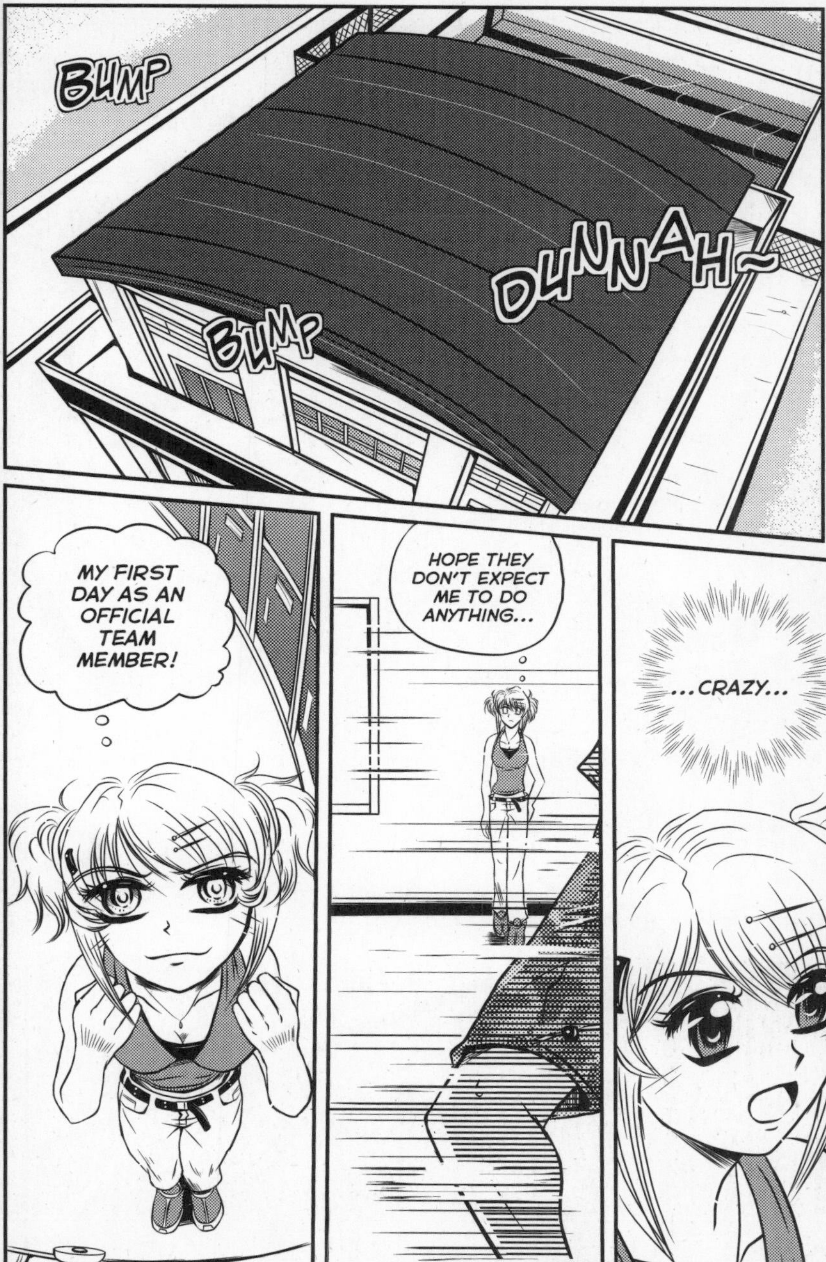
BUMP
BUMP
DUNNAH~
MY FIRST DAY AS AN OFFICIAL TEAM MEMBER!
HOPE THEY DON'T EXPECT ME TO DO ANYTHING...
...CRAZY...

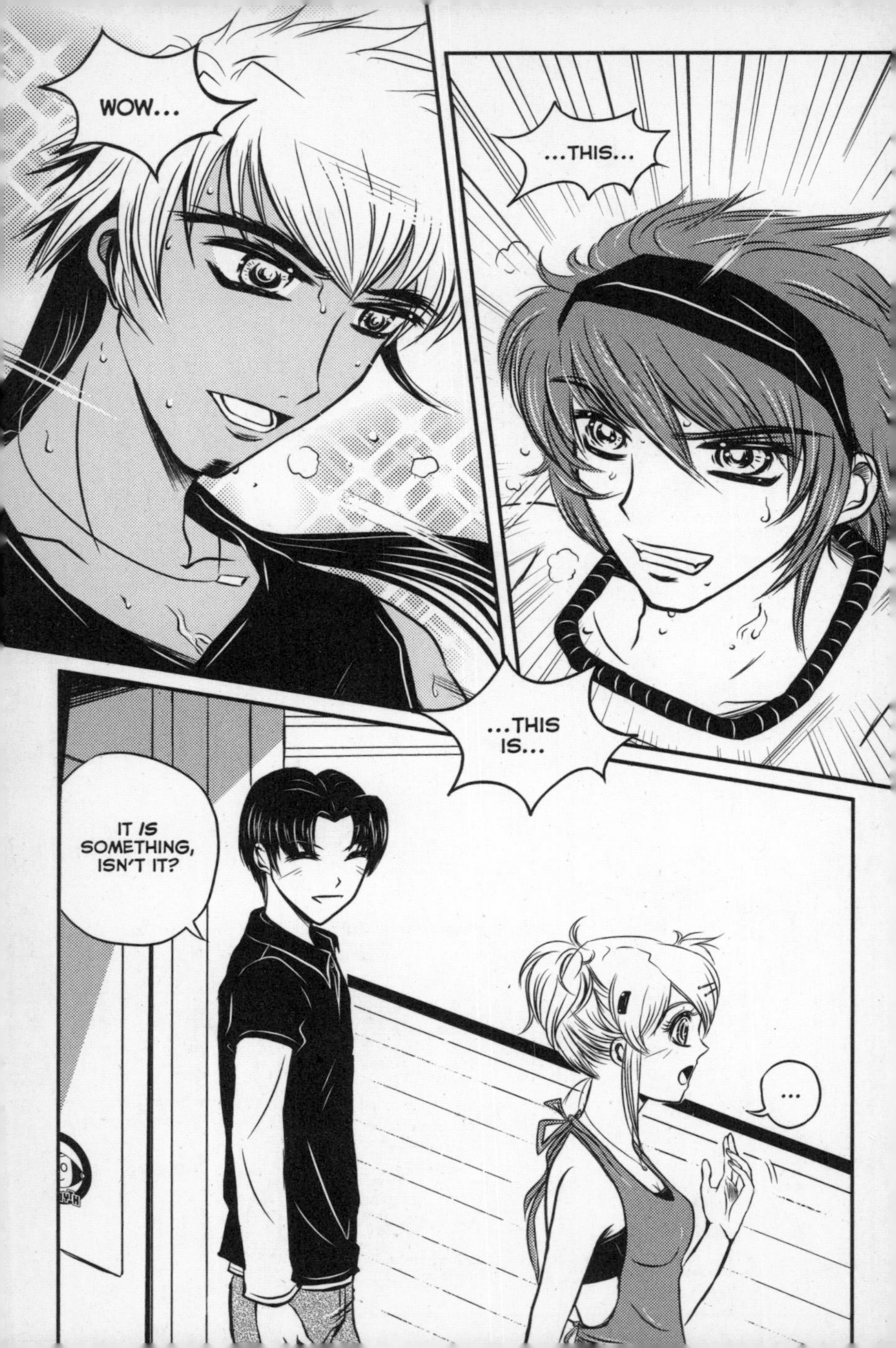
WOW...
...THIS...
...THIS IS...
IT *IS* SOMETHING, ISN'T IT?
...

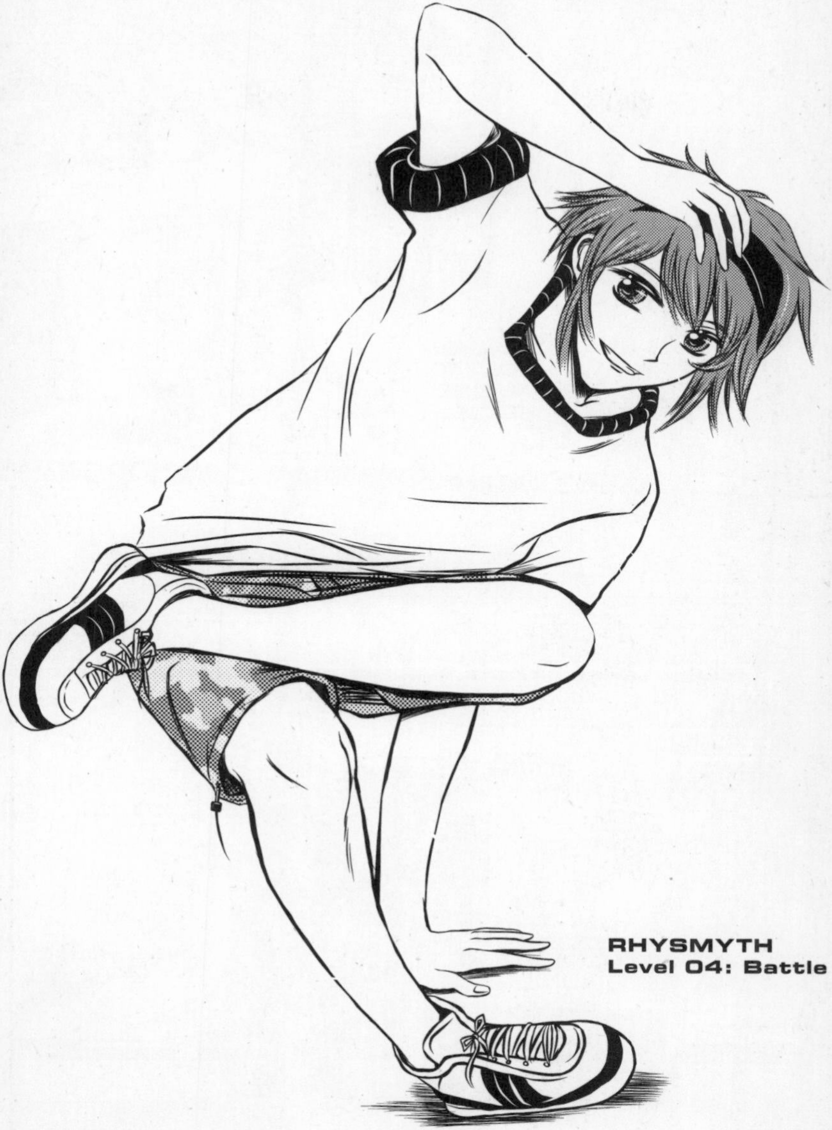

RHYSMYTH

Level 04: Battle

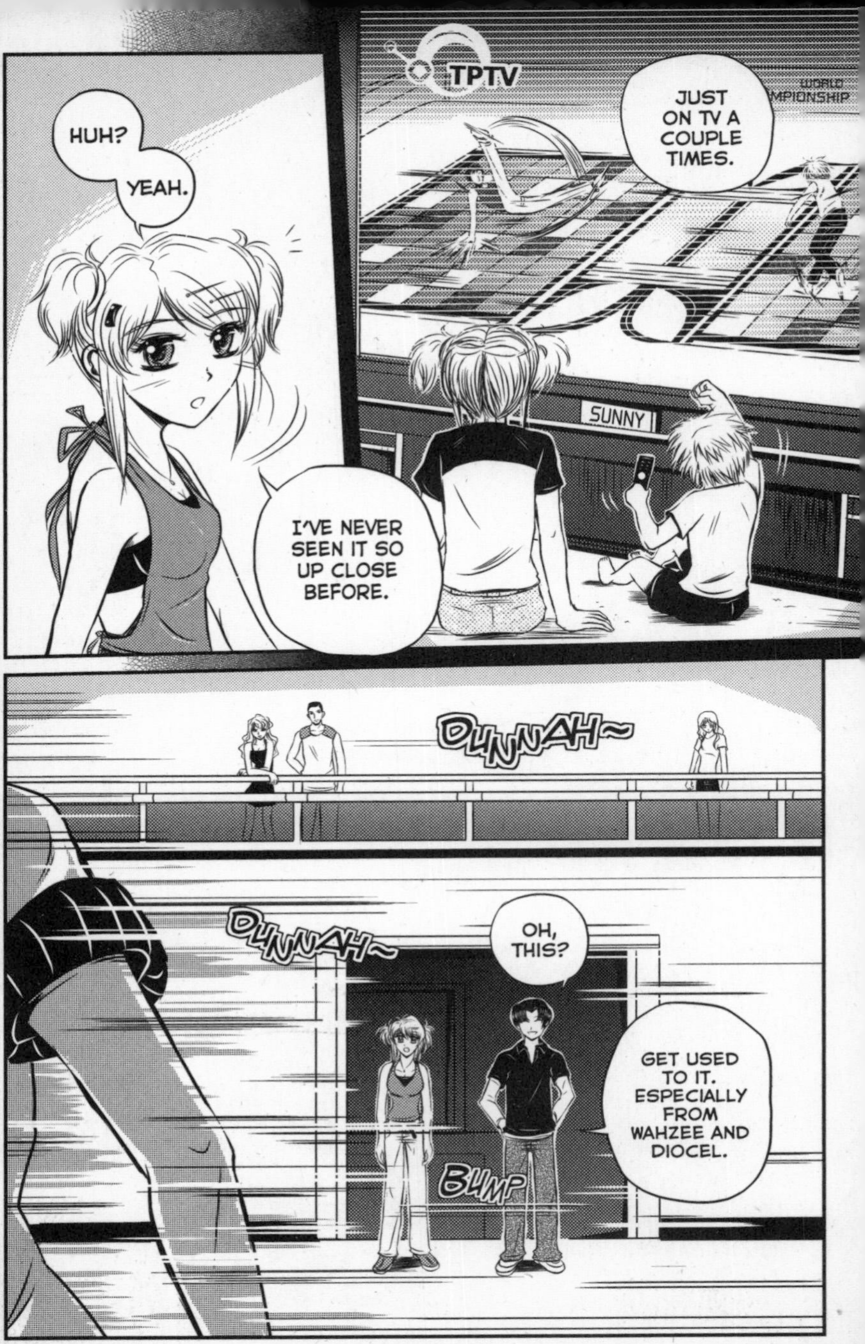
HUH?
YEAH.
TPTV
WORLD
MPIONSHIP
JUST ON TV A COUPLE TIMES.
SUNNY
I'VE NEVER SEEN IT SO UP CLOSE BEFORE.
DUNNAH~
DUNNAH~
OH, THIS?
GET USED TO IT. ESPECIALLY FROM WAHZEE AND DIOCEL.
BUMP

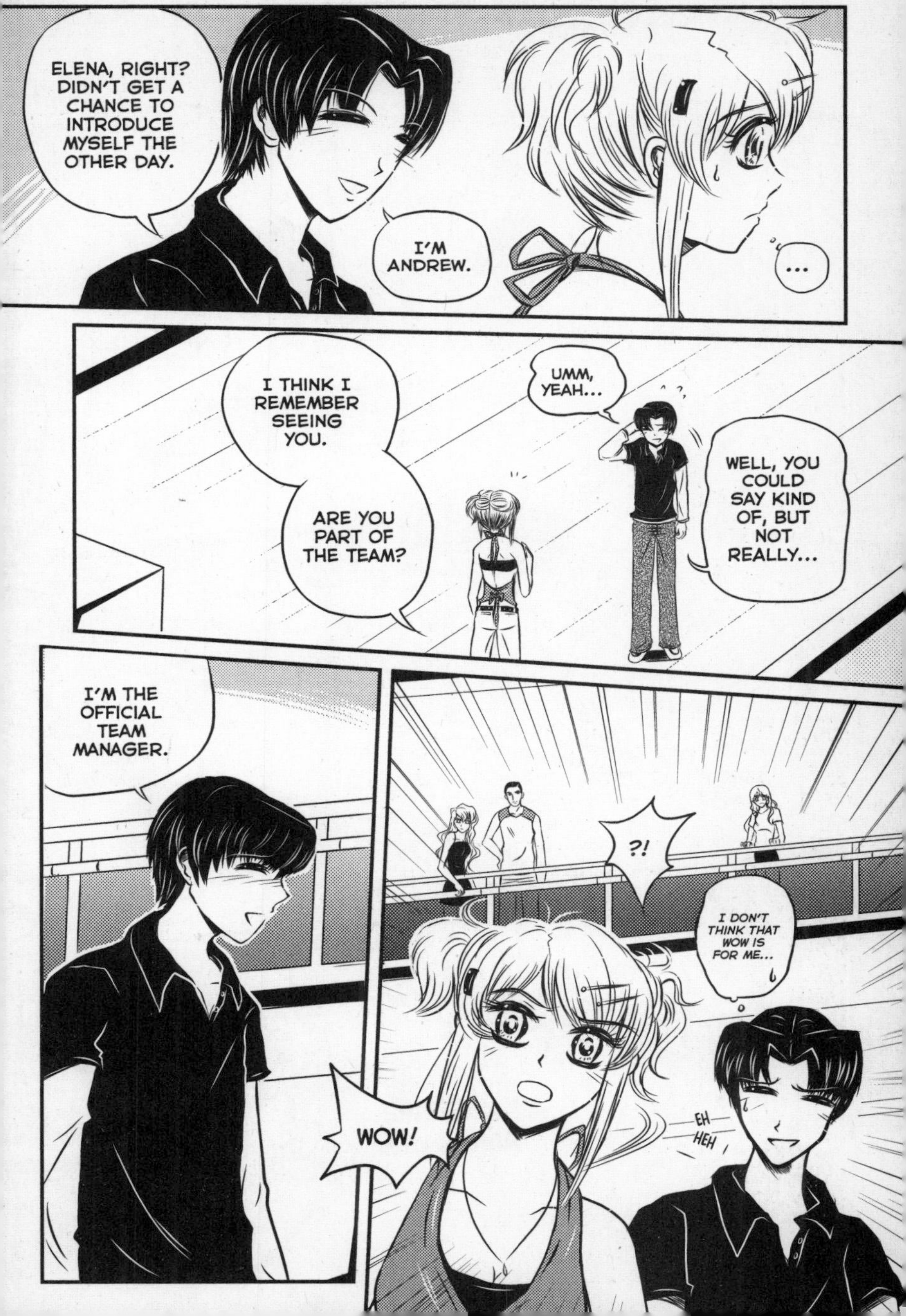
ELENA, RIGHT? DIDN'T GET A CHANCE TO INTRODUCE MYSELF THE OTHER DAY.
I'M ANDREW.
...
I THINK I REMEMBER SEEING YOU.
ARE YOU PART OF THE TEAM?
UMM, YEAH...
WELL, YOU COULD SAY KIND OF, BUT NOT REALLY...
I'M THE OFFICIAL TEAM MANAGER.
?!
WOW!
I DON'T THINK THAT WOW IS FOR ME...
EH HEH

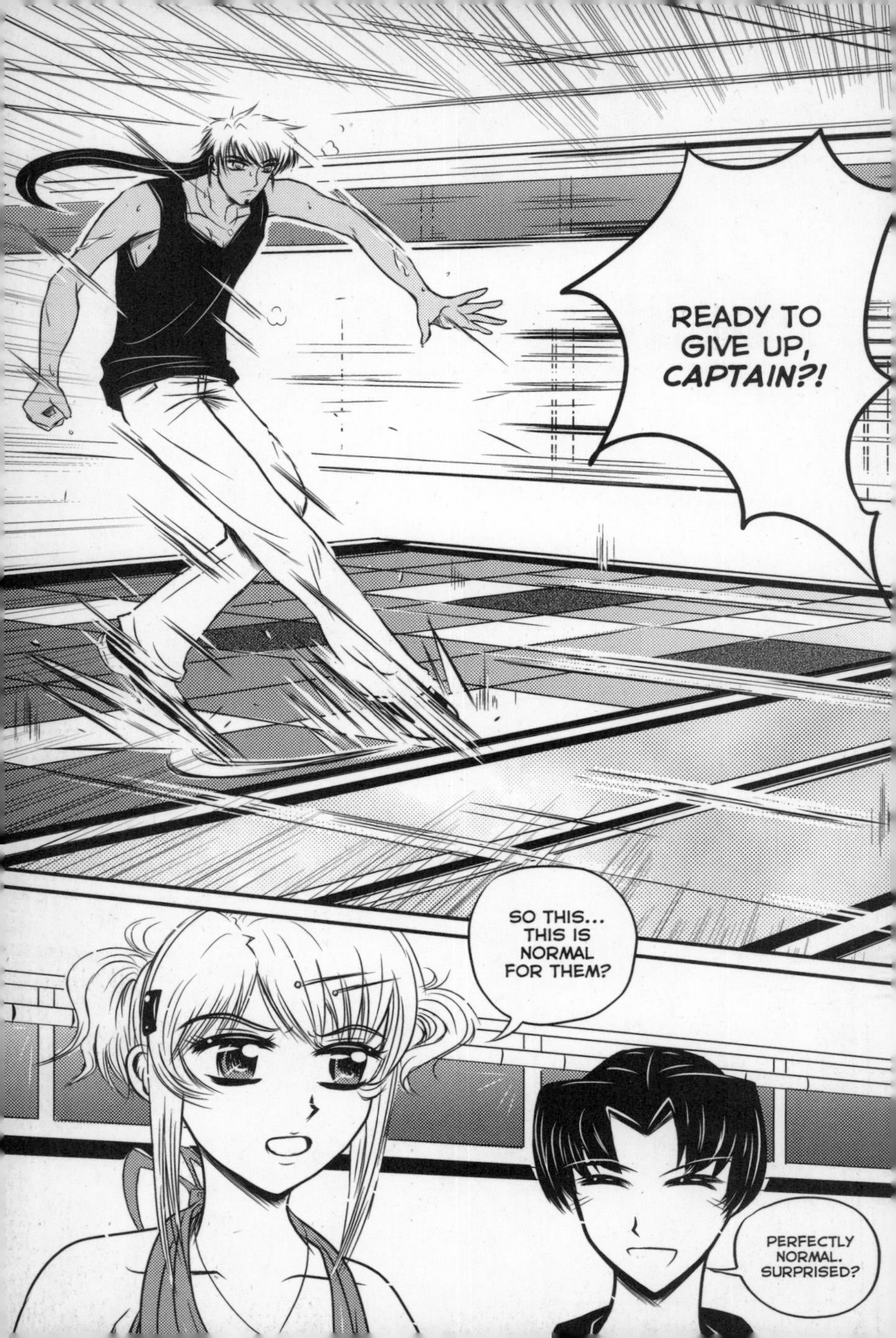
READY TO GIVE UP, *CAPTAIN?!*
SO THIS... THIS IS NORMAL FOR THEM?
PERFECTLY NORMAL. SURPRISED?

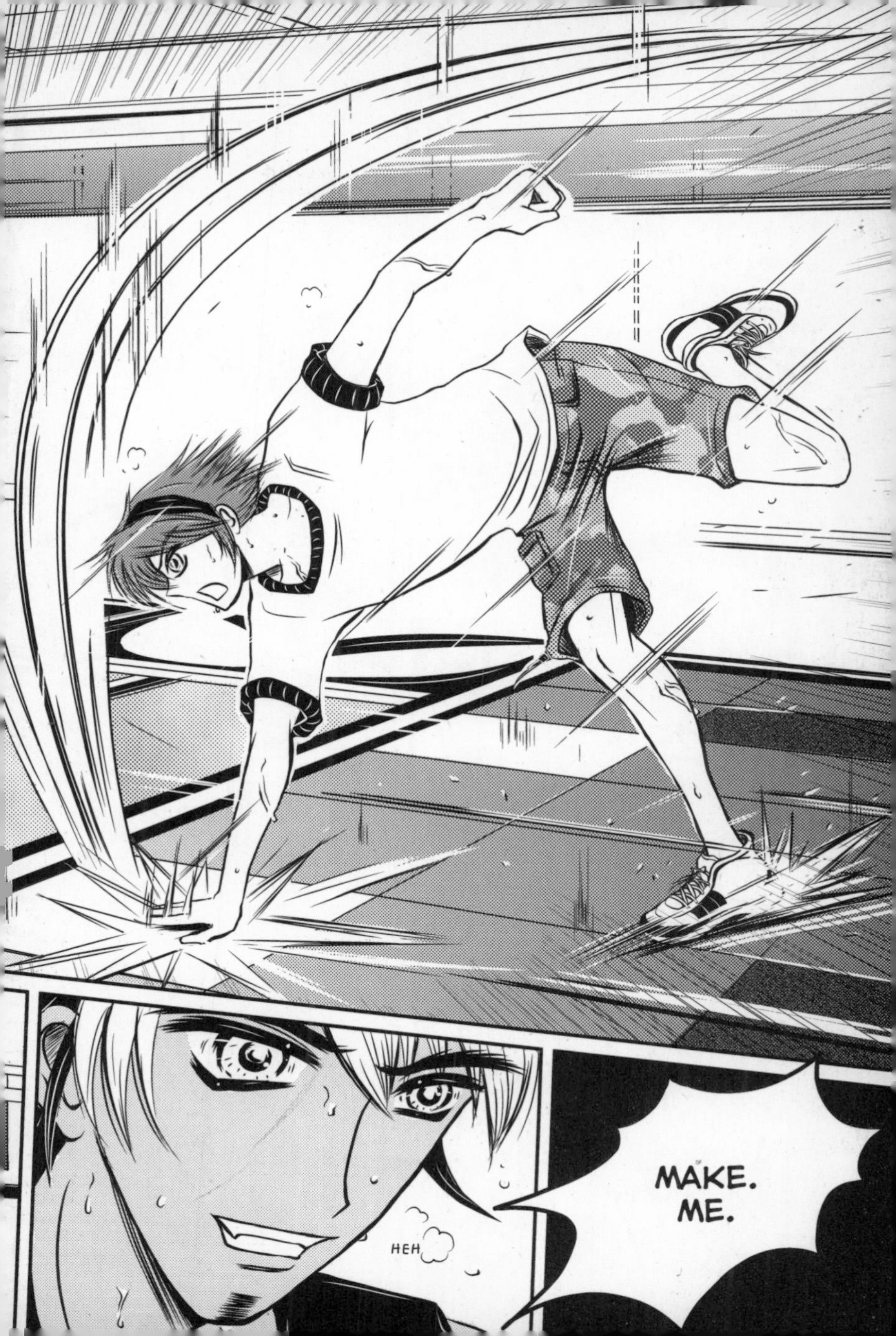
HEH
MAKE. ME.

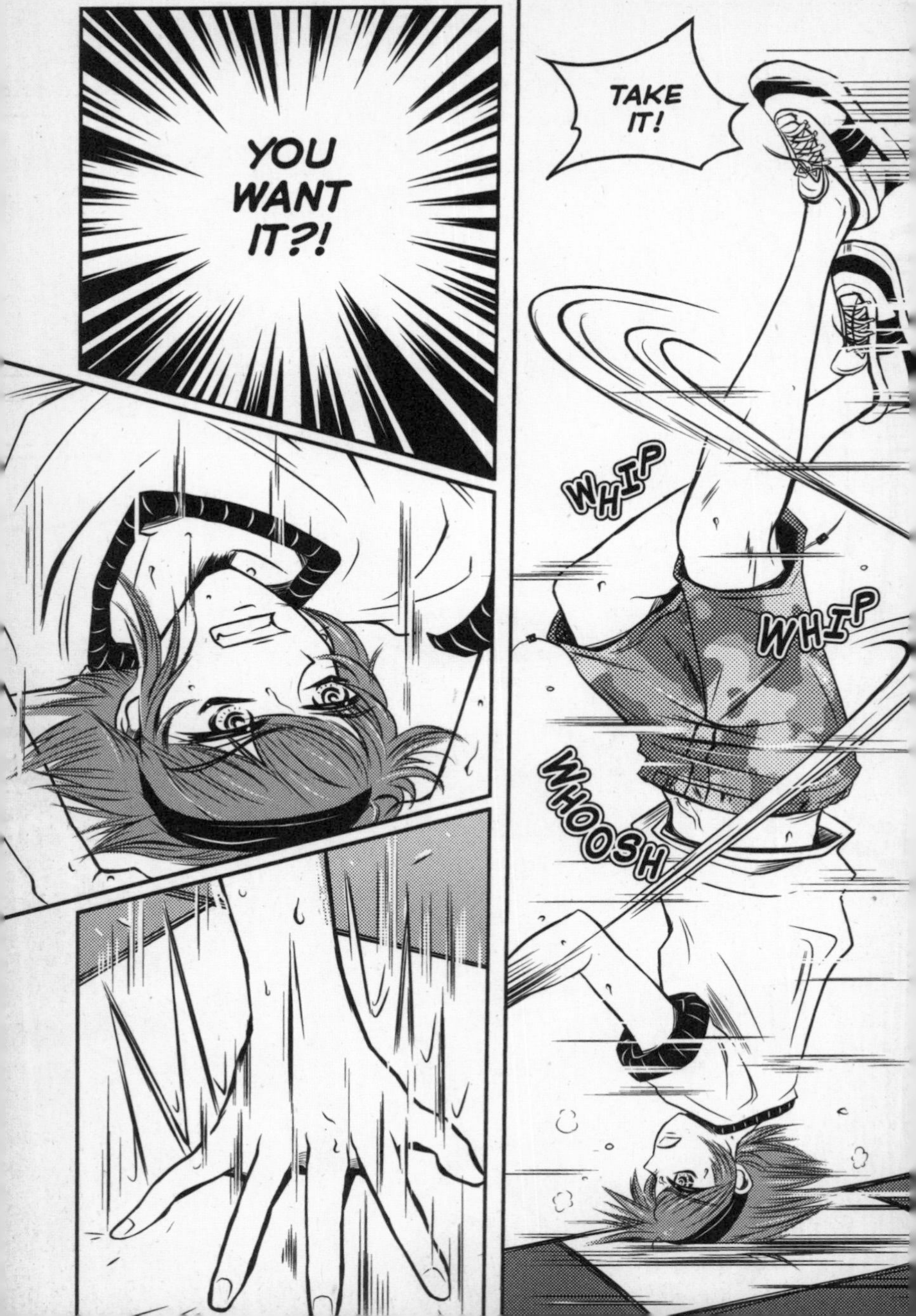
YOU WANT IT?!
TAKE IT!
WHIP
WHIP
WHOOSH

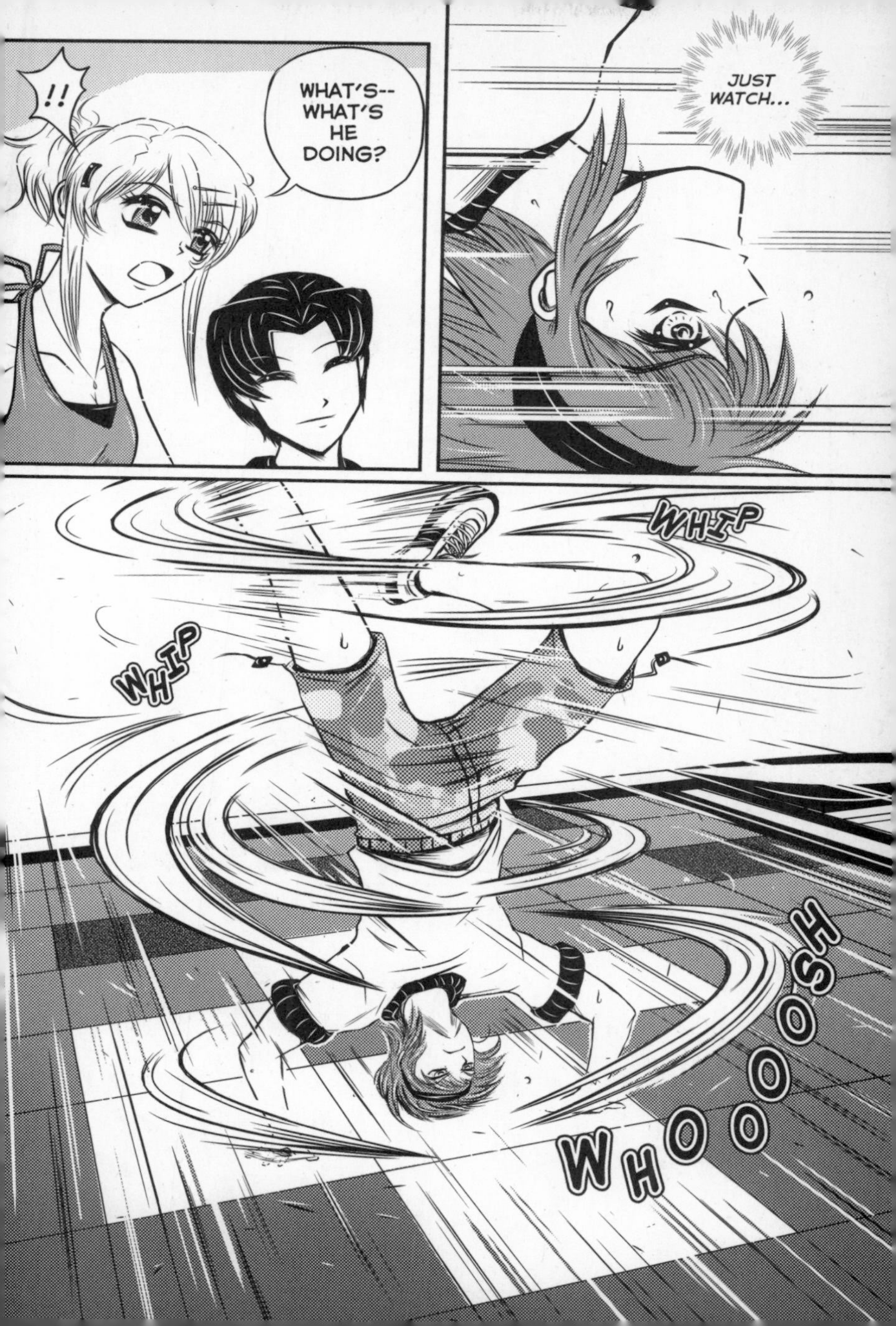
!!
WHAT'S-- WHAT'S HE DOING?
JUST WATCH...
WHIP
WHIP
WHOOOOSH

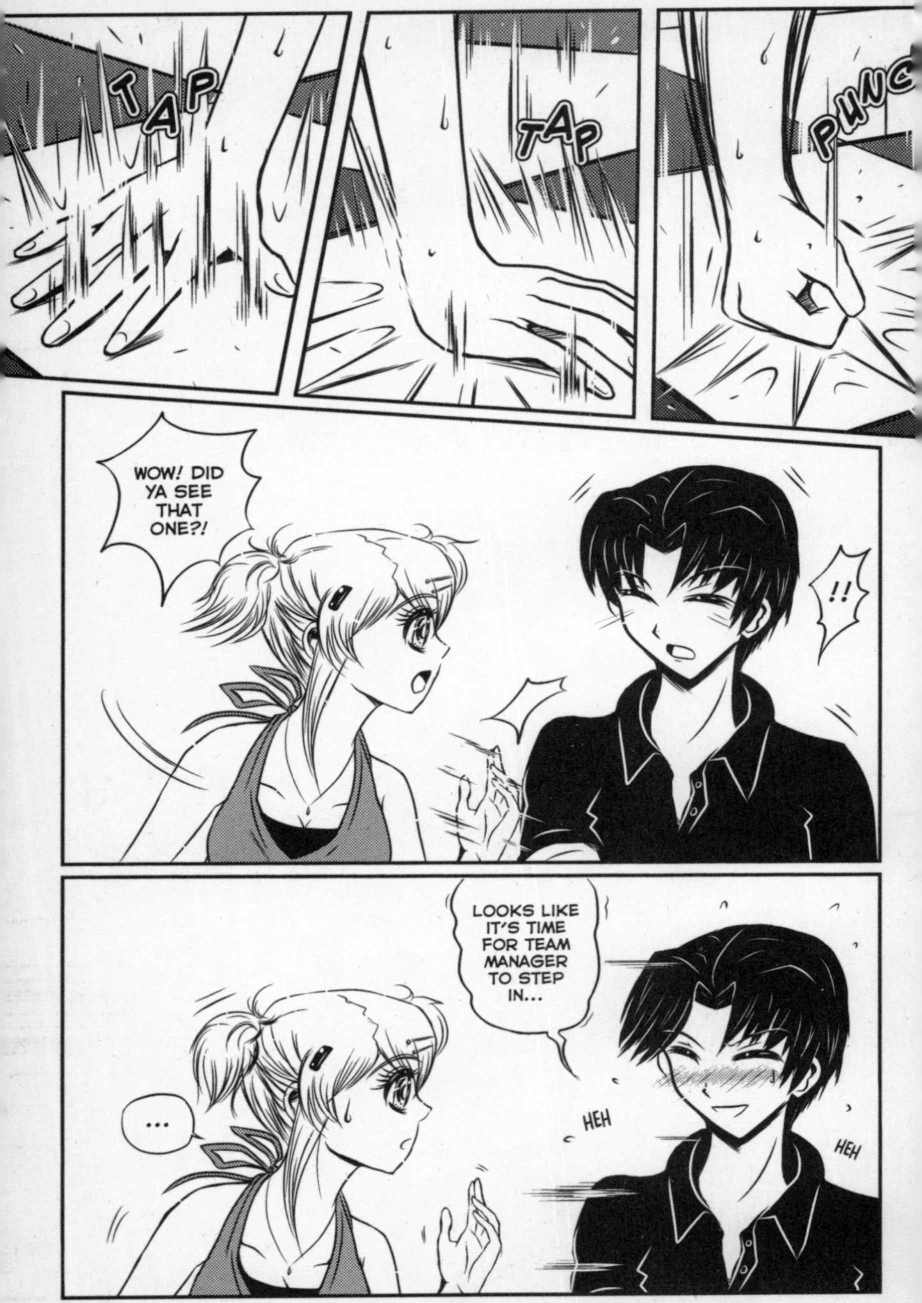
TAP
TAP
PUNC
WOW! DID YA SEE THAT ONE?!
!!
LOOKS LIKE IT'S TIME FOR TEAM MANAGER TO STEP IN...
...
HEH
HEH

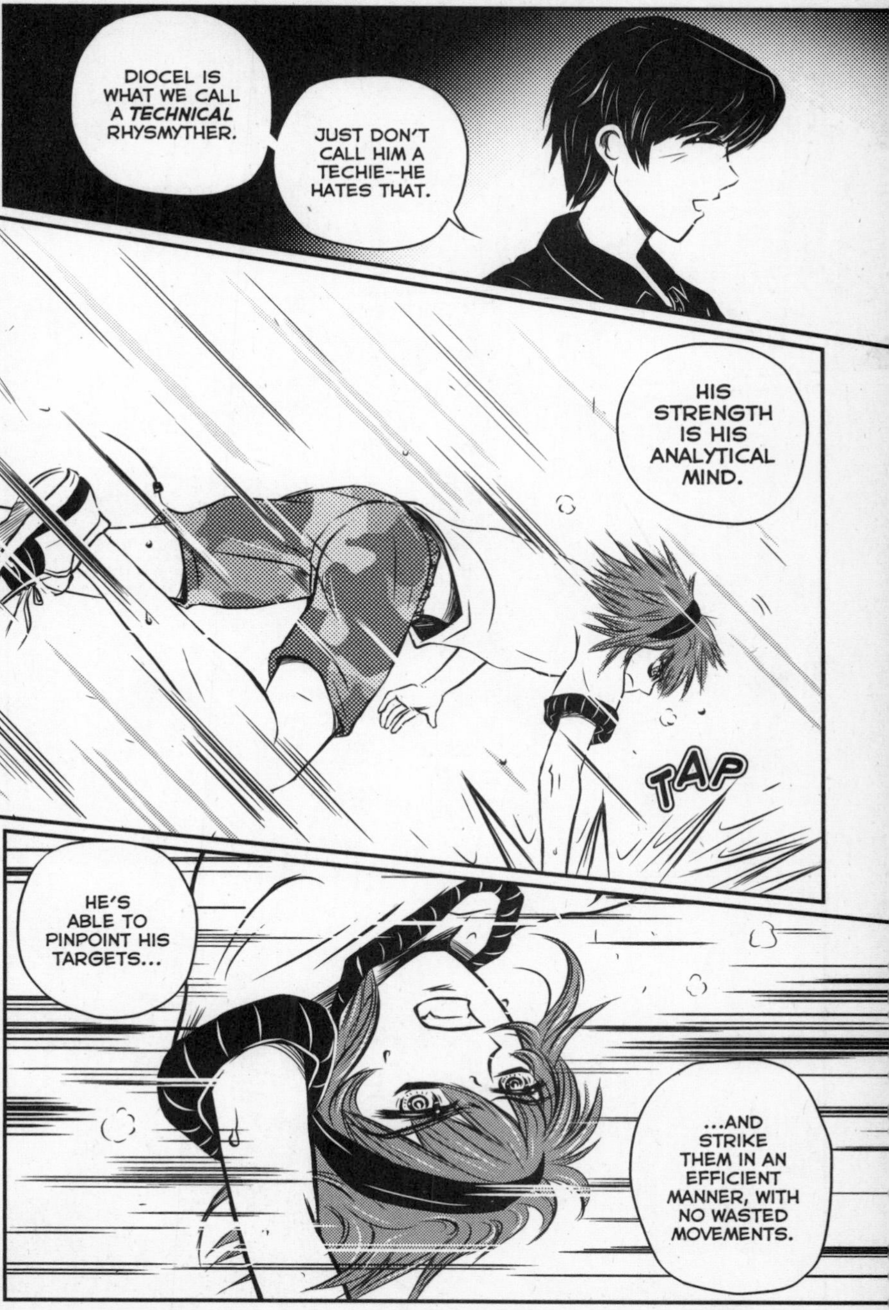
DIOCEL IS WHAT WE CALL A *TECHNICAL* RHYSMYTHER.
JUST DON'T CALL HIM A TECHIE--HE HATES THAT.
HIS STRENGTH IS HIS ANALYTICAL MIND.
TAP
HE'S ABLE TO PINPOINT HIS TARGETS...
...AND STRIKE THEM IN AN EFFICIENT MANNER, WITH NO WASTED MOVEMENTS.

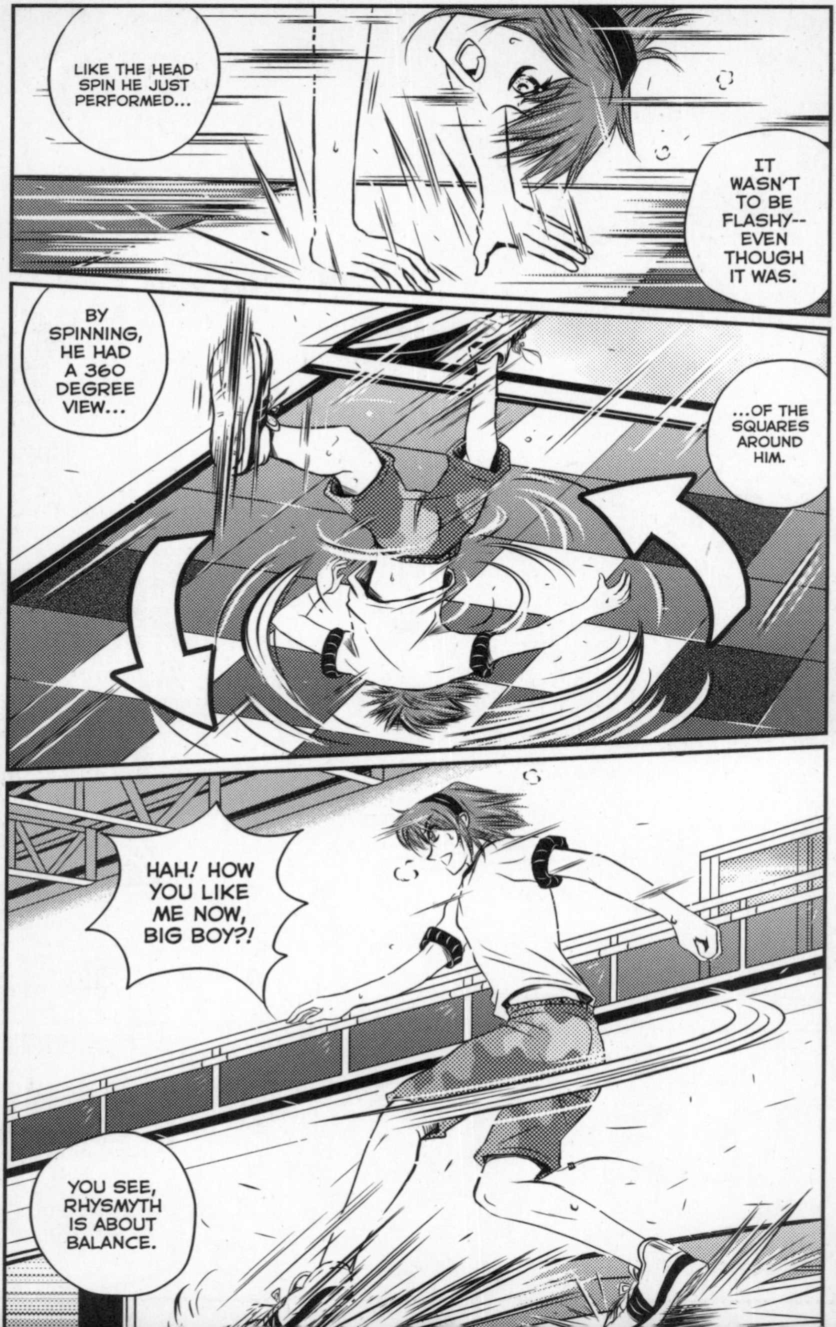
LIKE THE HEAD SPIN HE JUST PERFORMED...
IT WASN'T TO BE FLASHY--EVEN THOUGH IT WAS.
BY SPINNING, HE HAD A 360 DEGREE VIEW...
...OF THE SQUARES AROUND HIM.
HAH! HOW YOU LIKE ME NOW, BIG BOY?!
YOU SEE, RHYSMYTH IS ABOUT BALANCE.

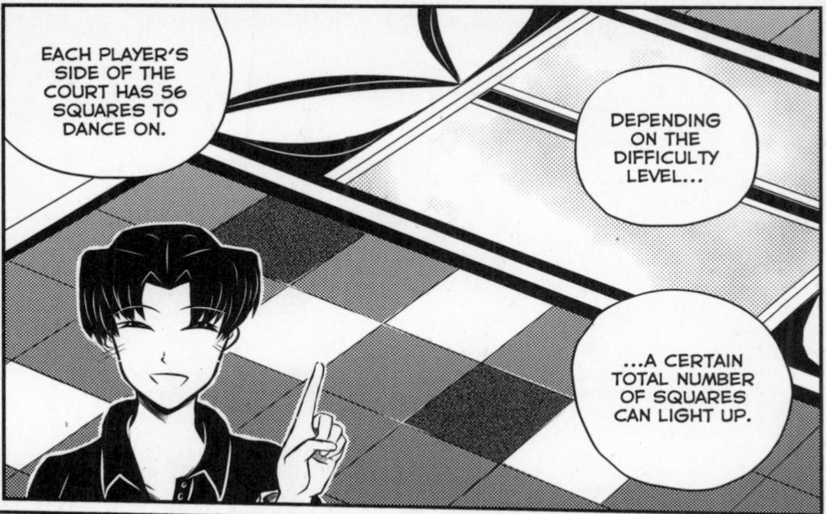
EACH PLAYER'S SIDE OF THE COURT HAS 56 SQUARES TO DANCE ON.
DEPENDING ON THE DIFFICULTY LEVEL...
...A CERTAIN TOTAL NUMBER OF SQUARES CAN LIGHT UP.
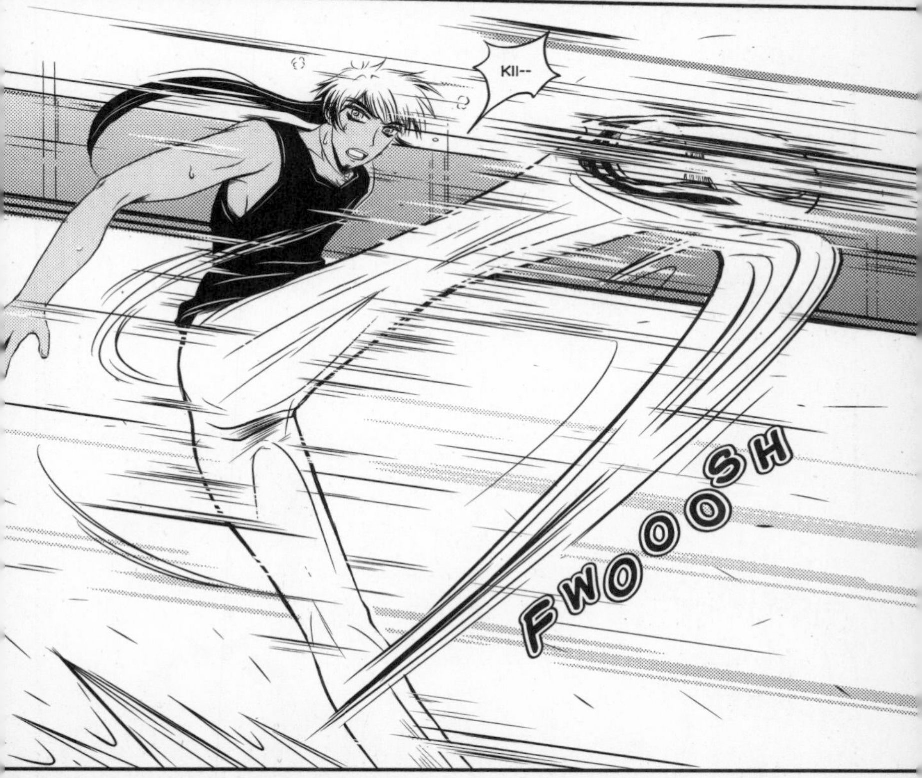
KII--
FWOOOSH

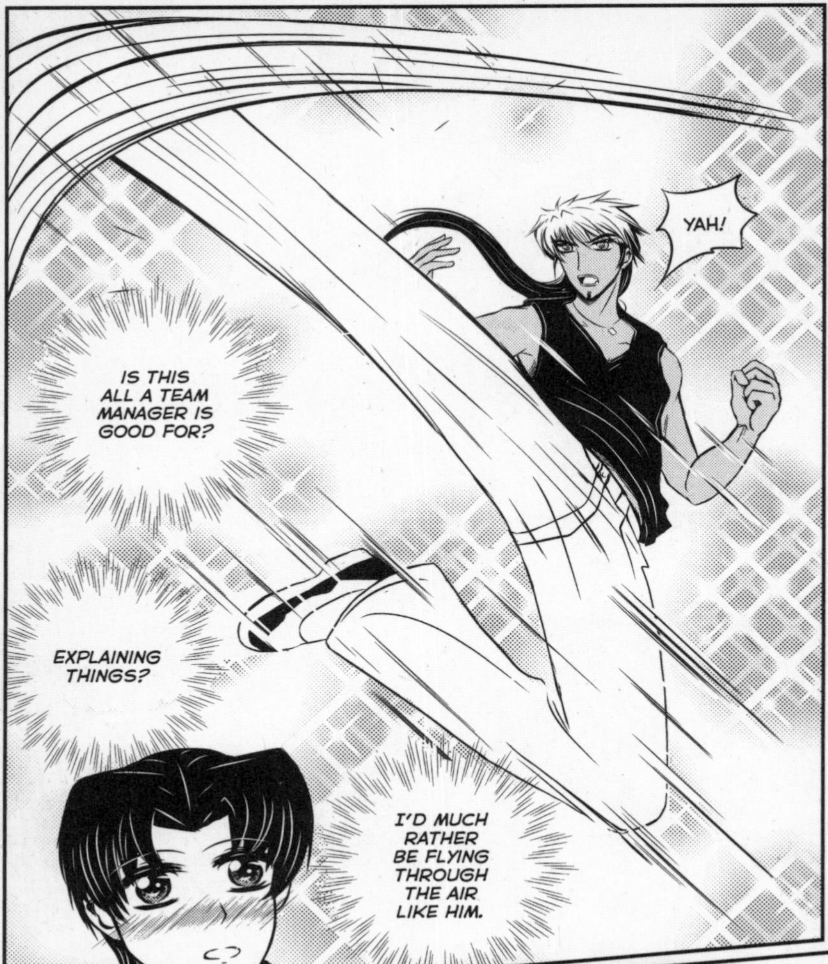
YAH!
IS THIS ALL A TEAM MANAGER IS GOOD FOR?
EXPLAINING THINGS?
I'D MUCH RATHER BE FLYING THROUGH THE AIR LIKE HIM.
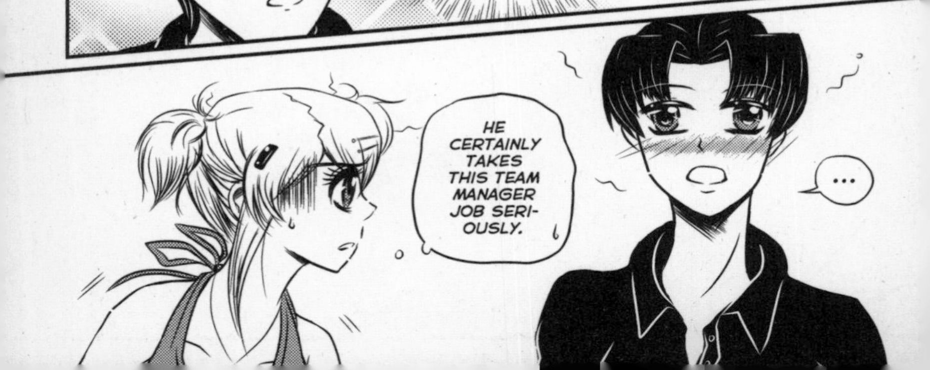
HE CERTAINLY TAKES THIS TEAM MANAGER JOB SERI-OUSLY.
...

EXCUSE ME...

KOFF

AS I WAS SAYING...

EACH PLAYER STARTS WITH EVERY SQUARE LIGHTABLE.

SINCE THIS IS COMPETITION MODE, EACH OF THEM HAS EIGHT RANDOMIZING LIGHT SQUARES.

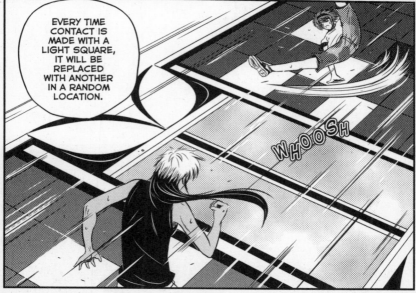

EVERY TIME CONTACT IS MADE WITH A LIGHT SQUARE, IT WILL BE REPLACED WITH ANOTHER IN A RANDOM LOCATION.

WHOOSH

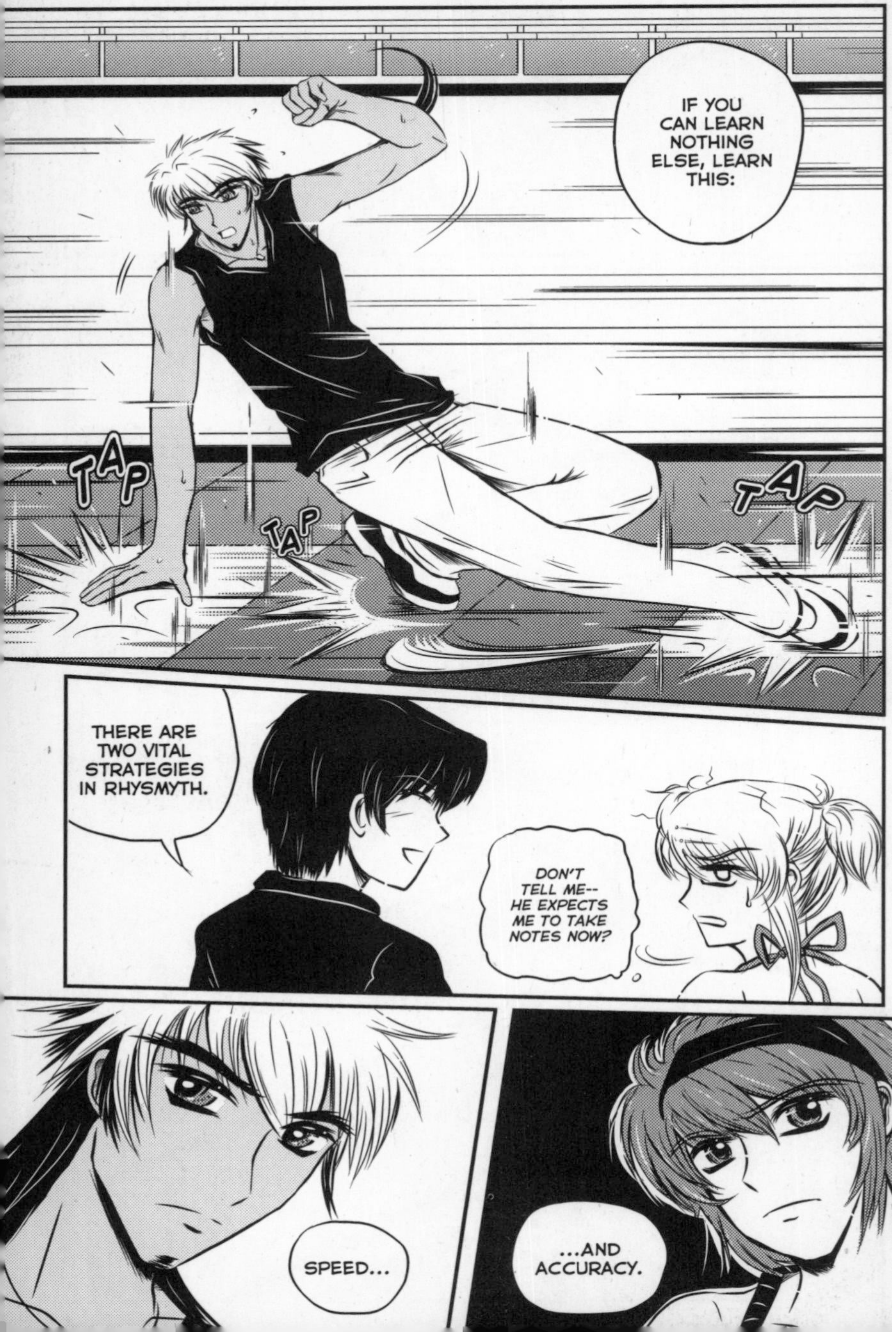
IF YOU CAN LEARN NOTHING ELSE, LEARN THIS:
TAP
TAP
TAP
THERE ARE TWO VITAL STRATEGIES IN RHYSMYTH.
DON'T TELL ME-- HE EXPECTS ME TO TAKE NOTES NOW?
SPEED...
...AND ACCURACY.

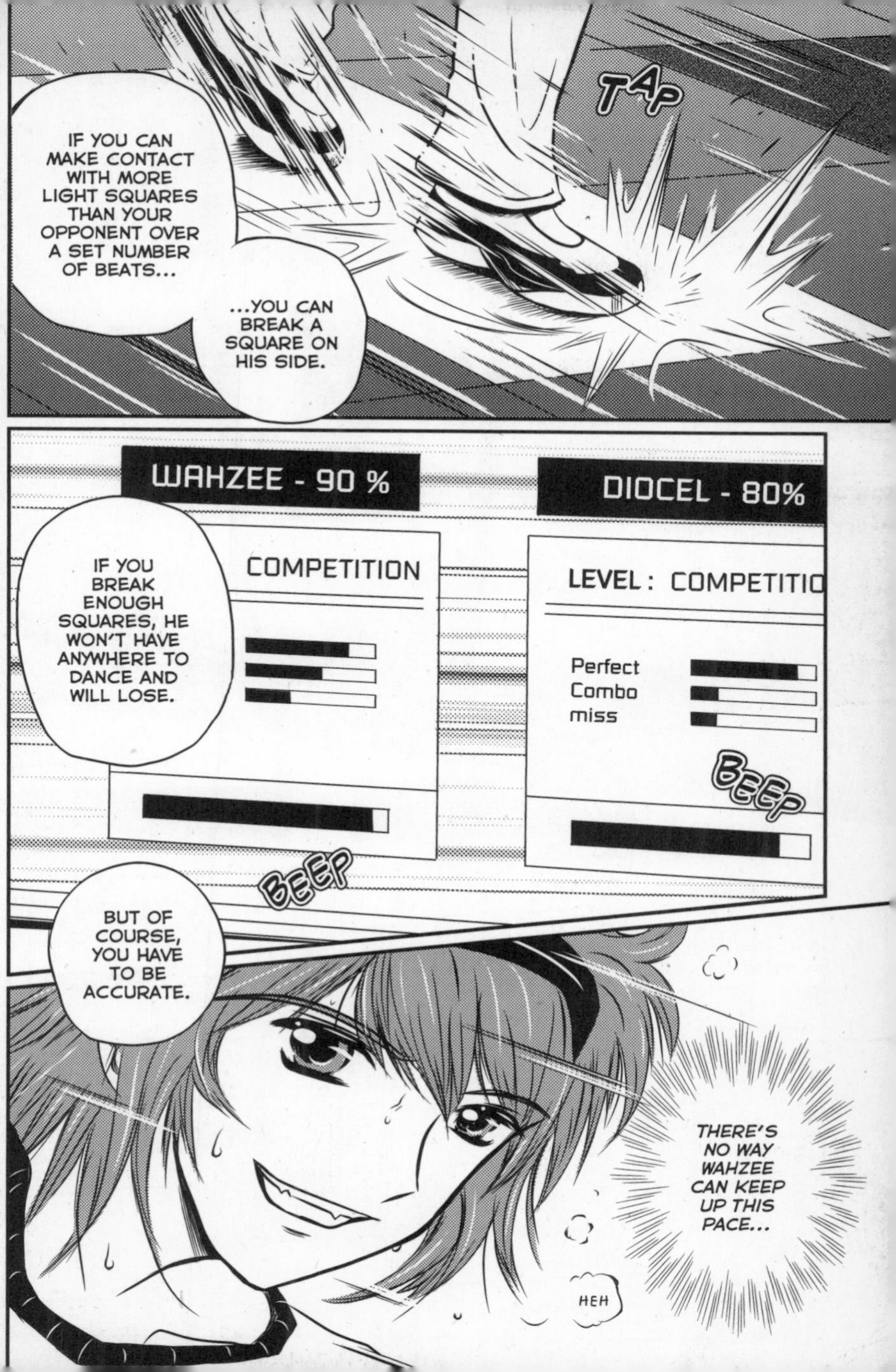
TAP
IF YOU CAN MAKE CONTACT WITH MORE LIGHT SQUARES THAN YOUR OPPONENT OVER A SET NUMBER OF BEATS...
...YOU CAN BREAK A SQUARE ON HIS SIDE.
WAHZEE - 90 %
DIOCEL - 80%
IF YOU BREAK ENOUGH SQUARES, HE WON'T HAVE ANYWHERE TO DANCE AND WILL LOSE.
COMPETITION
LEVEL : COMPETITIO
Perfect
Combo
miss
BEEP
BEEP
BUT OF COURSE, YOU HAVE TO BE ACCURATE.
THERE'S NO WAY WAHZEE CAN KEEP UP THIS PACE...
HEH

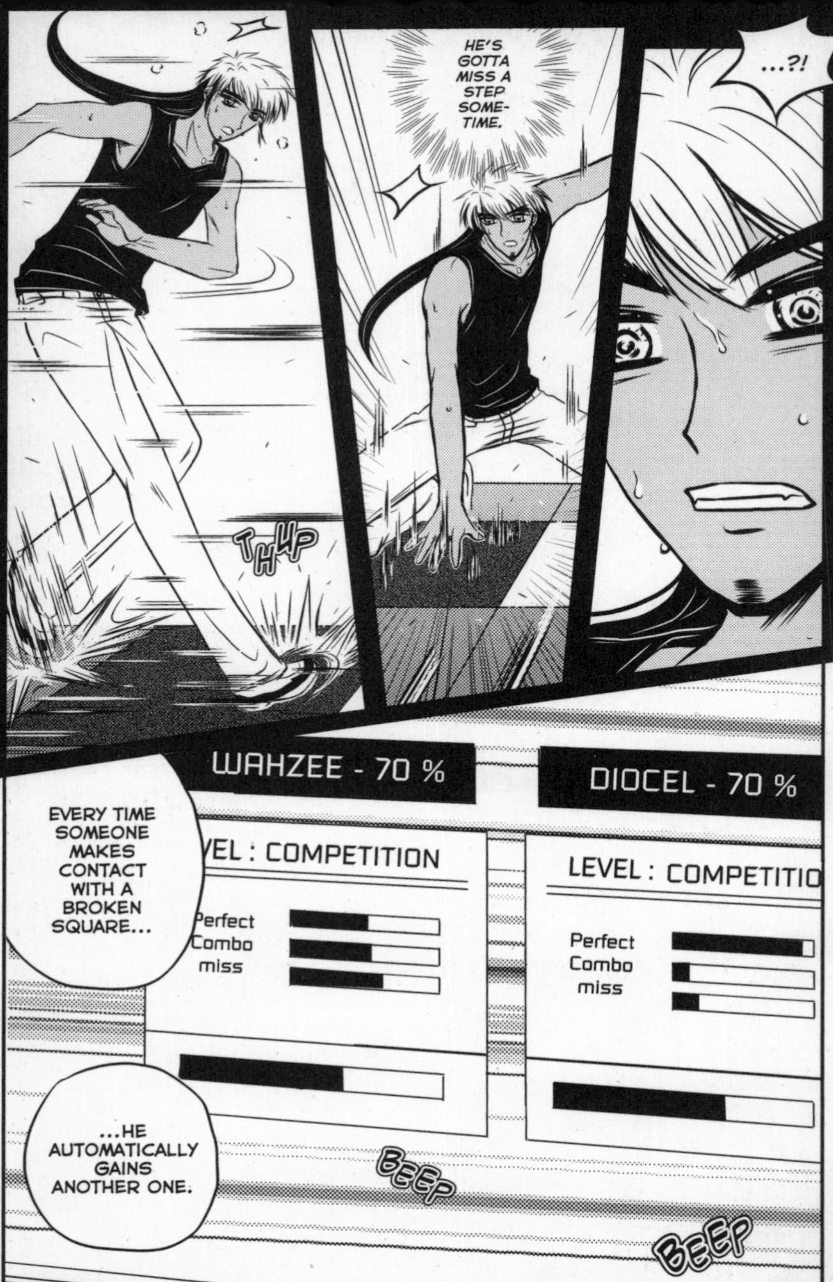
...?!
HE'S GOTTA MISS A STEP SOME-TIME.
THUP
DIOCEL - 70 %
LEVEL : COMPETITIO
Perfect
Combo
miss
WAHZEE - 70 %
VEL : COMPETITION
Perfect
Combo
miss
EVERY TIME SOMEONE MAKES CONTACT WITH A BROKEN SQUARE...
...HE AUTOMATICALLY GAINS ANOTHER ONE.
BEEP
BEEP

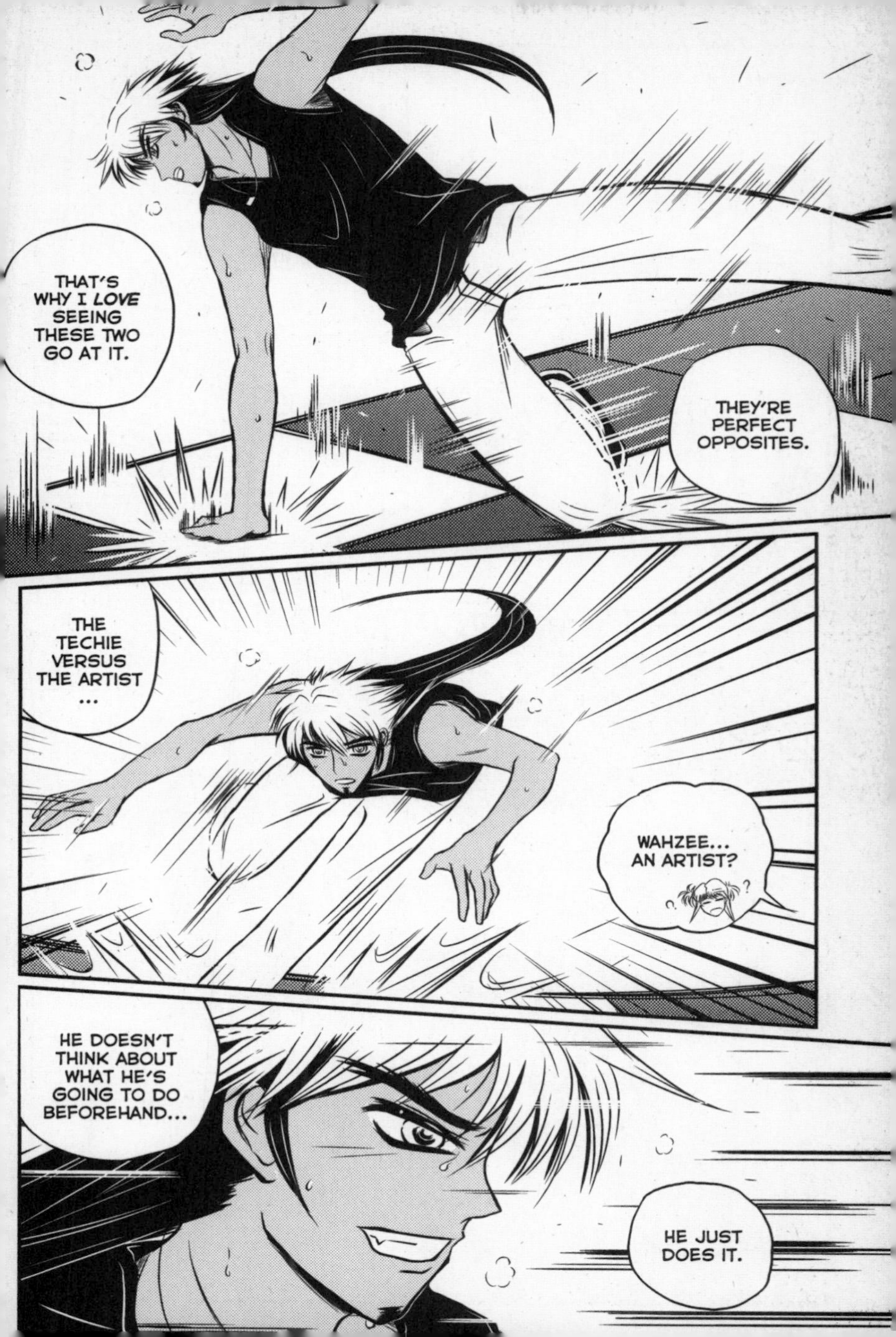
THAT'S WHY I *LOVE* SEEING THESE TWO GO AT IT.
THEY'RE PERFECT OPPOSITES.
THE TECHIE VERSUS THE ARTIST ...
WAHZEE... AN ARTIST?
HE DOESN'T THINK ABOUT WHAT HE'S GOING TO DO BEFOREHAND...
HE JUST DOES IT.

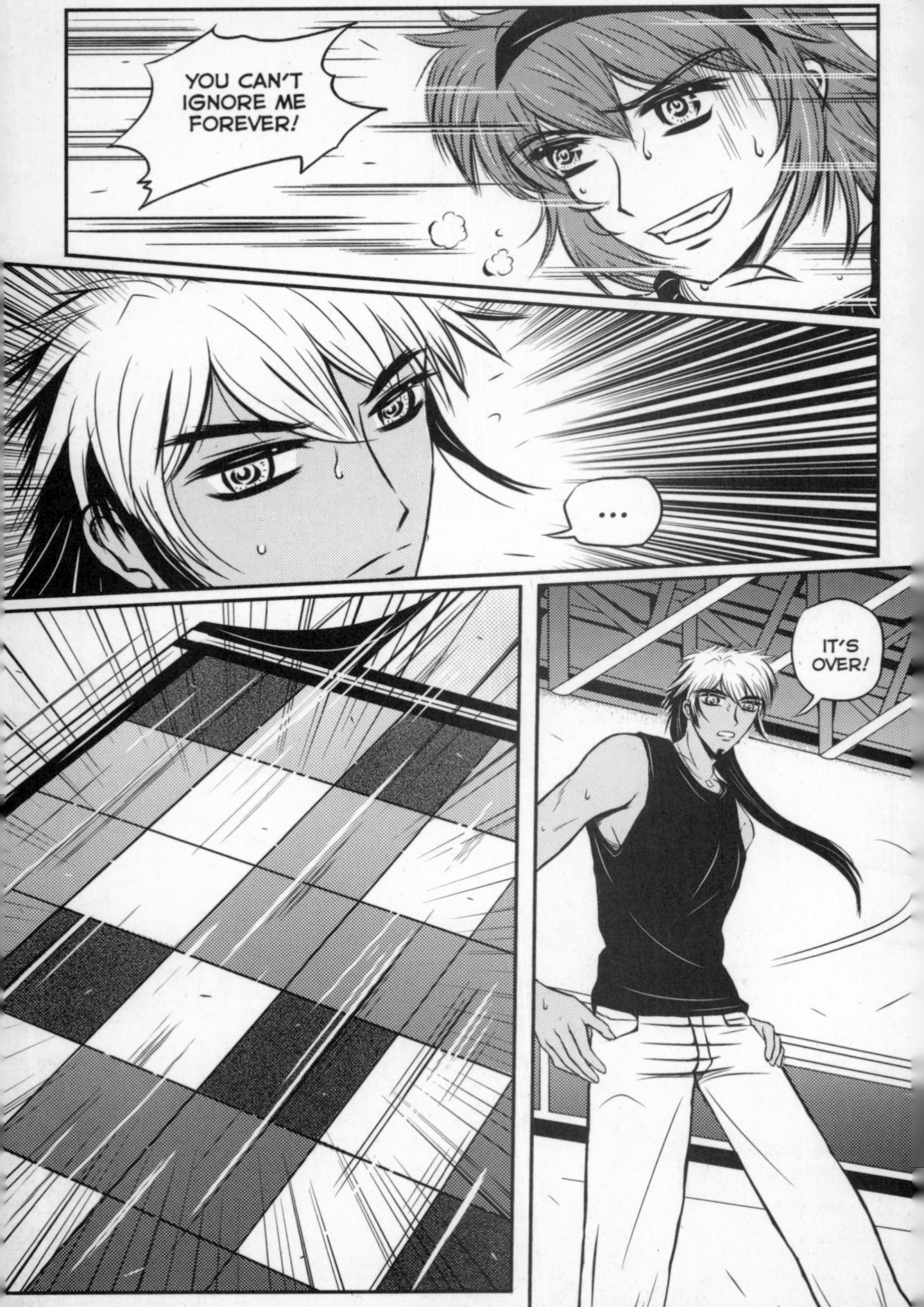
YOU CAN'T IGNORE ME FOREVER!
...
IT'S OVER!

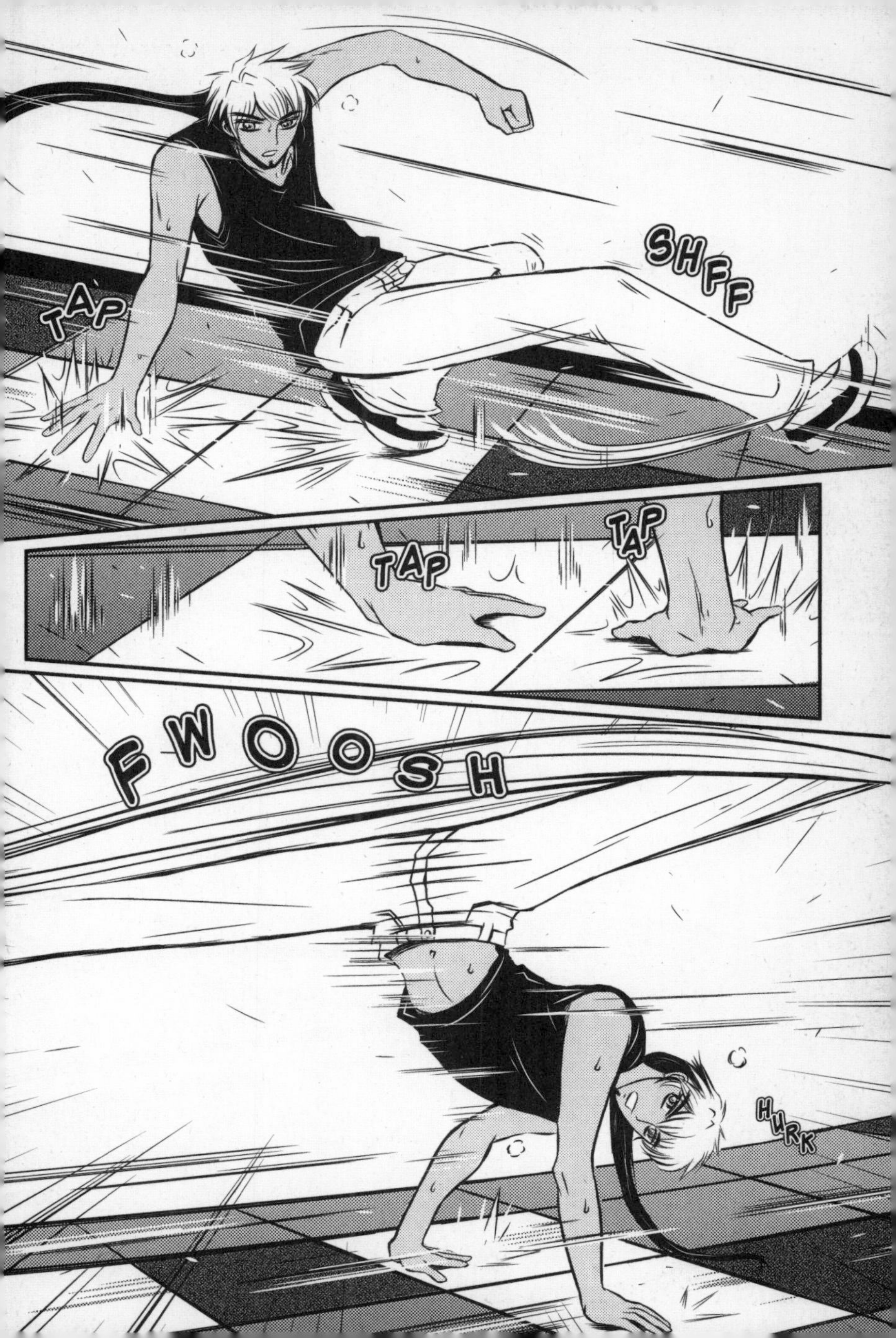
TAP
SHFF
TAP
TAP
FWOOSH
HURK

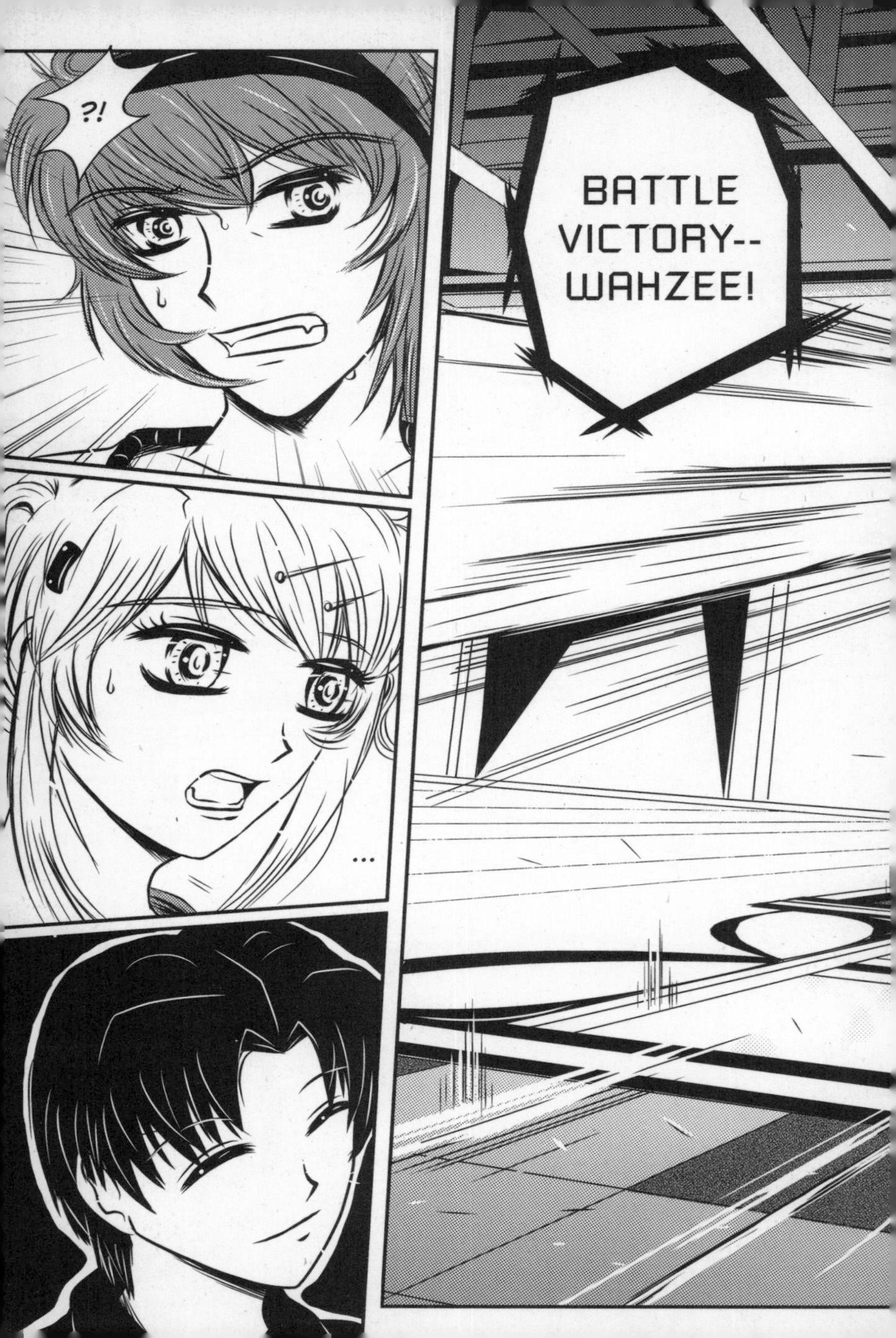
?!
...
BATTLE VICTORY-- WAHZEE!

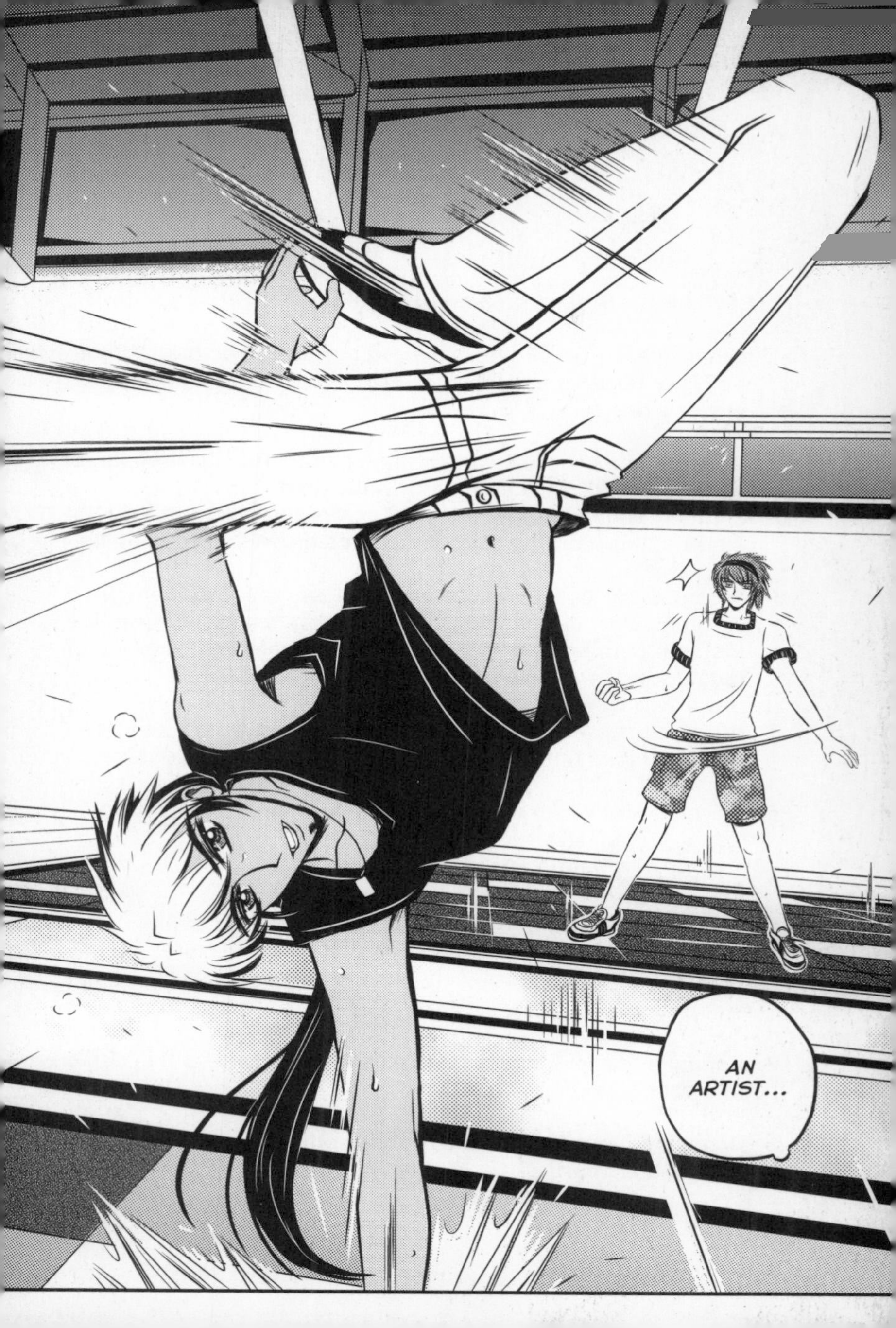
AN ARTIST...

REGULAR RHYSMYTH BATTLE RULES

1. Each player dances on a court made up of 56 squares (8x7).

2. When the battle begins, each square is capable of lighting up. This is represented by the 100% on the screen by each player's name.

3. When the music starts, eight random squares will light up on either side. When a lit square is touched it will turn off and another random square will light up. At any given time during a battle, there will be eight lit squares on each player's side.

4. Every eight beats, each player's progress is compared via computer. Depending on the difference of light square touches between them, the player with the least amount of touches gains a broken square.

5. A broken square is permanent (will not move location), can no longer light up and detracts from a player's percentage.

6. Contact with a broken square adds another broken square.

VICTORY CONDITIONS

Rhysmyth player wins when:

1. Opposing player does not touch a lit square within an eight beat period.

2. Opposing player's percentage dips to 14.5% or less (i.e. down to eight unbroken squares).

3. Opposing player crosses over onto other player's court (i.e. breaks half court).

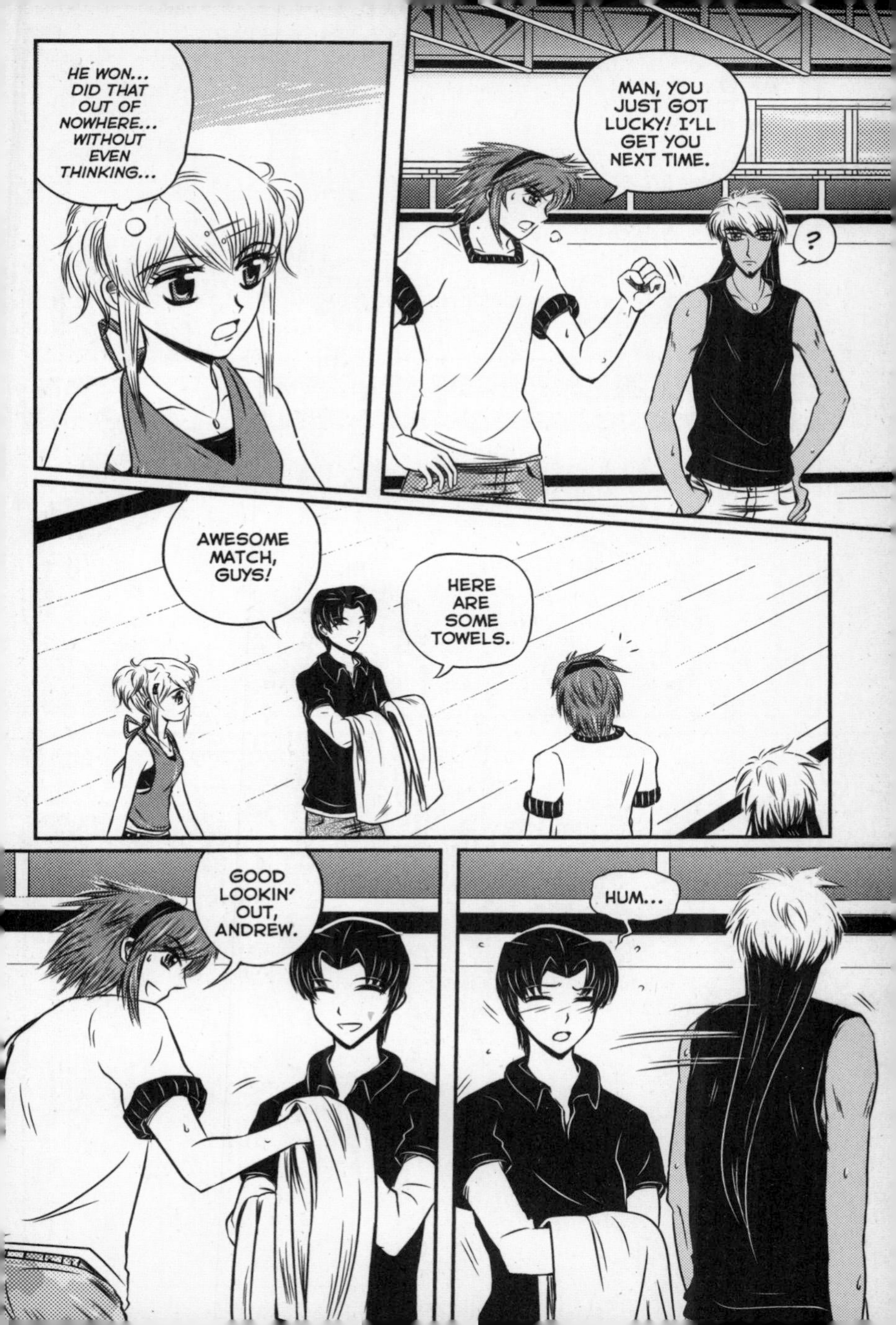
HE WON... DID THAT OUT OF NOWHERE... WITHOUT EVEN THINKING...
MAN, YOU JUST GOT LUCKY! I'LL GET YOU NEXT TIME.
?
AWESOME MATCH, GUYS!
HERE ARE SOME TOWELS.
GOOD LOOKIN' OUT, ANDREW.
HUM...

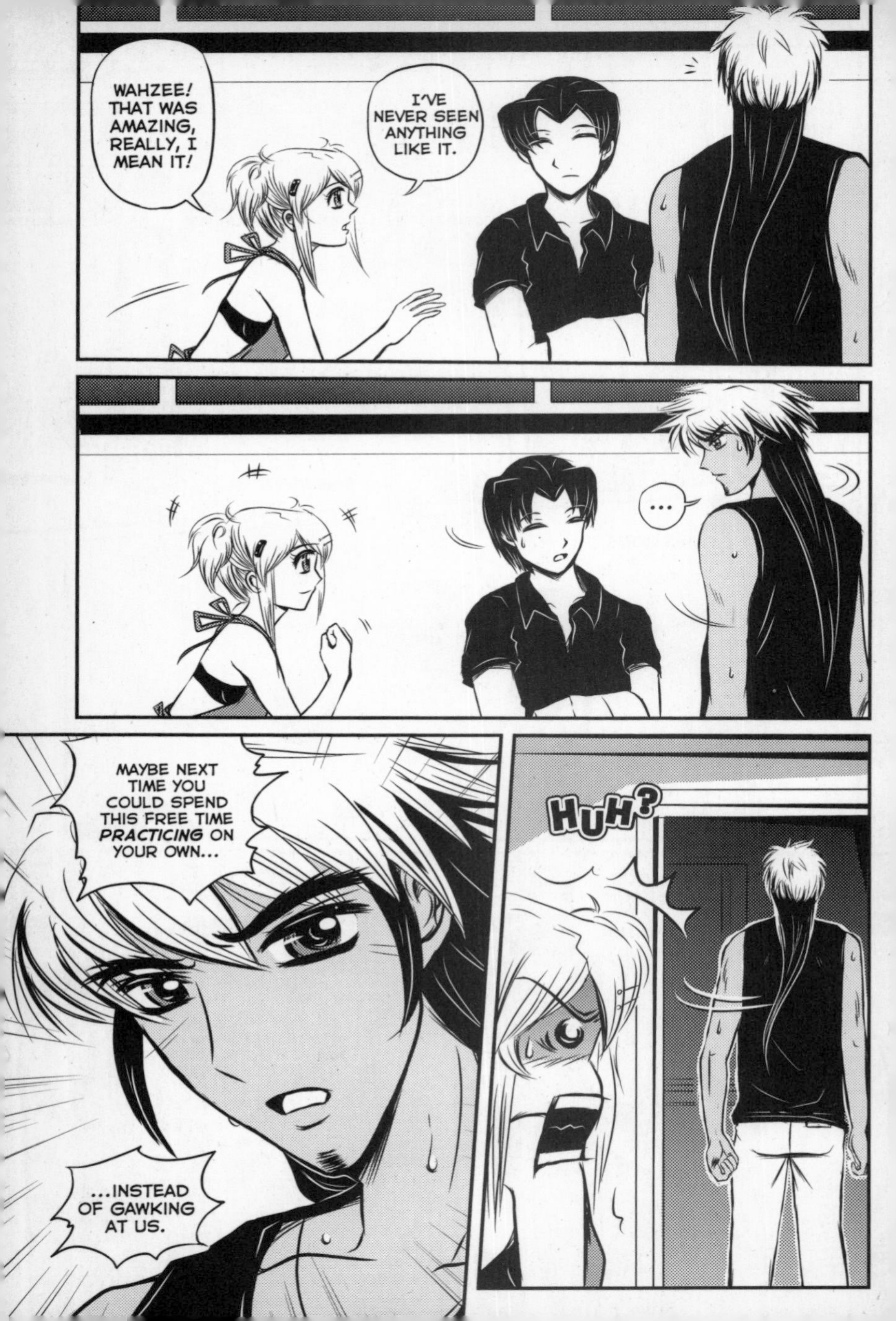
WAHZEE! THAT WAS AMAZING, REALLY, I MEAN IT!
I'VE NEVER SEEN ANYTHING LIKE IT.
...
MAYBE NEXT TIME YOU COULD SPEND THIS FREE TIME PRACTICING ON YOUR OWN...
...INSTEAD OF GAWKING AT US.
HUH?

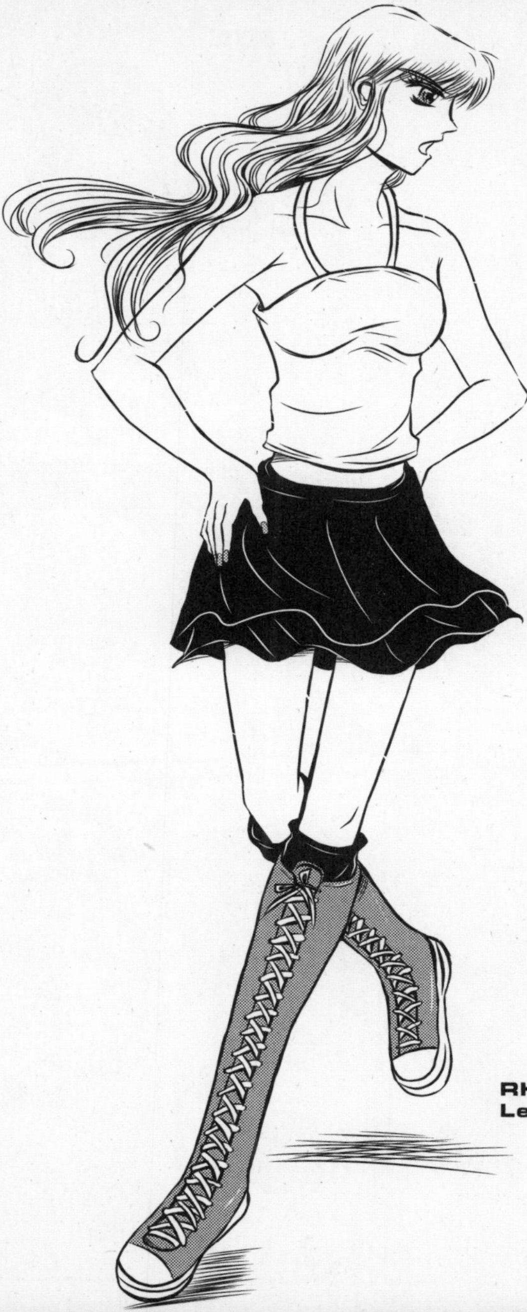

RHYSMYTH
Level 05: Notice

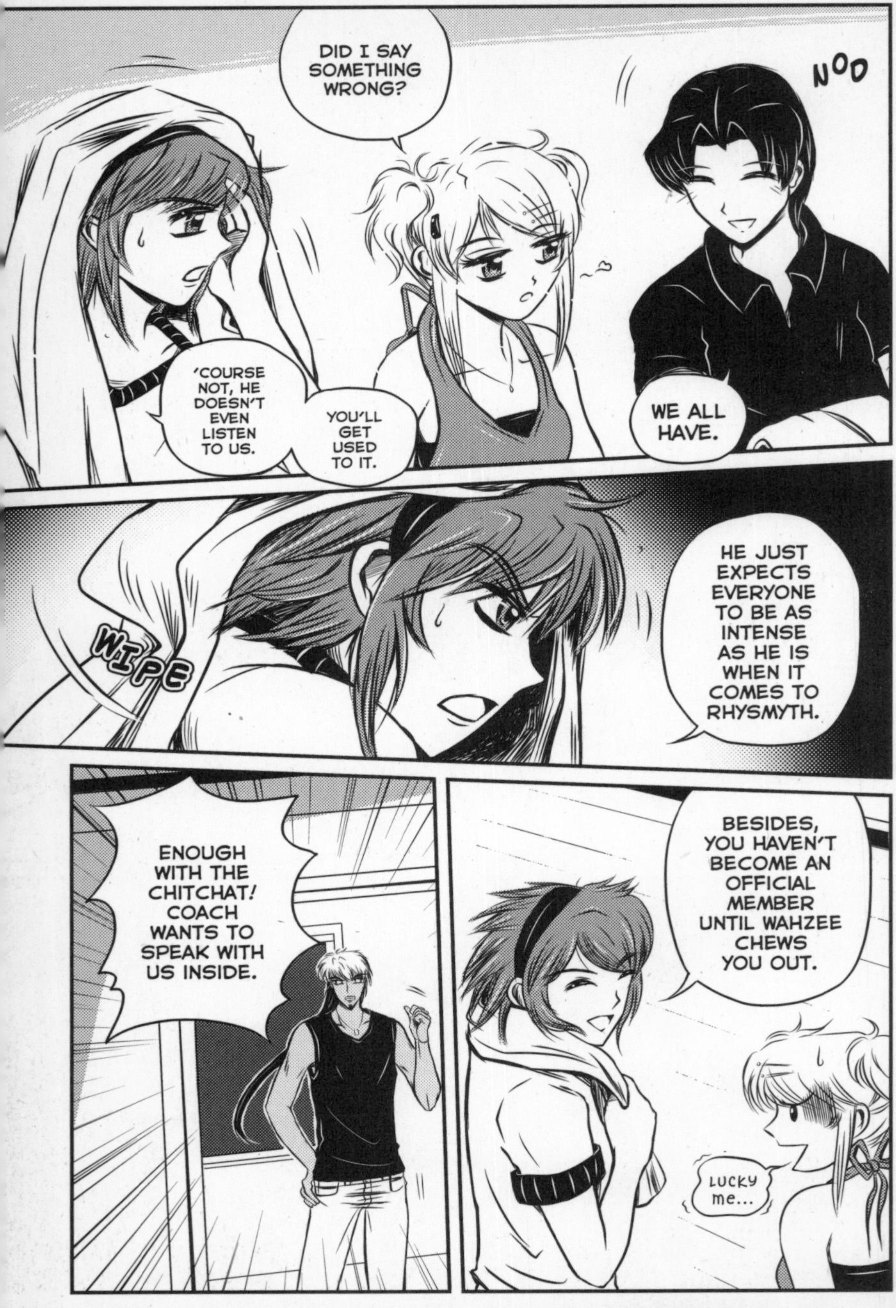
DID I SAY SOMETHING WRONG?
NOD
'COURSE NOT, HE DOESN'T EVEN LISTEN TO US.
YOU'LL GET USED TO IT.
WE ALL HAVE.
WIPE
HE JUST EXPECTS EVERYONE TO BE AS INTENSE AS HE IS WHEN IT COMES TO RHYSMYTH.
ENOUGH WITH THE CHITCHAT! COACH WANTS TO SPEAK WITH US INSIDE.
BESIDES, YOU HAVEN'T BECOME AN OFFICIAL MEMBER UNTIL WAHZEE CHEWS YOU OUT.
LUCKY me...

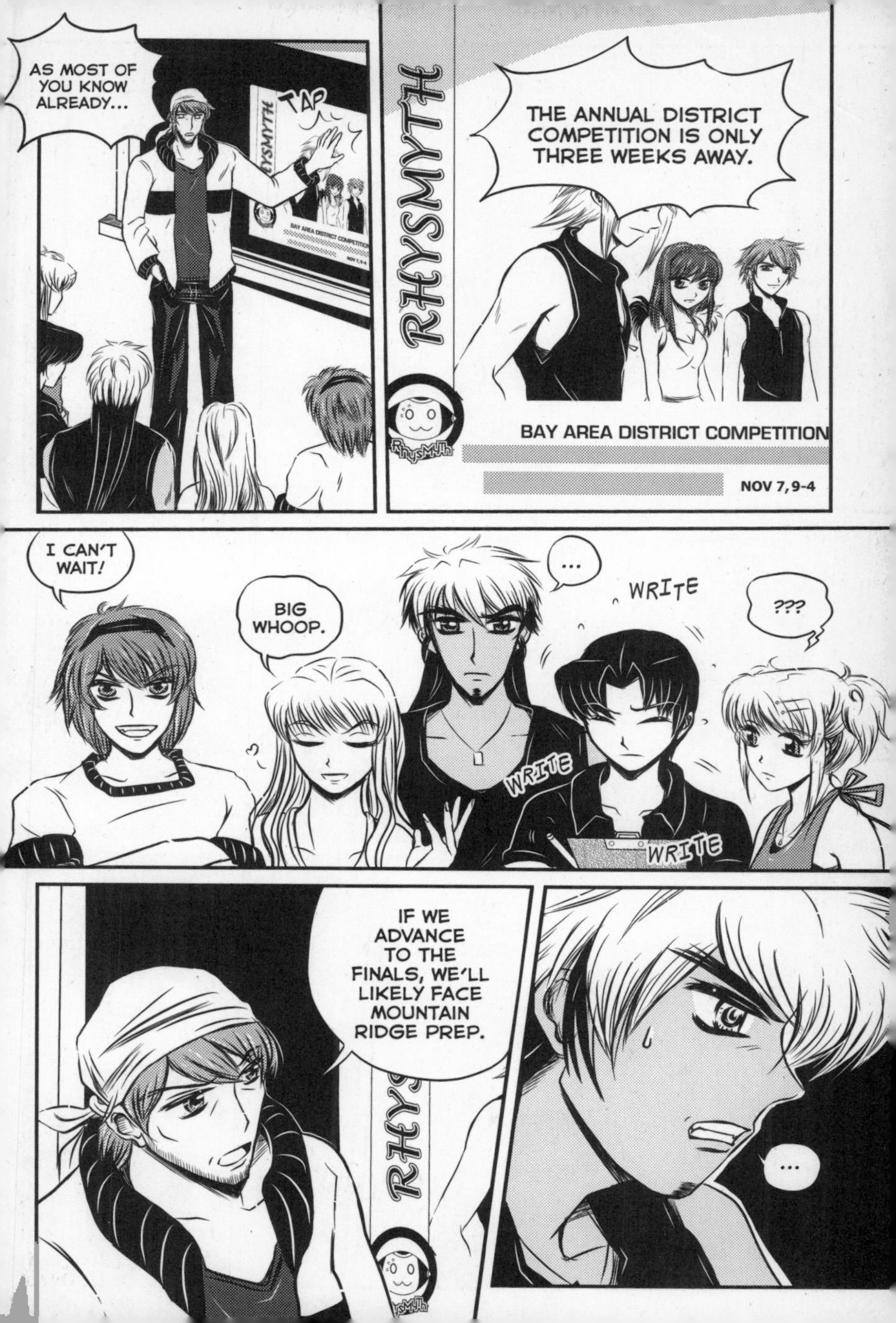
AS MOST OF YOU KNOW ALREADY...
TAP
RHYSMYTH
BAY AREA DISTRICT COMPETITION
NOV 7, 9-4
THE ANNUAL DISTRICT COMPETITION IS ONLY THREE WEEKS AWAY.
RHYSMYTH
RhysMyTh
BAY AREA DISTRICT COMPETITION
NOV 7, 9-4
I CAN'T WAIT!
BIG WHOOP.
...
WRITE
???
WRITE
WRITE
IF WE ADVANCE TO THE FINALS, WE'LL LIKELY FACE MOUNTAIN RIDGE PREP.
...

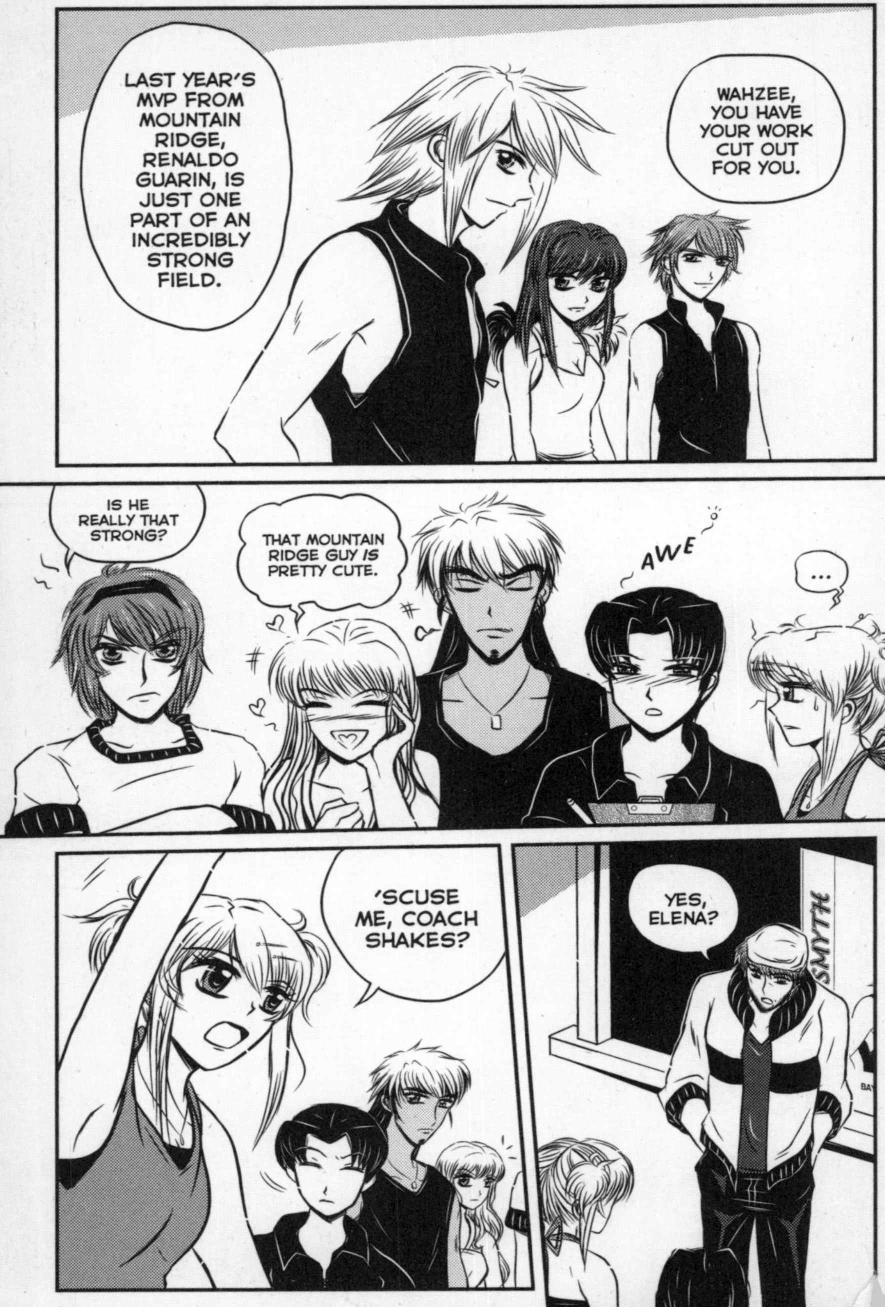
LAST YEAR'S MVP FROM MOUNTAIN RIDGE, RENALDO GUARIN, IS JUST ONE PART OF AN INCREDIBLY STRONG FIELD.
WAHZEE, YOU HAVE YOUR WORK CUT OUT FOR YOU.
IS HE REALLY THAT STRONG?
THAT MOUNTAIN RIDGE GUY *IS* PRETTY CUTE.
AWE
...
'SCUSE ME, COACH SHAKES?
YES, ELENA?
SMYTH

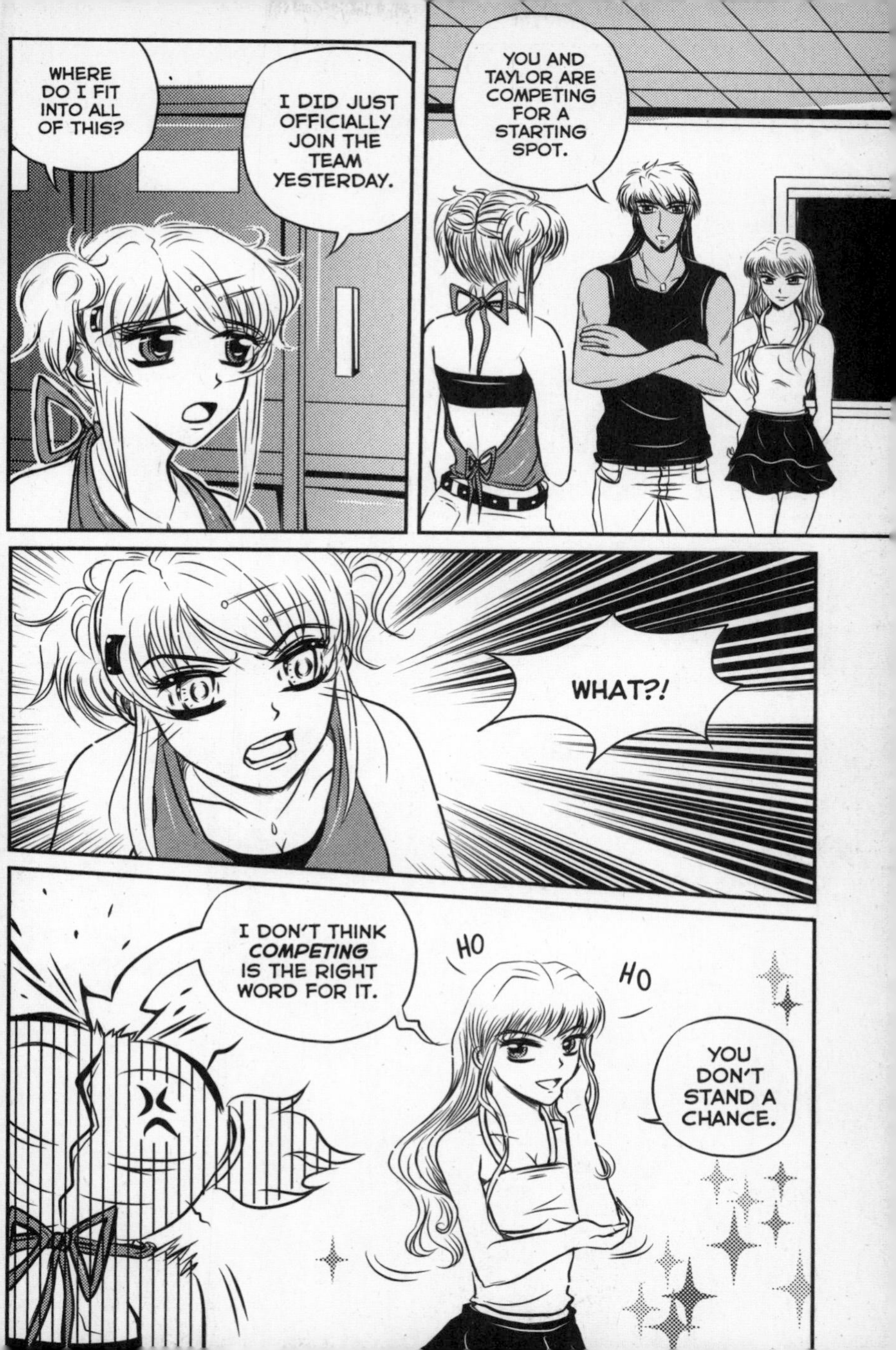
WHERE DO I FIT INTO ALL OF THIS?
I DID JUST OFFICIALLY JOIN THE TEAM YESTERDAY.
YOU AND TAYLOR ARE COMPETING FOR A STARTING SPOT.
WHAT?!
I DON'T THINK *COMPETING* IS THE RIGHT WORD FOR IT.
HO
HO
YOU DON'T STAND A CHANCE.

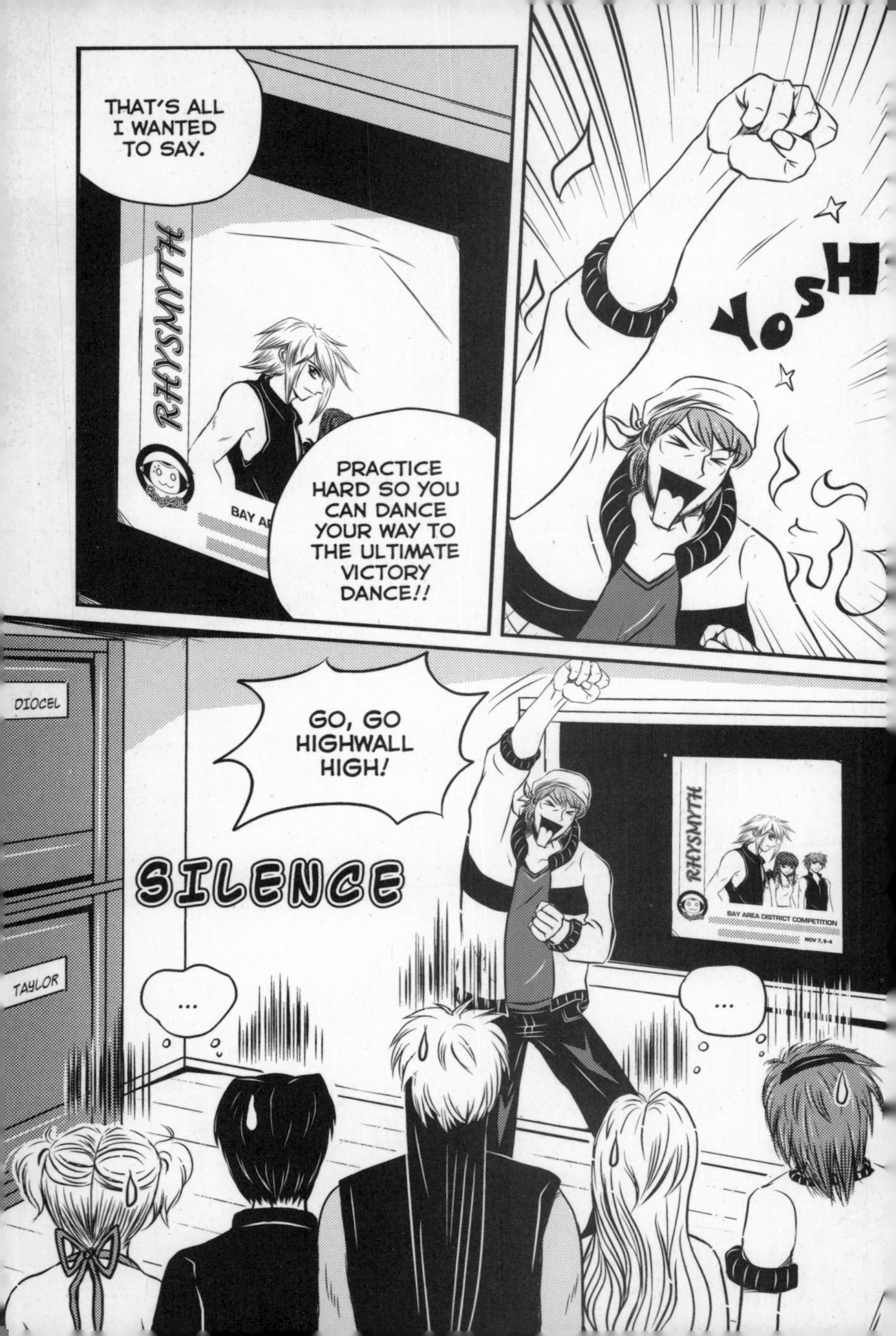
THAT'S ALL I WANTED TO SAY.
RHYSMYTH
PRACTICE HARD SO YOU CAN DANCE YOUR WAY TO THE ULTIMATE VICTORY DANCE!!
YOSH
GO, GO HIGHWALL HIGH!
DIOCEL
TAYLOR
SILENCE
RHYSMYTH
BAY AREA DISTRICT COMPETITION
NOV 7, 9-4
...
...

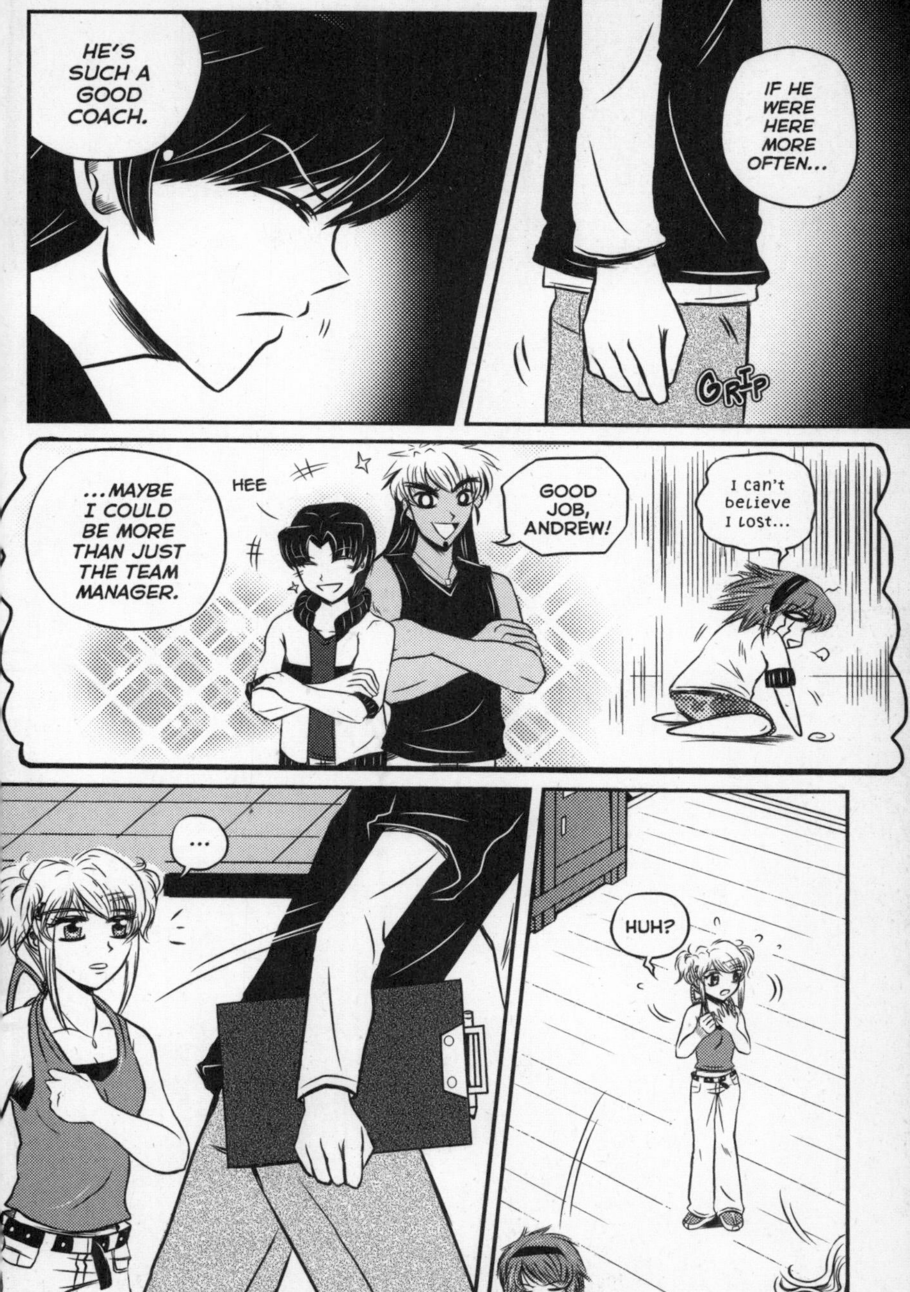
HE'S SUCH A GOOD COACH.
IF HE WERE HERE MORE OFTEN...
GRIP
...MAYBE I COULD BE MORE THAN JUST THE TEAM MANAGER.
HEE
GOOD JOB, ANDREW!
I can't believe I lost...
...
HUH?

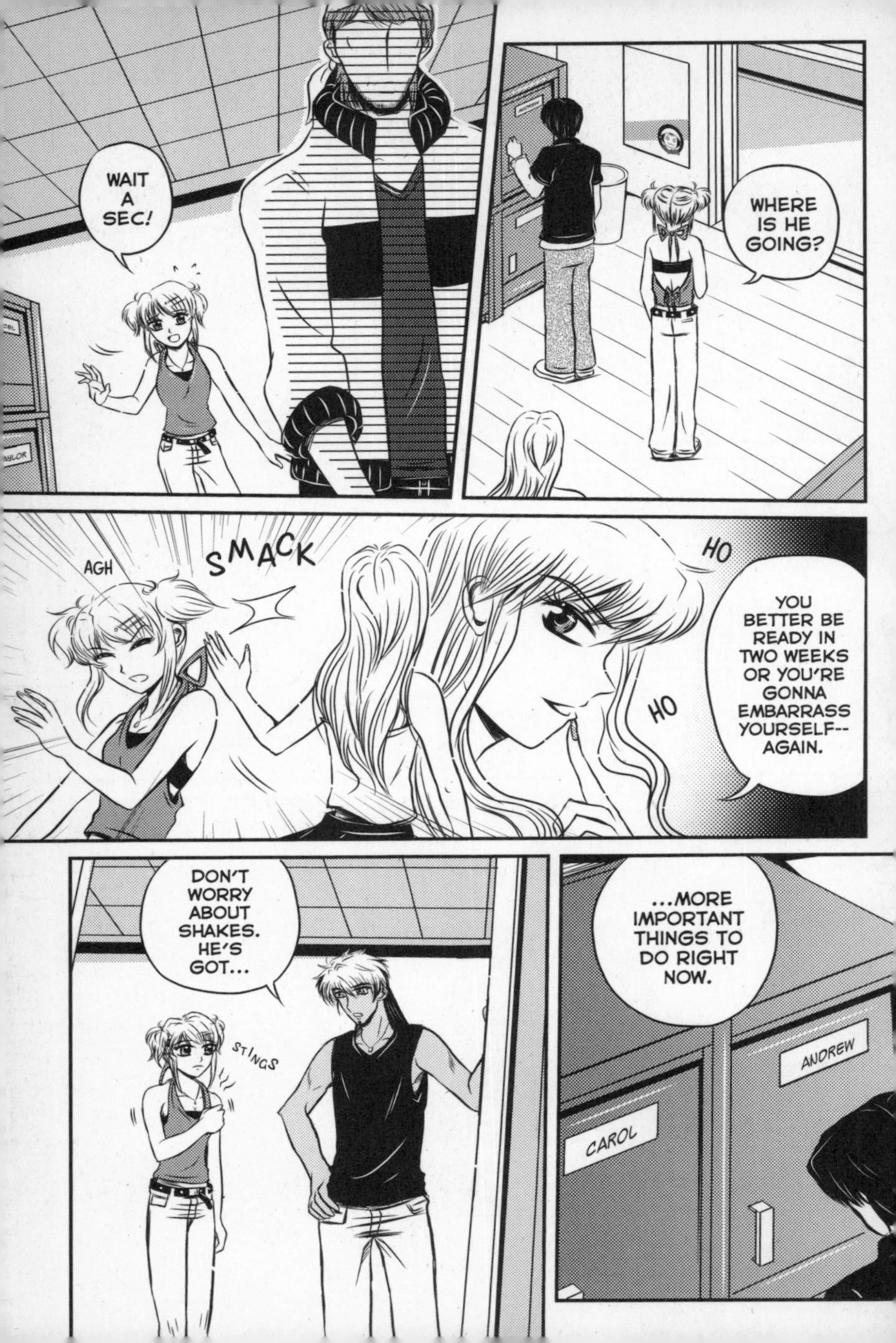
WAIT A SEC!
WHERE IS HE GOING?
AGH
SMACK
HO
YOU BETTER BE READY IN TWO WEEKS OR YOU'RE GONNA EMBARRASS YOURSELF--AGAIN.
HO
DON'T WORRY ABOUT SHAKES. HE'S GOT...
STINGS
...MORE IMPORTANT THINGS TO DO RIGHT NOW.
ANDREW
CAROL

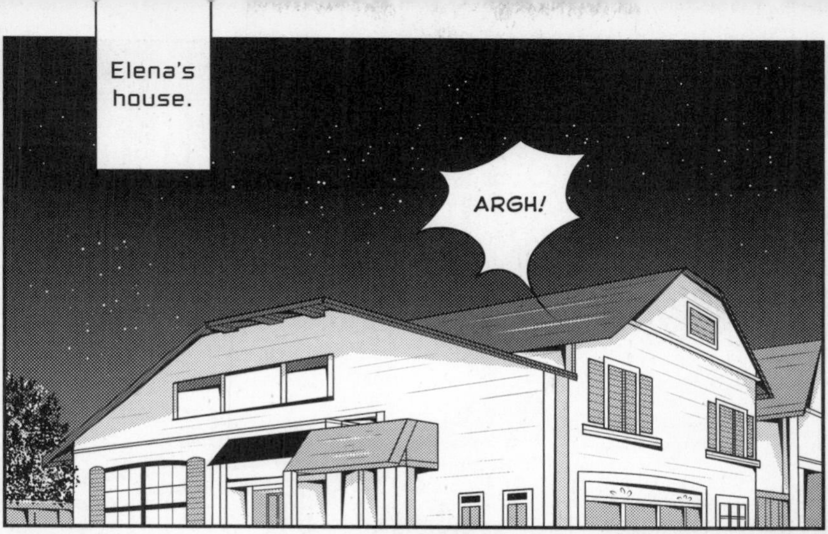
Elena's house.
ARGH!

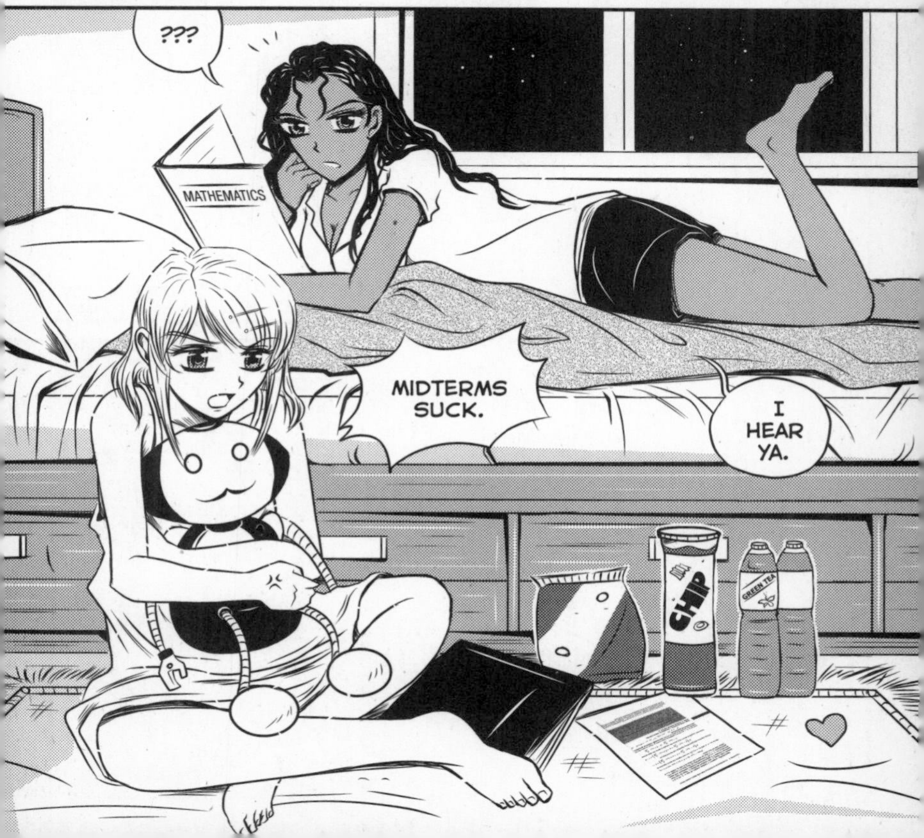
???
MATHEMATICS
MIDTERMS SUCK.
I HEAR YA.
CHIP
GREEN TEA

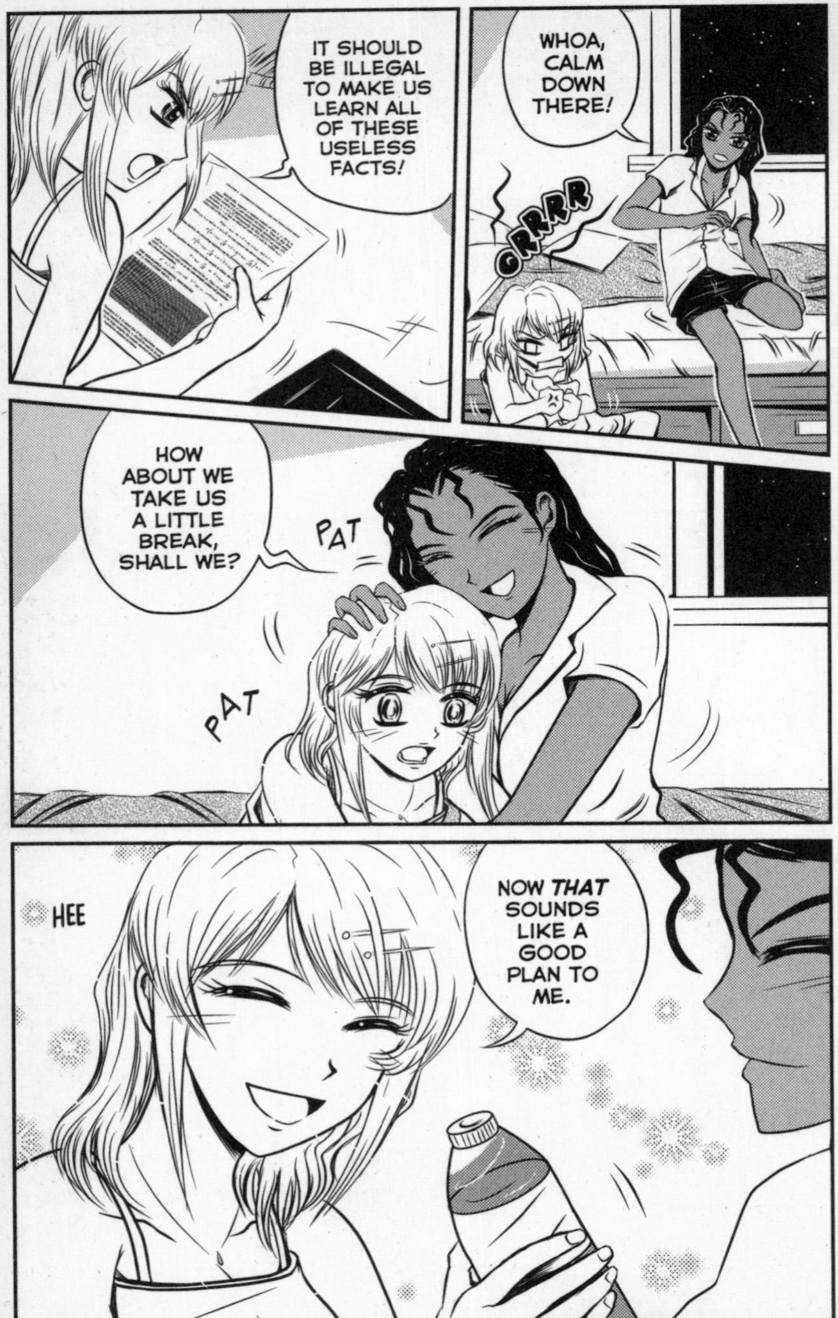
IT SHOULD BE ILLEGAL TO MAKE US LEARN ALL OF THESE USELESS FACTS!
WHOA, CALM DOWN THERE!
GRRRR
HOW ABOUT WE TAKE US A LITTLE BREAK, SHALL WE?
PAT
PAT
HEE
NOW THAT SOUNDS LIKE A GOOD PLAN TO ME.

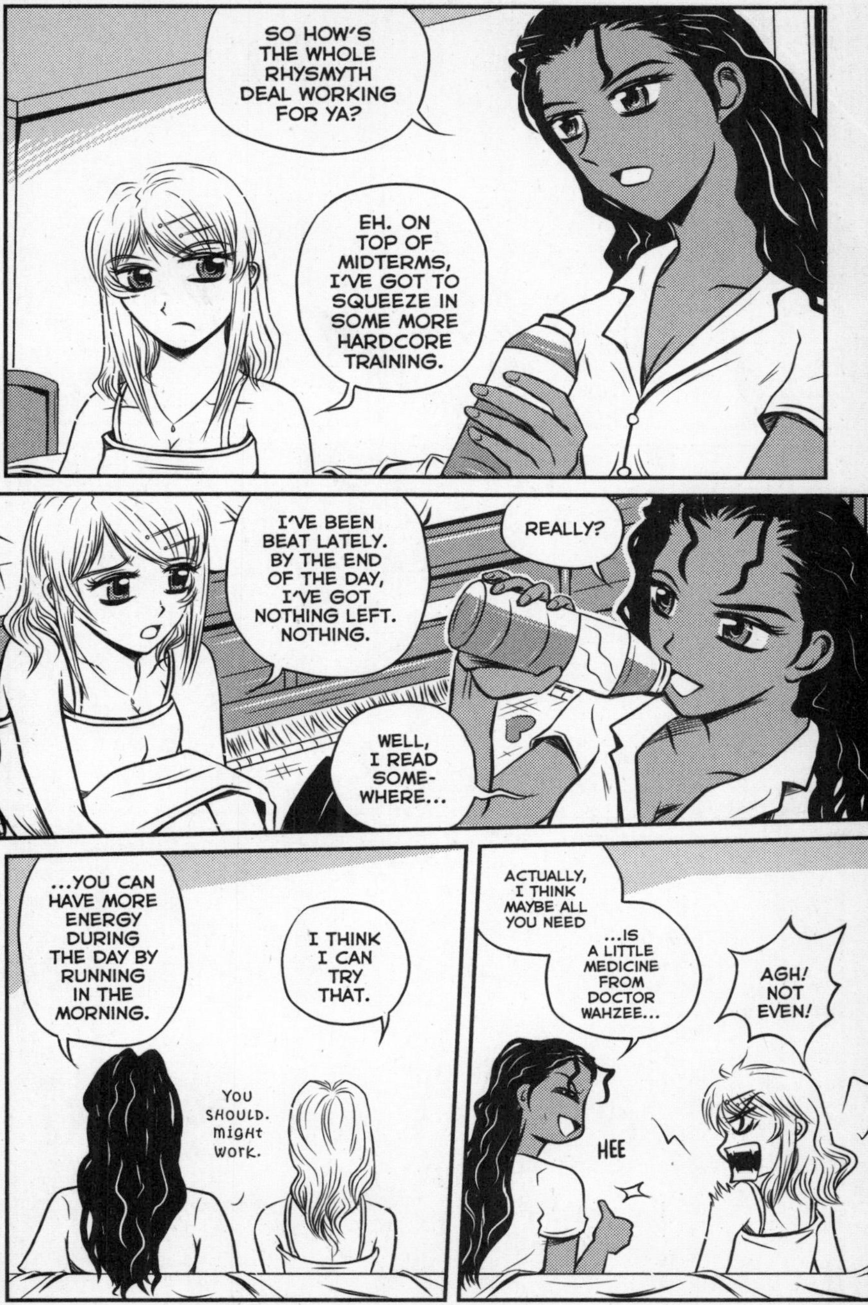
SO HOW'S THE WHOLE RHYSMYTH DEAL WORKING FOR YA?
EH. ON TOP OF MIDTERMS, I'VE GOT TO SQUEEZE IN SOME MORE HARDCORE TRAINING.
I'VE BEEN BEAT LATELY. BY THE END OF THE DAY, I'VE GOT NOTHING LEFT. NOTHING.
REALLY?
WELL, I READ SOME-WHERE...
...YOU CAN HAVE MORE ENERGY DURING THE DAY BY RUNNING IN THE MORNING.
I THINK I CAN TRY THAT.
YOU SHOULD. MIGHT WORK.
ACTUALLY, I THINK MAYBE ALL YOU NEED
...IS A LITTLE MEDICINE FROM DOCTOR WAHZEE...
AGH! NOT EVEN!
HEE

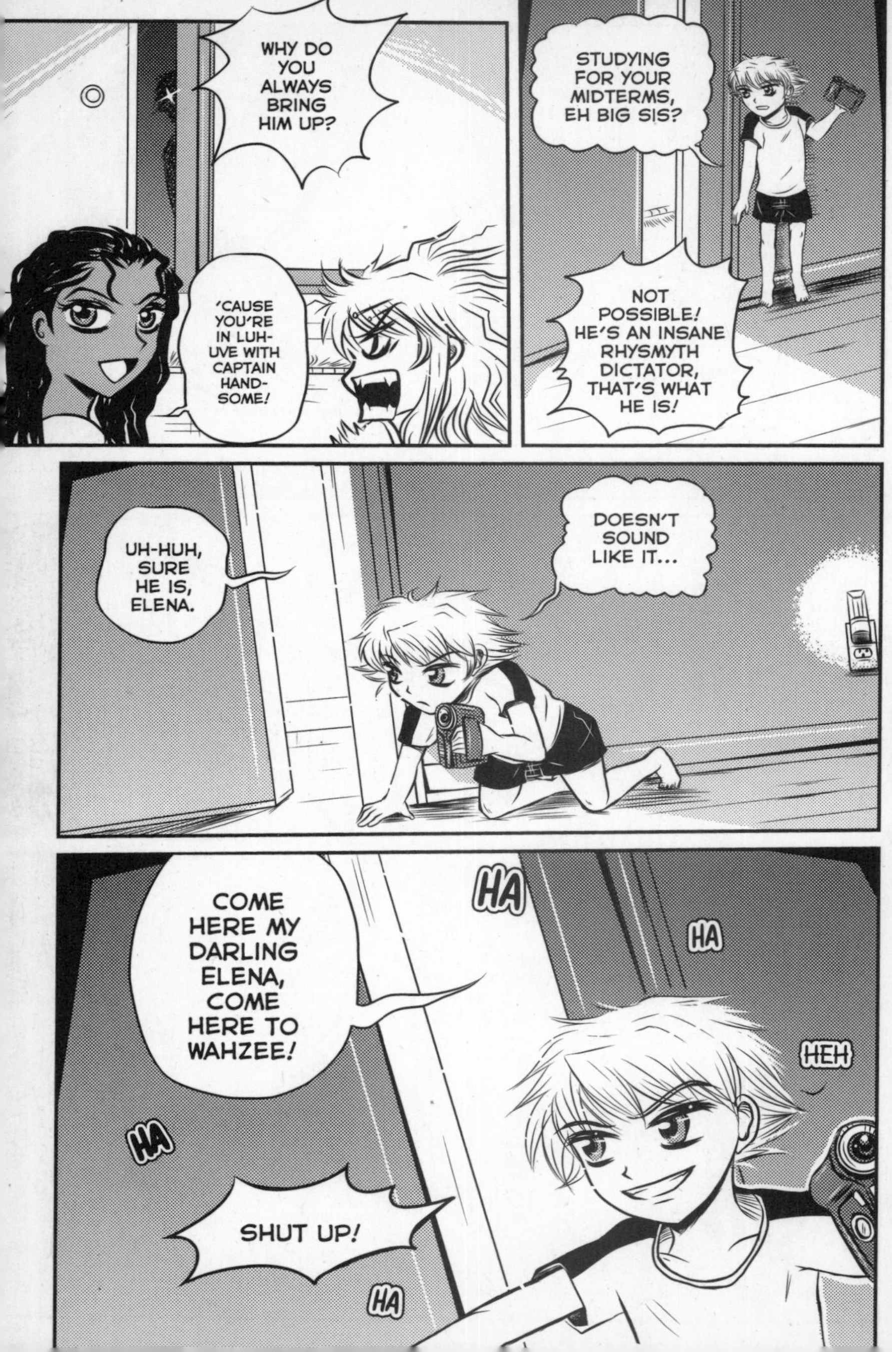
WHY DO YOU ALWAYS BRING HIM UP?
'CAUSE YOU'RE IN LUH-UVE WITH CAPTAIN HAND-SOME!
STUDYING FOR YOUR MIDTERMS, EH BIG SIS?
NOT POSSIBLE! HE'S AN INSANE RHYSMYTH DICTATOR, THAT'S WHAT HE IS!
UH-HUH, SURE HE IS, ELENA.
DOESN'T SOUND LIKE IT...
COME HERE MY DARLING ELENA, COME HERE TO WAHZEE!
HA
HA
HEH
HA
SHUT UP!
HA

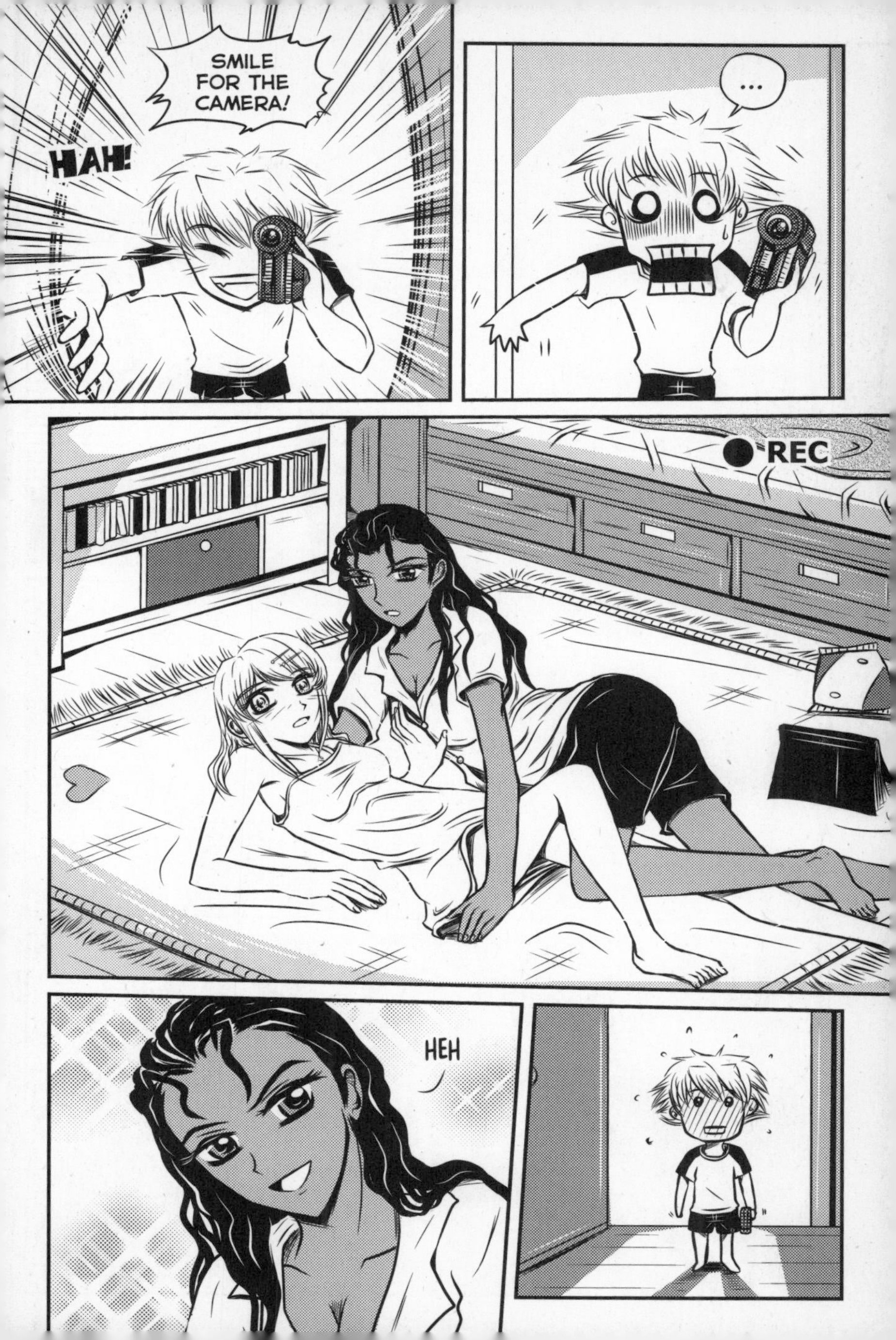
SMILE FOR THE CAMERA!
HIAH!
...
REC
HEH

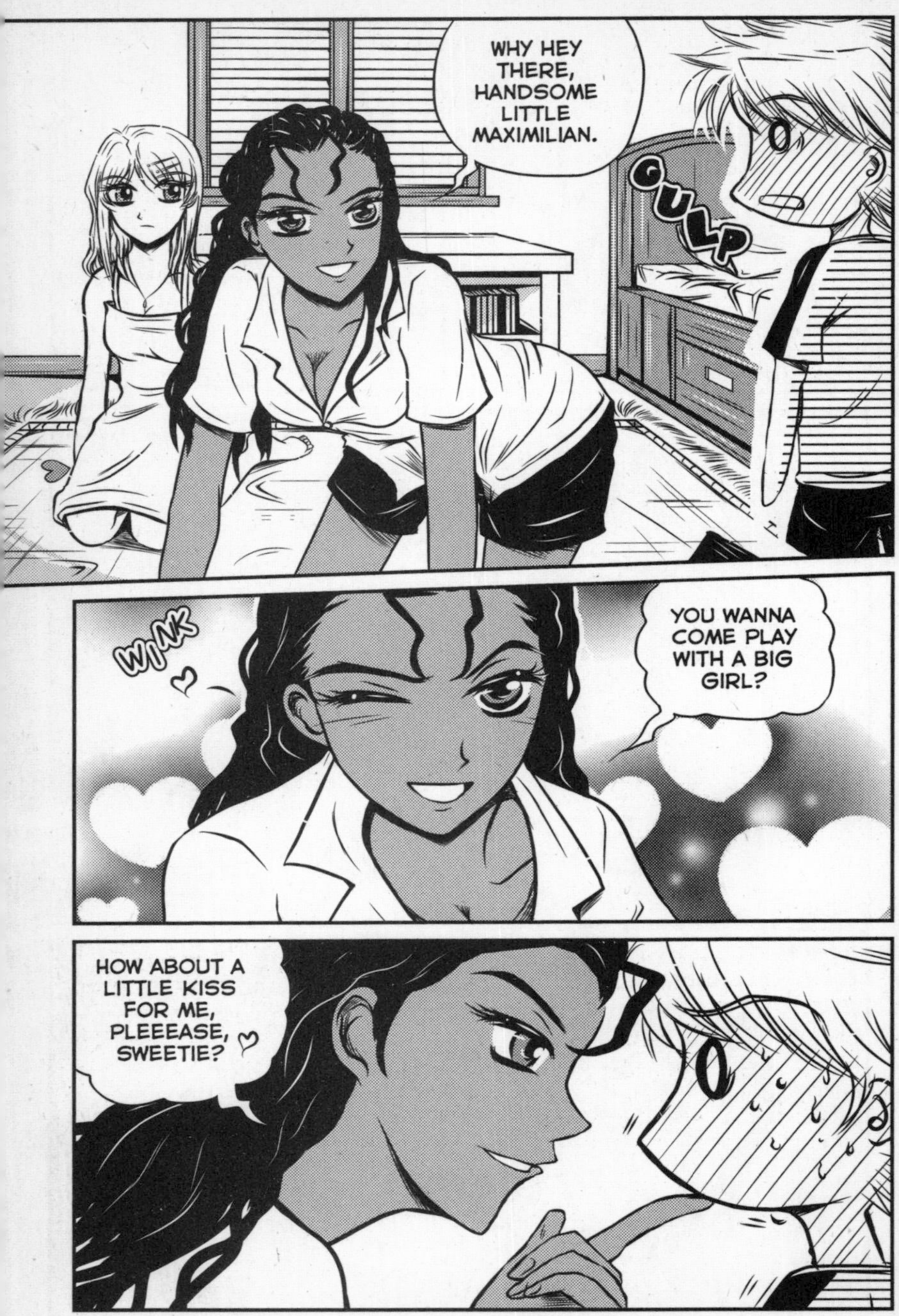
WHY HEY THERE, HANDSOME LITTLE MAXIMILIAN.
GULP
YOU WANNA COME PLAY WITH A BIG GIRL?
WINK
HOW ABOUT A LITTLE KISS FOR ME, PLEEEASE, SWEETIE?

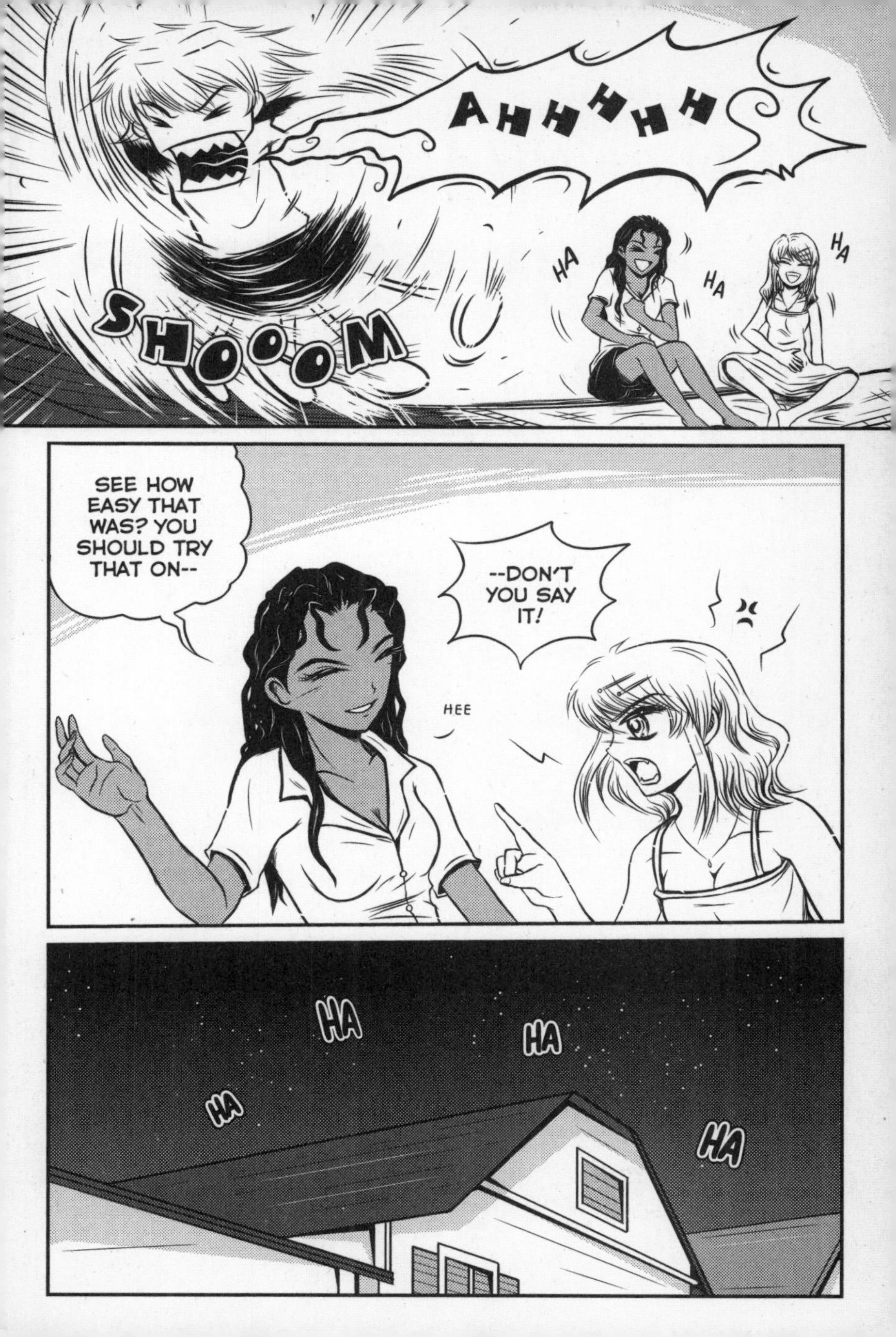
AHHHHHH
SHOOOM
HA
HA
HA
SEE HOW EASY THAT WAS? YOU SHOULD TRY THAT ON--
--DON'T YOU SAY IT!
HEE
HA
HA
HA
HA

3RD ANNUAL RHYSMYTH

BAY AREA DISTRICT COMPETITION

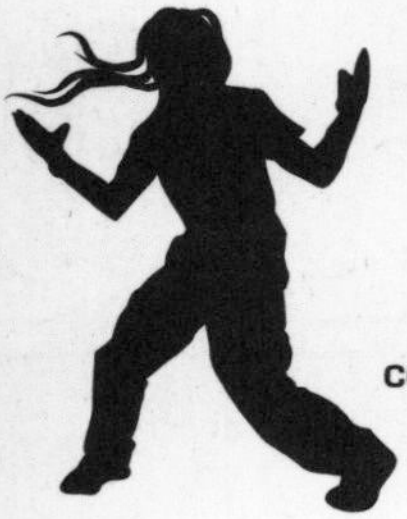

See the area's youngest and brightest Rhysmyth stars compete for a berth in the State Championship tournament.

November 7, 9am - 4pm

Catch last year's local phenom, Mountain Ridge's own Renaldo Guarin, and the best schools in the city battle it out for the title!

Admission:
Adults - $6
Students - $3
Children under 6 - free w/ paying adult

RhysMyTh

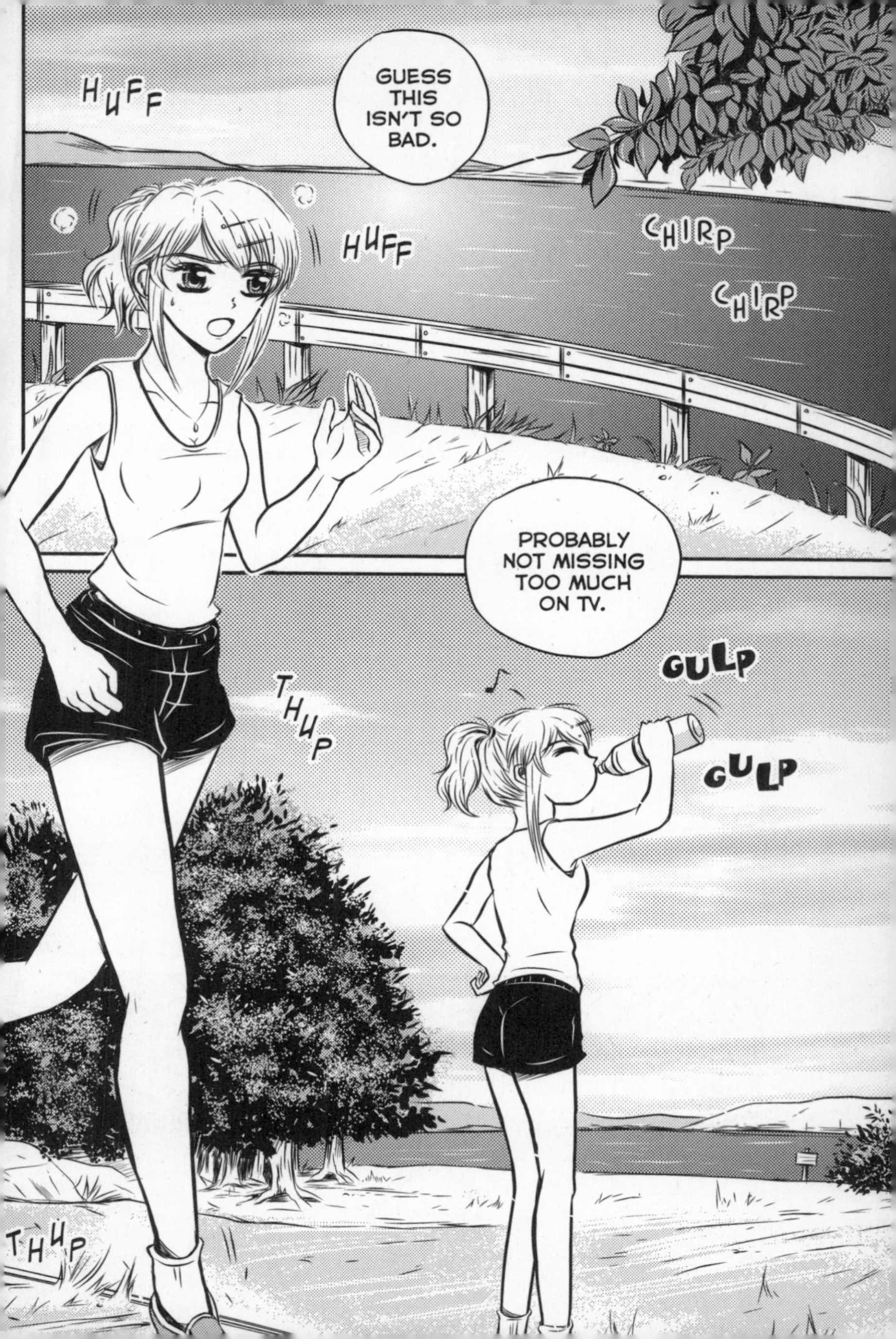
HUFF
GUESS THIS ISN'T SO BAD.
HUFF
CHIRP
CHIRP
PROBABLY NOT MISSING TOO MUCH ON TV.
GULP
THUP
GULP
THUP

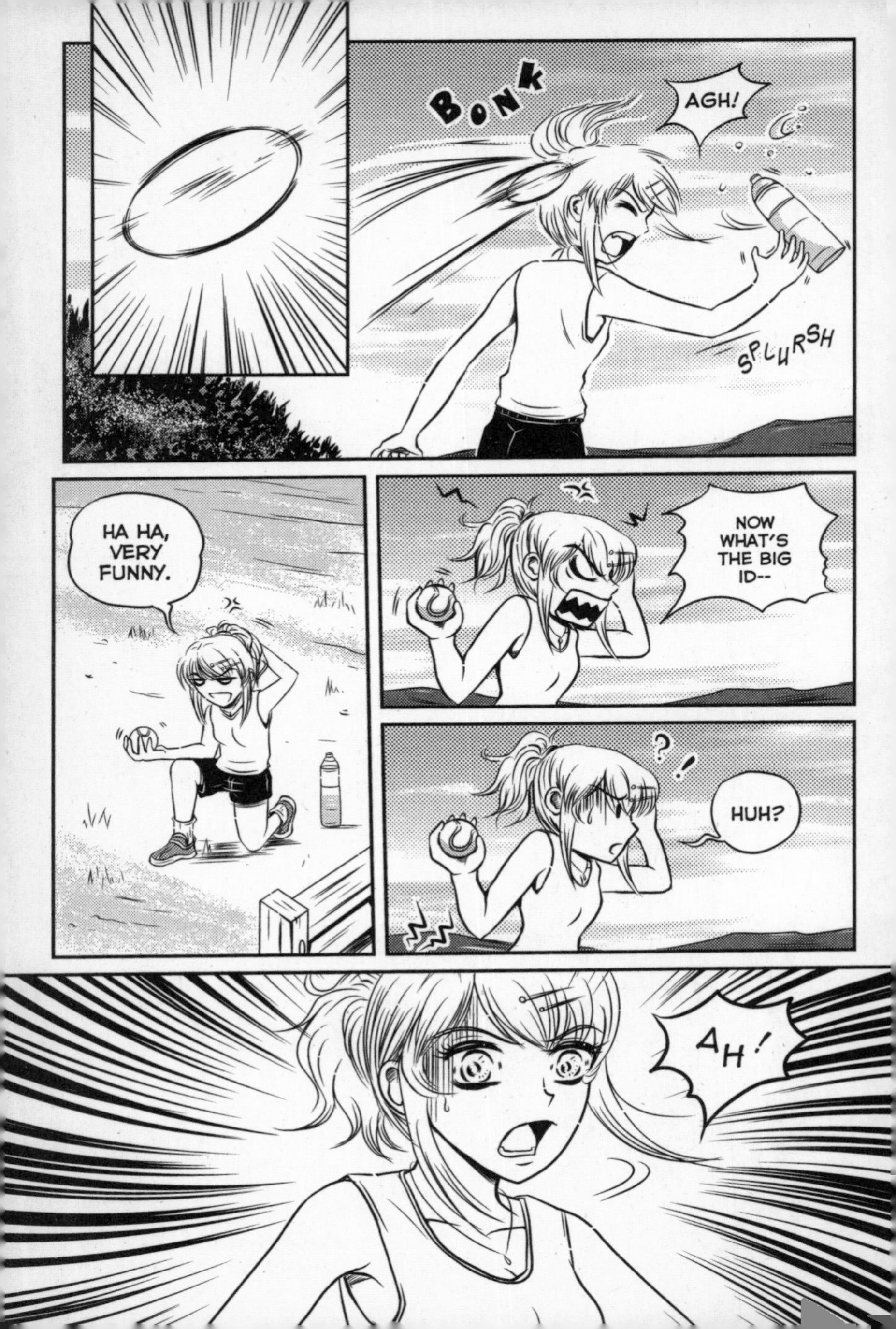
BONK
AGH!
SPLURSH
HA HA, VERY FUNNY.
NOW WHAT'S THE BIG ID--
?!
HUH?
AH!

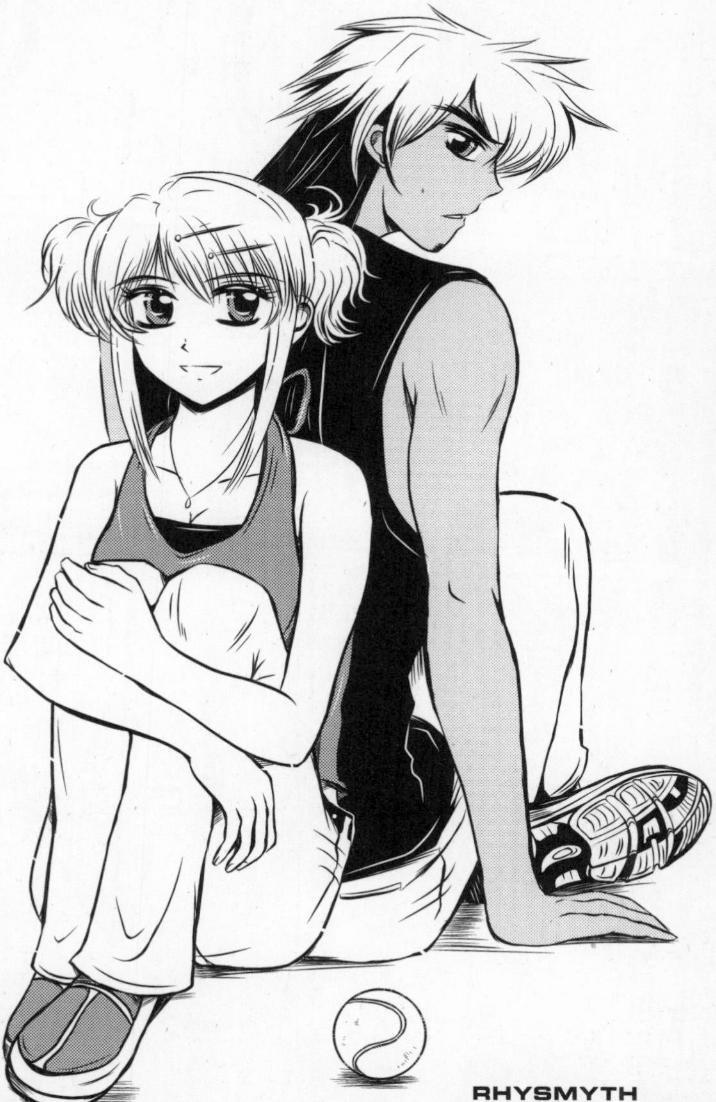

RHYSMYTH
Level 06: About Face

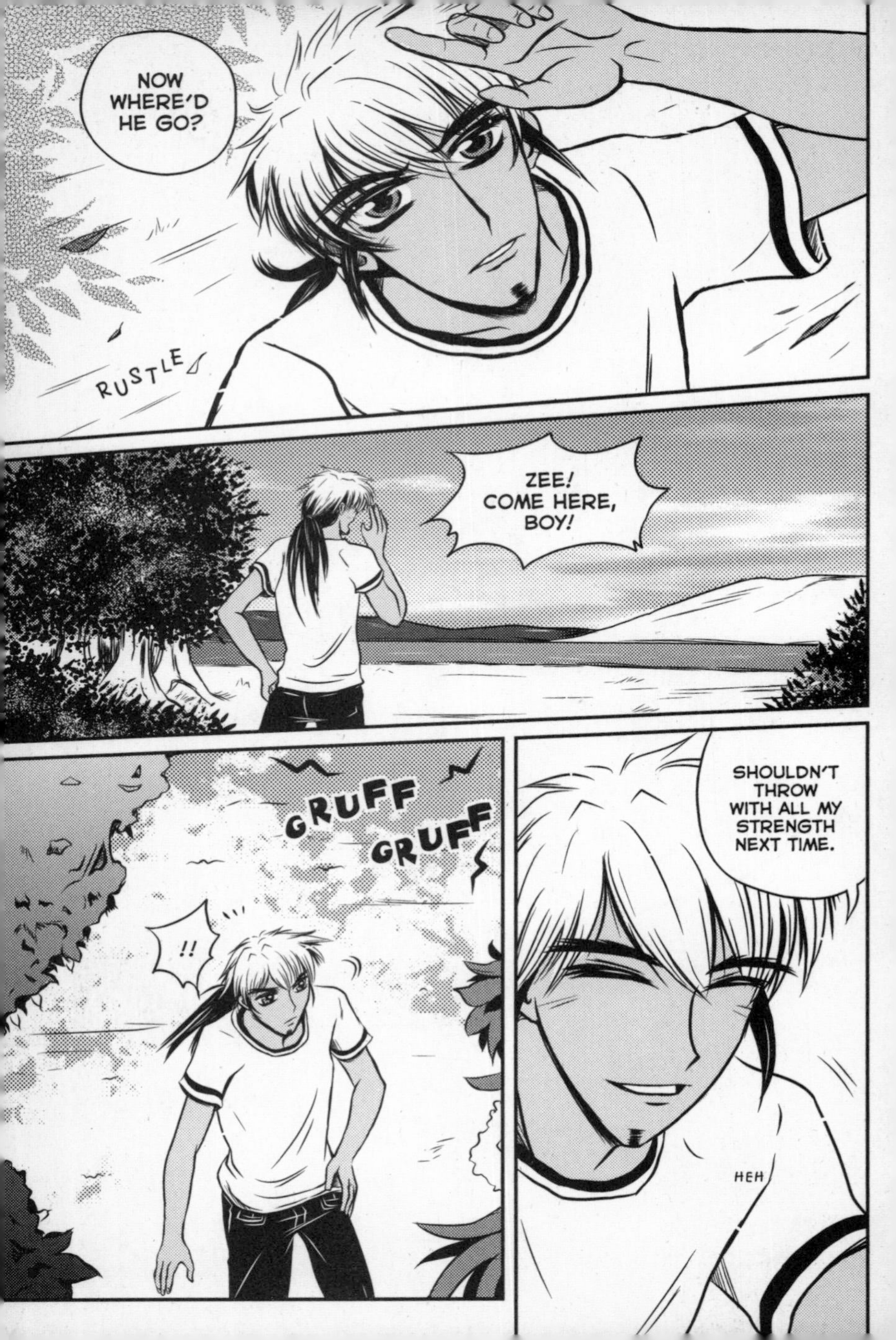
NOW WHERE'D HE GO?
RUSTLE
ZEE! COME HERE, BOY!
GRUFF
GRUFF
!!
SHOULDN'T THROW WITH ALL MY STRENGTH NEXT TIME.
HEH

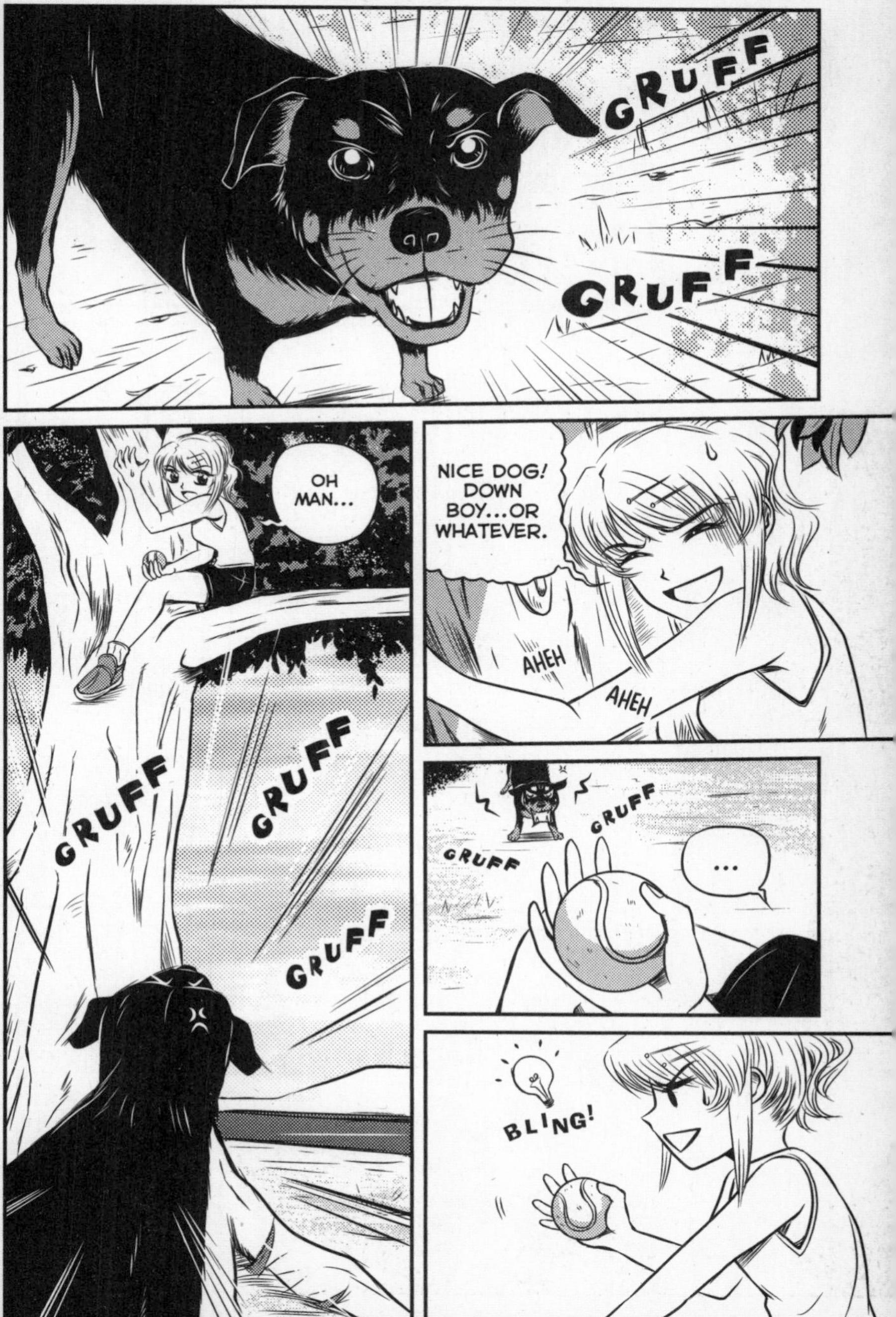
GRUFF
GRUFF
OH MAN...
GRUFF
GRUFF
GRUFF
NICE DOG! DOWN BOY...OR WHATEVER.
AHEH
AHEH
GRUFF
GRUFF
...
BLING!

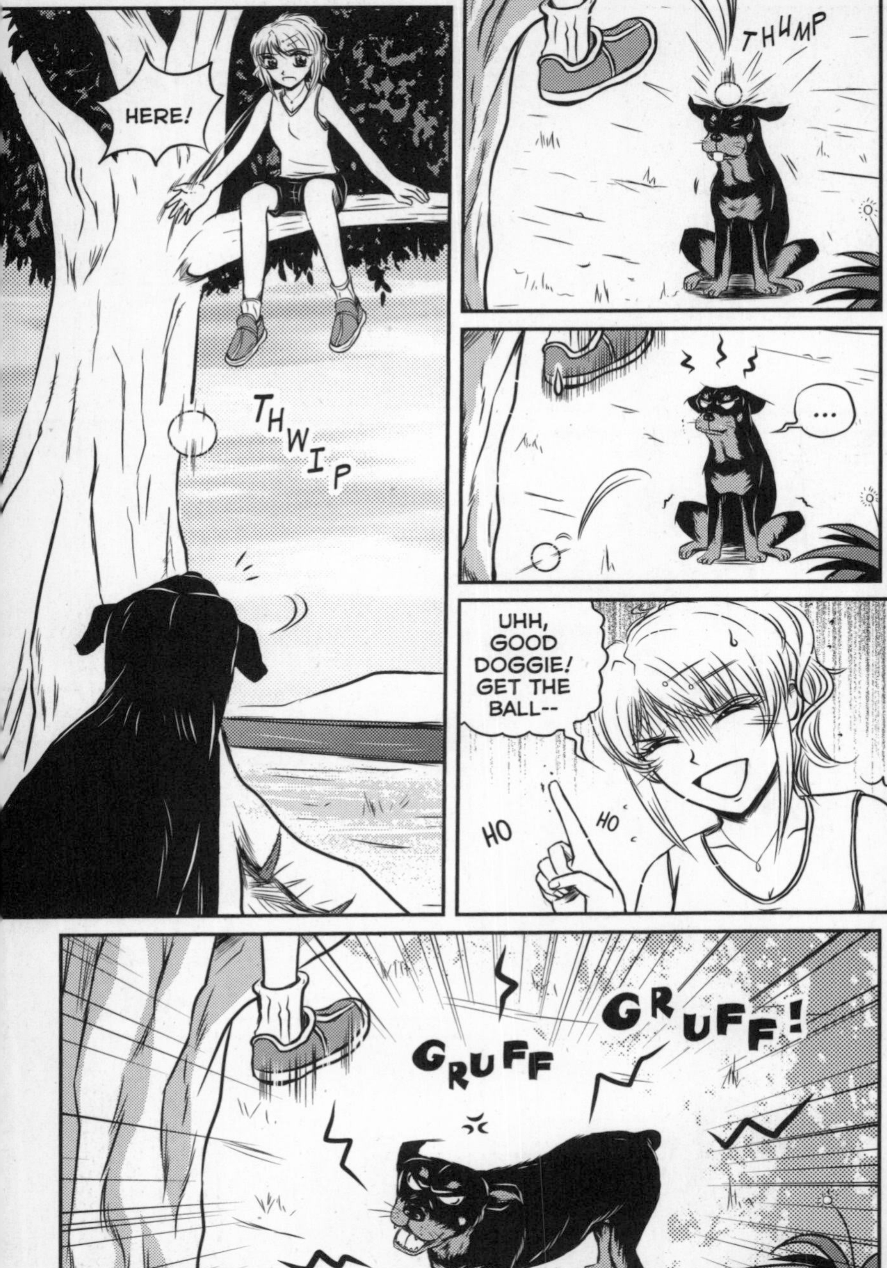
HERE!
THWIP
THUMP
...
UHH, GOOD DOGGIE! GET THE BALL--
HO HO
GRUFF
GRUFF!

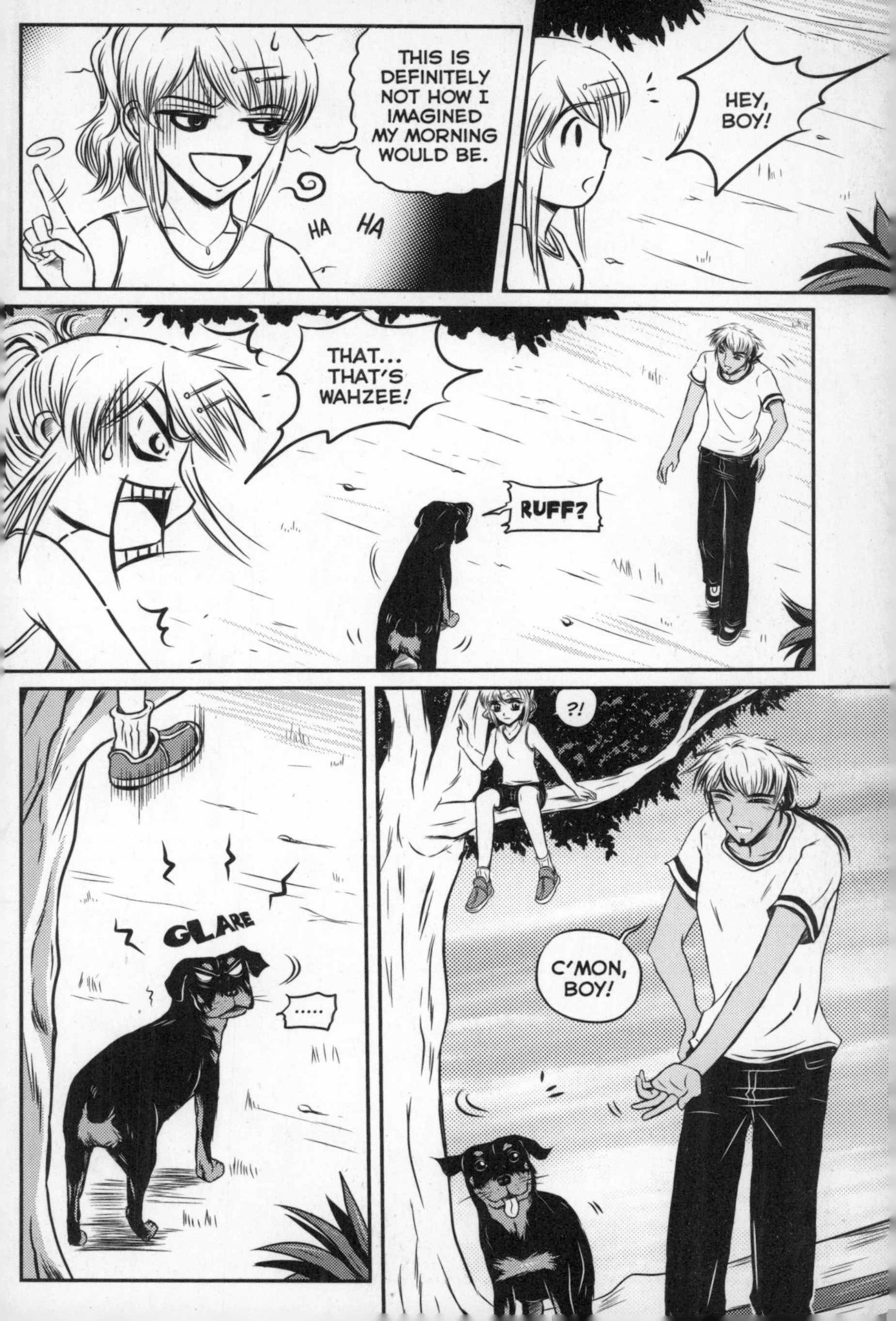
THIS IS DEFINITELY NOT HOW I IMAGINED MY MORNING WOULD BE.
HA HA
HEY, BOY!
THAT... THAT'S WAHZEE!
RUFF?
GLARE
......
?!
C'MON, BOY!

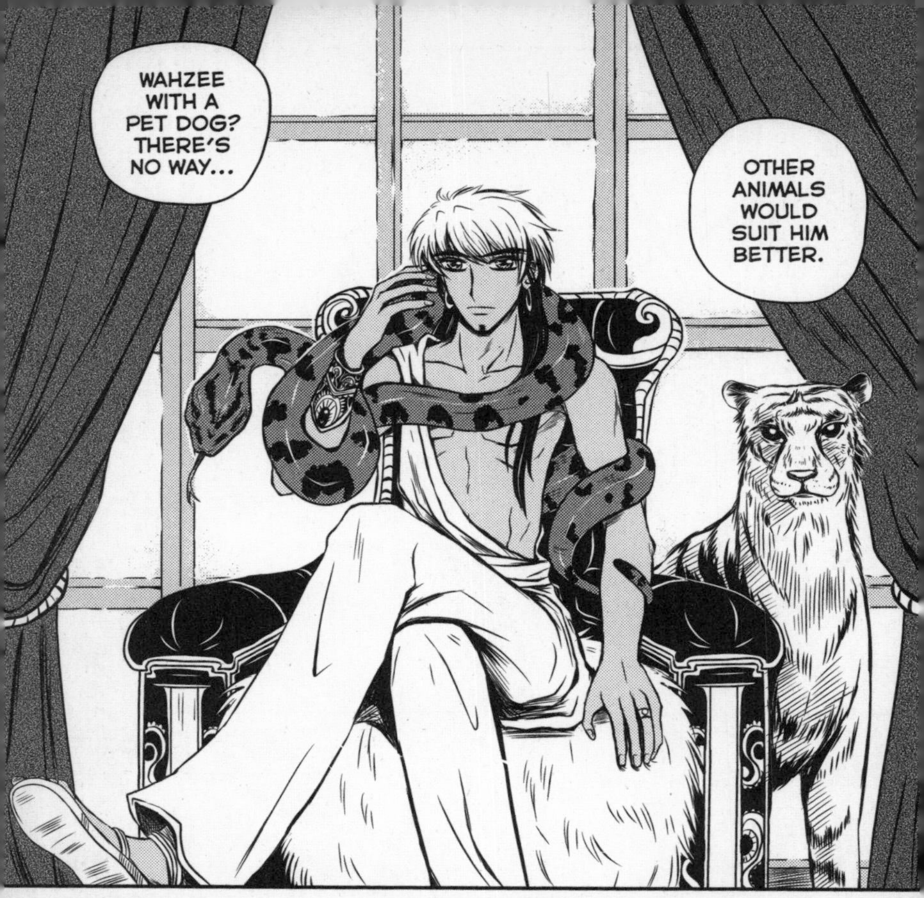
WAHZEE WITH A PET DOG? THERE'S NO WAY...
OTHER ANIMALS WOULD SUIT HIM BETTER.
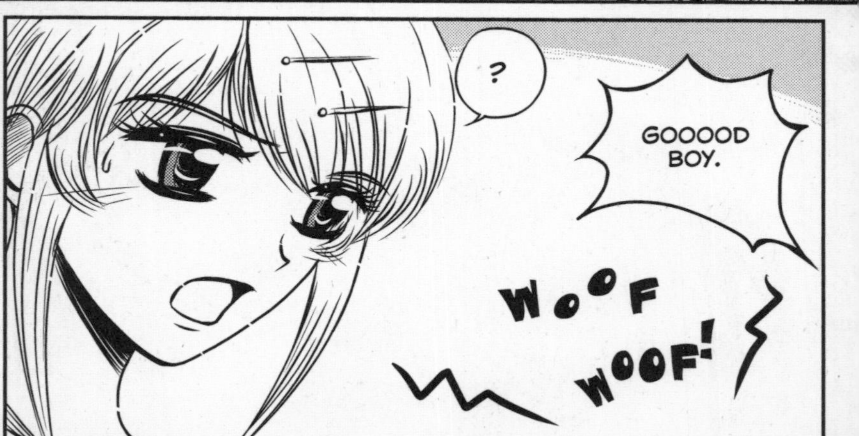
?
GOOOOD BOY.
WOOF WOOF!

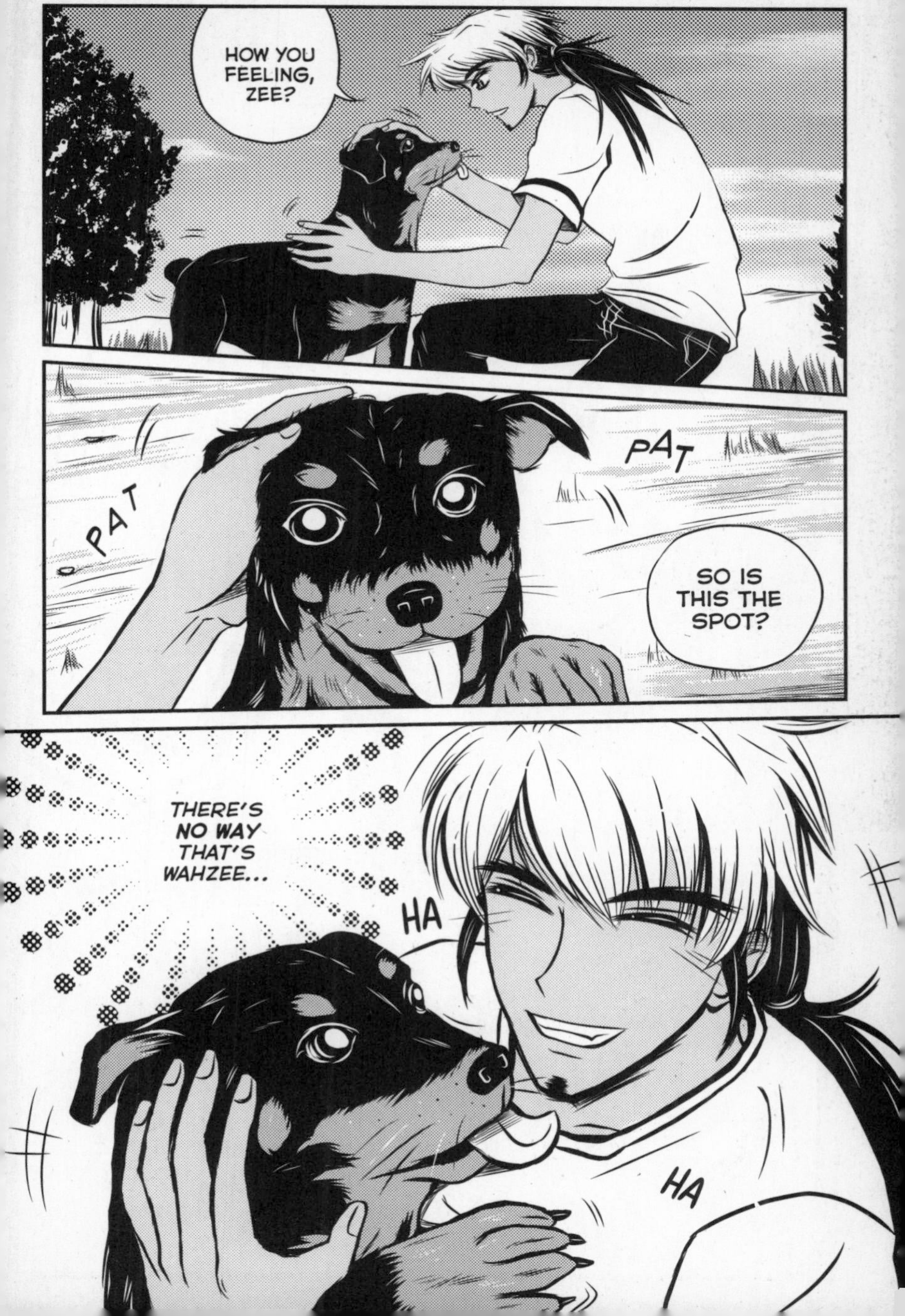
HOW YOU FEELING, ZEE?
PAT
PAT
SO IS THIS THE SPOT?
THERE'S NO WAY THAT'S WAHZEE...
HA
HA

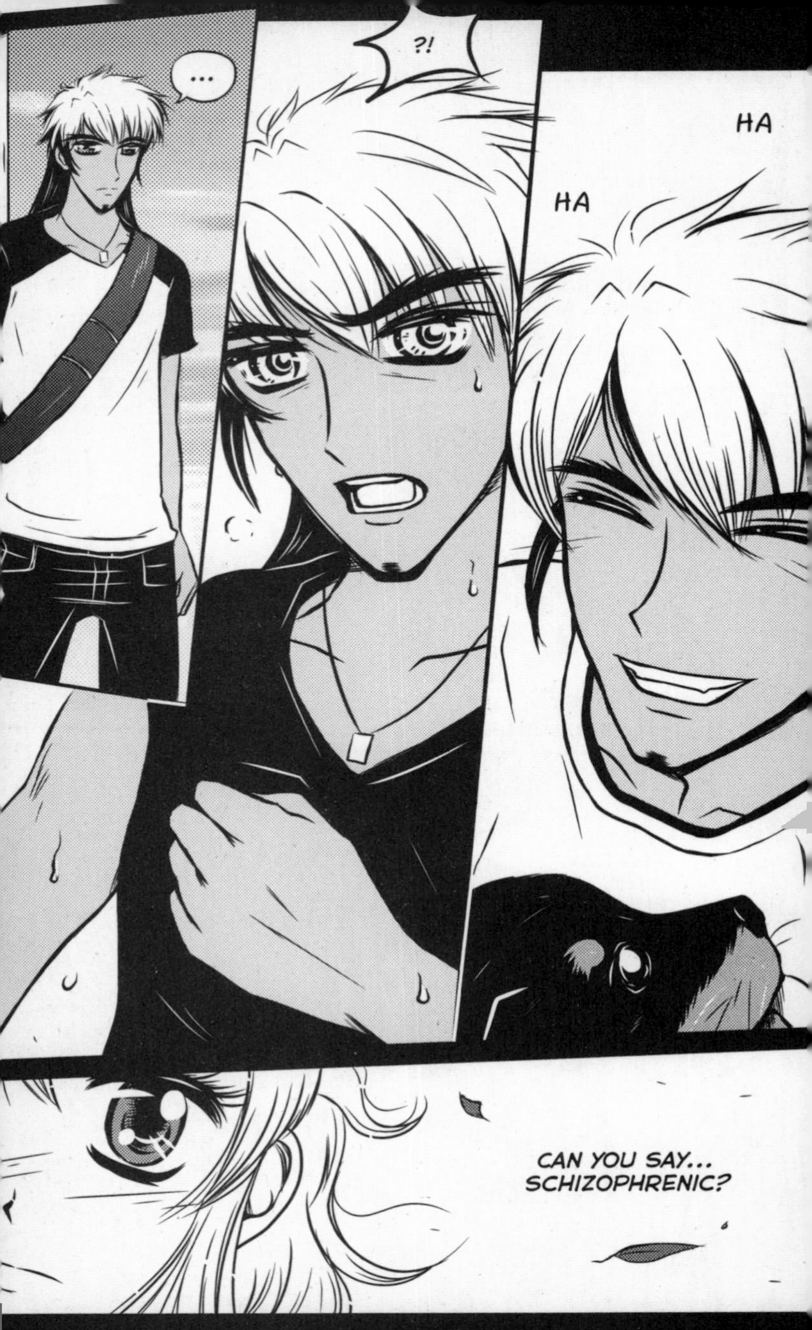
...
?!
HA
HA
CAN YOU SAY...
SCHIZOPHRENIC?

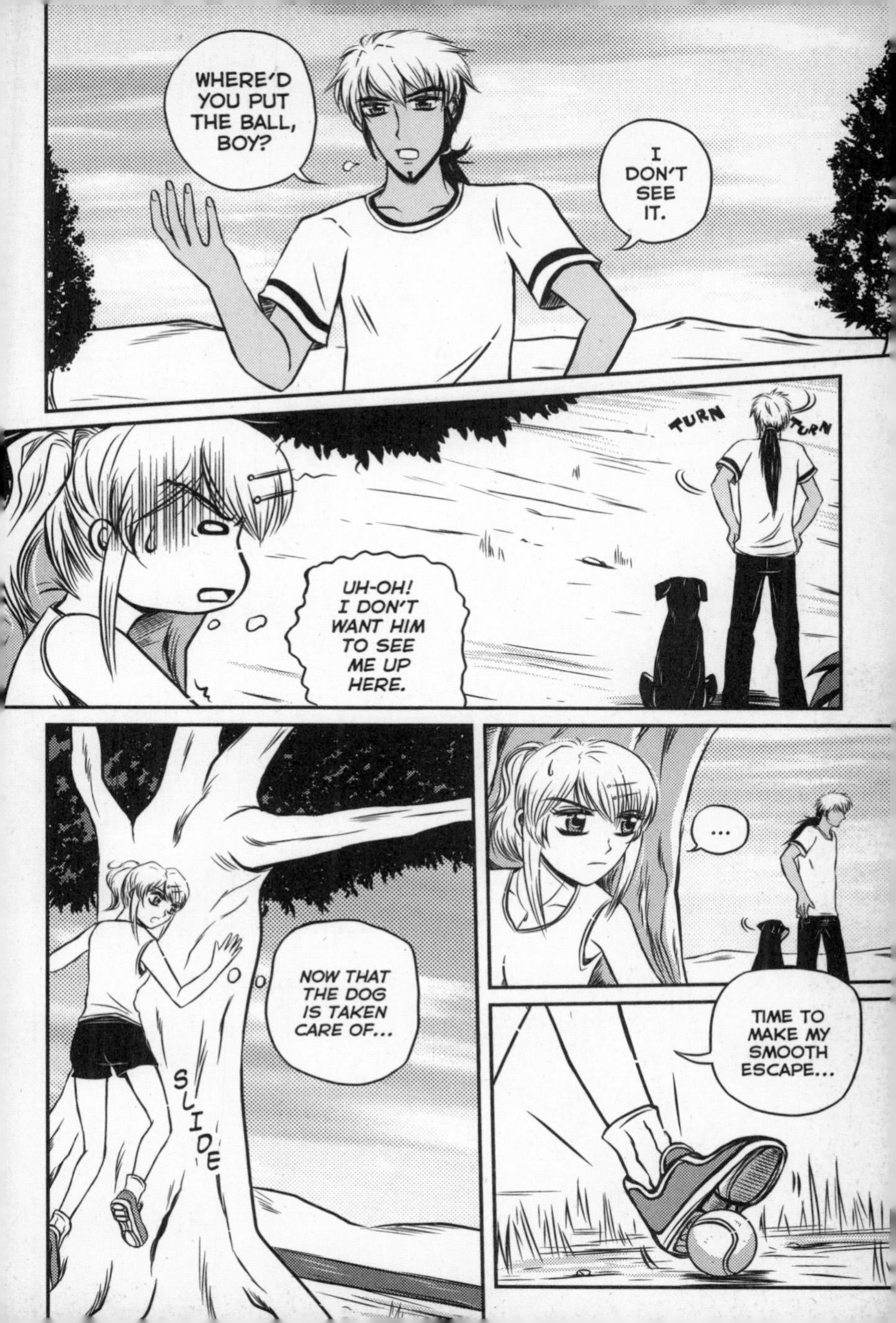
WHERE'D YOU PUT THE BALL, BOY?
I DON'T SEE IT.
TURN TURN
UH-OH! I DON'T WANT HIM TO SEE ME UP HERE.
NOW THAT THE DOG IS TAKEN CARE OF...
SLIDE
...
TIME TO MAKE MY SMOOTH ESCAPE...

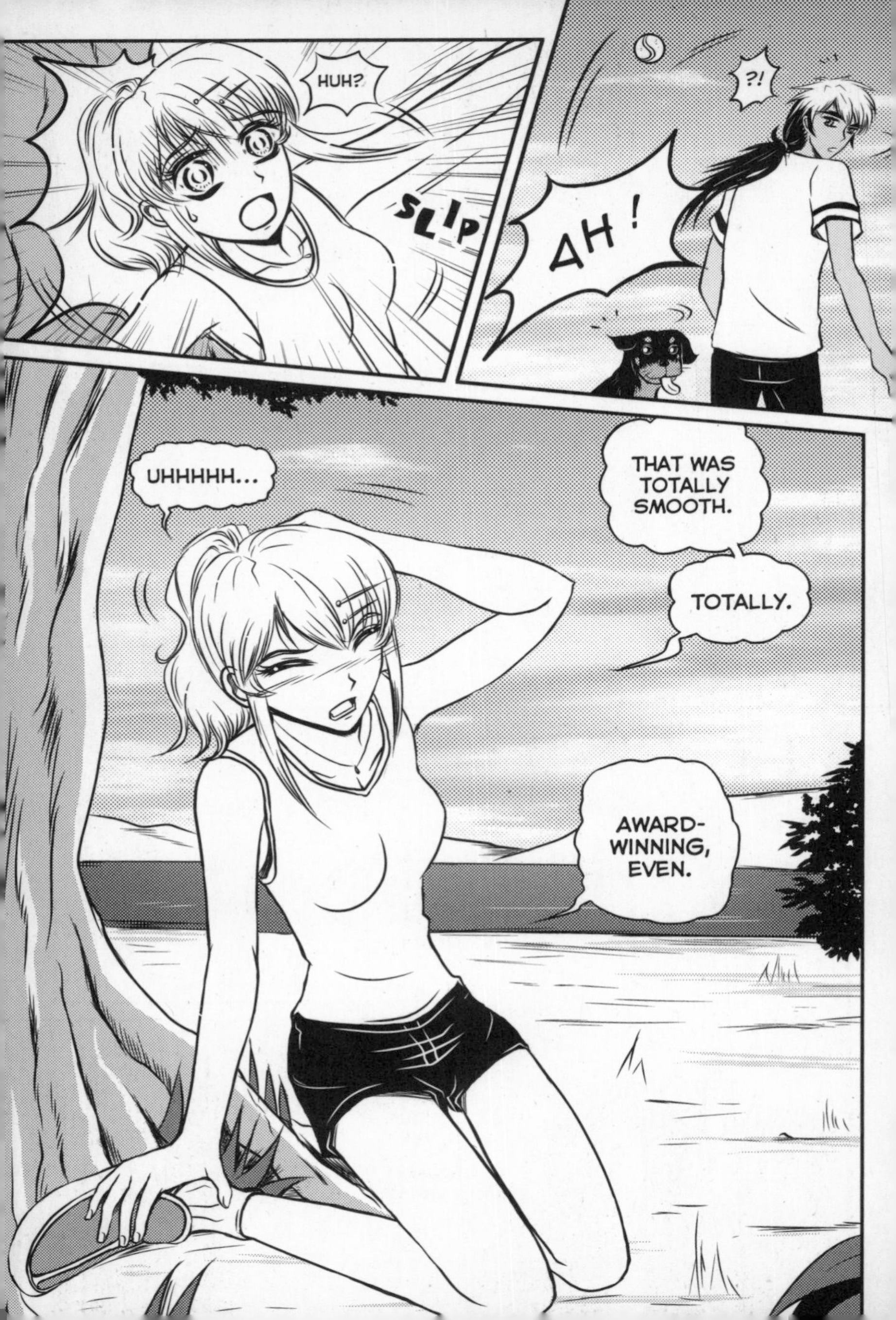
HUH?
SLIP
?!
AH!
UHHHHH...
THAT WAS TOTALLY SMOOTH.
TOTALLY.
AWARD-WINNING, EVEN.

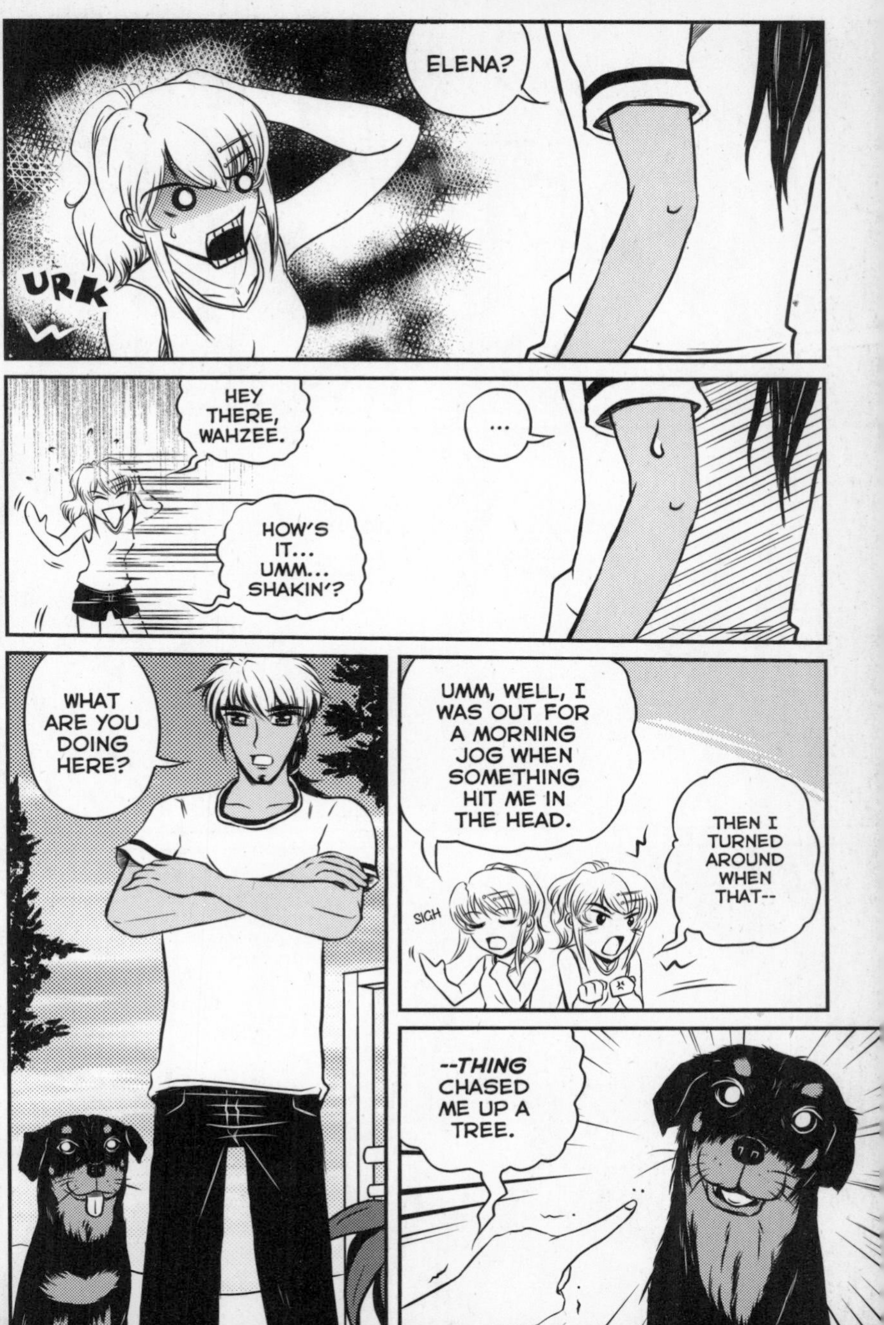
ELENA?
URK
HEY THERE, WAHZEE.
HOW'S IT... UMM... SHAKIN'?
...
WHAT ARE YOU DOING HERE?
UMM, WELL, I WAS OUT FOR A MORNING JOG WHEN SOMETHING HIT ME IN THE HEAD.
SIGH
THEN I TURNED AROUND WHEN THAT--
--*THING* CHASED ME UP A TREE.

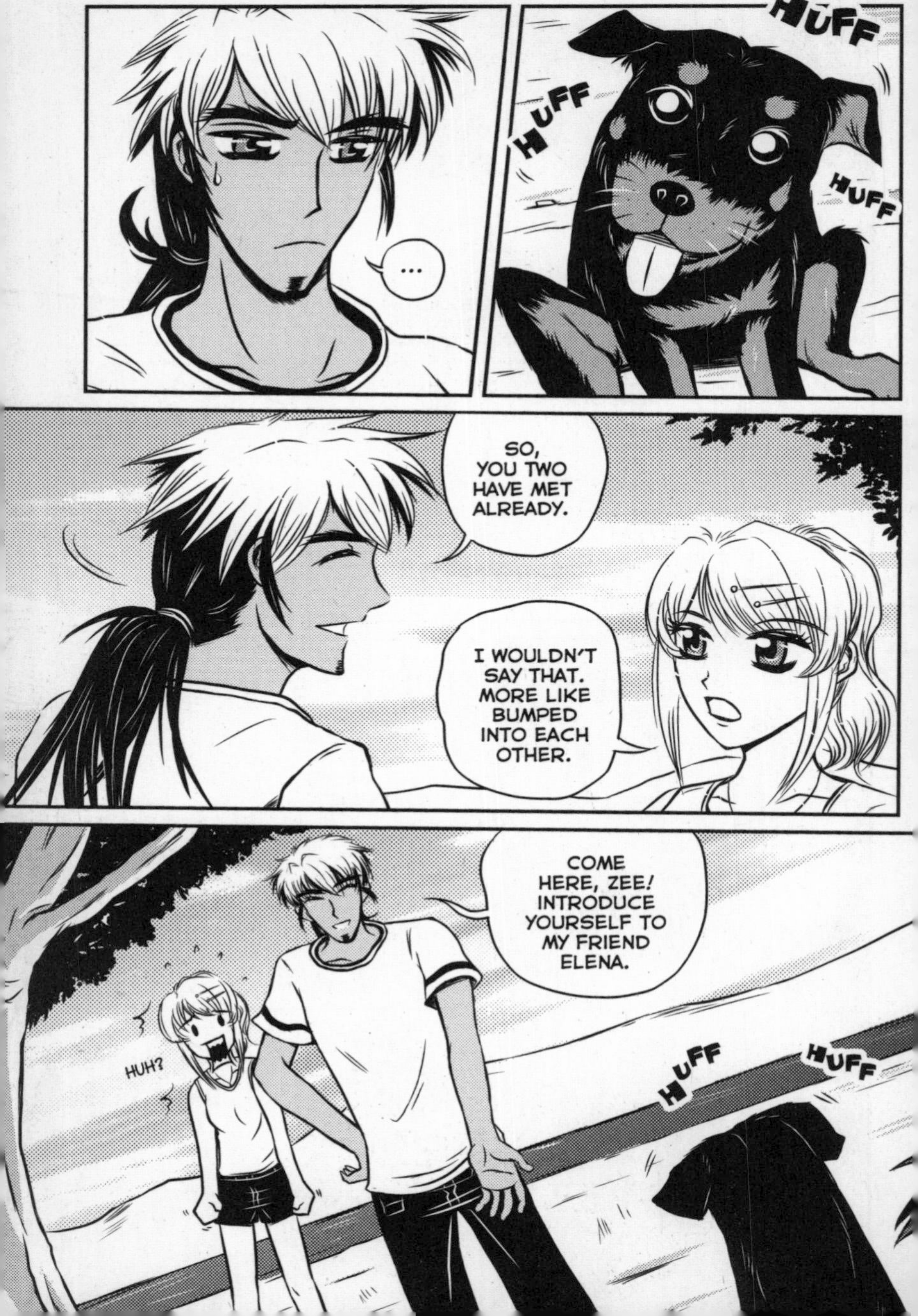
...
HUFF
HUFF
HUFF
SO, YOU TWO HAVE MET ALREADY.
I WOULDN'T SAY THAT. MORE LIKE BUMPED INTO EACH OTHER.
COME HERE, ZEE! INTRODUCE YOURSELF TO MY FRIEND ELENA.
HUH?
HUFF
HUFF

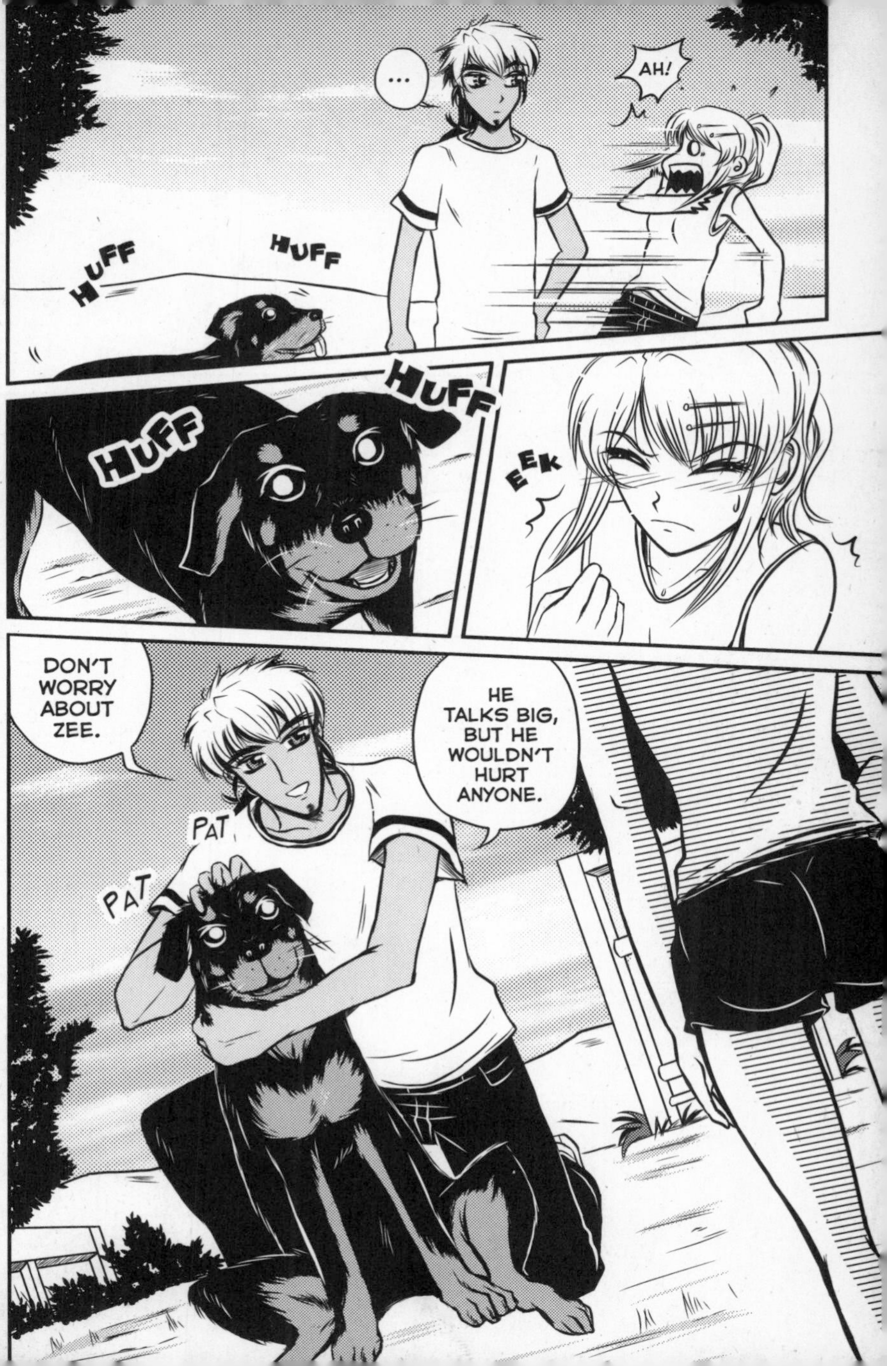
...
AH!
HUFF
HUFF
HUFF
HUFF
EEK
DON'T WORRY ABOUT ZEE.
HE TALKS BIG, BUT HE WOULDN'T HURT ANYONE.
PAT
PAT

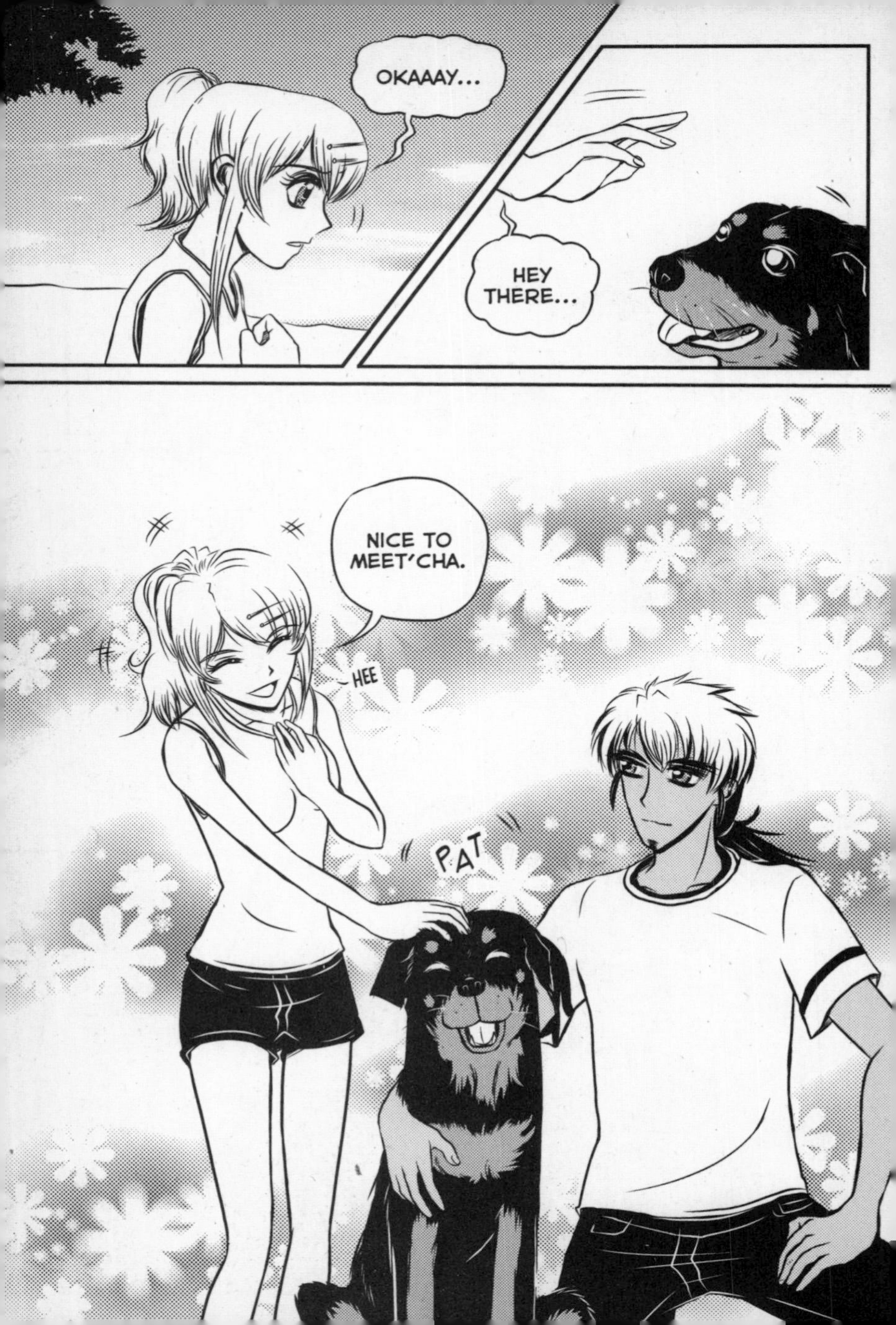
OKAAAY...
HEY THERE...
NICE TO MEET'CHA.
HEE
PAT

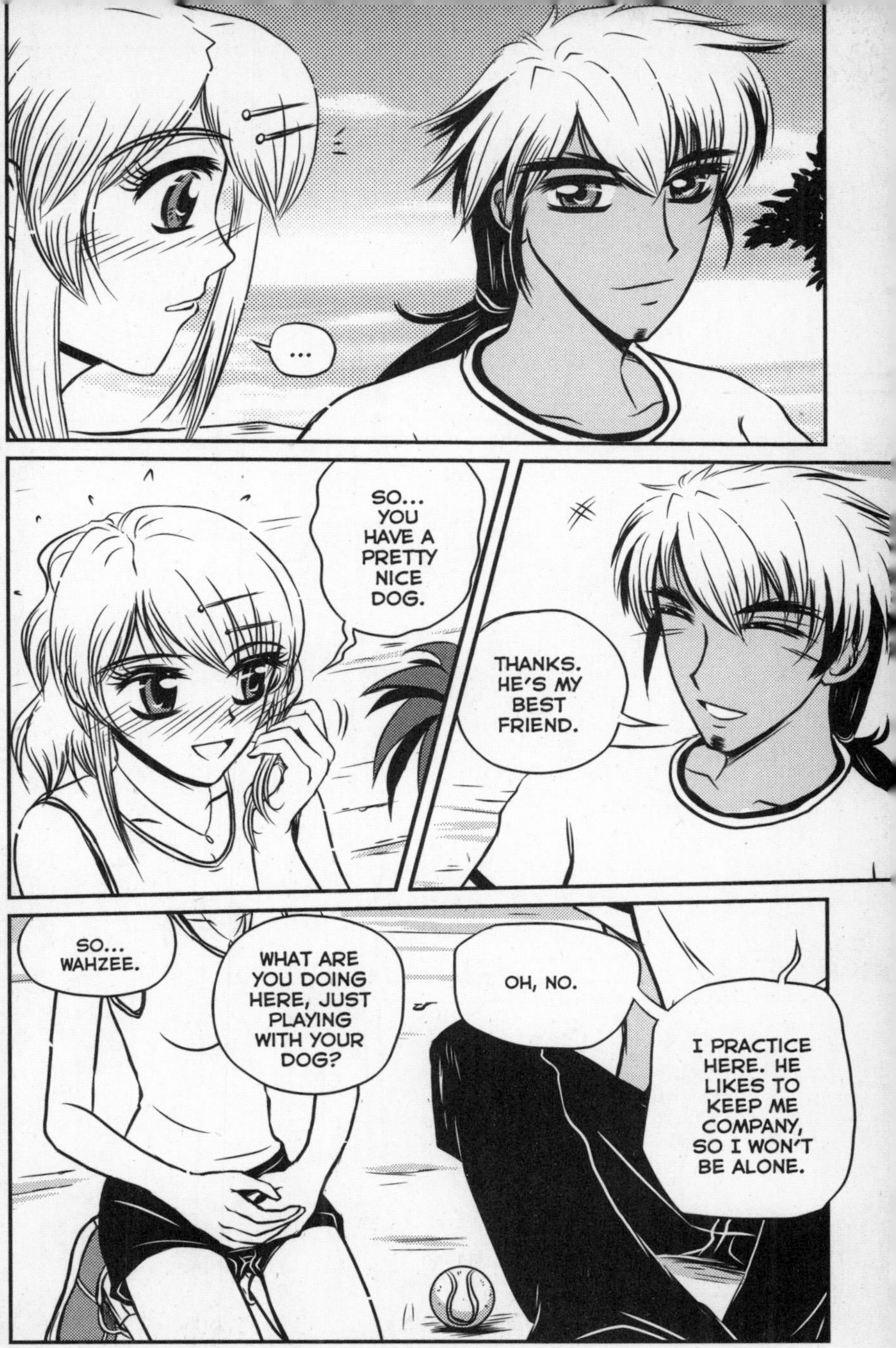
...
SO... YOU HAVE A PRETTY NICE DOG.
THANKS. HE'S MY BEST FRIEND.
SO... WAHZEE.
WHAT ARE YOU DOING HERE, JUST PLAYING WITH YOUR DOG?
OH, NO.
I PRACTICE HERE. HE LIKES TO KEEP ME COMPANY, SO I WON'T BE ALONE.

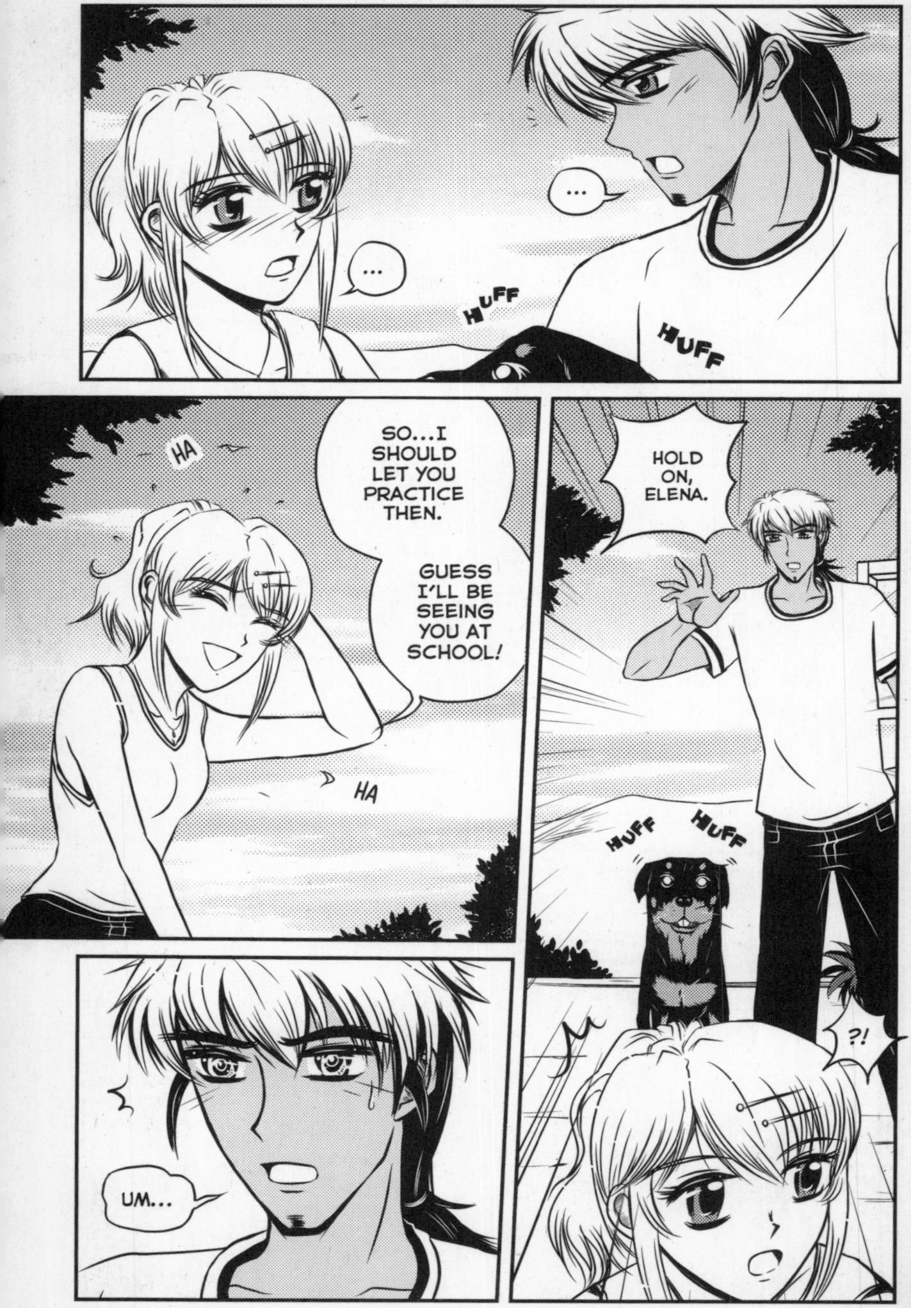
...
...
HUFF
HUFF
HA
SO...I SHOULD LET YOU PRACTICE THEN.
GUESS I'LL BE SEEING YOU AT SCHOOL!
HA
HOLD ON, ELENA.
HUFF
HUFF
UM...
?!

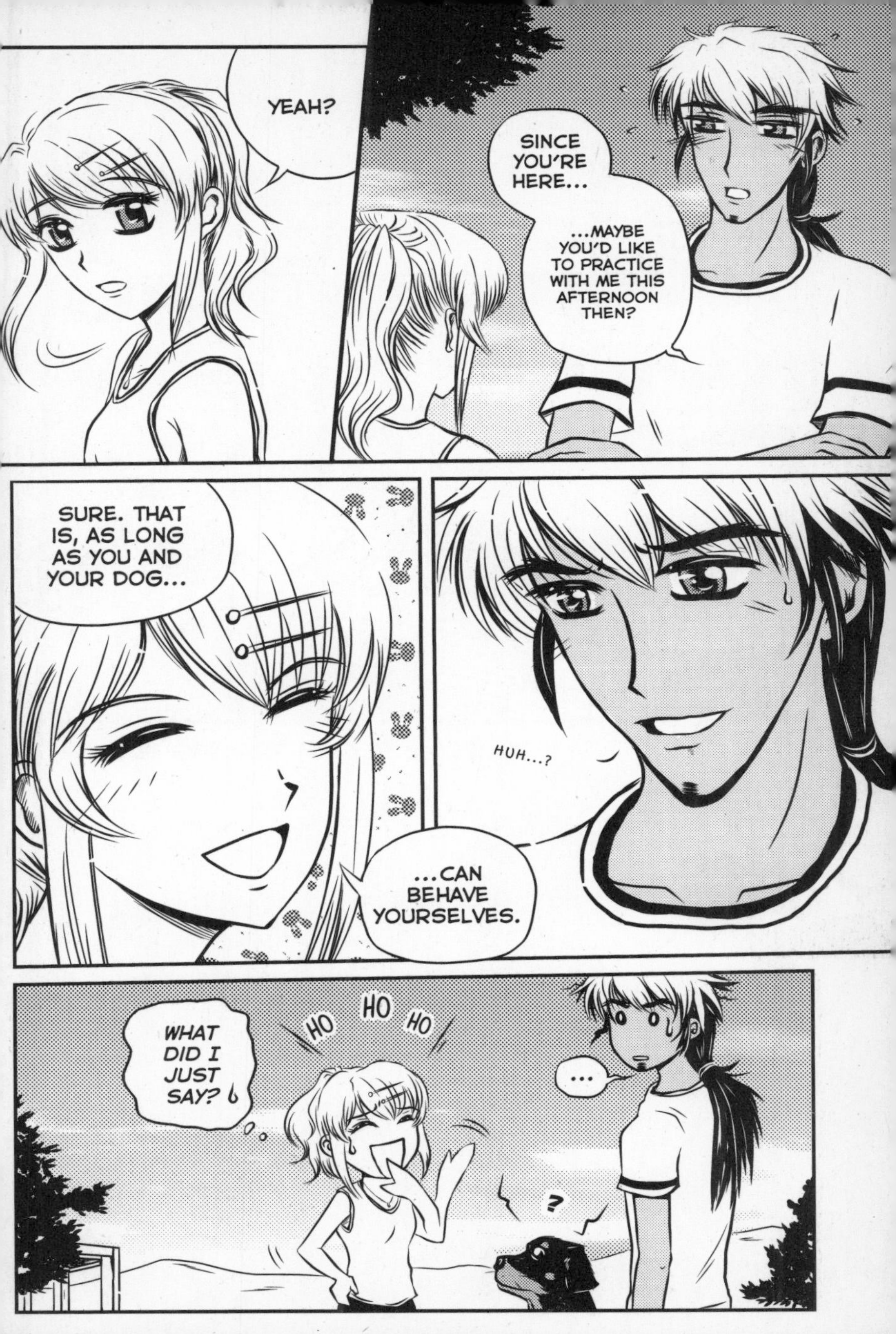
YEAH?
SINCE YOU'RE HERE...
...MAYBE YOU'D LIKE TO PRACTICE WITH ME THIS AFTERNOON THEN?
SURE. THAT IS, AS LONG AS YOU AND YOUR DOG...
...CAN BEHAVE YOURSELVES.
HUH...?
WHAT DID I JUST SAY?
HO HO HO
...
?

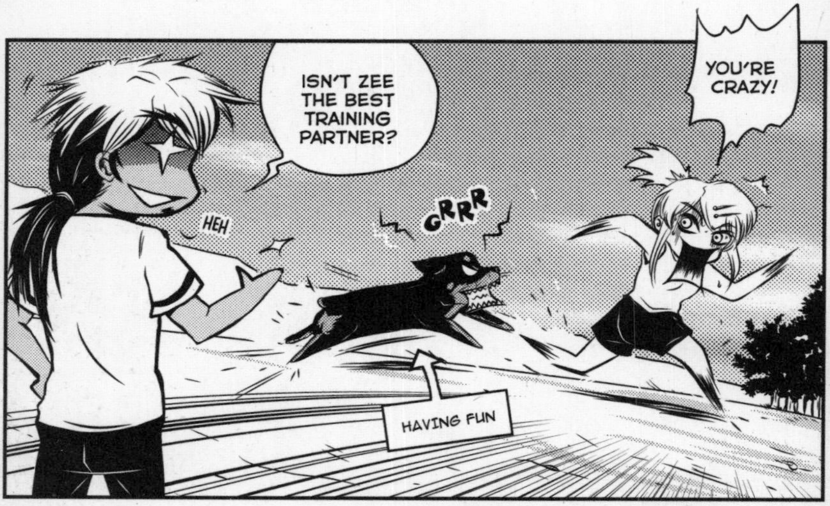
ISN'T ZEE THE BEST TRAINING PARTNER?
YOU'RE CRAZY!
HEH
GRRR
HAVING FUN

WAHZEE'S SECRET TRAINING SESSION

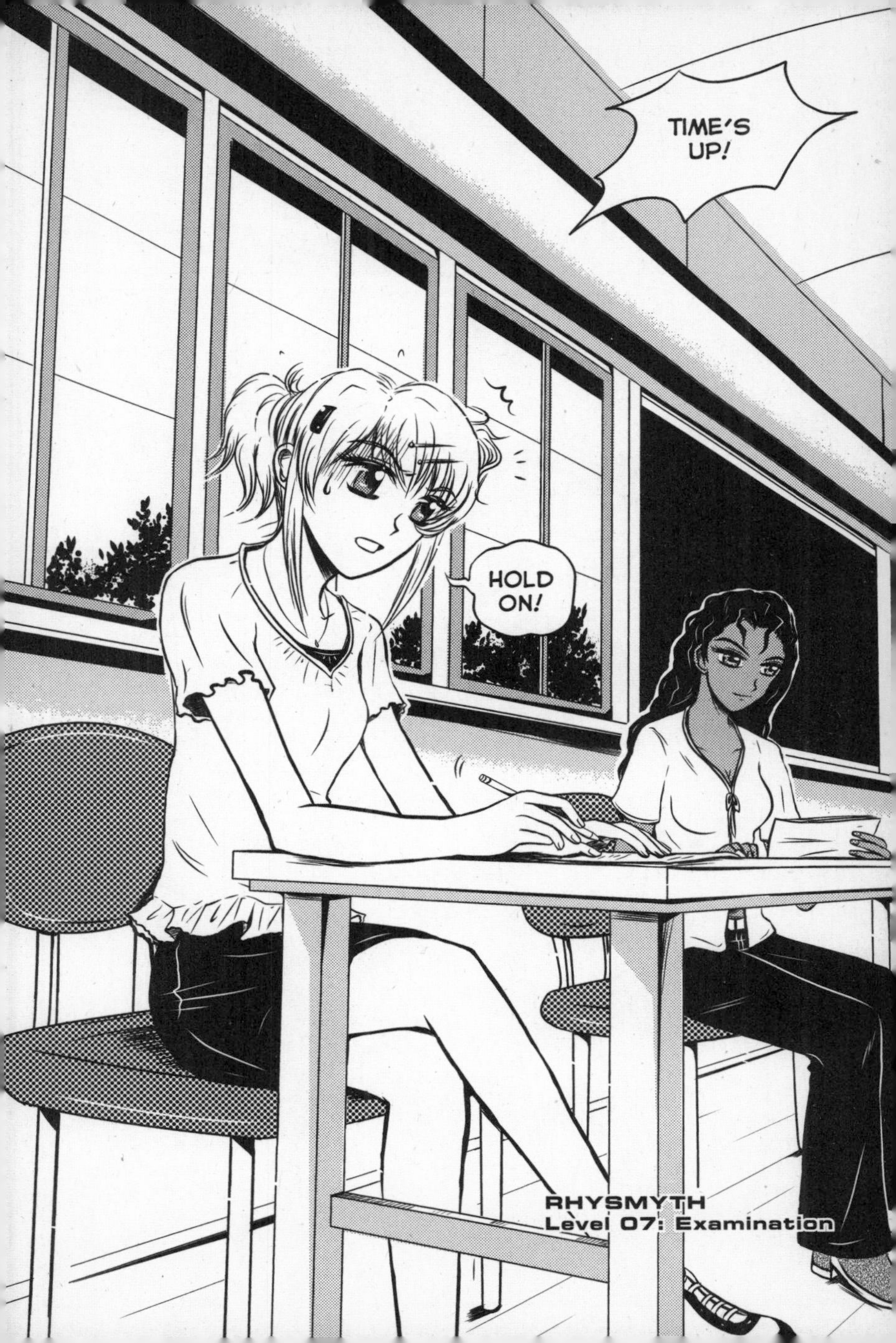
TIME'S UP!
HOLD ON!
RHYSMYTH
Level 07: Examination

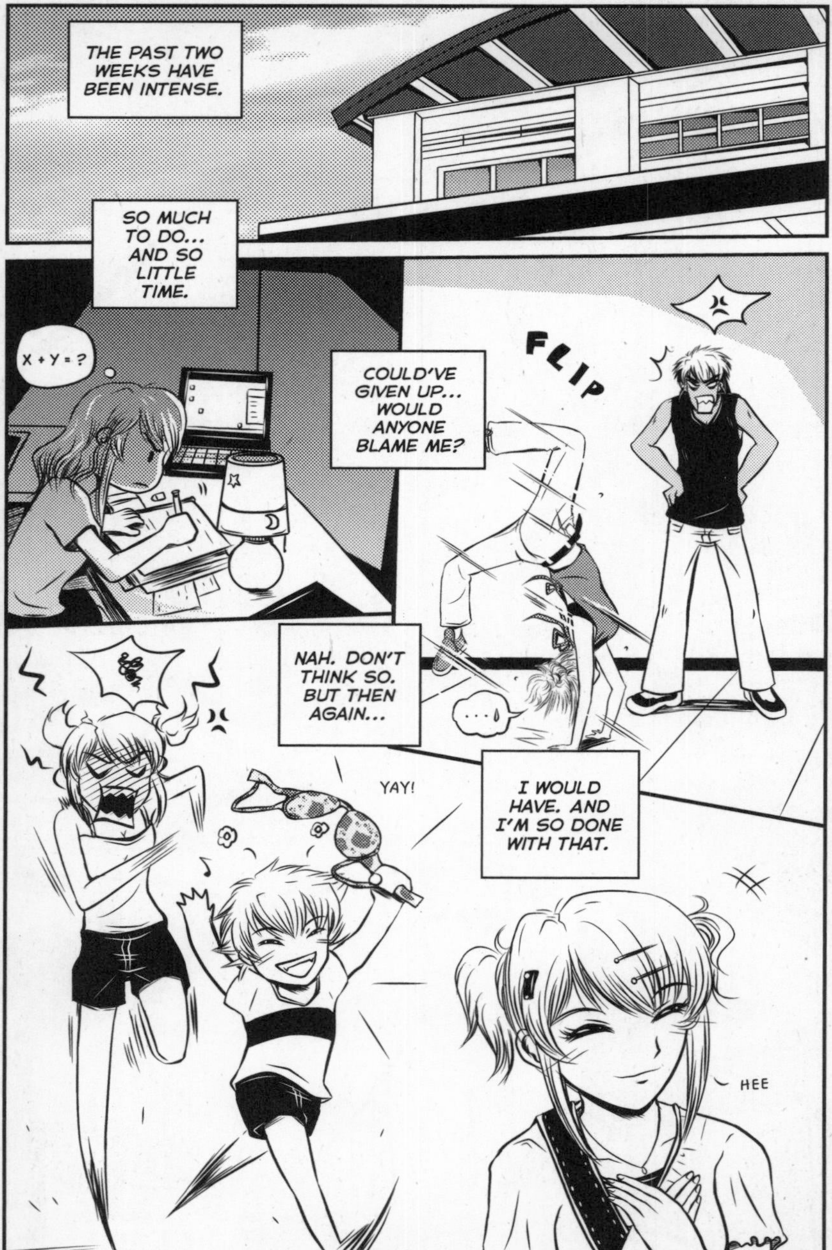
THE PAST TWO WEEKS HAVE BEEN INTENSE.
SO MUCH TO DO... AND SO LITTLE TIME.
X + Y = ?
COULD'VE GIVEN UP... WOULD ANYONE BLAME ME?
FLIP
NAH. DON'T THINK SO. BUT THEN AGAIN...
YAY!
I WOULD HAVE. AND I'M SO DONE WITH THAT.
HEE

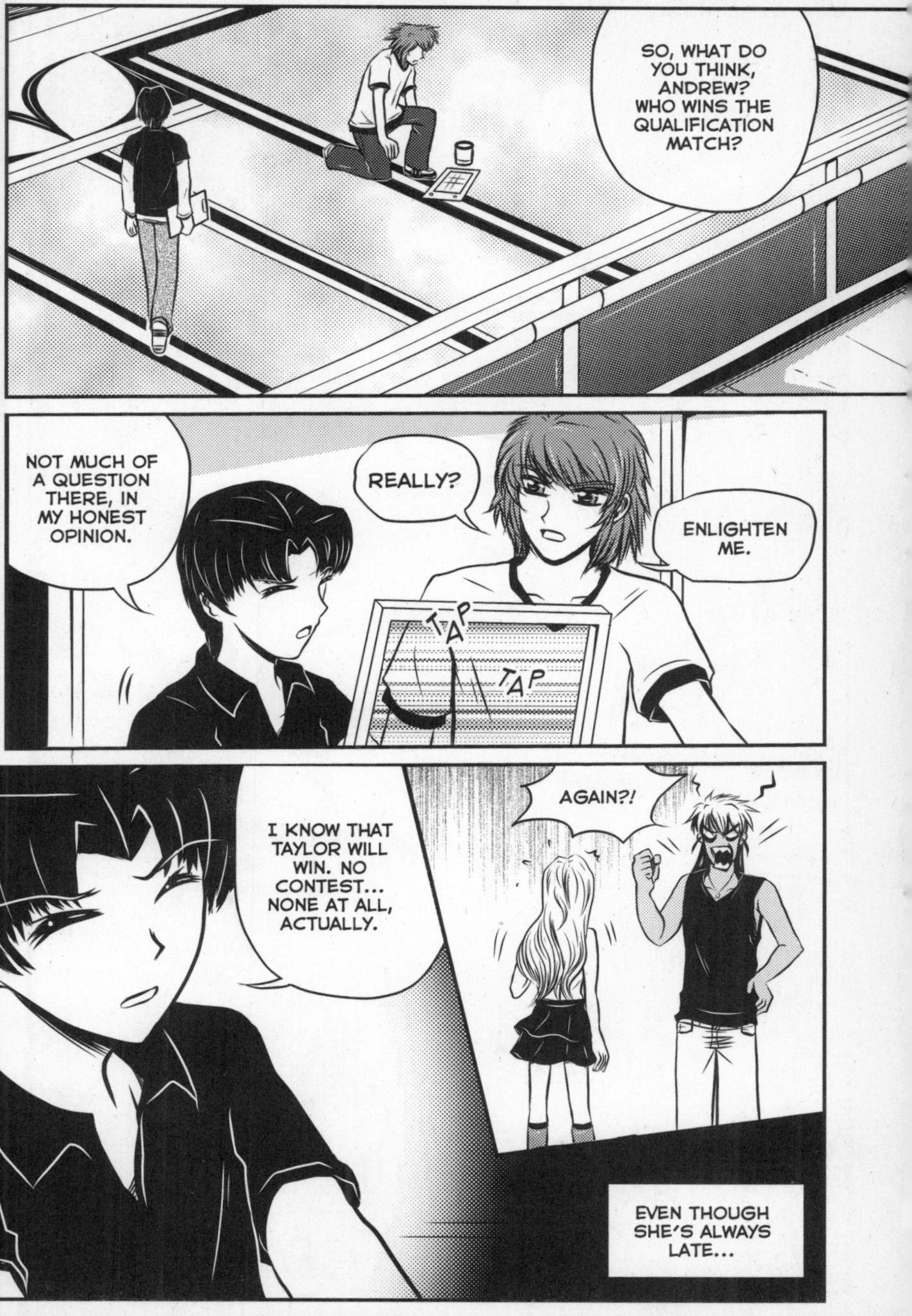

SO, WHAT DO YOU THINK, ANDREW? WHO WINS THE QUALIFICATION MATCH?
NOT MUCH OF A QUESTION THERE, IN MY HONEST OPINION.
REALLY?
ENLIGHTEN ME.
TAP
TAP
I KNOW THAT TAYLOR WILL WIN. NO CONTEST... NONE AT ALL, ACTUALLY.
AGAIN?!
EVEN THOUGH SHE'S ALWAYS LATE...

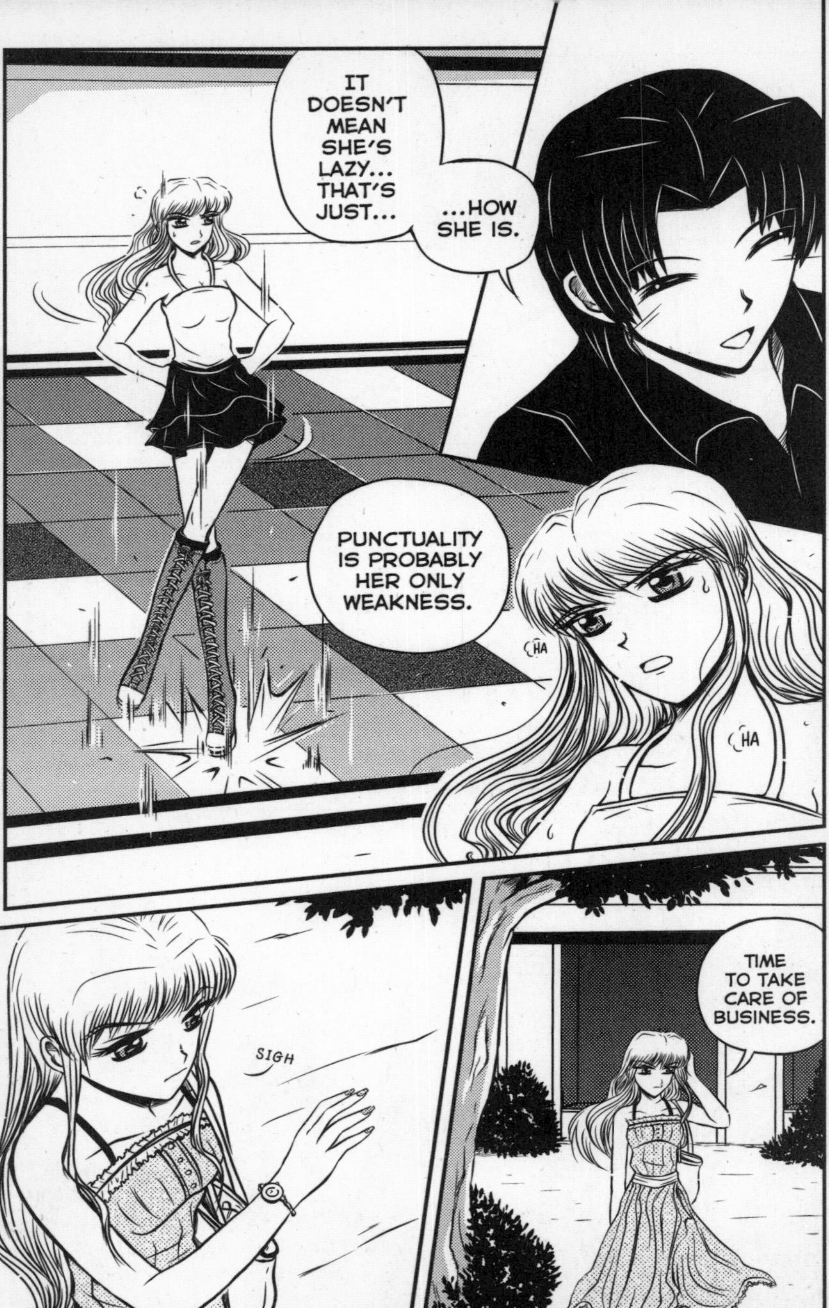
IT DOESN'T MEAN SHE'S LAZY... THAT'S JUST...
...HOW SHE IS.
PUNCTUALITY IS PROBABLY HER ONLY WEAKNESS.
HA
HA
SIGH
TIME TO TAKE CARE OF BUSINESS.

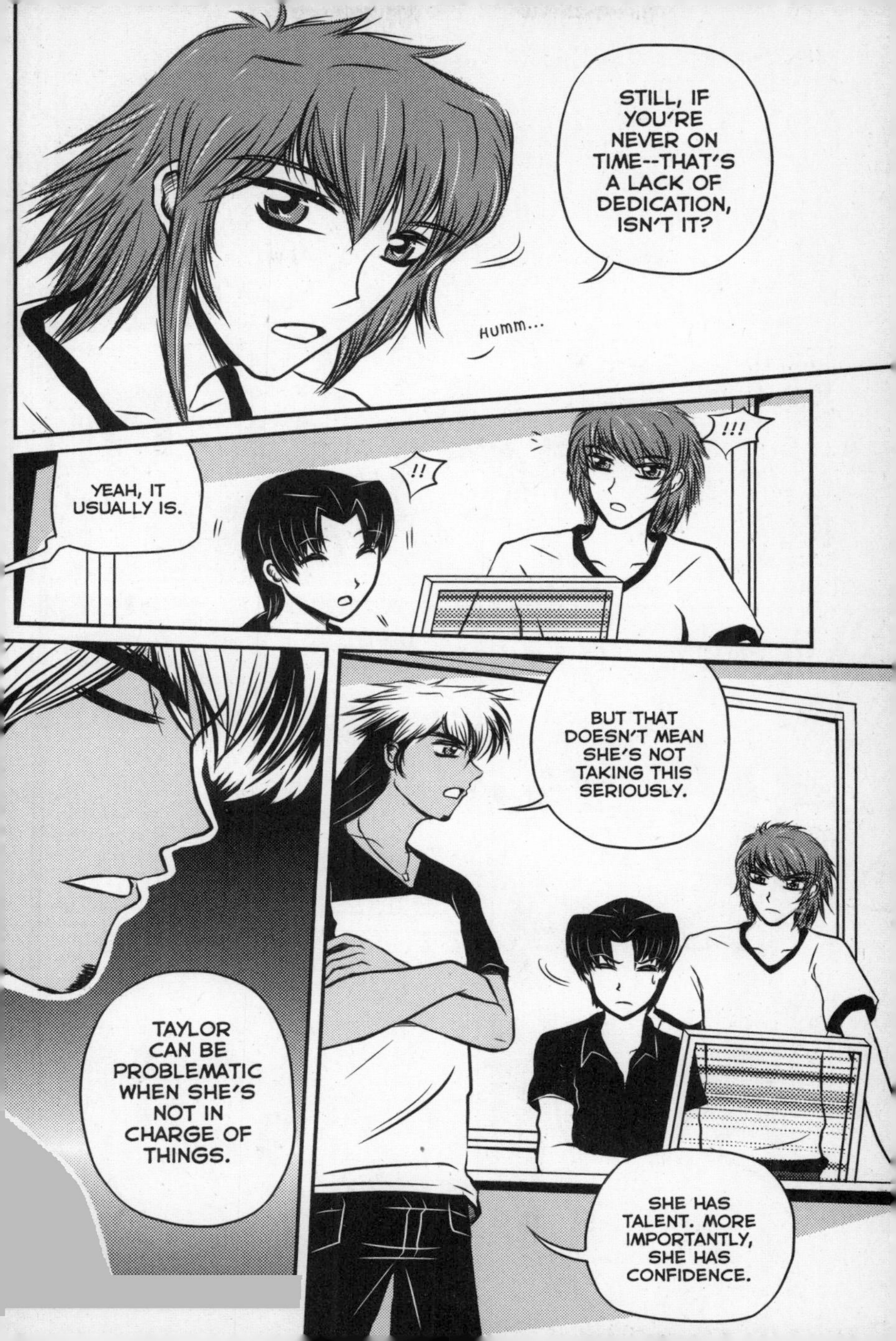
STILL, IF YOU'RE NEVER ON TIME--THAT'S A LACK OF DEDICATION, ISN'T IT?
HUMM...
YEAH, IT USUALLY IS.
!!
!!!
TAYLOR CAN BE PROBLEMATIC WHEN SHE'S NOT IN CHARGE OF THINGS.
BUT THAT DOESN'T MEAN SHE'S NOT TAKING THIS SERIOUSLY.
SHE HAS TALENT. MORE IMPORTANTLY, SHE HAS CONFIDENCE.

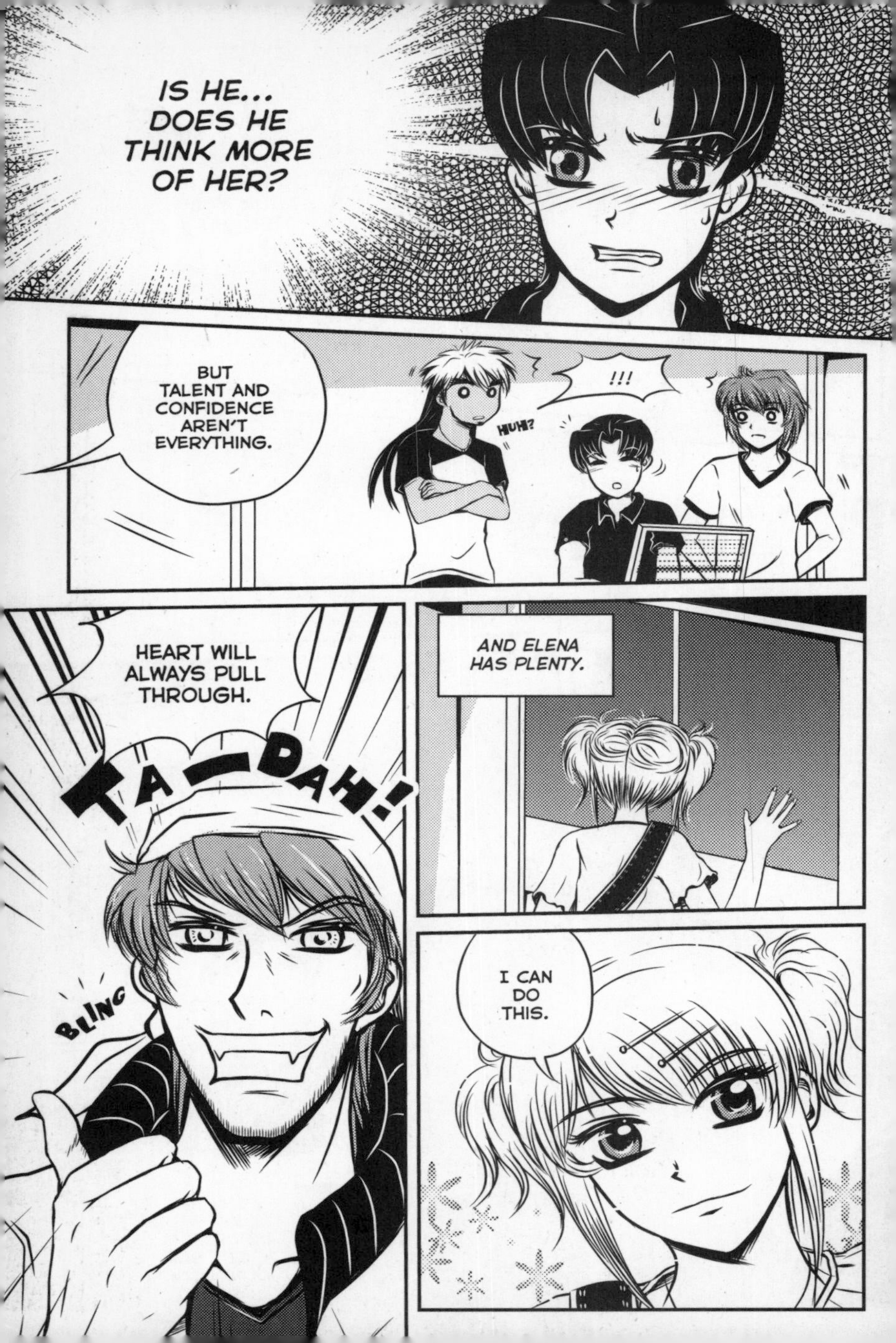
IS HE... DOES HE THINK MORE OF HER?
BUT TALENT AND CONFIDENCE AREN'T EVERYTHING.
HUH?
!!!
HEART WILL ALWAYS PULL THROUGH.
TA—DAH!
BLING
AND ELENA HAS PLENTY.
I CAN DO THIS.

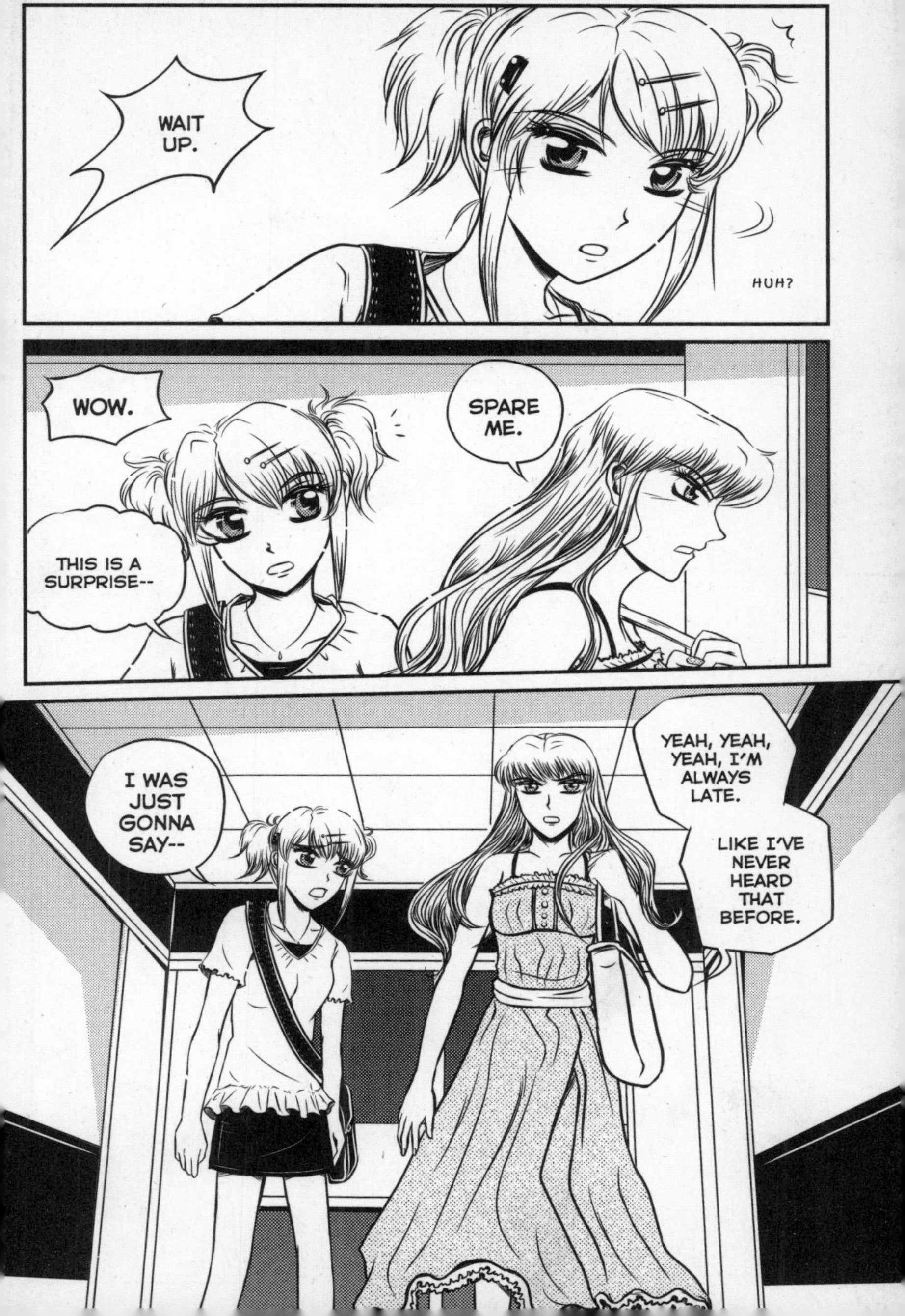
WAIT UP.
HUH?
WOW.
THIS IS A SURPRISE--
SPARE ME.
I WAS JUST GONNA SAY--
YEAH, YEAH, YEAH, I'M ALWAYS LATE.
LIKE I'VE NEVER HEARD THAT BEFORE.

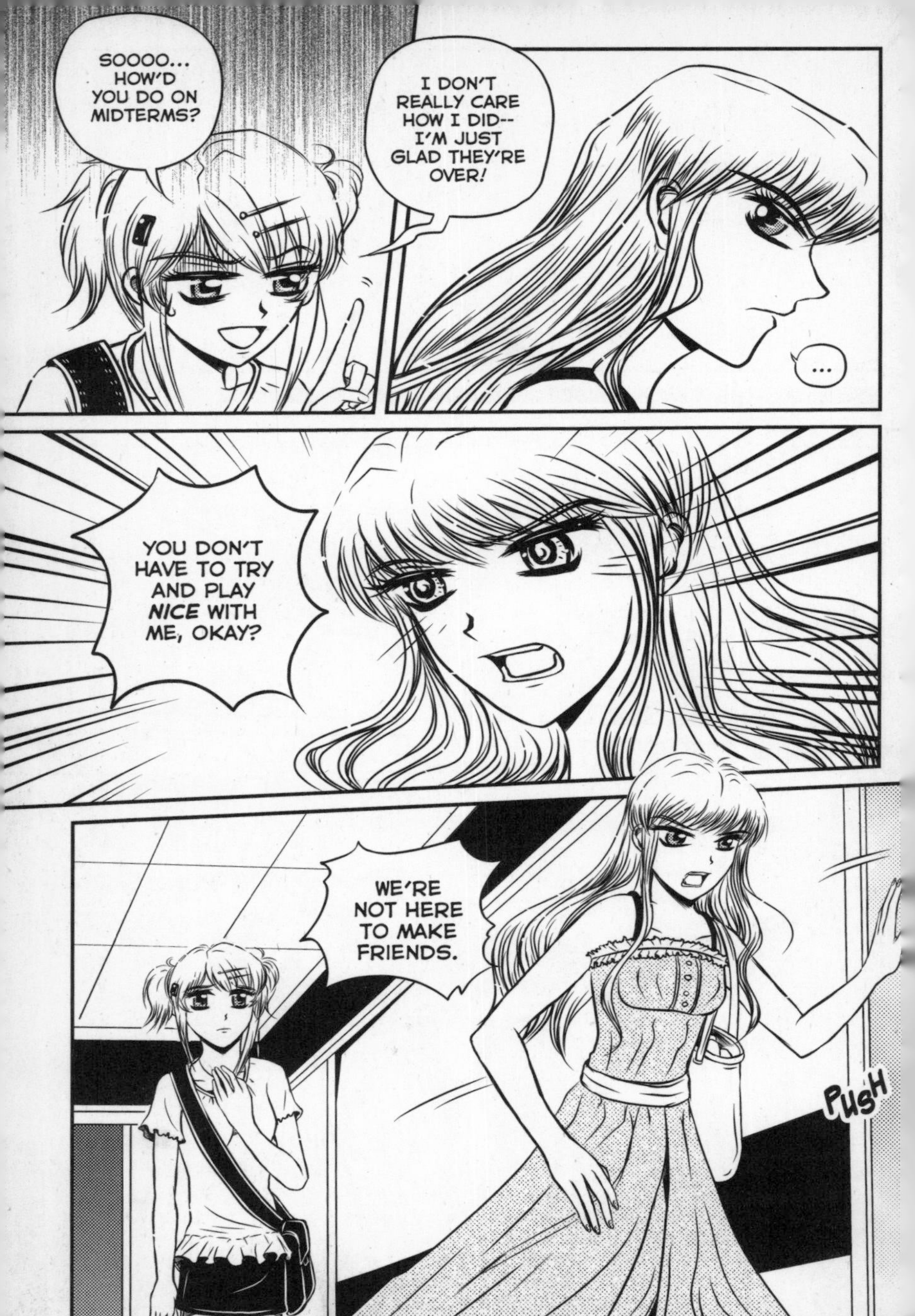
SOOOO... HOW'D YOU DO ON MIDTERMS?
I DON'T REALLY CARE HOW I DID-- I'M JUST GLAD THEY'RE OVER!
...
YOU DON'T HAVE TO TRY AND PLAY *NICE* WITH ME, OKAY?
WE'RE NOT HERE TO MAKE FRIENDS.
PUSH

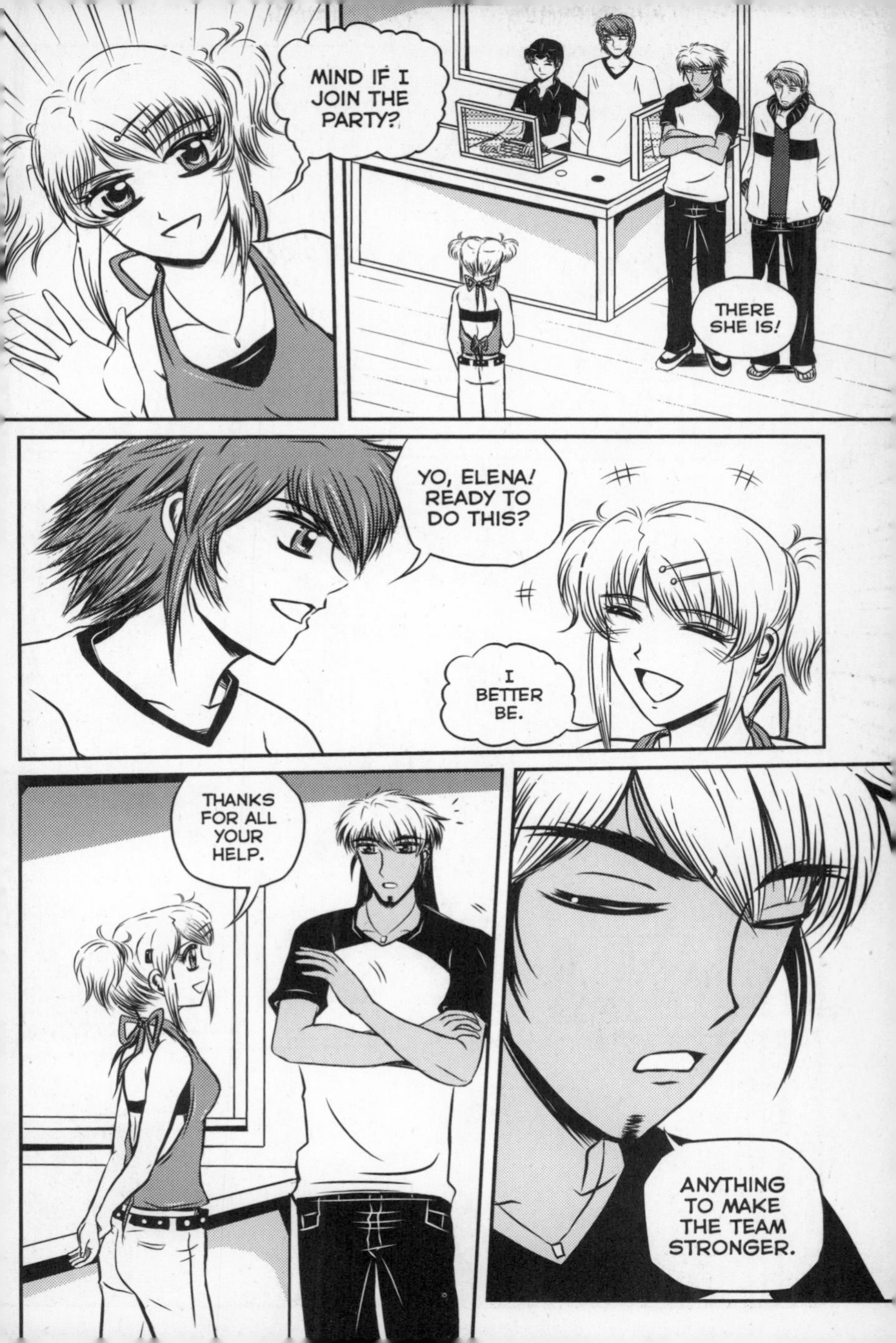
MIND IF I JOIN THE PARTY?
THERE SHE IS!
YO, ELENA! READY TO DO THIS?
I BETTER BE.
THANKS FOR ALL YOUR HELP.
ANYTHING TO MAKE THE TEAM STRONGER.

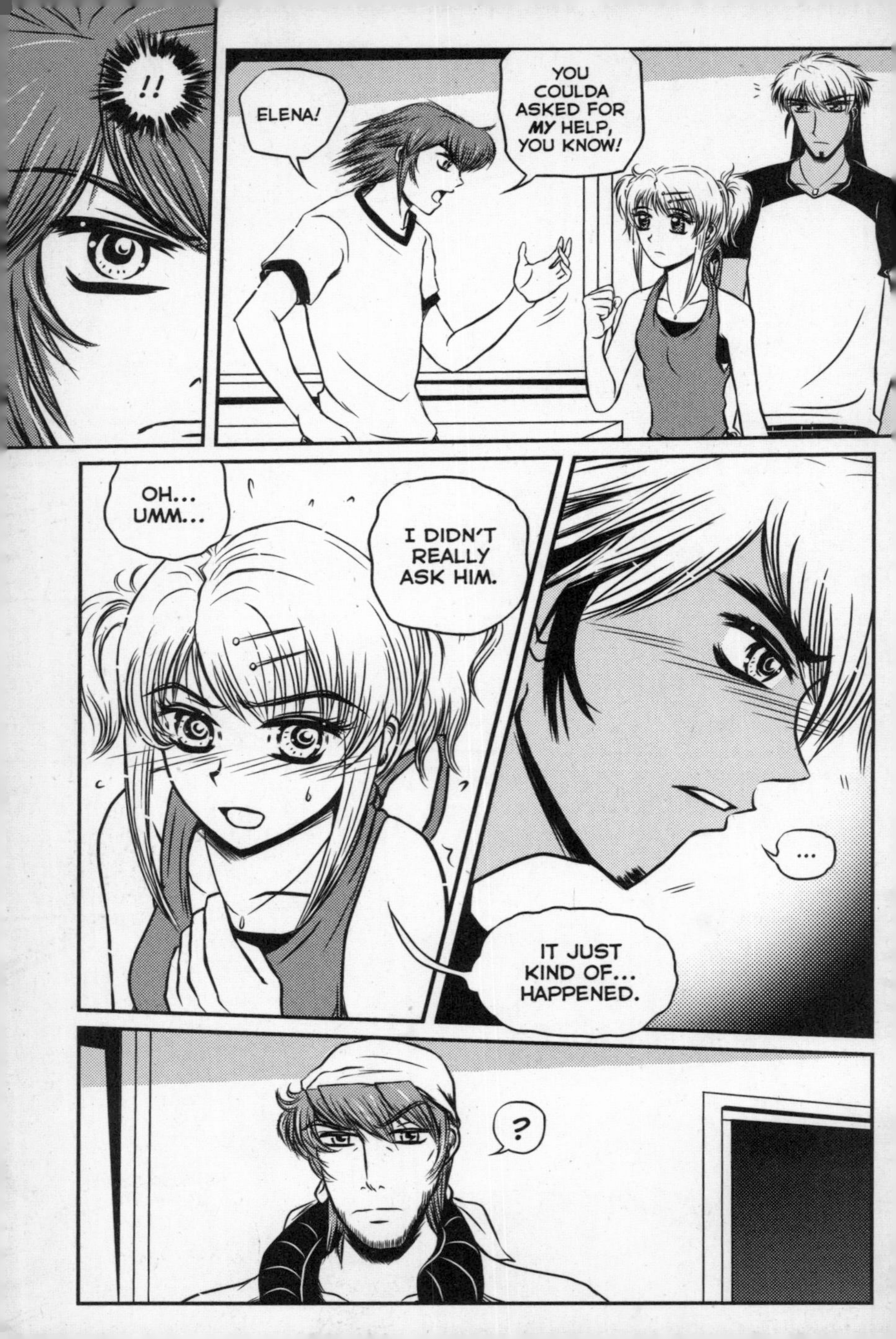
!!
ELENA!
YOU COULDA ASKED FOR MY HELP, YOU KNOW!
OH... UMM...
I DIDN'T REALLY ASK HIM.
...
IT JUST KIND OF... HAPPENED.
?

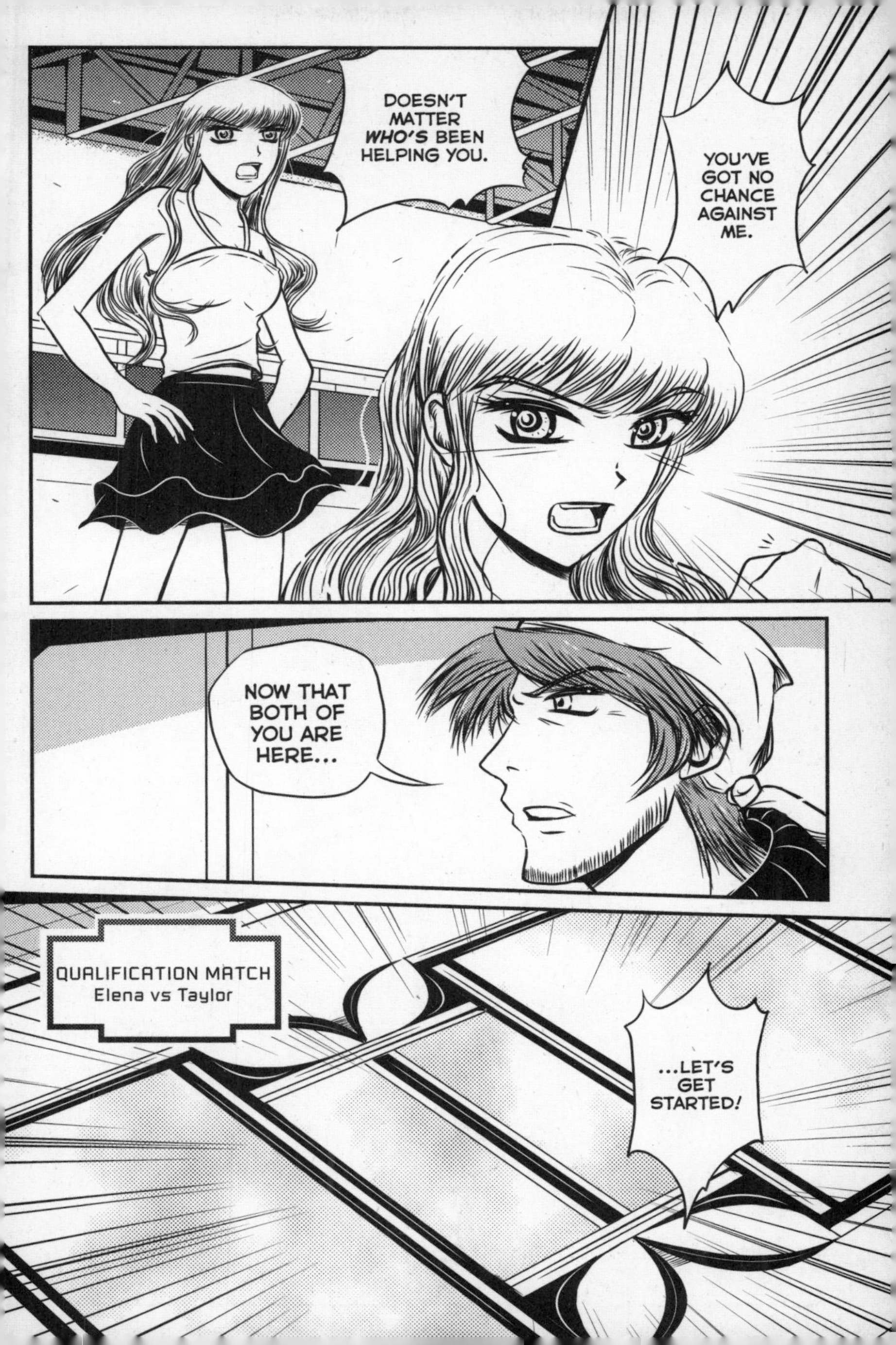
DOESN'T MATTER *WHO'S* BEEN HELPING YOU.
YOU'VE GOT NO CHANCE AGAINST ME.
NOW THAT BOTH OF YOU ARE HERE...
QUALIFICATION MATCH
Elena vs Taylor
...LET'S GET STARTED!

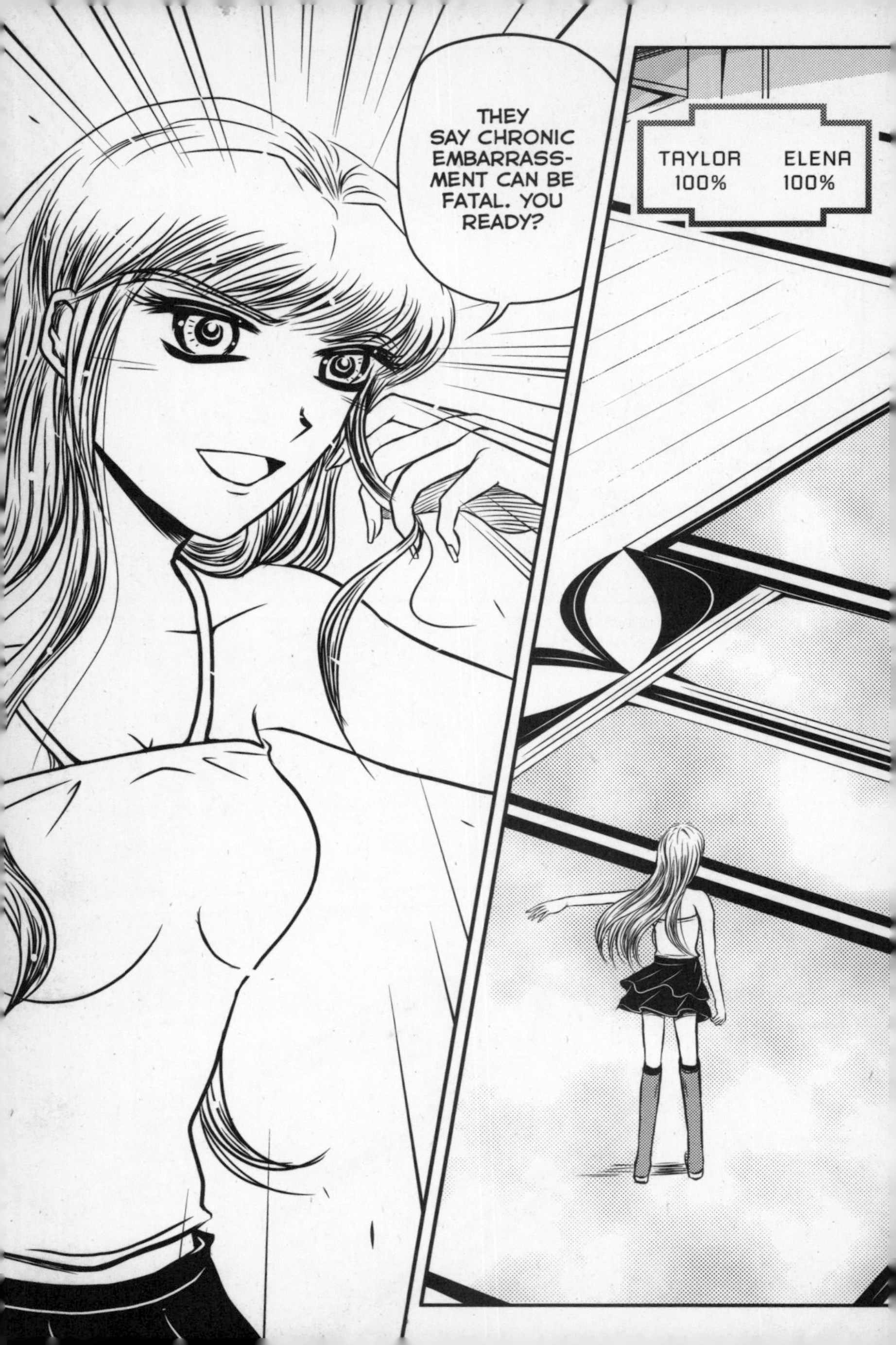
THEY SAY CHRONIC EMBARRASS-MENT CAN BE FATAL. YOU READY?
TAYLOR 100%
ELENA 100%

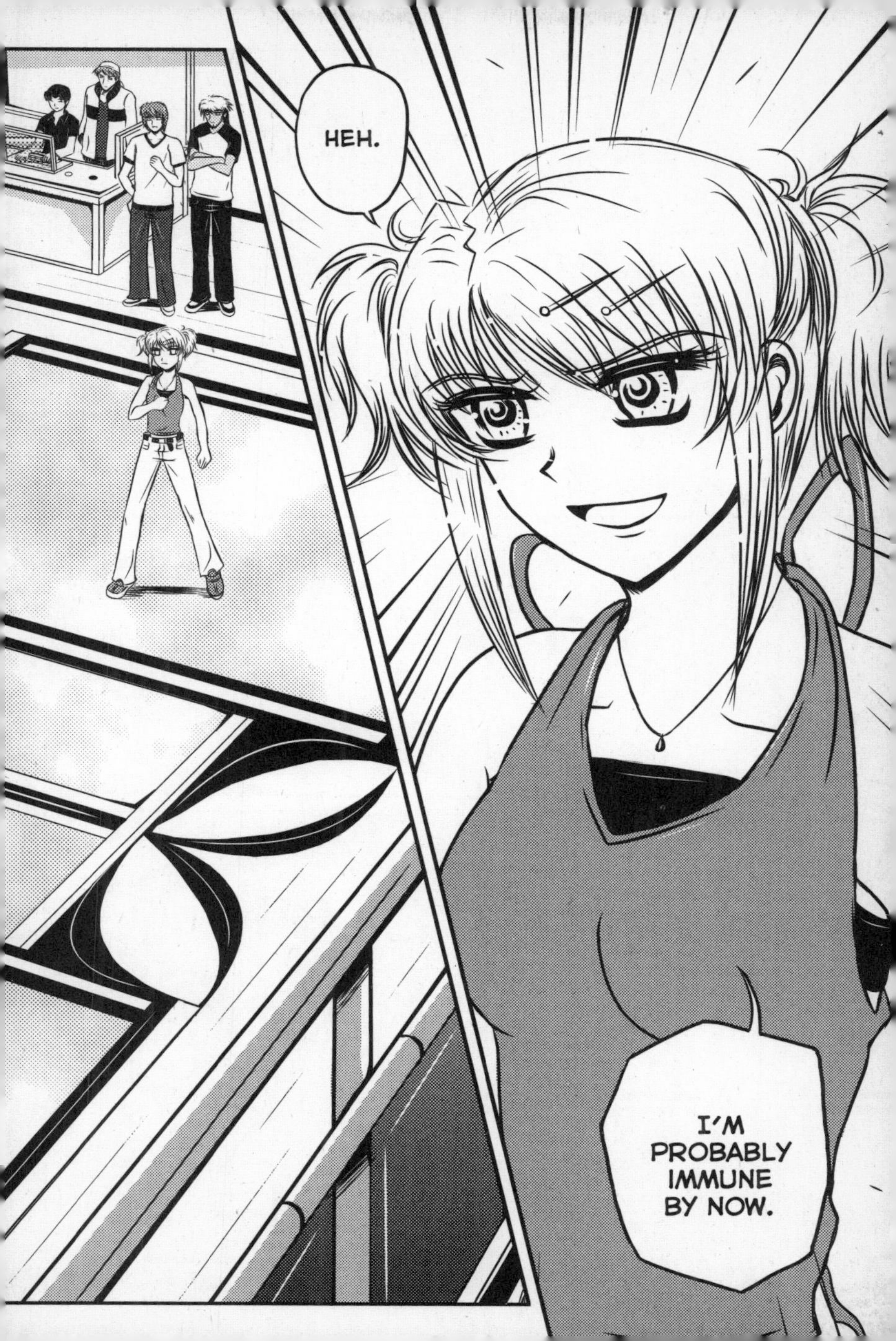
HEH.
I'M PROBABLY IMMUNE BY NOW.

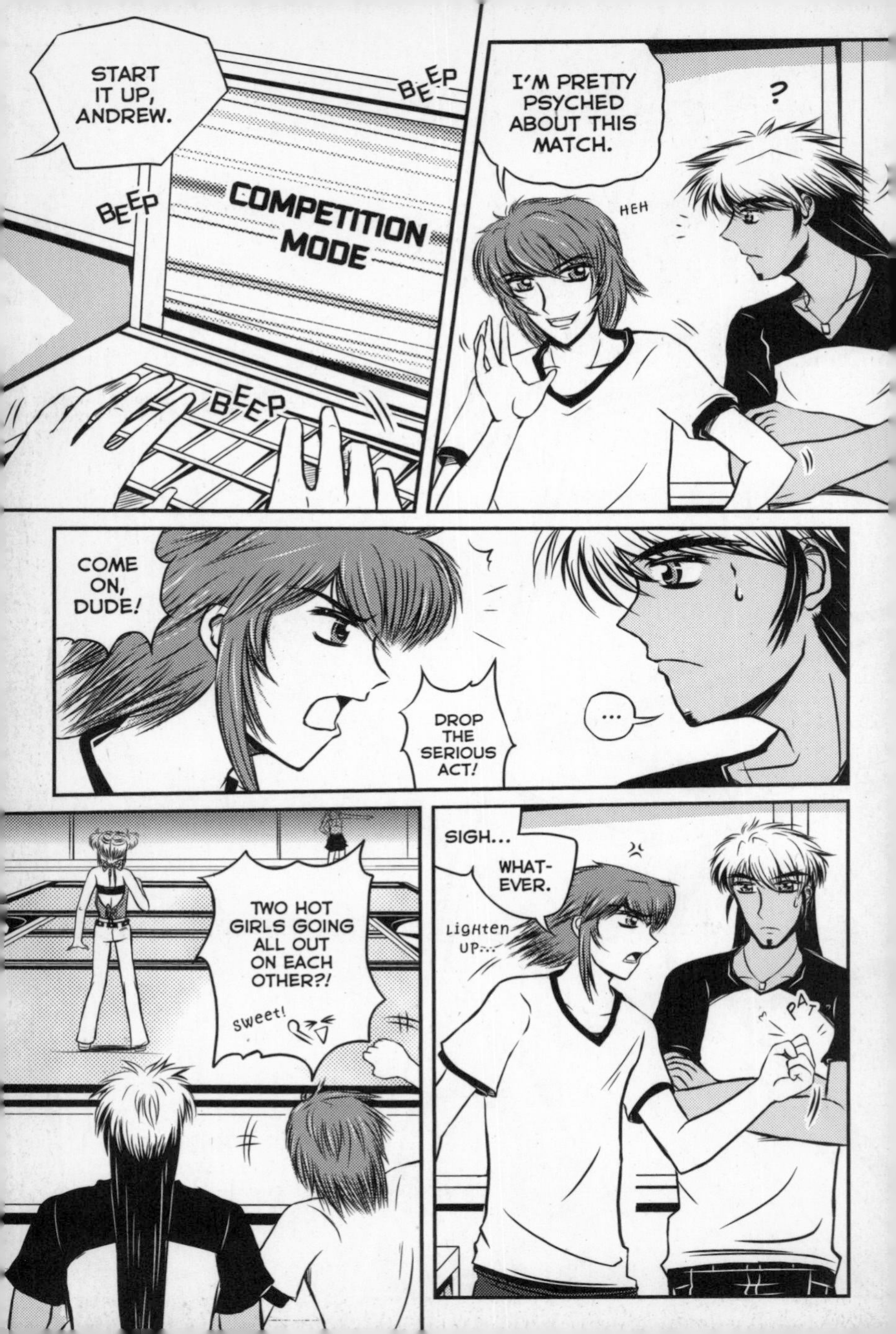
START IT UP, ANDREW.
BEEP
BEEP
COMPETITION MODE
BEEP
I'M PRETTY PSYCHED ABOUT THIS MATCH.
HEH
?
COME ON, DUDE!
DROP THE SERIOUS ACT!
...
TWO HOT GIRLS GOING ALL OUT ON EACH OTHER?!
Sweet!
SIGH...
WHAT-EVER.
LIGHTEN UP...
PAT

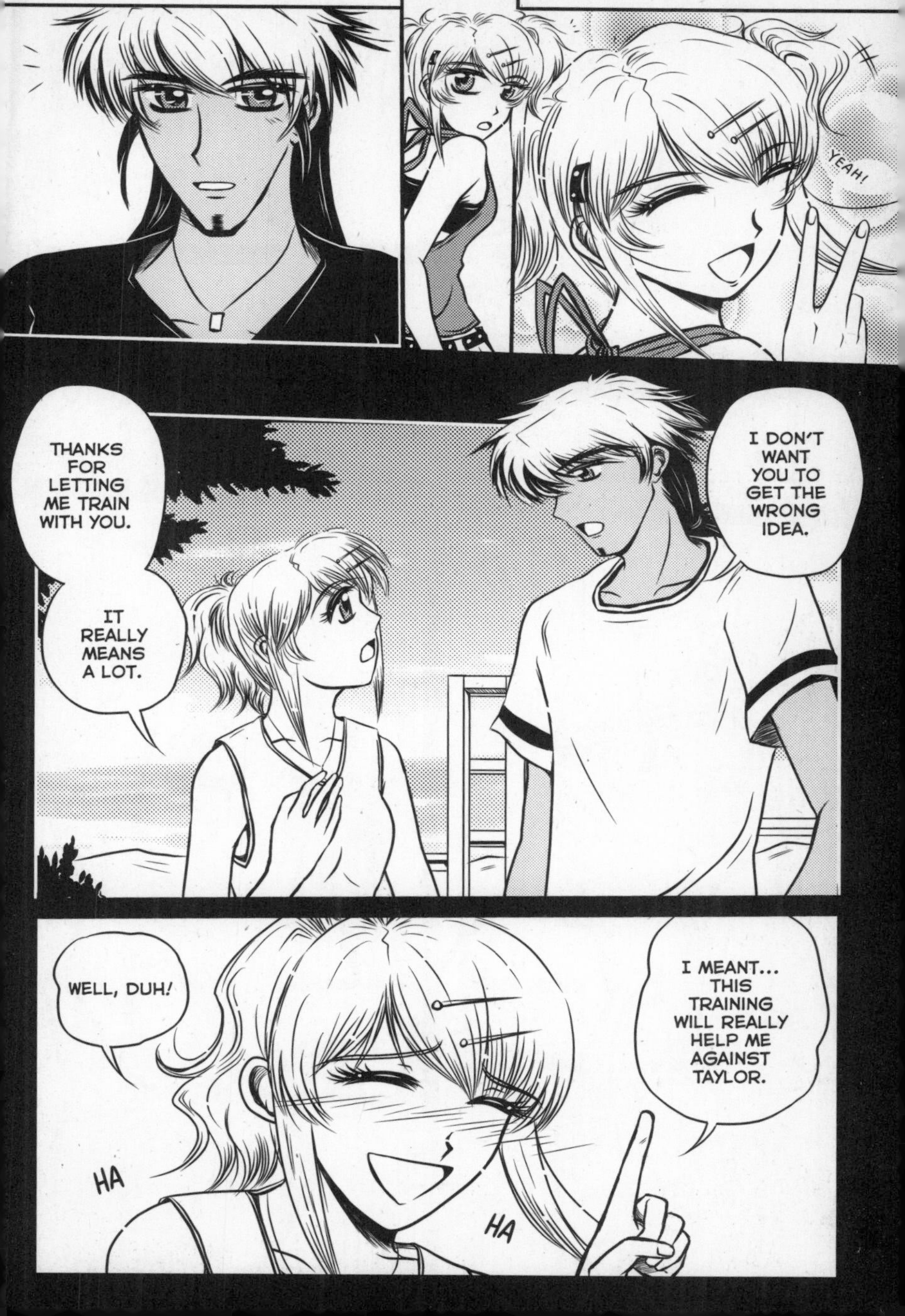
YEAH!
THANKS FOR LETTING ME TRAIN WITH YOU.
IT REALLY MEANS A LOT.
I DON'T WANT YOU TO GET THE WRONG IDEA.
WELL, DUH!
I MEANT... THIS TRAINING WILL REALLY HELP ME AGAINST TAYLOR.
HA
HA

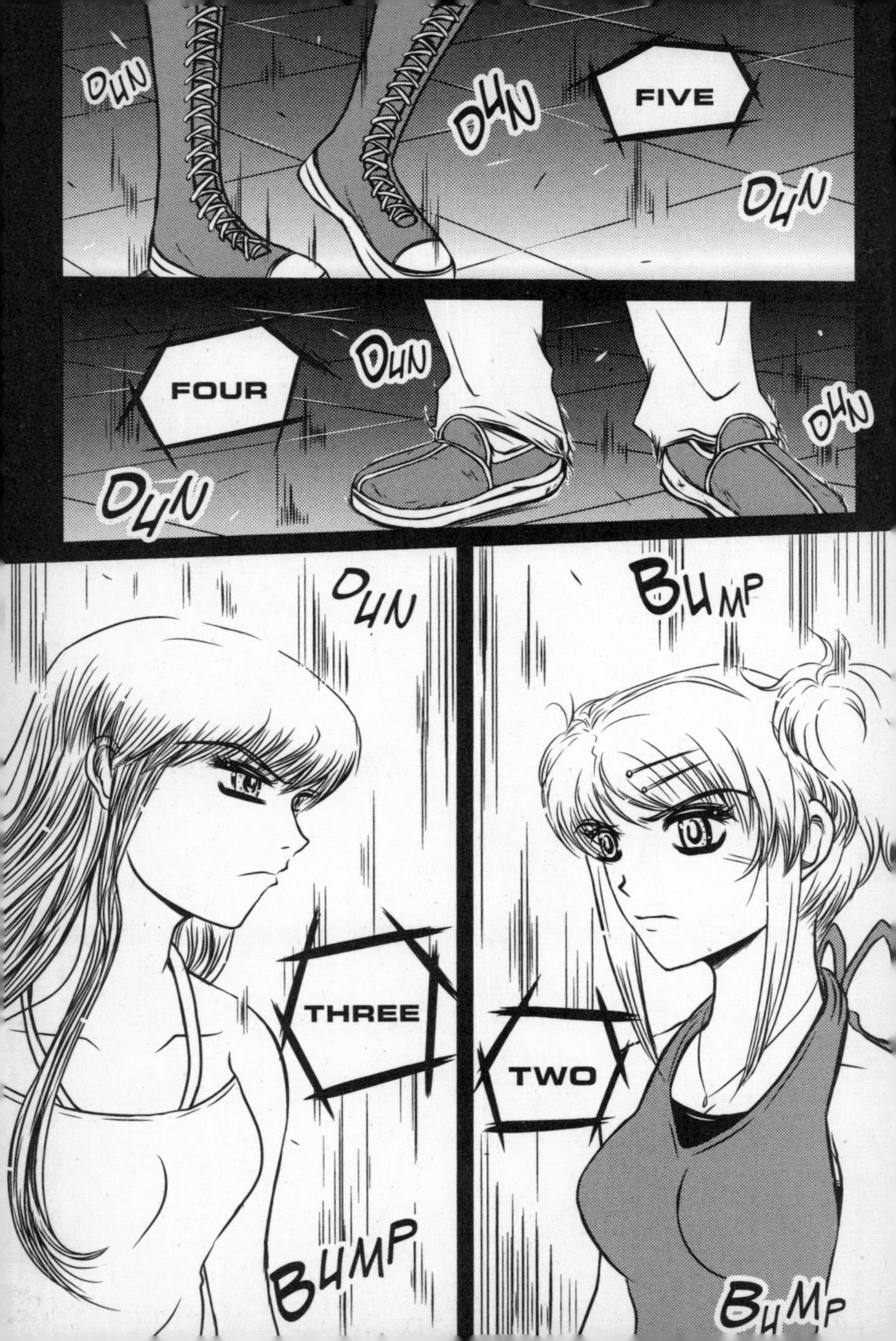

DUN
DUN
FIVE
DUN
FOUR
DUN
DUN
DUN
DUN
THREE
BUMP
BUMP
TWO
BUMP

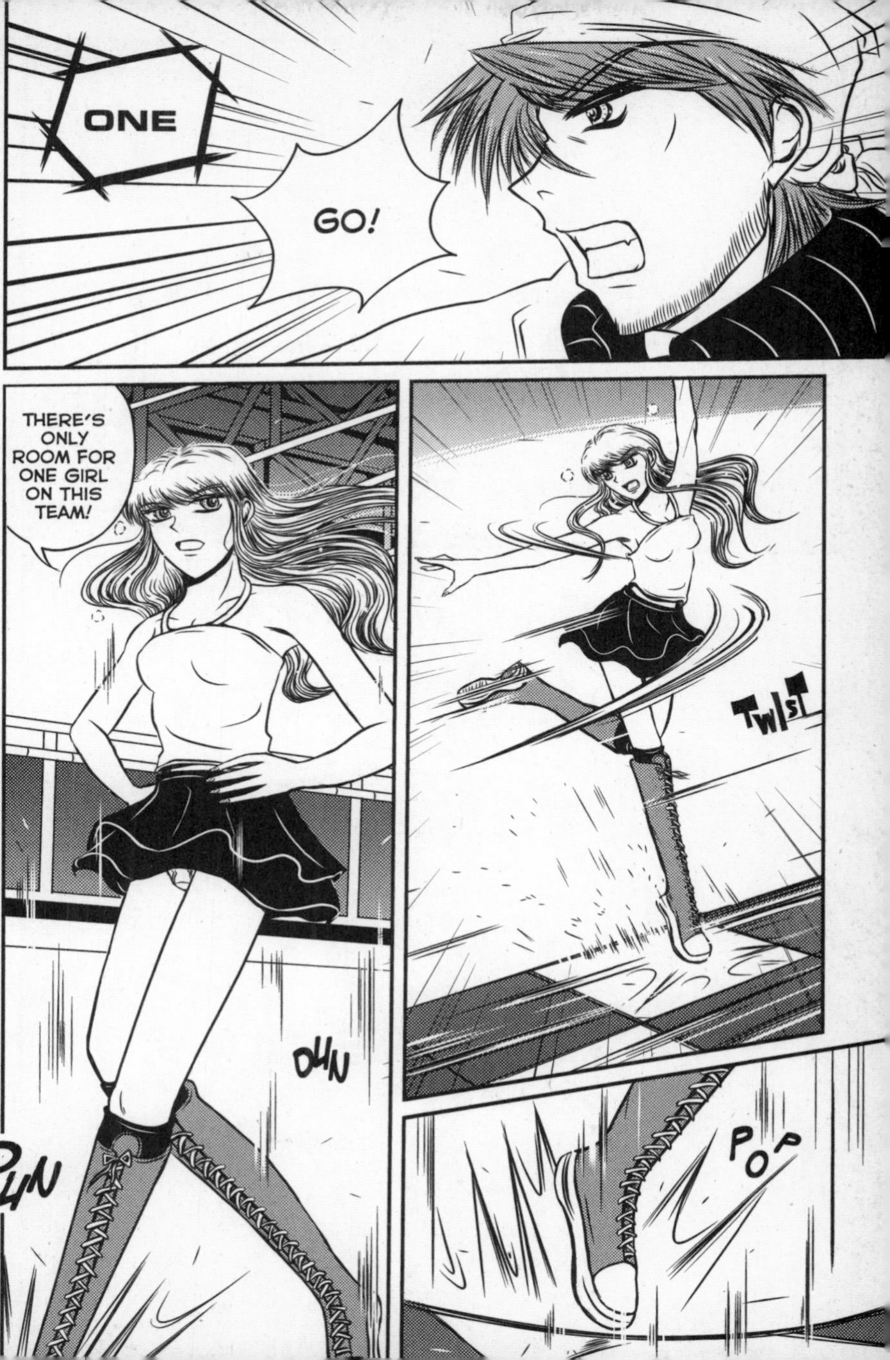
ONE
GO!
THERE'S ONLY ROOM FOR ONE GIRL ON THIS TEAM!
DUN
DUN
TWIST
POP

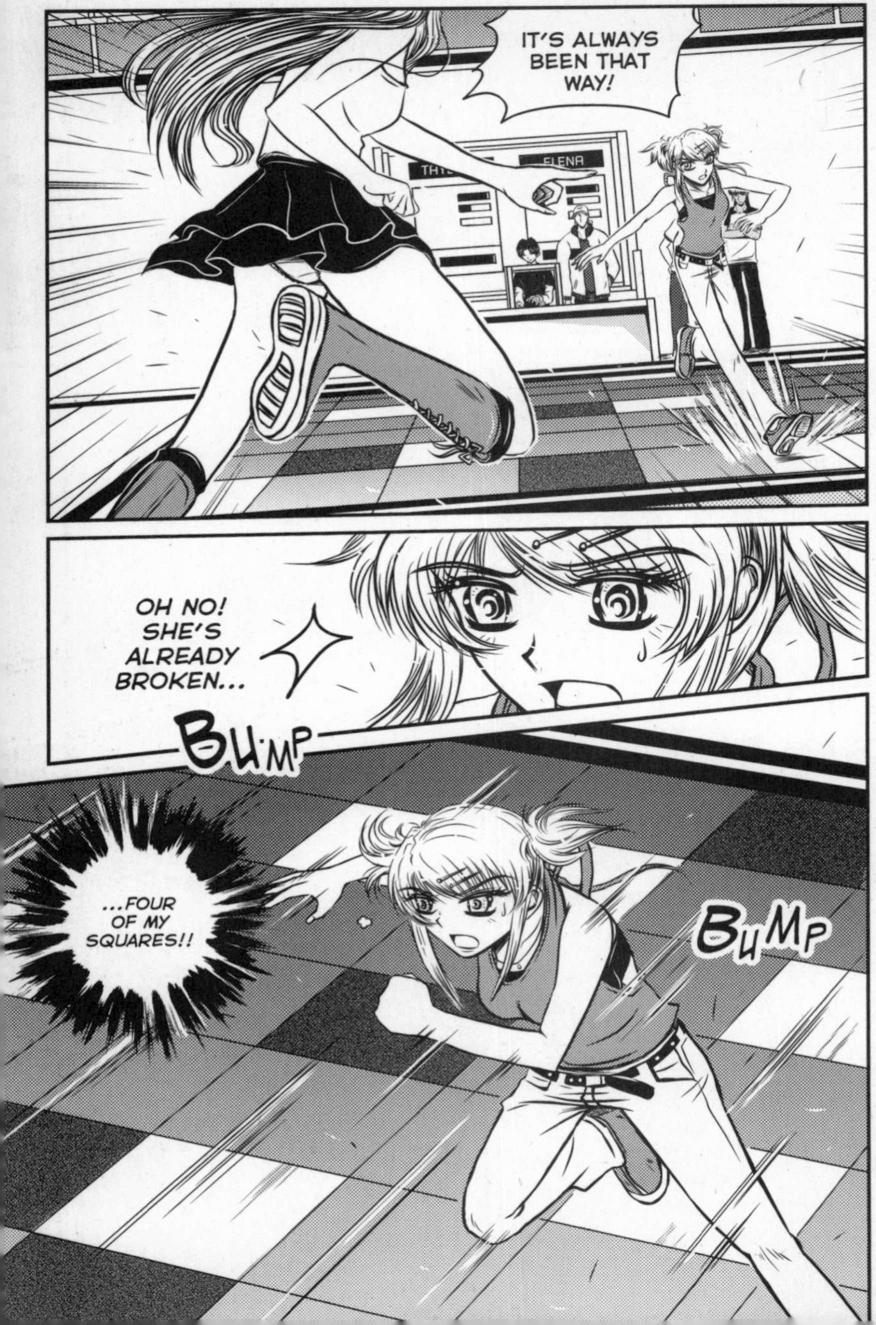
IT'S ALWAYS BEEN THAT WAY!
ELENA
OH NO! SHE'S ALREADY BROKEN...
BUMP
...FOUR OF MY SQUARES!!
BUMP

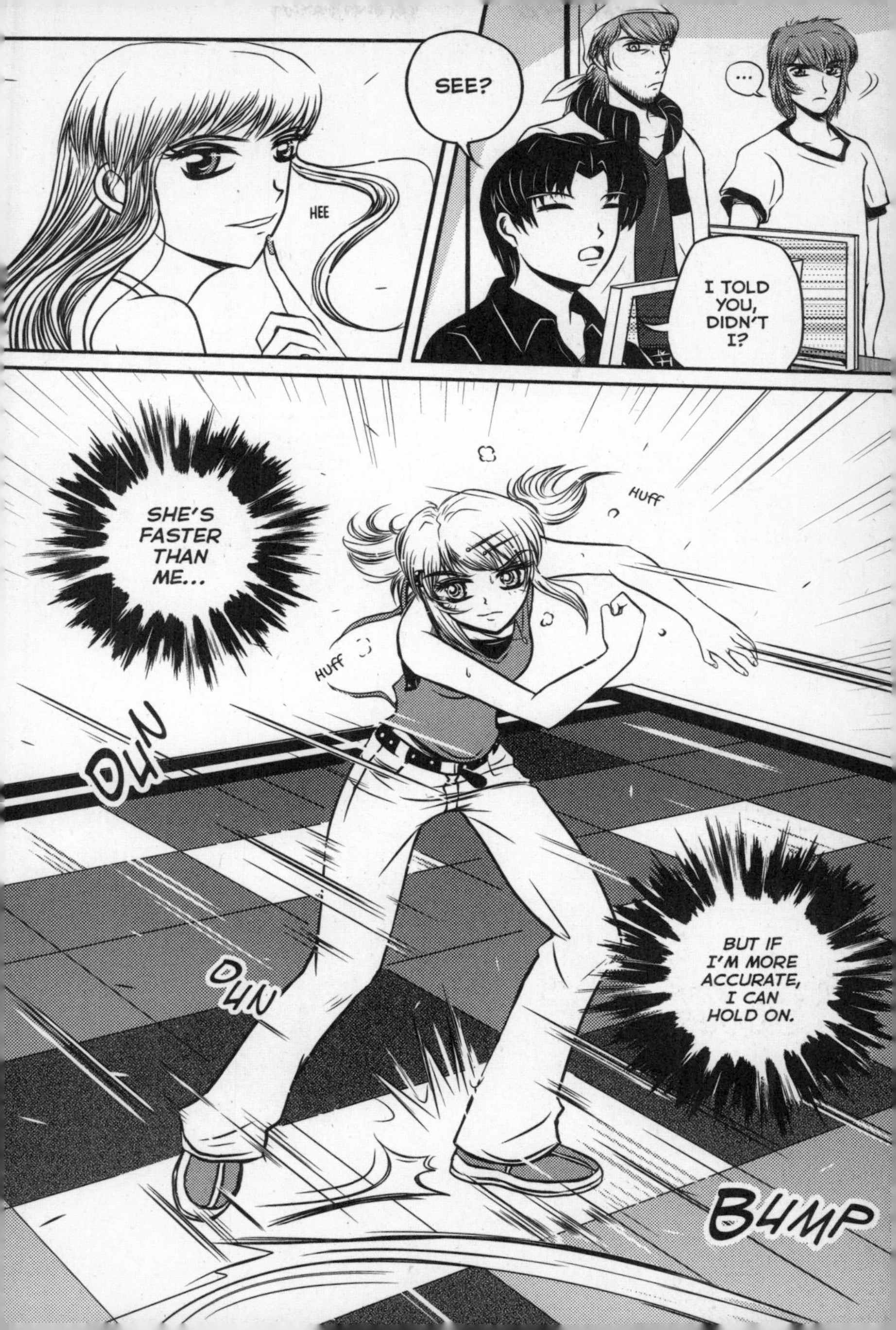
HEE
SEE?
...
I TOLD YOU, DIDN'T I?
SHE'S FASTER THAN ME...
HUFF
HUFF
DUN
DUN
BUT IF I'M MORE ACCURATE, I CAN HOLD ON.
BUMP

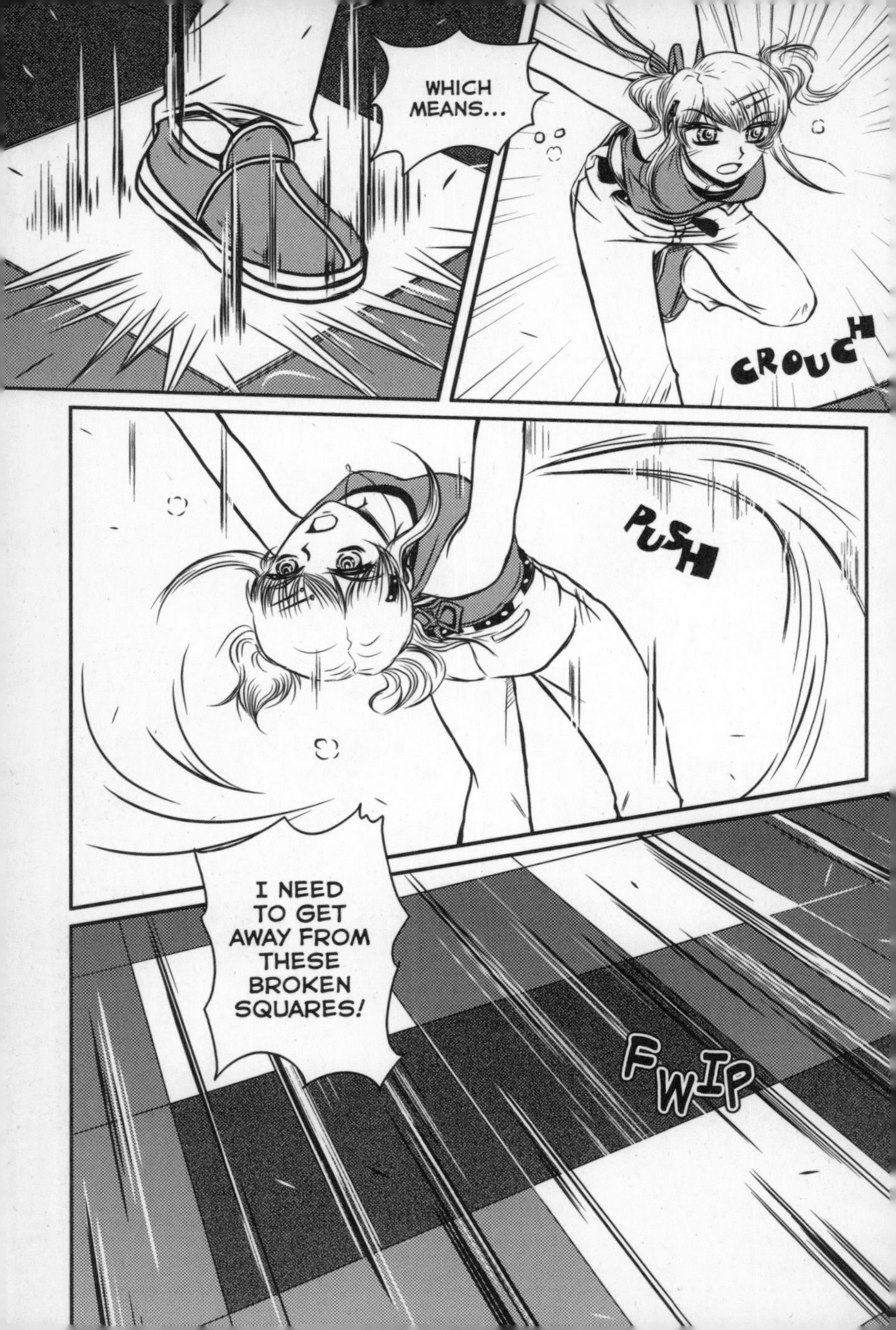
WHICH MEANS...
CROUCH
PUSH
I NEED TO GET AWAY FROM THESE BROKEN SQUARES!
FWIP

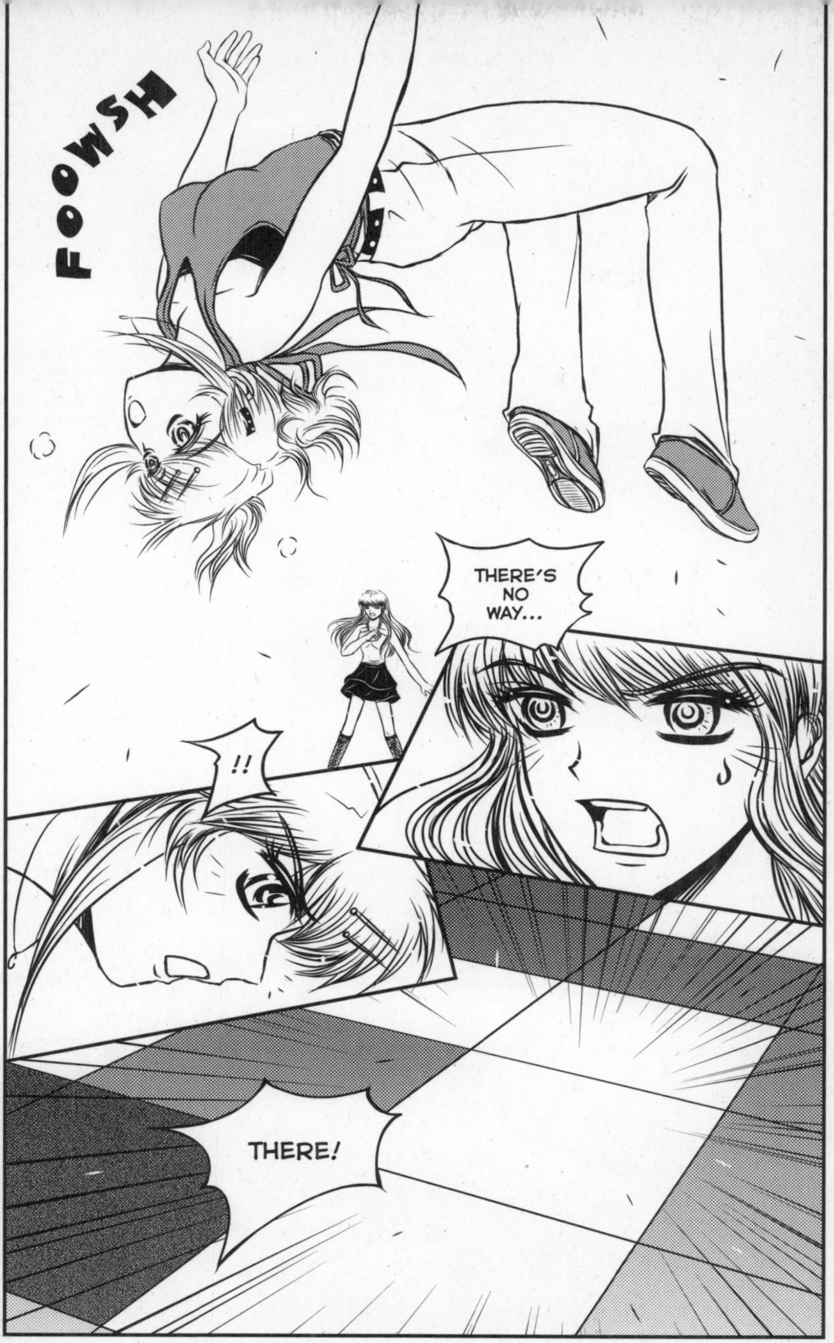
FOWSH
THERE'S NO WAY...
!!
THERE!

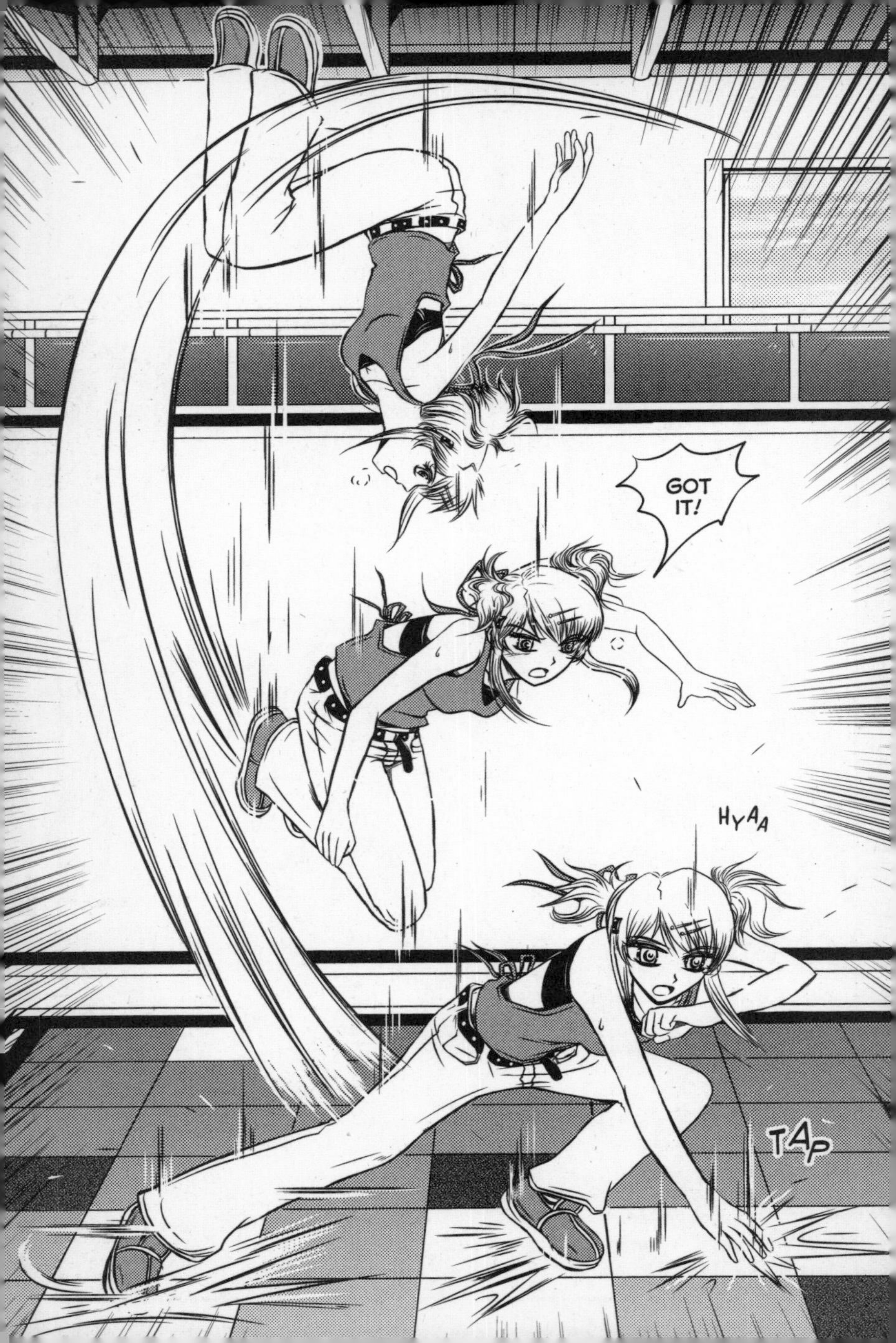
GOT IT!
HYAA
TAP

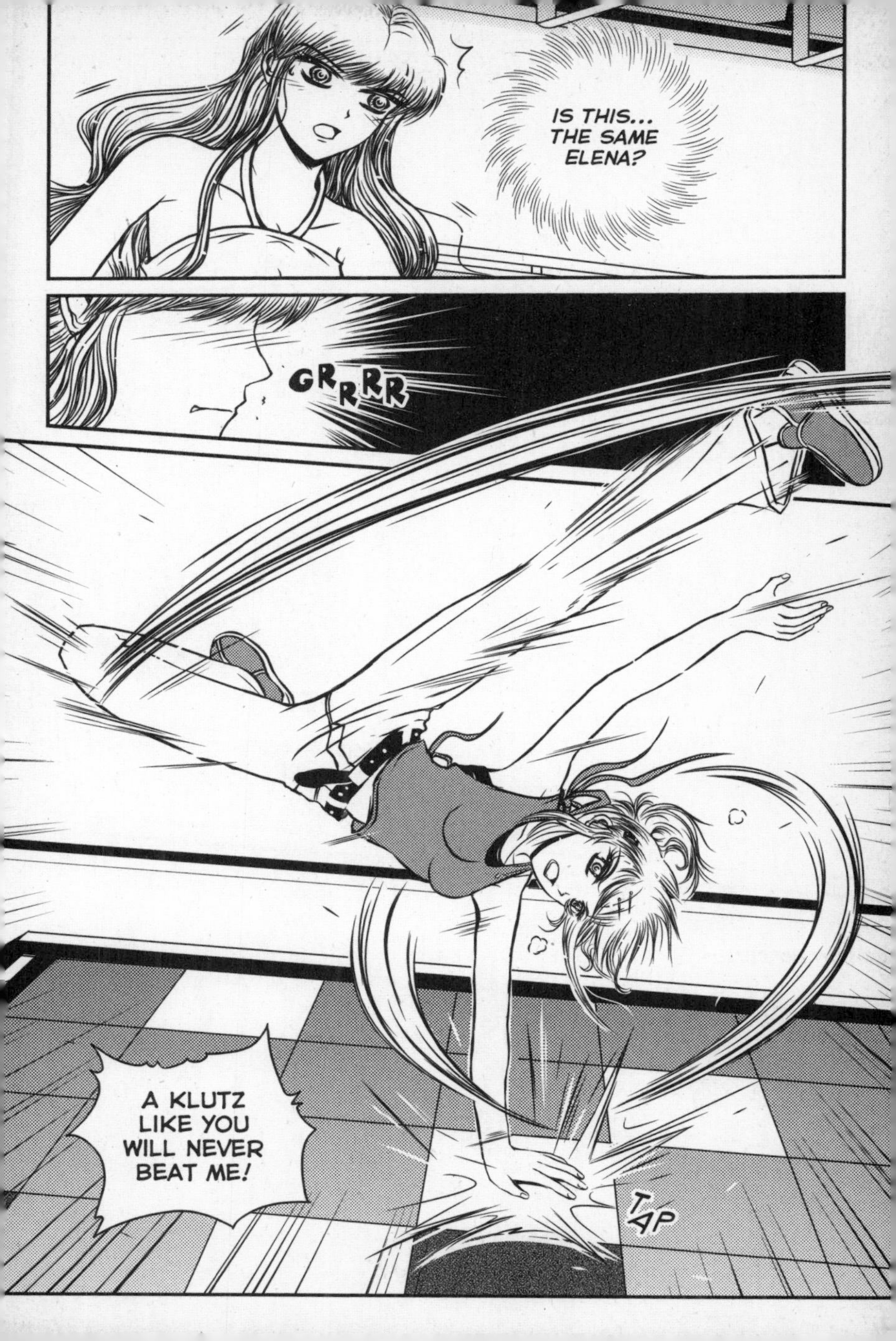
IS THIS... THE SAME ELENA?
GRRRRR
A KLUTZ LIKE YOU WILL NEVER BEAT ME!
TAP

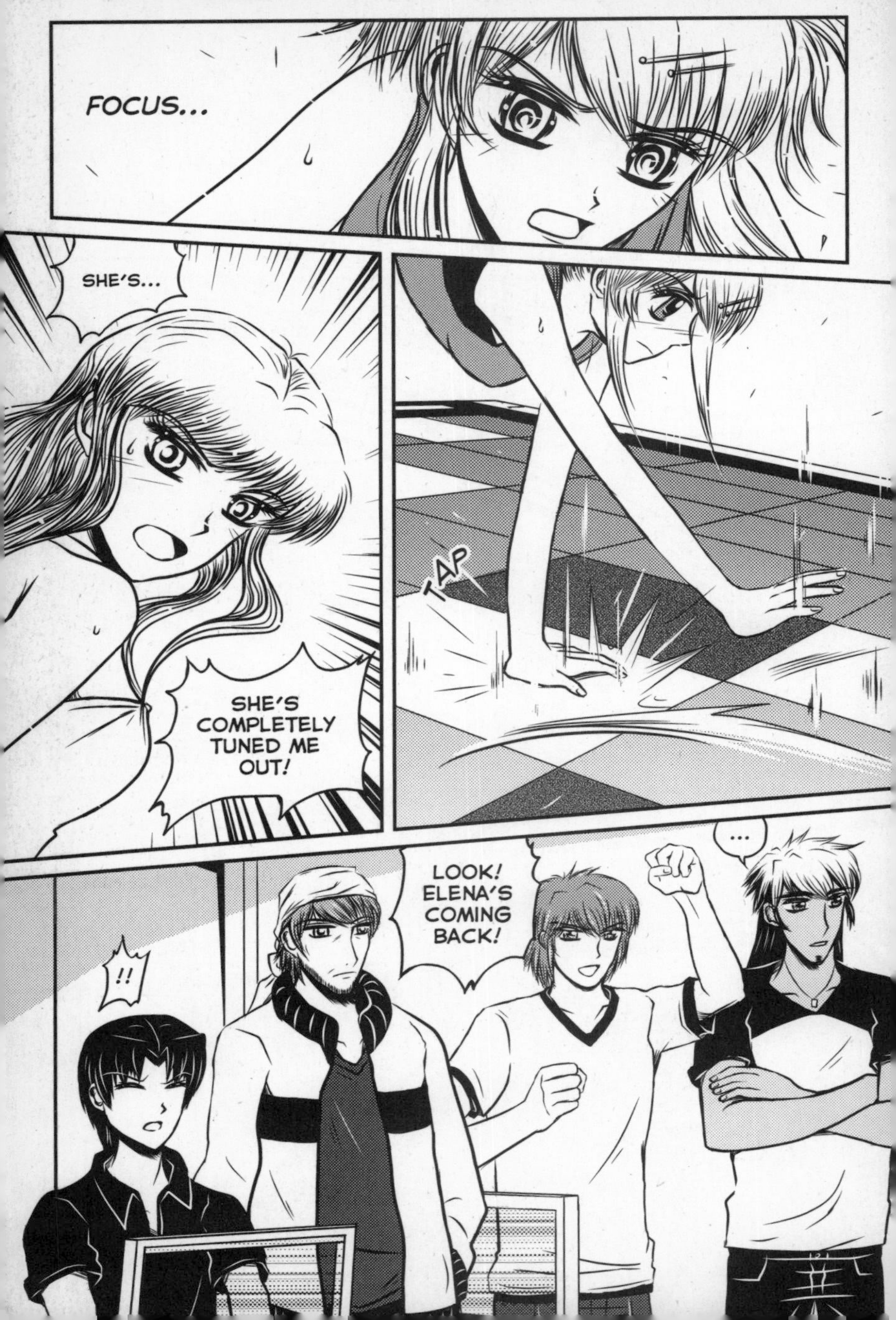
FOCUS...
SHE'S...
SHE'S COMPLETELY TUNED ME OUT!
TAP
!!
LOOK! ELENA'S COMING BACK!
...

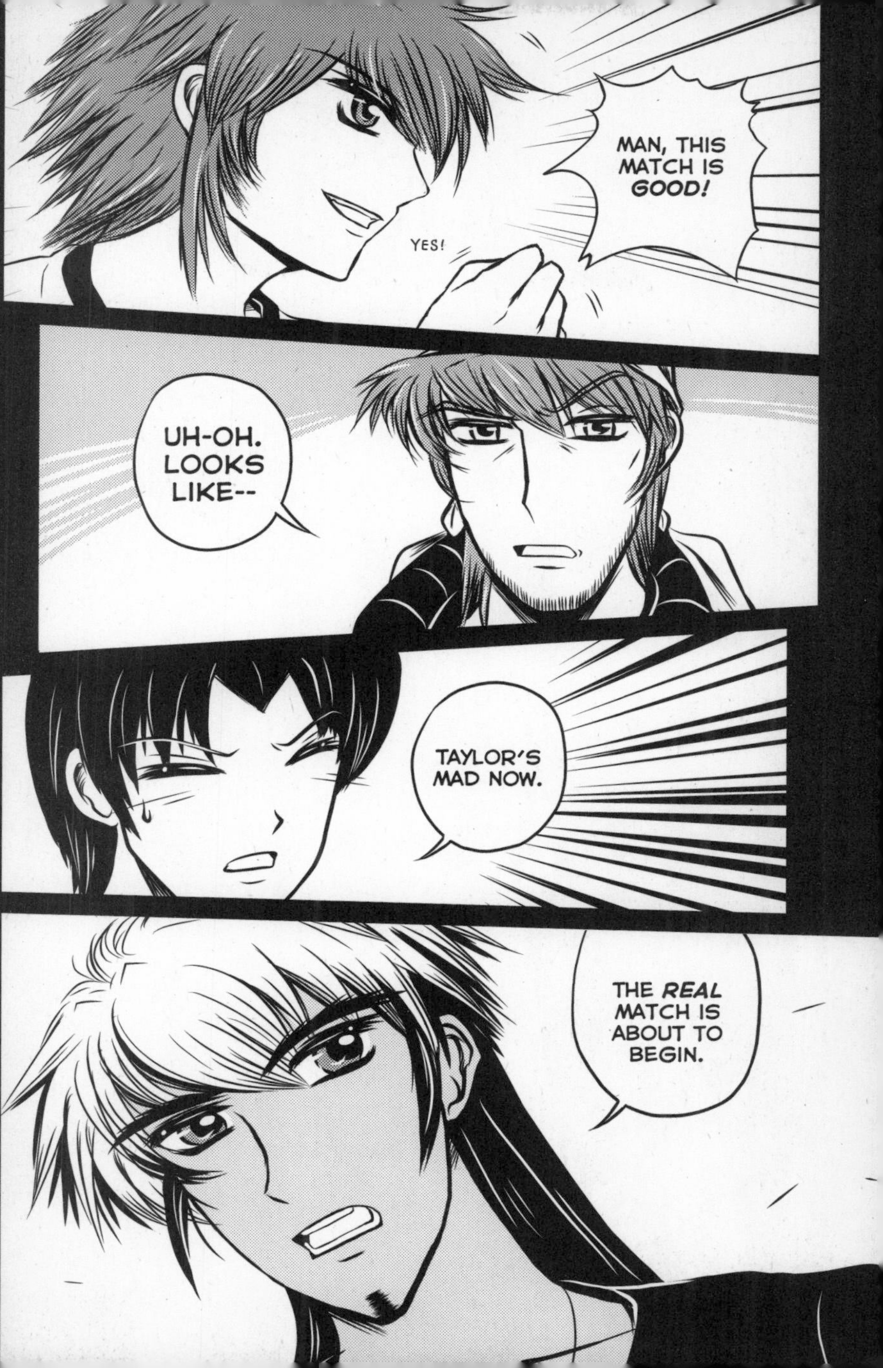
MAN, THIS MATCH IS GOOD!
YES!
UH-OH. LOOKS LIKE--
TAYLOR'S MAD NOW.
THE REAL MATCH IS ABOUT TO BEGIN.

In the next volume

If only joining the team made life simpler for Elena! Her qualification match against Taylor is the chance to prove that she truly belongs. But there's no rest after that when the District Tournament rolls around. Will she be able to help her team against the best Rhysmythers in the Bay Area? No simple answers here, especially when Wahzee's rival and a mysterious girl from his past step onto the court and turn up the beat!

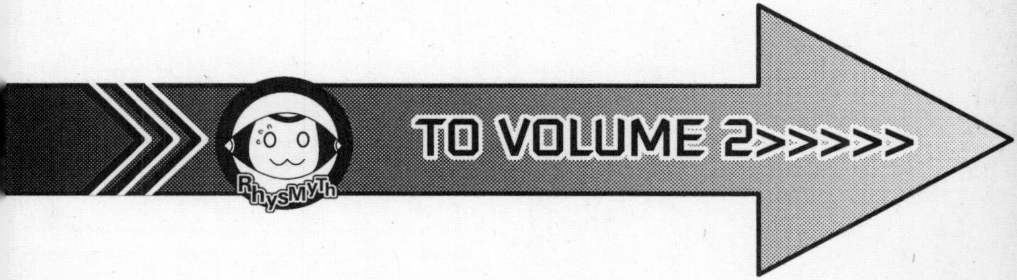
RhysMyTh
TO VOLUME 2>>>>>>

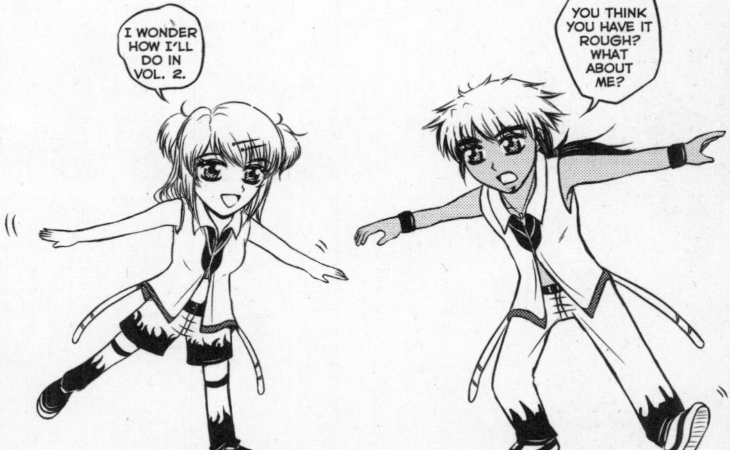
I WONDER HOW I'LL DO IN VOL. 2.
YOU THINK YOU HAVE IT ROUGH? WHAT ABOUT ME?

RHYSMYTH

BONUS LEVEL

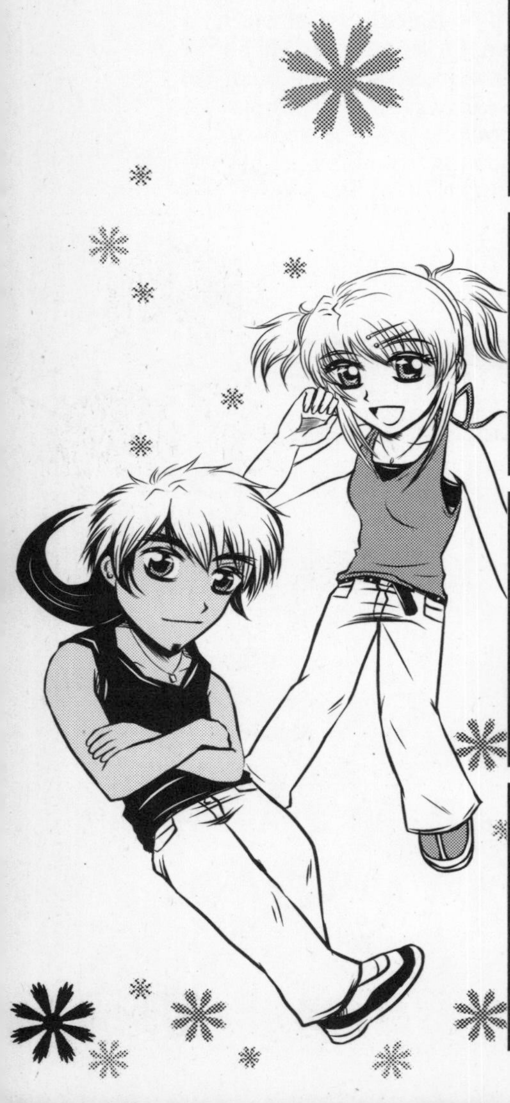

COACHING RUMORS

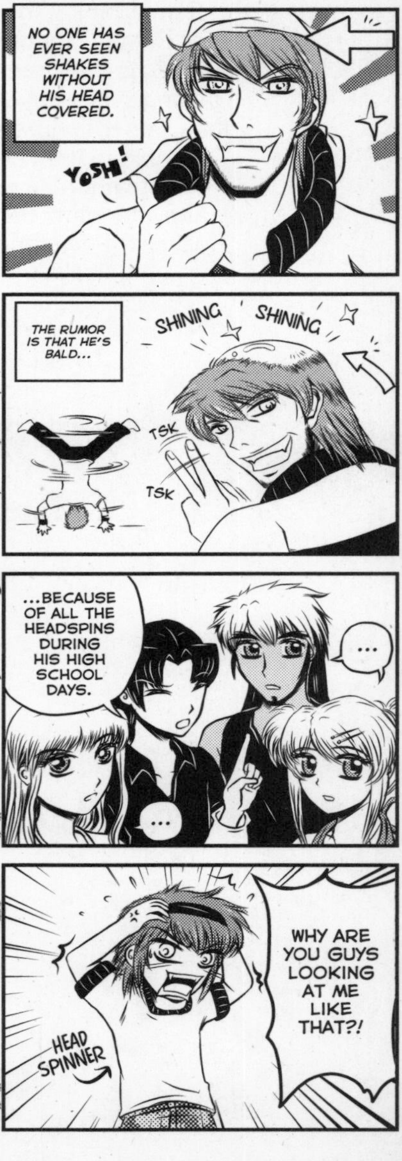
NO ONE HAS EVER SEEN SHAKES WITHOUT HIS HEAD COVERED.
YOSHI!
THE RUMOR IS THAT HE'S BALD...
SHINING
SHINING
TSK
TSK
...BECAUSE OF ALL THE HEADSPINS DURING HIS HIGH SCHOOL DAYS.
...
...
WHY ARE YOU GUYS LOOKING AT ME LIKE THAT?!
HEAD SPINNER

DIOCEL'S DEPRESSION

DIOCEL IS UPSET BECAUSE OF THE RUMOR.
BUT THE TEAM HAS TRIED TO CHEER HIM UP.
HOW TO PREVENT HAIR LOSS
PREVEN-TION IS THE KEY!
GET A WIG!
HEE
A HAIR GROWTH SPRAY SHOULD DO IT!
HUMM...
OR YOU CAN BE FASHIONABLE LIKE SHAKES!
SO MUCH TO DO...
HA
HA
TESTING... TESTING...
SPRAY
SPRAY

MAGNETIC HEAD

BONK
WHY IS MY HEAD A TARGET?
THIS NEEDS AN EXPLANATION!
WHEN IN DOUBT, PAIN = FUNNY.
Camera this way
TSK
TSK
Anthony, the writer.
Lincy, the artist.
BECAUSE YOUR PONYTAILS ARE MADE OF TWO GIANT MAGNETS THAT ATTRACT ROUND OBJECTS.
I'm a genius!
HUH?
GRRRR

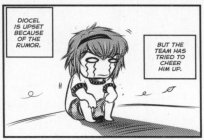

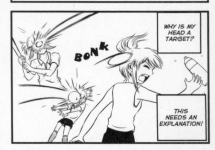

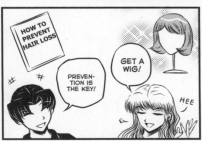

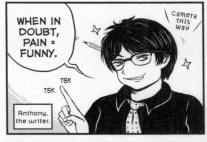

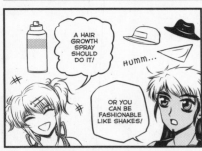

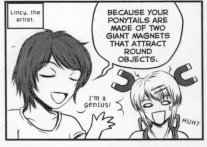

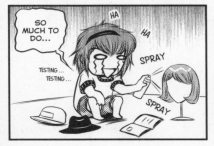

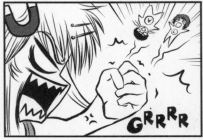

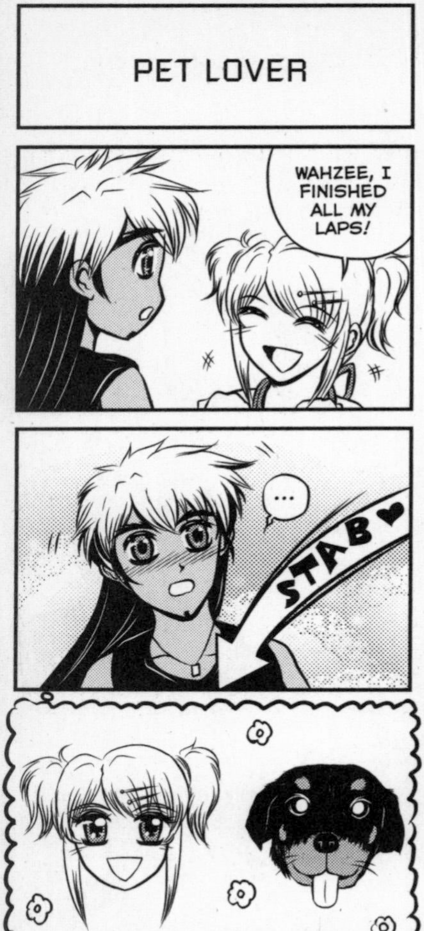
PET LOVER
WAHZEE, I FINISHED ALL MY LAPS!
...
STAB
ELENA = ZEE
GOOD GIRL, ELENA!
PAT PAT
HE'S... NOT BEHAVING HIMSELF.
HA HA
WAHZEE DOESN'T KNOW HOW TO TREAT THE LADIES...

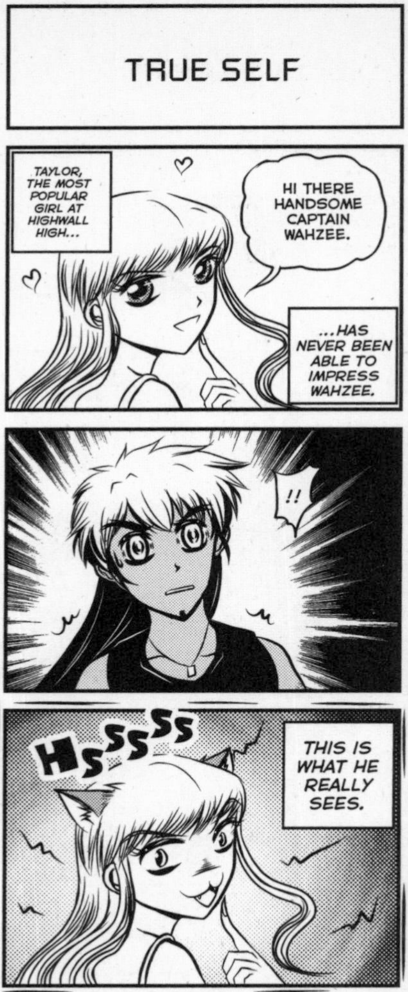
TRUE SELF
TAYLOR, THE MOST POPULAR GIRL AT HIGHWALL HIGH...
HI THERE HANDSOME CAPTAIN WAHZEE.
...HAS NEVER BEEN ABLE TO IMPRESS WAHZEE.
!!
HSSSSS
THIS IS WHAT HE REALLY SEES.
HERE, KITTY KITTY! CATCH THE MOUSE!
I'M NOT A CAT!!
WAHZEE HAS A STRONG ANIMALISTIC SENSE.

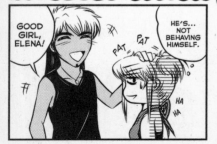

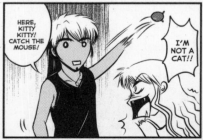

EYESIGHT

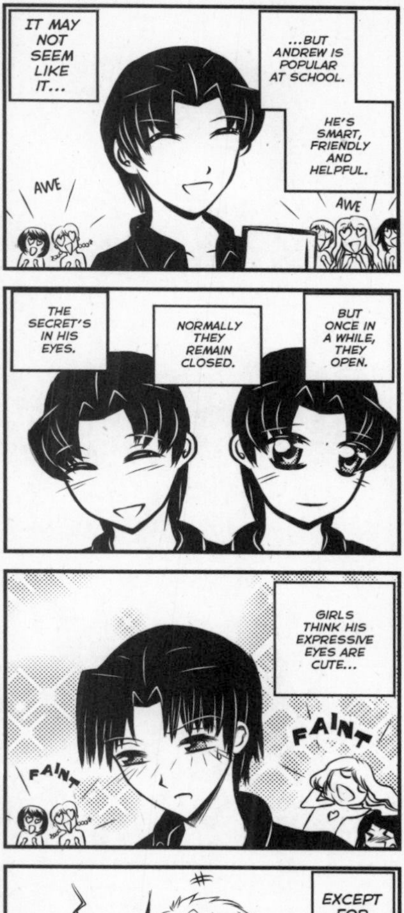
IT MAY NOT SEEM LIKE IT...
...BUT ANDREW IS POPULAR AT SCHOOL.
HE'S SMART, FRIENDLY AND HELPFUL.
AWE
AWE
THE SECRET'S IN HIS EYES.
NORMALLY THEY REMAIN CLOSED.
BUT ONCE IN A WHILE, THEY OPEN.
GIRLS THINK HIS EXPRESSIVE EYES ARE CUTE...
FAINT
FAINT
EXCEPT FOR ELENA.
SCARY.

BONUS

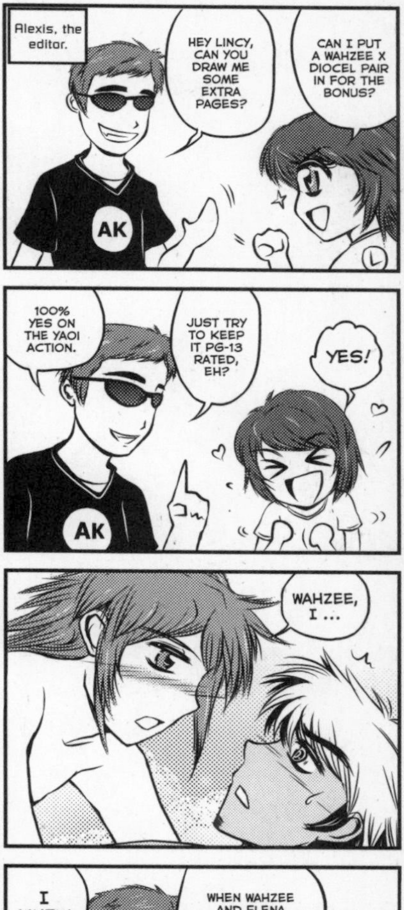
Alexis, the editor.
HEY LINCY, CAN YOU DRAW ME SOME EXTRA PAGES?
CAN I PUT A WAHZEE X DIOCEL PAIR IN FOR THE BONUS?
AK
100% YES ON THE YAOI ACTION.
JUST TRY TO KEEP IT PG-13 RATED, EH?
YES!
AK
WAHZEE, I ...
I KNEW IT!
WHEN WAHZEE AND ELENA ARE FRIENDLY, DIOCEL IS JEALOUS OF ELENA, NOT OF WAHZEE!
YES!

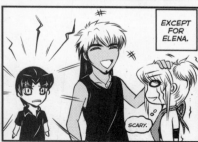

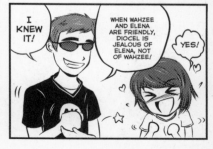

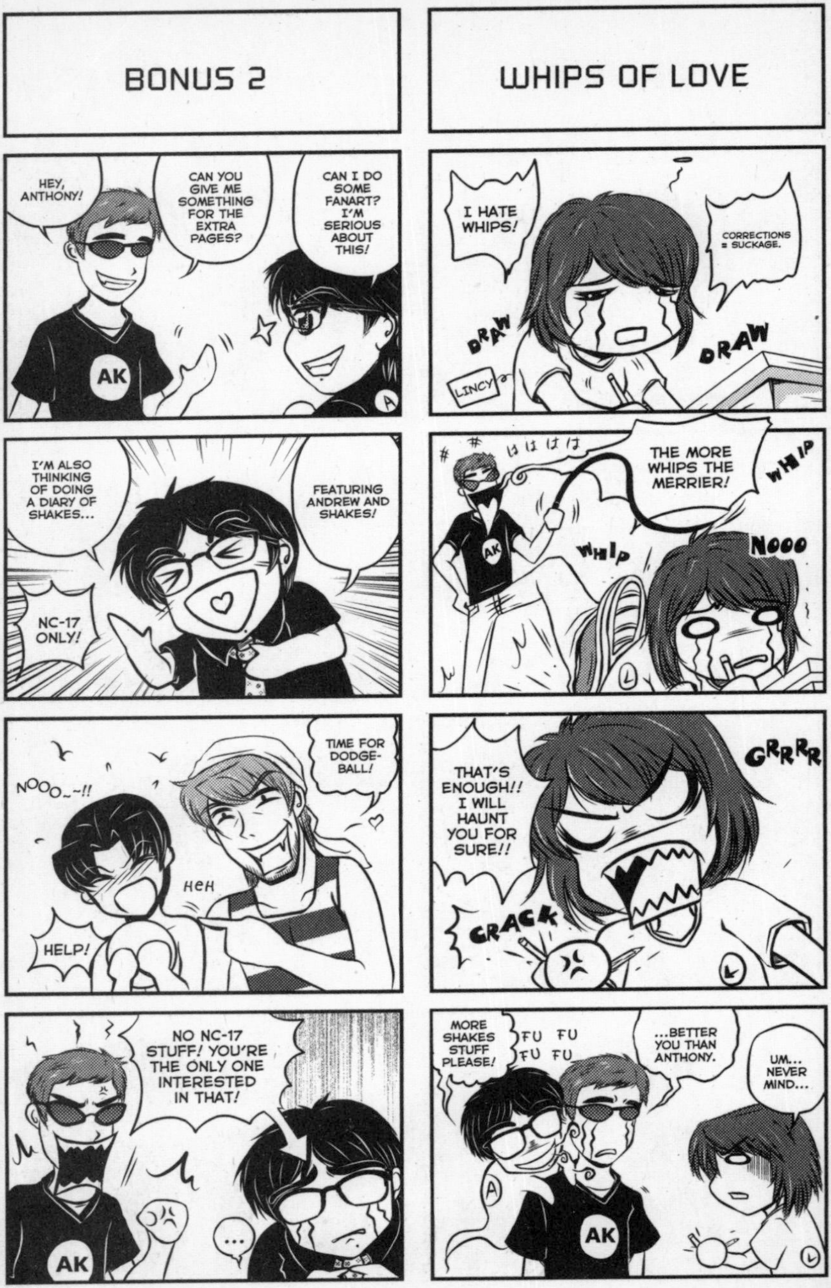
BONUS 2
HEY, ANTHONY!
CAN YOU GIVE ME SOMETHING FOR THE EXTRA PAGES?
CAN I DO SOME FANART? I'M SERIOUS ABOUT THIS!
I'M ALSO THINKING OF DOING A DIARY OF SHAKES...
FEATURING ANDREW AND SHAKES!
NC-17 ONLY!
NOOO~~!!
TIME FOR DODGE-BALL!
HEH
HELP!
NO NC-17 STUFF! YOU'RE THE ONLY ONE INTERESTED IN THAT!
...
WHIPS OF LOVE
I HATE WHIPS!
CORRECTIONS = SUCKAGE.
DRAW
DRAW
LINCY
はははは
THE MORE WHIPS THE MERRIER!
WHIP
WHIP
NOOO
THAT'S ENOUGH!! I WILL HAUNT YOU FOR SURE!!
GRRRR
CRACK
MORE SHAKES STUFF PLEASE!
FU FU FU FU
...BETTER YOU THAN ANTHONY.
UM... NEVER MIND...

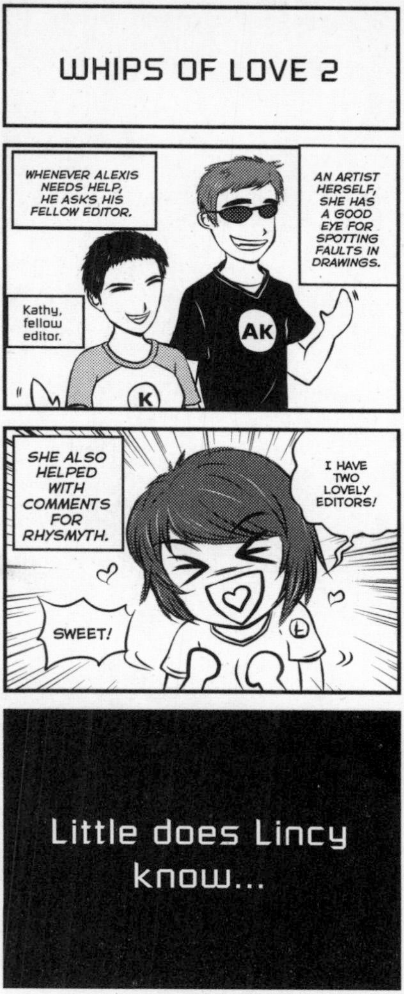
WHIPS OF LOVE 2
WHENEVER ALEXIS NEEDS HELP, HE ASKS HIS FELLOW EDITOR.
AN ARTIST HERSELF, SHE HAS A GOOD EYE FOR SPOTTING FAULTS IN DRAWINGS.
Kathy, fellow editor.
SHE ALSO HELPED WITH COMMENTS FOR RHYSMYTH.
I HAVE TWO LOVELY EDITORS!
SWEET!
Little does Lincy know...
ケケケケ
は、は、は、は
THEY BOTH LOVE TO WHIP.
NOOOO

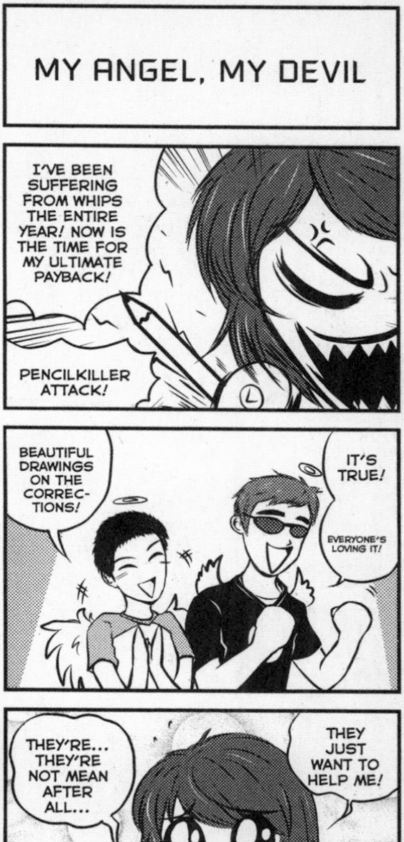
MY ANGEL, MY DEVIL
I'VE BEEN SUFFERING FROM WHIPS THE ENTIRE YEAR! NOW IS THE TIME FOR MY ULTIMATE PAYBACK!
PENCILKILLER ATTACK!
BEAUTIFUL DRAWINGS ON THE CORRECTIONS!
IT'S TRUE!
EVERYONE'S LOVING IT!
THEY'RE... THEY'RE NOT MEAN AFTER ALL...
THEY JUST WANT TO HELP ME!
THEY'RE ANGELS!!
BUT IN PANEL 1, ELENA LOOKS LIKE--
--SHE GOT HER THUMB SMASHED IN A CAR DOOR A THOUSAND TIMES.
NO, THEY'RE NOT ANGELS...

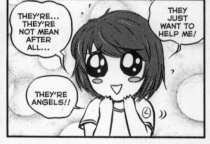

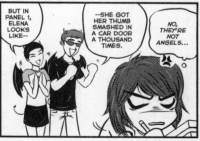

RHYSMYTH TRAINING SESSION

GEEZ IT STARTS AGAIN ...

IF YOU CAN LAST FOR MORE THAN *FOUR* TURNS, I'LL DO THE COOKING FOR A WEEK!

HEH

MAD

WAHZEE, YOU'RE SO MEAN SOMETIMES, YOU KNOW THAT?

I DON'T WANNA EAT ANYTHING YOU COOK ...

VS	
ELENA	WAHZEE
100%	100%
SP	SP

TEMPO 120

I'LL BE *MASTER WAHZEE'S* PROGRAMMER.

ALL RIGHT TONY. LET'S HAVE AT IT.

RUMBLE *RHYSMYTH* RUMBLE!

IN THE KE OF E

SKOOT

SCRATCH

SHAKES, ARE YOU *SURE* ABOUT *KATEY*?

OK!

IMPRISONED, MY WORDS BREAK THROUGH LIKE LIGHT THROUGH A *PRISM*

FWOOSH

MY BLOOD BOILS HOT CUZ I'M A MAN ON A *MISSION*

ZOOMMM

IN A *POSITION* TO TAKE YOU *DOWN* I'M NOT GONNA MESS *AROUND*

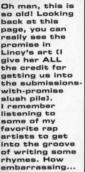

Oh man, this is so old! Looking back at this page, you can really see the promise in Lincy's art (I give her ALL the credit for getting us into the submissions-with-promise slush pile). I remember listening to some of my favorite rap artists to get into the groove of writing some rhymes. How embarrassing...

ANTHONY

ALEXIS

Anthony and Lincy's submission was sitting in the "stuff with promise" pile when I first took a look at it. Of all the submissions at the time, it was the only one that really grabbed me. I thought the concept of a dancing sport had real potential and could make for a really cool manga. It's interesting to look back on this and see all the improvements. Anthony really worked hard to improve the story, but as you can see, the characters mostly stayed the same. We may have to have a cat-hat wearing character in book two.

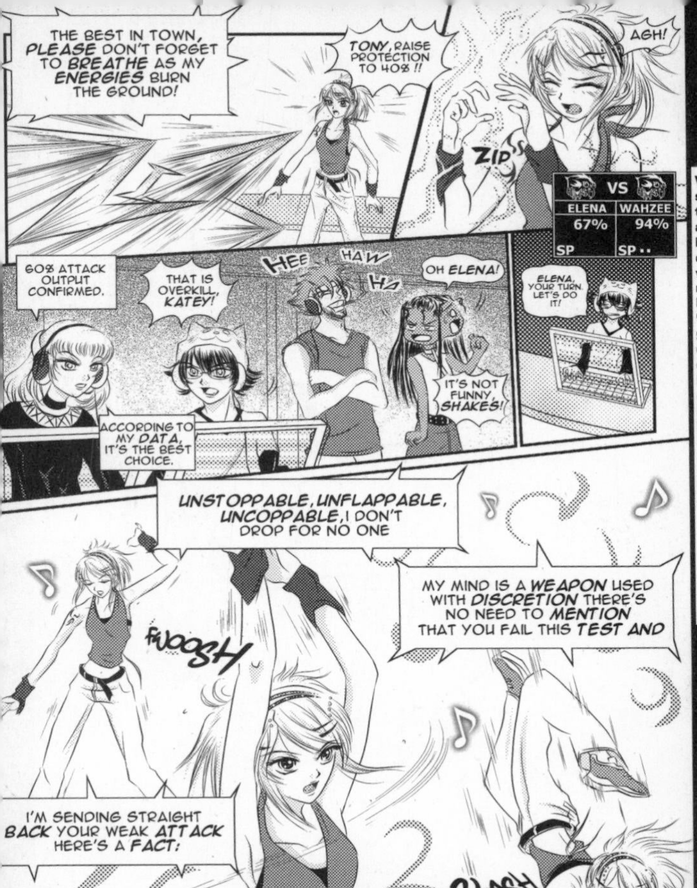
THE BEST IN TOWN, PLEASE DON'T FORGET TO BREATHE AS MY ENERGIES BURN THE GROUND!
TONY, RAISE PROTECTION TO 40% !!
AGH!
ZIP
VS
ELENA
WAHZEE
67%
94%
SP
SP ..
60% ATTACK OUTPUT CONFIRMED.
THAT IS OVERKILL, KATEY!
HEE HAW HA
OH ELENA!
IT'S NOT FUNNY, SHAKES!
ACCORDING TO MY DATA, IT'S THE BEST CHOICE.
ELENA, YOUR TURN. LET'S DO IT!
UNSTOPPABLE, UNFLAPPABLE, UNCOPPABLE, I DON'T DROP FOR NO ONE
FWOOSH
MY MIND IS A WEAPON USED WITH DISCRETION THERE'S NO NEED TO MENTION THAT YOU FAIL THIS TEST AND
I'M SENDING STRAIGHT BACK YOUR WEAK ATTACK HERE'S A FACT:
SLASH
YOU NEED TO LEARN HOW TO RAP!

When we first started working together, Lincy and I spent hours chatting online coming up with different manga ideas. Eventually a "rap battle game" became our prize concept-- Rhysmyth originally meant Rhyme Smyth. Fortunately, Alexis did a great editorial job guiding the story into something much more manageable for Lincy and I to do. Which meant no more pretentious raps!

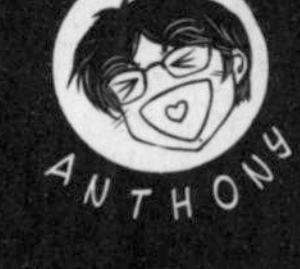
ANTHONY

You'll notice some of the big story changes we made by looking at this page. The original Rhysmyth game had characters rapping and getting attacked by various elements when they did poorly. I suggested Anthony try to make the sport more realistic. This meant that we had to come up with rules for the sport that actually made sense, and that was one of the harder tasks in the creation of the book. Oh, and Anthony was very sad that his "dope" rap lyrics were taken out of the story. Sorry, Anthony!

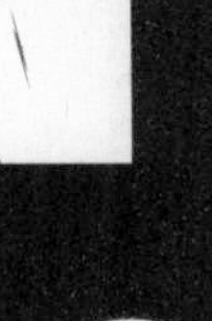
ALEXIS

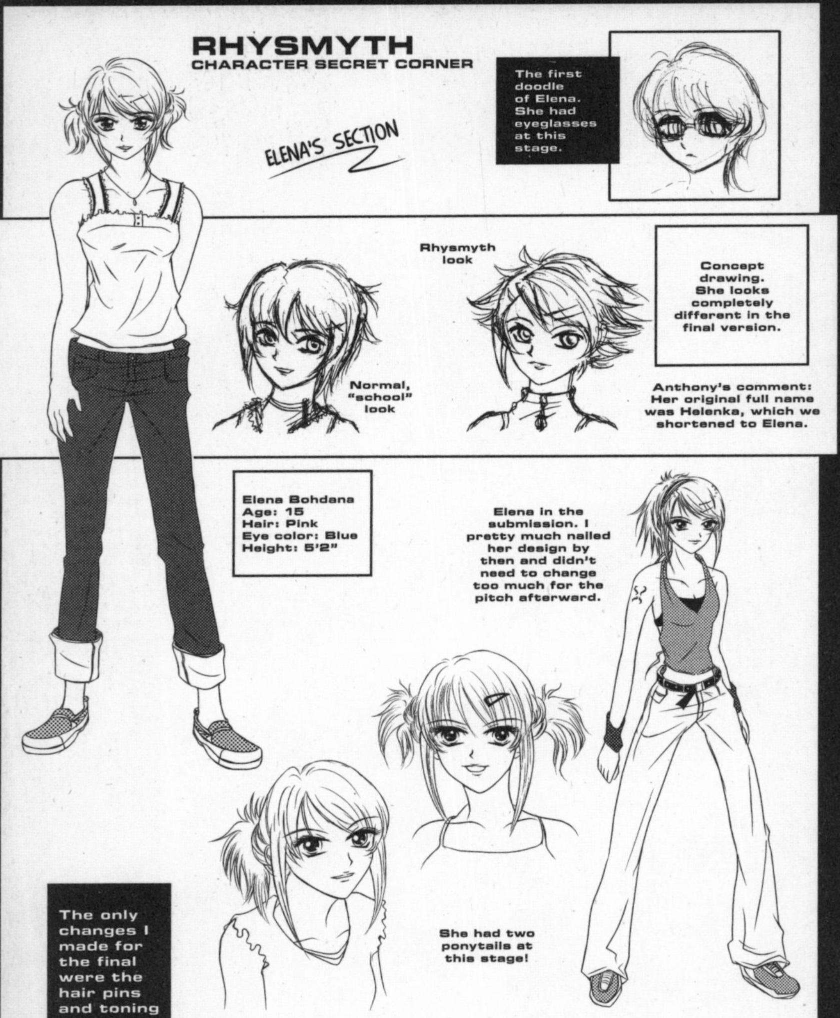
RHYSMYTH
CHARACTER SECRET CORNER
ELENA'S SECTION
The first doodle of Elena. She had eyeglasses at this stage.
Rhysmyth look
Concept drawing. She looks completely different in the final version.
Normal, "school" look
Anthony's comment: Her original full name was Helenka, which we shortened to Elena.
Elena Bohdana
Age: 15
Hair: Pink
Eye color: Blue
Height: 5'2"
Elena in the submission. I pretty much nailed her design by then and didn't need to change too much for the pitch afterward.
The only changes I made for the final were the hair pins and toning her eyes.
She had two ponytails at this stage!
Final design for the property bible.
In the manga, Elena looks a bit younger though...hee

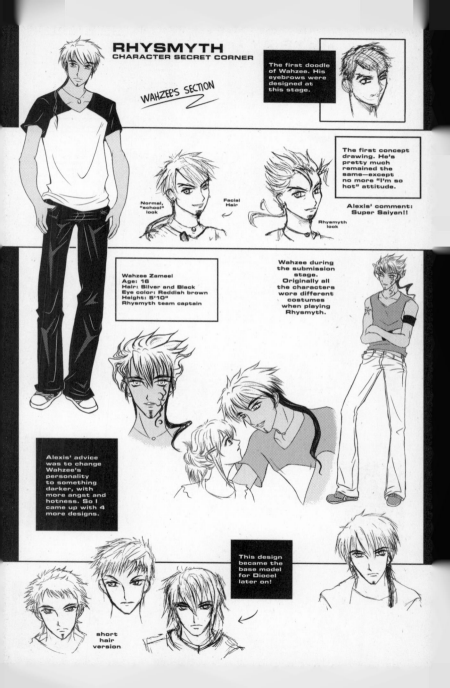

RHYSMYTH
CHARACTER SECRET CORNER

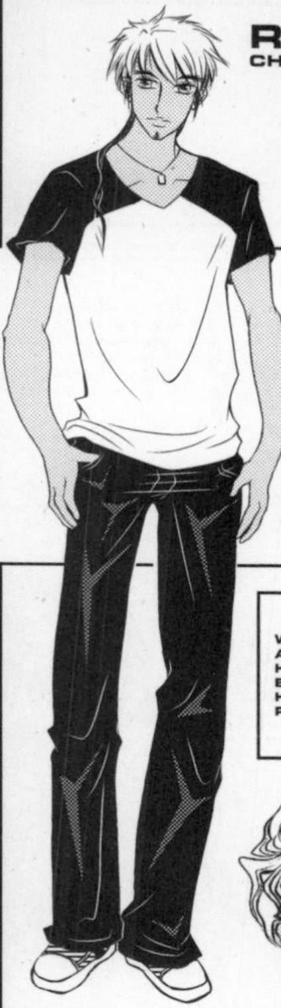

WAHZEE'S SECTION

The first doodle of Wahzee. His eyebrows were designed at this stage.

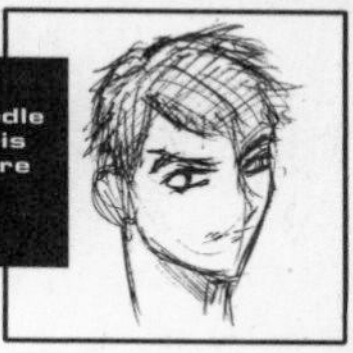

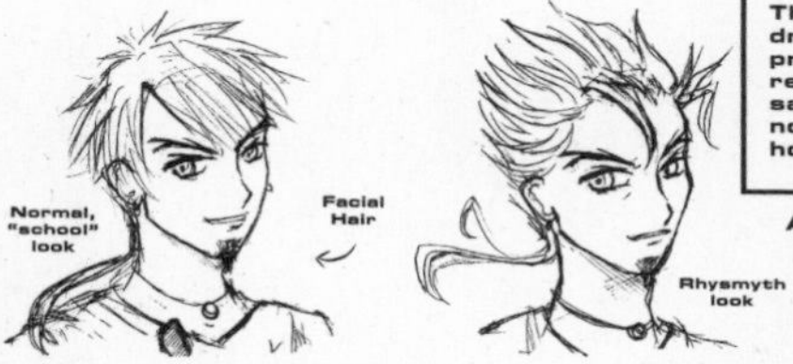
Normal, "school" look
Facial Hair
Rhysmyth look

The first concept drawing. He's pretty much remained the same—except no more "I'm so hot" attitude.

Alexis' comment: Super Saiyan!!

Wahzee Zameel
Age: 16
Hair: Silver and Black
Eye color: Reddish brown
Height: 5'10"
Rhysmyth team captain

Wahzee during the submission stage. Originally all the characters wore different costumes when playing Rhysmyth.

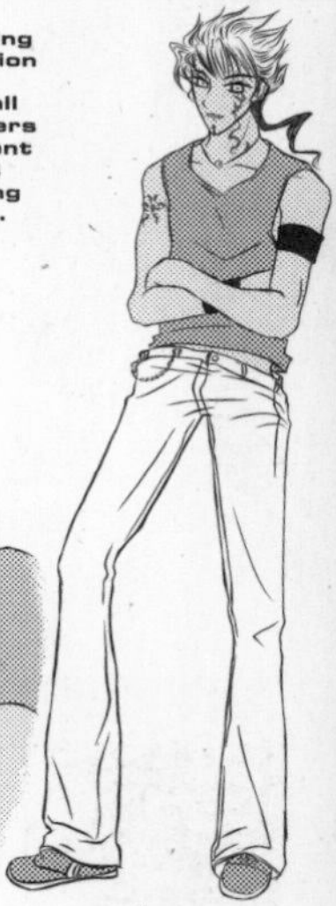

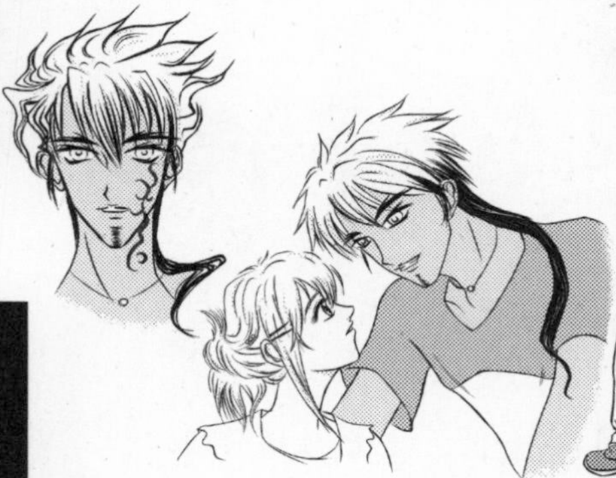

Alexis' advice was to change Wahzee's personality to something darker, with more angst and hotness. So I came up with 4 more designs.

This design became the base model for Diocel later on!

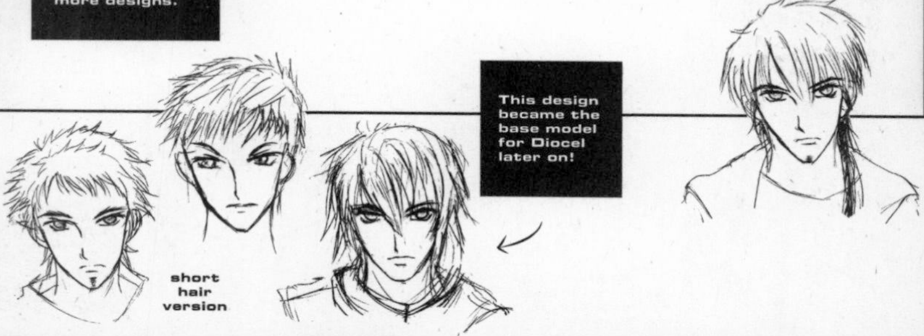
short hair version

RHYSMYTH
CHARACTER SECRET CORNER

DIOCEL'S SECTION

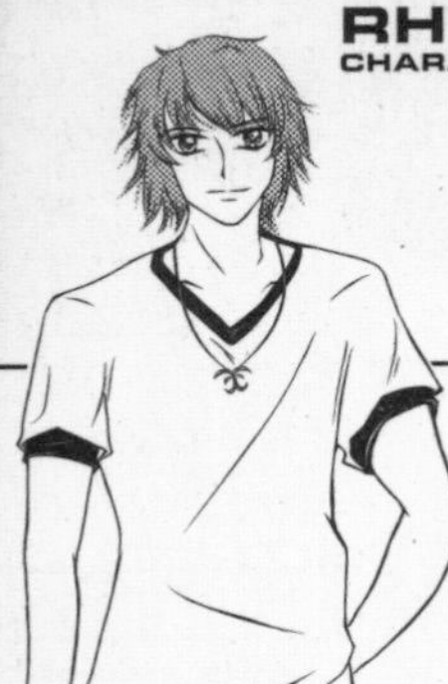

Originally an alternate design for Wahzee, Diocel gradually turned into his own character.

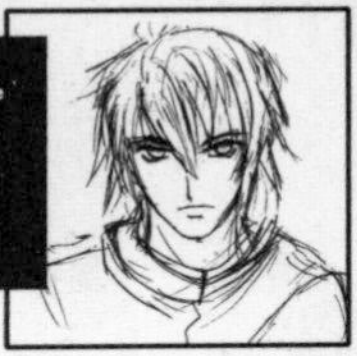

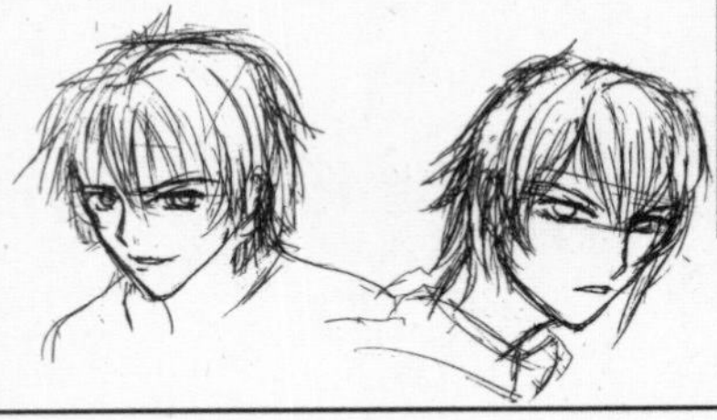

Out of all the angst-Wahzee designs, Anthony picked this one for me to work on.

Diocel Manibusan
Age: 16
Hair: Orange brown
Eye color: Brown
Height: 5'8"

Final angst-Wahzee design. After some deliberation we decided to stick with the original Wahzee allowing this design to become a new character.

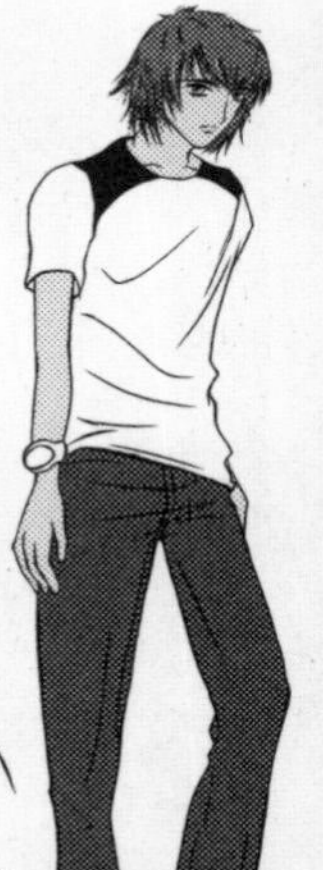

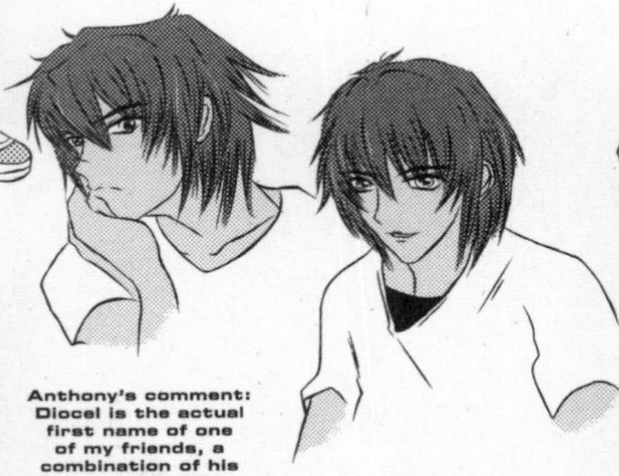

In the end we all decided that Elena needed another love interest and that's when Diocel was born!

Anthony's comment: Diocel is the actual first name of one of my friends, a combination of his parents' names.

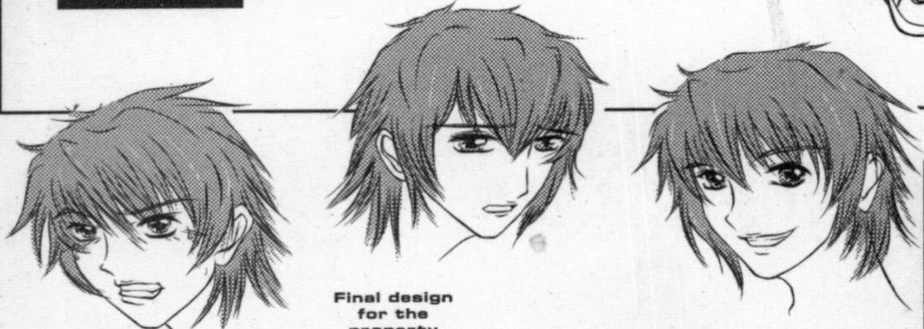

Final design for the property bible.

I lightened Diocel's character-istics to make him more of a contrast to Wahzee.

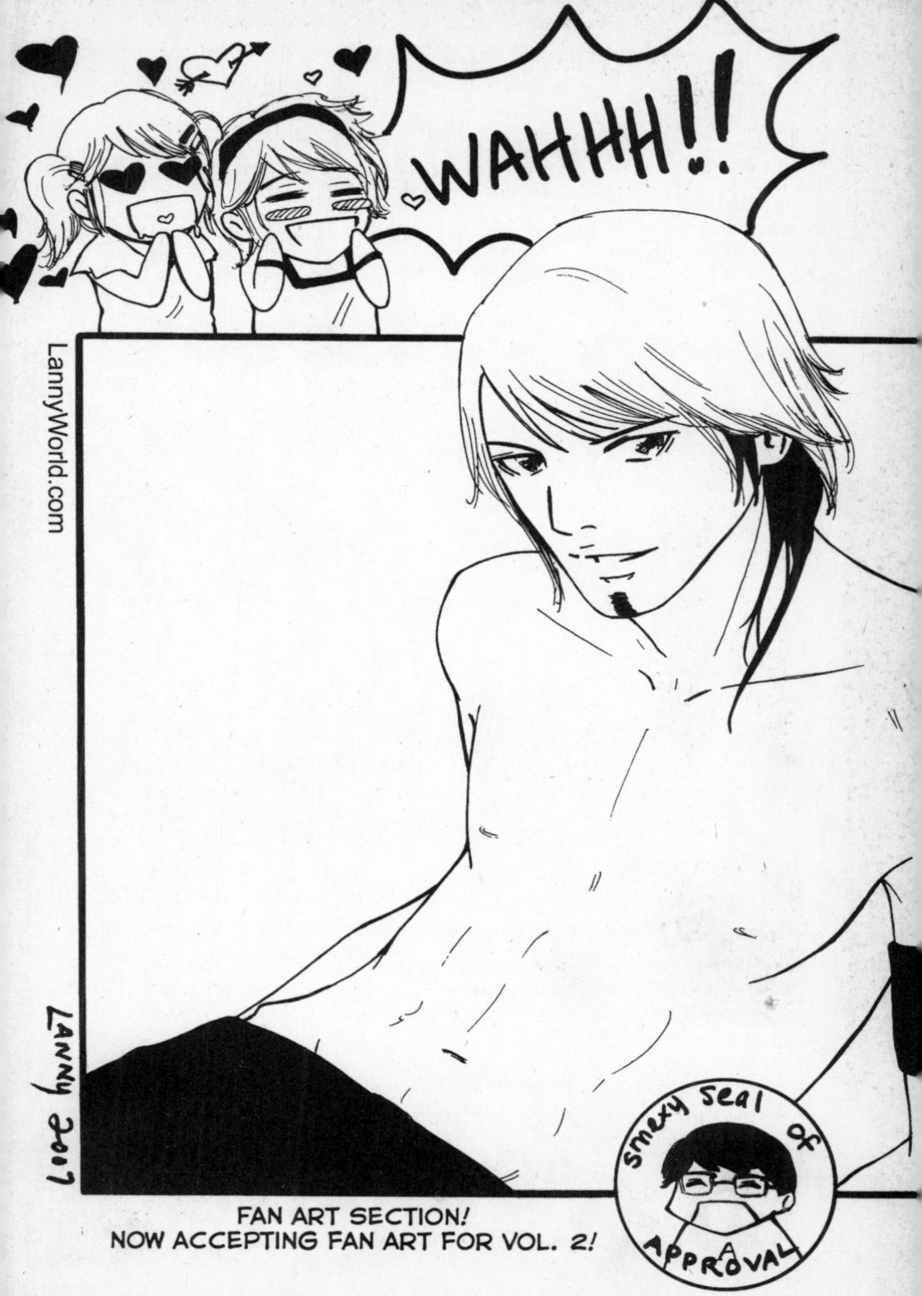
WAHHH!!
LannyWorld.com
LANNY 2007
smexy seal of
A
APPROVAL

FAN ART SECTION!
NOW ACCEPTING FAN ART FOR VOL. 2!

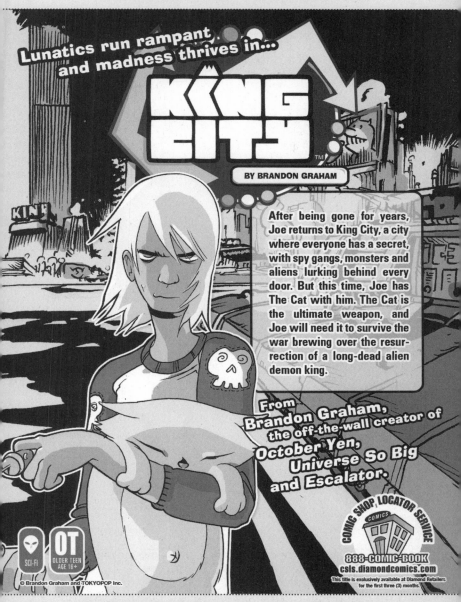

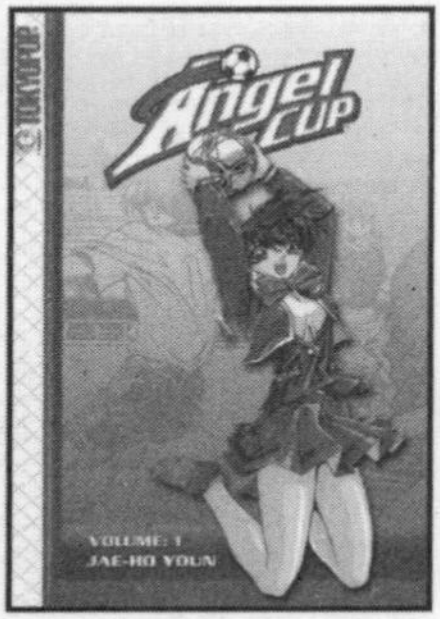
TOKYOPOP
Angel Cup
VOLUME: 1
JAE-HO YOUN

ACTION

T TEEN AGE 13+

ANGEL CUP

BY JAE-HO YOUN

Who's the newest bouncing broad that bends it like Beckam better than Braz—er, you get the idea? So-jin of the hit Korean manhwa, *Angel Cup!* She and her misfit team of athletic amazoness tear up the soccer field, whether it's to face up against the boys' team, or wear their ribbons with pride against a rival high school. While the feminist in me cheers for So-jin and the gang, the more perverted side of me drools buckets over the sexy bust-shots and scandalous camera angles... But from any and every angle, *Angel Cup* will be sure to tantalize the soccer fan in you... or perv. Whichever!

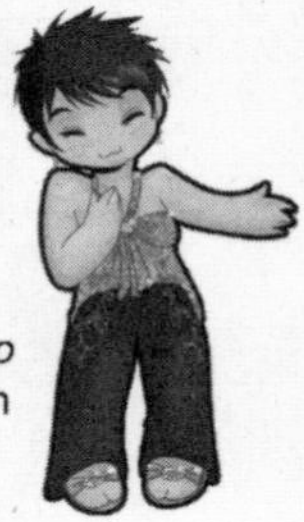

~Katherine Schilling, Jr. Editor

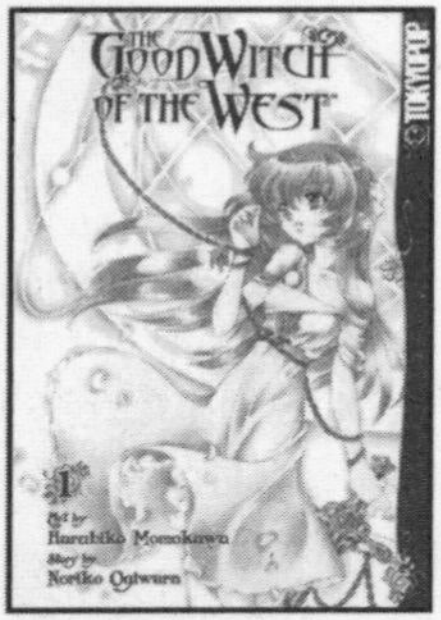
The Good Witch of the West
TOKYOPOP
1

FANTASY

T TEEN AGE 13+

GOOD WITCH OF THE WEST

BY NORIKO OGIWARA AND HARUHIKO MOMOKAWA

For any dreamers who ever wanted more out of a fairytale, indulge yourself with *Good Witch*. Although there's lots of familiar territory fairytale-wise—peasant girl learns she's a princess—you'll be surprised as Firiel Dee's enemies turn out to be as diverse as religious fanaticism, evil finishing school student councils and dinosaurs. This touching, sophisticated tale will pull at your heartstrings while astounding you with breathtaking art. *Good Witch* has big shoes to fill, and it takes off running.

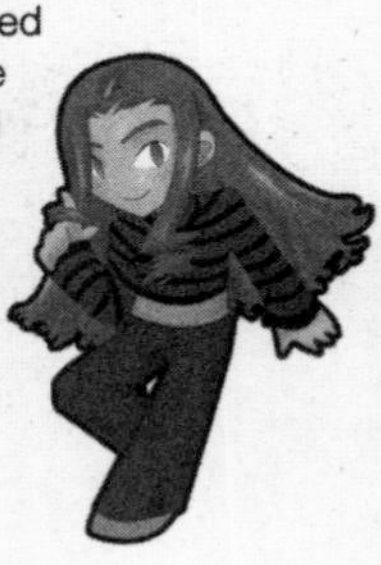

~Hope Donovan, Jr. Editor

SAKURA TAISEN
TOKYOPOP

ACTION

T
TEEN AGE 13+

SAKURA TAISEN

BY OHJI HIROI, IKKU MASA AND KOSUKE FUJISHIMA

I really, really like this series. I'm a sucker for steampunk-type stories, and 1920s Japanese fashion, and throw in demon invaders, robot battles and references to Japanese popular theater? Sold! There's lots of fun tidbits for the clever reader to pick up in this series (all the characters have flower names, for one, and the fact that all the Floral Assault divisions are named after branches of the Takarazuka Review, Japan's sensational all-female theater troupe!), but the consistently stylish and clean art will appeal even to the most casual fan.

~Lillian Diaz-Przybyl, Editor

BATTLE ROYALE 1
TOKYOPOP

ACTION

M
MATURE AGES 18+

BATTLE ROYALE

BY KOUSHUN TAKAMI AND MASAYUKI TAGUCHI

As far as cautionary tales go, you couldn't get any timelier than *Battle Royale*. Telling the bleak story of a class of middle school students who are forced to fight each other to the death on national television, Koushun Takami and Masayuki Taguchi have created a dark satire that's sickening, yet undeniably exciting as well. And if we have that reaction reading it, it becomes alarmingly clear how the students could so easily be swayed into doing it.

~Tim Beedle, Editor

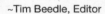